SHARDS

Shards

Published by The Conrad Press in the United Kingdom 2020

Tel: +44(0)1227 472 874
www.theconradpress.com
info@theconradpress.com

ISBN 978-1-911546-66-5

Typesetting and Cover Design by: Charlotte Mouncey, www.bookstyle.co.uk
Cover image created with details from photos of old man by Janko Ferlic and broken glass windows by Tara Evans both available on www.unsplash.com, and broken shattered glass pieces by Arsgera on www.istockphoto.com

The Conrad Press logo was designed by Maria Priestley.

SHARDS

STEPHEN KEEN

CHAPTER ONE

New Year's Eve 1979

Baines was late, Baines was always late.

Conor Christie lit his last fag, the one he had been saving all day and thought of Baines, Baines the gobshite, Baines the wastrel, Baines the apprentice criminal who did not think enough of himself to make something of himself. And now in the cold, Conor felt the cool blade in his trouser pocket and knew that soon the shudder would come and with it thoughts of the voice and the black. Quickly pulling his hand from the blade as if it were suddenly burning hot, he slowly rose from the broken chair and walked towards the light.

Outside, the snow, sickly-looking and sparse, was still falling from a cataract sky. Shivering slightly, he pulls the hood of his Parka over his head. Not merely to ward off the cold, but also because it offered him a kind of indefinable solace. A comfort in face obscured anonymity: an ephemeral normality. And now he was trying so hard not to think about thinking. But it was fatuous. The shudder was building up and would have to be sated.

Sitting back down he slowly pulls the knife from his pocket and here in his hand in his mind the blade becomes truth and redemption a shudder-slayer, a back alley Excalibur. And so, ritualistically, because he had done this a thousand times before, he pulls the left sleeve of his jacket up to his elbow. It feels tight he could feel the life pumping through his veins. A life he did not even want, not like this, not any more.

Pressing the shudder-slayer against his flesh, it skims slices and scythes a pale skin dead skin harvest. And in this way Demons are expurgated daily. But their spores run deep, cutting off the Serpents head merely means that two will grow in its place, but the ritual goes on and Conor was not even sure why any more. Suddenly dropping the knife to the floor, he looks at the scarlet slashes juxtaposed against such white skin. And knows this is as good as it gets. The thinking stops, the shudder stops, the world stops. Well, at least for a while.

And the while was short, for after a few precious minutes the worlds pulse starts to beat again, and trance time is over. And with that Conor knows that he must start to think about thinking again. And now in the afternoon gloom of this winter squat the boy looks at his watch and then at the blood still trickling down his arm. Slowly walking to the window once more he looks outside at snow still falling lethargically across a sombre as sheet iron vista.

Out the corner of his eye he sees a dead pigeon laying in grey slush that used to be grass. From above limp snow fall was forming it a shroud. Standing a few feet from the bird a stringy looking cat, both pall bearer and executioner, glances a glance at the bird as if to say. 'Did I do that?'

Then, wearying of the cold, wearying of the game, the cat turns and skulks away. Conor watches its departure and cannot help wondering who he would rather be. Wondering who he would eventually become: the cat or the pigeon? Then turning himself to face himself, he looks down at the bloodstained floor, scarlet and dust.

Bringing with himself dusk and the stench of scrounged cigarettes and park bench cider, Baines finally arrives, swaying slightly and with a slack jaw. He gazes down at the crimson dripped floor. 'So, you have been outing the devils again then?' Conor stayed silent, just looking coldly at Baines through those strange crippled eyes; squint damaged amber, hating and hated.

As ever, Conor's silence unnerves him, until finally he turns away. He can never look at those eyes for too long.

They were not friends. They were not anything really. But they were all they had. It is practically impossible to define or describe their relationship. It would be somehow glib to say that they were together because they were outcasts, a cliché but a truism nevertheless. The bottom line is they were together because no one wanted them, so, better to drift in plurality as singularly. And drift is what they did, day in and day out. And they appeared on no official records. No National Insurance numbers for they. Seventeen years old and perfectly invisible.

Lazarus Glick's large and rambling suburban home was a stopped clock. Within its four walls time had seemingly stood still somewhere around the early 1950s and then henceforth refused to budge another inch. And each and every cluttered room was mothball deep, suffocated in a prosaic mosaic of memories that Lazarus could not or would not let go of. And to call the house a home would be spurious. To term it a museum of memories would be more apt.

However, artefacts and exhibits in a museum are routinely rearranged, removed and replaced. But here nothing was moved, nothing was changed. Dust gathered upon dust and each memory good or bad was compartmentalised, preserved forever in the aspic of his mind.

But neither collecting dust nor gathering it amongst the relics was Lazarus' state-of-the-art stereo sound system. Incongruous by its modernity, this musical concession to the modem world was his pride and joy and sat snugly and smugly in a corner of the capacious sparsely furnished front room. Indeed, to highlight its precedence it was set on its very own polished walnut pedestal, where it was as lovingly tended as any suburban aspidistra. And within this expensive box of wires, stylus and turntable: well not to put too fine a point on it, a life was soothed, saved and salvaged. Indeed, time and time again Lazarus' old friends, Basie, Ellington, Armstrong and Fitzgerald had hauled and pulled him back from the very edge of the abyss.

Time and again they had been there for him through long days and even longer nights when he would emerge horrified and panic stricken after a nightmarish descent into himself. But there they would be their pure golden sounds the only thing that could silence the terror screams of his fellow inmates. Their sweet Jazz strains were all that could quieten the coarse shouts of the guards and their baying, snarling dogs, and when Lazarus finally closed his eyes the sublime music was all that stopped him feeling like less than nothing. Stopped him from wondering why he was one of the saved and not the drowned.

But, would it not have been better to have been one of the drowned and not the saved? To have died with loved ones, to have shared the fate of so many Millions, and not to have become this, what he was today… For over thirty years this thought never left his mind.

Decades ago he had given up trying to work out why what had happened had taken place. Because this dialogue. Or more accurately monologue from Hell never gave him any answers, just more questions, more reasons for self-recrimination. And so, he had reached the conclusion that perhaps there were no answers to explain the horrors and insanity that had occurred.

After all, madness often only merits silence. And yes, his world was just that, a place of madness and silence in equal measure. And the silence bred a coldness in him which fuelled the madness. Over time he became of granite, a cold heart, stone heart, no heart.

Stripped of compassion and humanity, the laughing face of the sun now avoided him like the plague. And so, here, sitting in the darkness, set like a slab of marble, this stone man that used to be Lazarus Glick, tries to cry, to howl, but he knows nothing will answer his cry. For God was not listening... again.

Closing his eyes, he cast his mind back a thousand years to when he was a boy in Krakow. Rabbi Rabinowitz was talking. Rabbi Rabinowitz was always talking.

'Lazarus, when you grow up never become one of those men to whom joy happiness and warmth are a foreign land, an alien country they shall never visit or know. Do you hear? Do you understand?' Suddenly from outside the beery bonhomie of the first of the night's New Year's revellers broke Lazarus' mental step. Rising slowly from the armchair he walks over to the bay window. He briefly watches the dark figures starkly defined against the snow. He hears their joy and their happiness but cannot feel their warmth. Then this foreigner in their country, this alien in their world closes the curtains and darkness is his once more.

By mid-evening the snow had departed and so too had the late shoppers from the soulless town centre. Just merely to be replaced by gaggles of young people determined to be at least halfway to Lager oblivion by the first chimes of midnight.

Despite the New Year festivities, the town centre had a depressed air. The High Street especially wore it pedestrianised Piazza like a millstone around its smug, cobble-stoned neck. At the far end of the High Street near to the Ornamental Gardens, which were were not especially ornamental, nor in the strictest sense of the word gardens, walked Conor and Baines in a silence of strangers. And despite their footsteps being in unison their minds are a thousand miles apart. And as they trudge slush puddles lit gold blaze by street lights. Baines zips his Harrington jacket up to his throat and ducks an icy wind blast direct from the Urals or some such place. And as he listens, the sound of the wind reminds him of the desolate sound the wind makes in Westerns when the Tumble weed is blown around.

Raising his head slightly he looks across at Conor. 'D'you think it's possible for your eyebrows to freeze solid? You know, so they could snap off?' Conor does not reply.

Baines continues undeterred. Just what Conor feared he let out a heavy sigh. 'Anyway, I saw this film once where this geezer was in the North Pole and got lost. It was forty below or something. Anyway, when he was finally found he was frozen stiff as a board. When they tried to move his head his hair snapped off, I wonder if his pubes did too?' Conor sighs even louder, he turns and faces Baines. 'Christ, you do talk some old pony sometimes!' Baines stops in his tracks.

'No. Straight up it's true, it was on the BBC.' Conor can

barely be bothered to hide the sarcasm in his voice. 'Oh well, if they say it's true it's clinched it. Got to be a hundred per cent banker.' Shaking his head he walks slowly away. Baines follows a few paces behind, his voice fighting the icy wind for supremacy. 'You know your trouble? The only truth you see or think you see is in that blade! So, go on, how many demon voices you killed today?' Conor does not rise to the bait he had heard it all before. Instead he pulls the hood of his Parka up and tries again to stop thinking about thinking.

On the steps of the War Memorial the theological polemic was in full swing. Pastor Pat, bottle of Scotch in one hand and crucifix in the other, was in fine form, rapier like in attack yet stoical in defence he was both believer and non believer, Anti Christ and Messiah. 'I am Alpha and Omega.' His rasping Whisky tones were for anyone and everyone. For this was his Church Pulpit and Altar.

And now in the near distance he spots the approach of his congregation, shaped black against the snow. And at the sight of them Pat's face registered a broad smile. 'Boys, boys, come join me in prayer. Bow your heads and raise your hearts to our Saviour, Lord Jesus Christ!'

That old Pat was as mad as a fish was of little consequence to Baines. The man always had a supply of cigs and booze and that was all that mattered. It gave him instant currency, if not credence and cool. And as ever by his side was an old banjo from which he made a precarious living by busking outside various locales around the town. And where, always half-drunk and plucking and picking hymns on the instrument, he would invariably end up playing outside St Bartholomews Church, in between nipping inside to get a light for his fag off of an altar candle.

Now, the priest was a patient man known for his altruism and piety amongst other equally noble attributes, however after a couple of hours of Catholic 'Cabaret', which always included a drunken one man Conga up the Nave, not to mention singing tunelessly, filthy and obscene lyrics to the hymns he was playing on his banjo, the priest, his sensibilities duly offended for the day, would bung Pat a fiver and tactfully suggest he perhaps go entertain the good folk at the Anglican Church across town. This Pat duly did, after replenishing his stocks of booze at the nearest Off Licence.

But the 'gig' at the Anglican Church was never as profitable. Invariably they only slipped him two or three quid and a few tired looking ham sandwiches left over from the Mother and Toddler Group. Insulted by the paltry rewards for his musical talents he would unleash a volley of invective at the vicar. Indeed, such was his passion and anger that half munched lumps of sandwich would take on the mantle of offensive weapons as they shot out of his mouth, spraying anyone within a three yard radius.

Finally, the vicar, a timid Welshman, would slip Pat another couple of quid to placate him. Whereupon Pat would pocket the money, smile cheerily, and utter the words the vicar dreaded. 'Okay then Boss, see you same time tomorrow then.' With that this diminutive, bible-bashing, blaspheming busker would sway and saunter off in the general direction of The Hope and Anchor Public House.

But here and now on this bitterly cold New Year's Eve, Pat was ignoring the elements because he was in his element. This small man in the big Ex-Army great coat that more resembled a shroud, was happy in his War Memorial Church with his congregation of two. And with Epiphany looming he had the child like expectation that a listening God was looking in too.

Whether or not an omnipotent deity was listening in of course was open to conjecture. However, what was certain was that his congregation were no longer listening in. Indeed, with Pat's booze rapidly disappearing, Baines could no longer be bothered to feign interest at the fire and brimstone tub-thumping.

It no longer registered a pulse. And as for Conor, silent and hooded, resembling a disinterested novice monk, truth was, stray and random images of hate were seeping into his mind. Disturbing and disturbed he tried to cut them out shut them out of his mind; but the shudder was upon him, insidious and all powerful.

With logic and rationality drifting away with the tide, he attempted to recall just when he had first traded love for hate; when he had first apprenticed himself to hatred. He attempted to enumerate one by one all the past and present reasons for hating. But always, just always it came back to the soul deep loathing, repulsion of self. The way he felt, the way he looked, the way he…

'I am the WAY the TRUTH and the LIFE.' Pat's voice was strong and defiant. His grey-blue rainbowed eyes flamed briefly like those of the patriarchs of old. Suddenly sinking to his knees in the snow his voice became a windblown rasp, 'Lord, take my body take my flesh!' With that, the pavement preacher keeled over. As if one, Baines and Conor rise to their feet and walk over to the supine figure. Kneeling down in the snow Baines takes the man's wrist, feeling for a pulse. Looking on Conor asks quietly.

'Is he dead?' Baines shakes his head. 'No, just dead drunk.' With that, Baines ever the opportunist starts to rifle through Pat's pockets which brings a small moan from the man but no more than that. Conor eyes Baines disdainfully. 'What the hell do you think you are doing?' The boy doesn't reply; instead, pulling out not a plum from the man's coat pocket but a little cash, ten cigs and a small crucifix, he proceeds to pocket the money, light a cig and throw the crucifix into kerb side slush the colour of dirty rags. Walking over to where Pat's banjo lay sleeping in its battered case, Baines slowly picked it up, Conor's normally quiet and soft voice grew louder and harsher. 'Leave it! Don't even think about taking it. At least leave the poor old sod that.'

As snow once more started to fall apologetically from this suburban sky, Conor and Baines just stared at each other both uncertain of what to do next. It was the latter who blinked first, faced down, was forced to look away. Truth was he could no longer bear to look at those eyes, that face, it sickened, repelled even terrified him. He slowly started to walk away. But not before firing back petulantly on the wind.

'Okay, let him keep the poxy banjo, it's crap anyway.' Conor watches his departure in silence, and then bends down next to Pat and tries to rouse him. But the little man with the big coat had found heavenly oblivion. Taking him under either arm Conor drags him across the steps of the War Memorial and props him up against its giant marble plinth. Carefully he goes through Pat's rucksack and takes out a blanket and wraps it around the comatose preacher.

Descending the steps he takes one last look back at Pat and then turns and walks over to the kerbside, and there lying face down was the broken body of Christ. Without knowing why, he gently lifts the crucifix from the cold grey slush. He thinks he should feel something, anything but he does not. Well, maybe something he cannot quite understand or explain. So, he simply offers the crushed body of his Saviour sanctuary, a refuge in the back pocket of his jeans.

If nothing else the youthful parents of Dina Gina Molina had a wicked sense of humour; hence the child's name. But, and it's sad to say they had scarce little else in the way of parental responsibility, common sense and maturity. However, for a brief time after coming back from the Maternity Ward at the hospital baby Dina was a brand new toy for her parent's vacant minds, a break from their routine of cold takeaways, Coronation Street and fortnightly dole cheques.

But as weeks turned into months these playground parents wearied of the toy in the corner. It was no longer new and shiny, just demanding and spewy. Things were starting to unravel. And as the parents Saturday night rows became seven days a week brawling binges, so little Dina forsaken and forgotten would be left to crawl amongst the carnage on dirty threadbare carpets.

The red-letter day was overdue, but it had to come. And come it did one cool September afternoon sixteen years ago. Dina's father, if not exactly thinking the grass would be greener elsewhere, at least thought it would be clear of baby sick, full nappies and adult responsibilities. And with this in mind as mother and baby were napping, he did a runner. This paragon of paternal and parental dependability before vacating himself forever from the lives of baby and mother, took the TV, the housekeeping money, and as a final cheery adieu even broke open the electricity meter and relieved it of its meagre contents.

To a child with a child, Social Services in the early Sixties were more of a moral and didactic body than a helpful one. And the simple truth was that this particular child with a child could not cope, emotionally, physically or mentally. But do not get the wrong impression of this seventeen year old child, she tried she really did. And freed from the influence of Dina's superfluous and feckless father, the girl attempted to be the perfect little mother.

But one way or another, the odds were stacked against her. Firstly, rationality and common sense had never exactly been close allies of hers; in fact they kept their distance from her. Secondly, and perhaps more importantly, history was repeating itself. You see, the girl's Mother, who by the way, after the desertion of her daughter by Dina's father, took mother and infant into her modest home, was in a sense the facsimile, the blueprint by which her daughters life was seemingly preordained, because just like her daughter, she too had been a teenage mum. And also just like her daughter, she too had chosen as her lover a young man who would change his aimless drifting ways on that no way day when the Sun would rise in the west and set in the east.

And so, as the months passed turning into years, this little family, like any family, had its train of tears and occasional joys. But somehow, some way they survived, kept their heads above water. Well, survived until a man of nothing cut the thread of their fragile lives. A thread so fine that once severed it could never be properly repaired.

For a long time, every Friday after collecting her wages from her packers job at the biscuit factory, Dina's mother would take her shopping. And invariably the highlight of this shopping trip would be the visit to the small, cluttered toy shop at the far end of the High Street. Now, this shop was like any other toy store anywhere else in the world. A place that with nostalgic, dewy eyes we look back on now and again when we revisit that place in our minds that will always be the child, the pure, the innocent. Likewise, the owner of this particular toy shop was an exaggerated version, a caricature of just how we imagine a toy shop owner should look.

Because Annie Bridges was small, chubby, rosy cheeked and cheerful and you would swear to God that no expletive had ever emanated from those cheery cherry pie lips. Or that any profane thought had tip toed across her mind. And so it was under Annie's gentle gaze that Dina with eyes as big as a bush baby's would slowly scan and survey shelves fit to burst with toys of every description.

Wide eyed she viewed fluffy koalas, jigsaws, train sets and dolls of every size, shape and hue. And was she tempted? No, she was not. For at the far end of the shop covering an entire wall was her glittering prize, shelves upon shelves of toy and model cars.

For any small child this myriad of Matchbox models, this cornucopia of Corgi cars was a pure delight. But for five year old Dina it somehow transcended this. For her it was Heaven on earth. Looking down at the child, her mother thought it odd that she should have such a profound fascination for the toy cars, but they were cheap enough to buy and they undoubtedly gave the little girl great pleasure. And so now, after much mental deliberation, the vital decision was made, Dina was now the proud owner of a shiny red 1964 E type Jaguar. And with palpable joy she clutched the small models box tightly in tiny hands.

Annie Bridges was the last adult to see Dina's mother alive. Well, apart from the man of nothing that is. After leaving the shop Dina and her mother had taken a short cut home due to the imminent threat of rain. Breaking her step to gaze up at the cracked cloud skies, she viewed the pink shades, blue flashes and crimson streaks with an awe and wonder that only small children can possess. It was certainly not possessed by her mother who gently hurried the girl along.

The road through the wasteland was desolate and deserted. And as mother and child walked it, a heavy rain began to drown the autumn dusk. On either side of the grey straight road skeletal remains of houses due for demolition loomed aggressively sad. But despite this, despite the rain Dina was content, she had a brand new car and much to her mother's annoyance, she was noisily puddle stamping in her new, red shiny Wellington boots. But the reflection of dark clouds that she saw gathering in those puddles, were now bearing down with intensity. For now, the sky was about ready to fall in on her.

In court, if it had ever gone to court, Michael Baines would have sworn blind that the deceased woman and her child, seemingly bereft of rhyme or reason, had suddenly left the pavement without looking and had started to cross the road, whereupon, despite the heavy rain and hazardous driving conditions, he had applied the brakes of the car but had not been able to avoid mother and child.

The actual truth of course was another matter. But the truth and Michael Baines were pretty much strangers to each other, they had barely ever met. Indeed, he was an inveterate liar whose lies had become his realities. So, what had really happened in that late afternoon deluge of rain and blood only a broken five year old was left to tell. But no court in the land would ever hear her, this child whose mother had been extinguished right in front of her eyes, and whose own injuries meant she would spend countless weeks in hospital, with a shattered leg and a fractured mind, of course in time the leg, after a fashion healed, but as for her mind.

Michael Baines, still 'upped' on Purple Hearts, torched the stolen car that evening in woods near Woking. Standing in mud, mulched leaves and rain of biblical proportions, he watches intently the fire catch hold, his narrow grey eyes darting left and right transfixed by the flames. Suddenly, something almost primeval, something unnerving grips him hard deep inside. And this man who lives only for the now, sinks down on his knees in the cold earth and cries. For himself.

The mud of the camp was the camp, a living thing voracious and insatiable. Everywhere it oozed malice, sucking and sapping the will, strength, and ultimately the humanity of the camp inmates, until all that was left was a shell of a human being, possessed of a sad indifference to the misery and suffering of his fellow tormented inmates. Spring, summer, autumn and winter, the mud of the camp was the camp. And from its poisonous slime buildings rose: the most striking being the mock Bavarian villa of the camp commandant, Jurgen Hassler.

Before the war he had been renowned for designing some of the most innovative and sought after residences in Southern Germany. But now, this builder of homes, creator of dreams had become the destroyer of lives and creator of nightmares. And as in the case of Himmler, so the term 'banality of evil' could equally be applied to him. Physically Hassler was of medium height and build, with sparse light brown hair and dark blue eyes. But his face would not have got lost in a crowd, because his face was the crowd, forgettable and unremarkable. And it was with bitter irony that the camps inmates called him 'Little Flower' because of his plethora of highly prized geraniums that he lovingly grew in pots around the exterior of his grandiose villa. Indeed, these flowers in there various hues and shades meant more to Hassler than most human life, most certainly the lives of the camps inmates.

Indeed, how incongruous it all was, for as Little Flower lovingly tended his little flowers, less than a hundred meters away in another world, men were being starved, worked and beaten to death. Should we laugh or cry at the madness of it? Perhaps best to cry, with the hope that our tears flow into the heart of God, better that than they fall for all eternity into an empty void, into nothingness.

With the last snows of winter finally melting away, Hassler was ready for his expansion. For germinating in his mind through the long winter months had been the idea of a geranium explosion. And now in his mind's eye he could clearly visualise the borders of his villa's garden resplendent with geraniums of every colour, shade and hue. He had a mental plan, a burning image of where each plant would be positioned. All five hundred of them! And in this madness, this bizarre obsession, he had an unlikely ally.

Lazarus knew that he could not last much longer in the Stone Quarry. Situated a mile from the camp, the quarry was a place of death, pure and simple. If the mud of the camp was the camp, then the dust of the quarry was the quarry. A living hell, where for twelve hours a day two hundred dust-covered spectral figures laboured incessantly with pickaxes breaking down huge stone more obdurate than granite. And when broken the stones were loaded onto wooden pulley carts and then heaved and pushed by teams of more dead then alive human animals.

Bullied, beaten and berated, many of these tormented visions would in desperation leap from the top of the quarry heights into oblivion. Hand in hand father and son, brother and brother would hurl themselves away from the nightmare they could no longer endure. The SS guards called these suicides 'parachutists' and with sardonic smiles they would encourage other inmates to go and follow suit. 'Learn to fly into the waiting arms of Abraham'. And many times Lazarus had been close to doing just that. But something stopped him at the edge strength, cowardice, perhaps an element of both?

Whatever it was, intrinsic in it was an overwhelming desire to live. After all, his mother had struggled, fought, and ultimately died giving him life, and he was not going to give it away so cheaply. It would be a betrayal to the woman he had never known but who had made the ultimate sacrifice in giving him life. But it wasn't enough holding on hope that the Red Army would be his and his fellow Jews saviour any time soon.

Admittedly, despite the lack of such luxuries as wireless or newspapers, he knew through the camp grapevine that the Germans were suffering defeats and setbacks in the East. But he also knew that they were far from beaten. And even if by some miraculous happening they did capitulate under the Russian onslaught, it would be months before they would reach this isolated camp in southern Poland. And by then he and the other camp inmates would long be dust in this place of mud and blood.

That evening in the barren opacity of the barrack, Lazarus sat on the bunk he shared with his old friend Yitzhak. As usual they were locked in a silence so familiar to them after a day's brutal, unforgiving labour, namely a silence of exhaustion, hunger and utter hopelessness.

Yitzhak did not work in the quarry, instead his days were spent labouring on a nearby SS run farm, where the crops were wheat and maize, and the harvest beaten and abused Jewish souls. Even in the darkness Lazarus could see the reflection of his own face in that of Yitzhak. Both knew the brutality and malnutrition was killing them. How quickly these gaunt, haunted old men of twentyfive had become barely flickering flames. He looked once more at his friend. He was unrecognisable as that bolshy kid back in Krakow who had always been up for a scrap, a scrape, an adventure. A dare devil who would fight kids twice his size if needed. But now the fight was going out of him just when he needed it most.

And so it would remain unspoken between them that they were living out their last days in hell. Unspoken it may have been, but both still had that spark left in them, a tiny spark nearly extinguished and diminished, but nevertheless still there.

A spark of life, a tiny flame of self preservation burned within each of them. They knew that if they did not escape this place of mud, dust and blood soon it would consume them body and soul.

Just then, in the darkness, serendipity appeared to show itself in the angular figure of Manny the barrack elder. A half-Jew in his early forties, Manny was a man of contradictions, kind, unkind, pleasant, unpleasant. Basically, he was a man who could never be what was in his heart, and this engendered in him a frustration and bitterness that would chase him to the grave. But now, and for whatever reason, he appeared to display a liking for Lazarus.

He never beat or bullied him as he did on occasion the other barrack inmates. Indeed, Manny seemed to possess a respect for the tall, studious looking young Jew. Unlike Lazarus, Manny was a veteran of this place of mud and blood. In fact he had been one of the slaves forced to construct it. And in those early wild east days of mud and blood, surreal and unreal, he and the other slaves had learnt only too well that the mud of the camp was the camp. And always would be.

Indeed, Hassler in his first address to his ragged, starving minions had promulgated it, had decreed it to be so. And in its final murderous birth pangs, bathed and swathed in tortuous torment, the last buildings the inmates barracks sprang forth from the cloying mud, so blind but so all seeing. And here now, from slave to barrack master, Manny was offering a thread, fine and fragile perhaps, but nevertheless a possible lifeline.

At his sudden appearance, Lazarus and Yitzhak went to rise from their bunk, but Manny motioned with his hand for them to remain seated. Around him the prosaic and nocturnal barrack noises echoed out, rasping coughs, hopeless sobbing, the first breaths of sleep and last breaths of life; another corpse for morning roll call. Cramped so close on the bunk Lazarus could smell the vodka on Manny's breath, and the strong aroma of Russian cigarettes also, the privileges of being the barrack elder.

When it came, Manny's voice was somehow dismembered because of the blackness. 'What do you boys know about flowers?' Lazarus was taken aback. Was it some kind of joke? He stammered a reply. 'Flowers, I don't understand?' The disembodied voice sighed impatiently. 'Yes, bloody flowers! You know those things that grow in the ground. Look, I don't know if you have heard or not, but that mad bastard Hassler is having five hundred geraniums delivered in the morning.' Lazarus and Yitzhak both shook their heads non-plussed. Not noticing, Manny continued.

'The thing is, Untersturmführer Overath has ordered me to pick three men to plant the bloody geraniums in Little Flower's garden.' He coughed a barrack room cough then spat at the wall. Remaining silent, Lazarus and Yitzhak were suddenly uneasy in the older man's presence. Manny's voice became hoarser. 'It's three days easy work. But perhaps you prefer the quarry and the farm?' His voice trailed off into the darkness.

Poison chalice or lifeline? These were the thoughts in both Lazarus and Yitzhak's mind. It was the former who spoke first, a hint of caution and reticence in his tone. 'So, it's just planting flowers? What about when the planting is finished?' Manny sighed wearily. 'How the hell should I know? Perhaps Hassler will like you and keep you on as his bloody housemaid! Look, do you want the job or not?' Finally, Lazarus spoke for them both... 'Yes!'

'The Arcade Buildings are without doubt the finest example of late eighteenth-century civic architecture in the town. For once the tourist brochure blurb was true. Situated in the centre of town, the Arcade was imperious, elegant and snobbishly Georgian, built in the 1790s by a wealthy benefactor of the town, now long forgotten even by those that never forget. The Arcade buildings today serve as ornate shop fronts for expensive but obscure independent retailers, whilst also housing a small theatre that showcases equally obscure performers.

A short distance from the Arcade was situated a Multi Storey car park. Decidedly Stalinist, Eastern bloc concrete block in appearance, its sad starkness is in total contrast to what was housed on its forlorn windswept ground thirty odd years ago. Back then, on New Years Eve 1979 to be precise, in its stead stood the Magenta Rooms. Supercilious and aloof, this elegantly furnished bar was the suave, suburban sets drinking establishment and posing palace of choice. And as ever, on this New Years Eve night the Magenta was kitted out wall to wall with smart young things, sublime, superior in body and mind. God forbid a High Street dress here or a catalogue suit.

In a darkened corner as incongruous as sobriety at an Irish wake, sit Conor and Baines. Somehow, some way they had slipped under the radar and actually managed to get served at the bar. Uncomfortable and forever insular, Conor keeps crippled eyes cast downwards, neither wishing to see or be seen. Nervously he thrusts his hands into his jeans pocket, feeling the blade with one hand and the crucifix with the other, he briefly feels a sense of calm that is as unexplainable as it is ephemeral. The patterns in the carpet, black swirls against burnt orange break in on that calm, giving him a headache. Closing amber eyes he pretends to float away.

Beside him, Baines was getting tanked on cheap Bulgarian Beaujolais or some such poison. Through narrow, green-grey eyes he eyes up the 'sacrosanct Sara's and divine Davinia's.' In every way, shape and form they are out of his league, reach and class. His 'revenge' is to stare hard and unflinching at them, his stare one of lust, loathing and cold menace. Never blinking, never averting his ice gaze the women's discomfort and unease excites the boy. Knowing he is in some small way fucking up their evening is reward enough. And this puerile pastime satisfies him. For an apprentice alcoholic, for a kid who did not think enough of himself to make something of himself, this was as good as it got. To play the part of the spoiler, the pisser on other peoples parades. Yeah, Sweet.

Getting lost in the trail of the hours, they finally left the Magenta an hour before midnight. And now back out in the bitter snow-slush night, they pass New Years revellers, boozy best mates who proclaim loudly that they will be best mates forever. But as it turns out their eternal friendship will end on the opening of bleary ten am eyes and to a hangover the size of Latvia.

Baines, brooding and belligerent sneers a snarl in their general direction. 'Wankers!' How dare they have the temerity to be happy, content with life when his was such a crock, still, all that would change, and soon, because with booze in his blood and delusions in his head he sees himself as some kind of criminal genius. A special one whose talents would see him safe, see him standing alone above the chaos and wreck.

That his father had been a criminal Baines wore as a badge of honour, an emblem of pride. That this criminality never extended beyond car theft and petty housebreaking the boy never elaborated upon. Because to this lost and impressionable kid, his old man was a player, a crony of the Richardson's, a major face on south London streets, streets that he had once killed on had now claimed him.

It happened one sultry September night when the boy was thirteen. The police version of events had been that Michael Baines, age thirtyeight years, had collapsed on a Deptford side street, probably due to his being heavily intoxicated, and had there died, choking on his own vomit. Of course, this sordid and ignominious version of events was not accepted by his son. Even though it was well known that his father often disappeared for days on end, haunting the less salubrious pubs and clubs of south London. Where invariably he indulged in massive spit and sawdust benders, where not only were days lost along with the rent and housekeeping money, but also any last vestiges of self respect he might once have possessed were pissed up the wall.

Whatever the exact circumstances of Michael Baines death were, it was palpable that he had become careless with his own life, a trait already evident in his son. A feckless legacy bestowed upon him by a feckless father.

CHAPTER TWO

For too long the plangent rattle of the anti-depressant bottle had been the soundtrack of her life. And now with the death of her daughter, for Dina's grandmother Peggy, a difficult life had suddenly become untenable. For even in the best of times this small, dark- eyed woman was melancholic and pessimistic in her outlook on life. But now with her daughter gone, the fragile threads of Peggy's life were unravelling. Every night in tormented dreams there were furious shout-outs with a God she now perceived as the Devil for taking her only child. And come morning the silent despair would find her lost somewhere between the two.

But it was not all gloom. Dina was home from the hospital now and the little girl was a solitary light against the darkness. Always inquisitive, seemingly cheerful and bright, she was Peggy's shadow, lost in a little world of awe and wonder always wanting to know anything and everything.

But neither would, could speak of their loss. Painful, open wounds are best left untouched. And Dina lived with a constant reminder of the 'accident.' Despite two operations and intense physiotherapy, her left leg would not mend correctly. Doctors could not understand why the limb would not heal properly, they had carried out numerous tests and procedures but the leg seemingly refused to heal. A few suggested that it was perhaps something psychological that still forced the girl to limp. Whatever it was that made her leg obdurately refuse to mend properly, in some respects it had little to do with her innocent mind.

Indeed, she had a mind that was only too happy to experience and learn new things. But just as this young mind was starting to open and flourish, so Peggy's mind was somehow slowly dying, closing down. In fact, as with the walls of Jericho, her mind was not merely closing, but was tumbling down. No longer were the anti-depressants able to paper over the cracks in her mind, and no longer was she able to negotiate the bends in that damaged mind.

She had become so weary of trying to find strength in pain. Always a quiet woman, now her quiet moods were heavy day long silences. Too many daylight hours spent pacing, and staring out of windows, and then the nights where purgatorial flames tortured and tormented her. And that which she so tenaciously fought to keep at the back of her mind now refused to stay there any longer, desperate to escape the confines of her shadowlands.

And although young, Dina could see her grandmother disappearing little by little with each passing day. Could see, sense and feel her falling down, until the role reversal was complete and the frail of body looked after the frail of mind, and in next to no time the child had become the adult and the adult the child. And Dina's school books took a back seat to rent books and shopping bags; homework to housework.

Soon consumed by the drudgery, Dina's still hungry and enquiring mind missed her books, missed the content and touch and feel of them. Her young heart cried out for study, for someone to talk to about serious things, trivial things, anything. For some days Peggy would go hours without uttering a word, her demons had seemingly removed her tongue without her even noticing, and this left Dina suffocating in the silent, stultifying drudgery of cleaning, caring, crying salt tears of frustration.

And of an evening when her nanny-child was fed, cleaned and put to bed, to dream of God and the Devil, Dina would lay down and write poetry, dark, desperate and sombre words of a girl, not waving but drowning.

In silence, the four Polish political prisoners unload the precious geraniums from the back of the black SS truck. A few yards from them the SS driver lies on the grass smoking and spitting occasionally. Now and then he shouts at them to slow down. He is enjoying the sunshine. And anyway, he was in no rush. His next job would be shifting corpses in the back of his truck. And no matter how well the truck was cleaned and hosed down afterwards, the stench of death clung to it for days after. And somehow it would linger on his clothes, in his hair, even seeping into the pores of his skin. No, he was not in any hurry.

From the balcony of the villa yet obscured from the view of those below, Hassler watches as his beloved geraniums are unloaded from the truck and placed by the capacious garden borders. As tense and as jumpy as any expectant father, he holds his rifle by his side. If one leaf on one geranium is damaged those four Polish bastards would pay with their lives. Taking a sip from his coffee cup his eyes pan across to the lounging driver. Now in full sunbathing mode, he has removed his shirt and lies on his back soaking up the rays.

Even as a child, Hassler had despised sloth and indolence. He recalled in his mind how as a boy he had come across one of the machinists in his father's textile factory sleeping on the job. He had instantly reported the man to his father, who in turn dismissed the man straight away. The young Hassler had felt no sympathy or sense of guilt for his actions, even when he later discovered that the man was the father of four small children and had a terminally ill wife. That the family would be destitute stirred not a modicum of remorse inside him. It was no concern of his, he had done the right thing by his father and by his conscience.

The rifle shot ripped through the quiet, tearing up the earth a few feet from the supine driver's legs. In a bemused panic he rolls underneath the truck. Squinting against the sun he tries to make out where the shot came from. He did not have long to find out. From the edge of the balcony Hassler makes himself visible. With the rifle still in his hands he stares silently at the driver. Crawling out from under the truck the driver tries to regain some lost dignity, by venting his ire at the still prostrate four Poles. 'Get up! Come on you idle shits, get back to work!' Hurriedly putting his shirt back on he casts a furtive glance towards the balcony. But it's empty now.

At just gone seven am, Lazarus, Yitzhak and a slight, silent Jew called Dawid were brought by Untersturmführer Overath to the villa garden. Hassler stands by the endless rows of geraniums, a proud father protective of his brood. The Poles and the driver were gone now, back on the corpse run, from the living to the dead, always such a bountiful harvest.

Hassler seems oblivious to the arrival of Overath and the three Jews. Transfixed by the geraniums, he had left the world. With a certain amount of discomfort Overath coughed to gain his superiors attention. Hassler did not tum to face the young

SS officer but continued to gaze admiringly at the plants.

'Are they not the most beautiful specimens you have ever seen, Overath?' The SS man hated being in the presence of Hassler. The man with his mad obsessions unnerved him. He just wanted to hand the three Yids over to him and then head back to the officer's mess for breakfast. 'Yes, Herr Commandant they are wonderful flowers. Sir, I have brought the three prisoners that you requested,' Hassler turning slowly interjects. He eyes the three Jews with a mixture of disdain and suspicion.

'What do you know about horticulture? Specifically geraniums, have you planted them before?' As if one the three men remove their caps, but remain quiet and uneasy. Finally, Lazarus cowed and hesitant stumble's a reply. 'Herr Commandant, every Spring I helped my mother plant geraniums in our garden in Krakow.' Hassler already turns to Yitzhak. 'And you?' The tension in Yitzhak's voice is palpable. 'Herr Commandant, I too helped my parents plant geraniums and lavender in our garden.'

Even before Yitzhak has finished speaking, Hassler's cold eyes are upon the small, frail figure of Dawid. 'So, Little Jew, what do you know of geraniums?' As if overawed, or simply not understanding the question, Dawid remains silent. With growing annoyance Hassler repeats the question. Still there is no response. Without another word Hassler grabs Dawid's hands and inspects them closely. Lazarus looks briefly at Yitzhak and then casts eyes downwards. Roughly turning Dawid's hands over in his Hassler speaks dismissively.

'These are not the hands of a nurturer of a gardener they have no sensitivity, no creativity, no soul. They are hands without life. Get back to the camp. There is no work for you here.' After a few seconds that seem an age, Dawid understands that he has been rejected, dismissed. So young, slight, fragile in his oversized rags, this lost little man boy glances across at Lazarus, his large dark eyes pleading for help. A help that is not forthcoming. Instead, ashamed and embarrassed at his helplessness, Lazarus looks at anything other than that face.

Finally, turning slowly, Dawid starts to walk tentatively away across the manicured grass back towards the camp. Hassler watches him briefly his face expressionless. Then in one swift movement he takes his Luger from his holster and fires twice in quick succession. Dawid falls instantly. Dying as he had lived, silently. Turning abruptly Hassler walks away towards the villa. Lazarus and Yitzhak remain rooted to the spot. Suddenly Hassler turns and faces them. Instinctively Lazarus closes his eyes and waits for the bullet. He feels the rapid beat of his heart thumping in his ears. He thinks of Esther. So, this is it? But instead of a bullet, Hassler's voice rings out.

'Before you start planting the flowers, plant him!' He glances disdainfully across at the prone figure of Dawid 'But nowhere near the geraniums. You understand?'

The car reeked of baby sick and harassed parents; but it offered sanctuary against the bitter cold night. Baines had hot wired the old Marina and driven it triumphantly out of the train station car park. He was buzzing, it was the first car he had actually been able to successfully hot wire. And now as he drives he swigs from a bottle of cheap red wine. On the crackling car radio 'In The City' by The Jam blasts out and Baines wonders if this is as good as it gets?...

Would he still be doing this, living like this in ten, twenty years time? For no reason at all or perhaps there was one but he just could not explain it, he remembered how in one English lesson at school he had had to read a text of the play 'Waiting for Godot'. At the time he had not been able to make sense of it. It was just these two blokes waiting, waiting for something to happen, but it never did. At the time he thought that the geezer who had written it was either nuts, or a sad muppet who should seriously consider getting out more often.

But now he thought he could kind of see where the guy was coming from. It's like he was saying that there is no point in waiting for someone or something, you have to make things happen. Well, that was the interpretation of a boozed up seventeen year old. And who is to say he is wrong? After all, is not all art and literature subjective? Turning his head, Baines briefly looks across at Conor as street lights rip a dead yellow across his long face. There dull light briefly illuminated his eyes.

Baines feels a passing sense of pity and revulsion, taking another swig from his bottle, as if to clear his mind of the imagery, he looks back out at the road ahead. Eerie, black and serpentine it stretches out far into the night. The boy had no idea where he was headed, where the road would eventually lead.

The warmth in the car made Conor feel sleepy, but he would not give in to it. For as long as he could remember, he had possessed an ambivalent attitude towards sleep. At times he would love how sleep afforded him dreamless oblivion, a sweet respite from not having to think about thinking, an ephemeral sanctuary against the shudders and the black. But equally he dreaded it when all that sleep offered him were dream terrors. Bizarre sleep visions where a voice, cold and mocking tormented him with its visionary hate. Over and over the rasping voice would tell him that the black cloak of suffering was sure to be his for all eternity. For his soul was cursed, cancerous, and for him there could never be the sweet release and tranquillity of death.

The irony was that the voice always emanated from flames but was always beyond cold, one minute it was a wrathful and vengeful God the next a loving, comforting Satan, and as much as Conor asked why? The more the voice mocked him. Sardonically gushing its bile in hateful floods from deep down in the flames. 'Who will bury you creature? Who would cast someone such as you, damaged of eye, face and soul into the frozen earth?' On and on the voice spat out its vitriol, 'All would be repelled by you, they would recoil in their revulsion' Conor had once tried to explain to Baines about the nightmares, but the boy had simply laughed, spat and looked away. So, Conor had never mentioned them again. But he knew that the voice and what it told him was real, he knew that now, knew that he could never die as others did.

Outside, the distant toll of church bells brought in the new year. Baines takes his eyes briefly off the road and turns to Conor. He wants to say something but realises he cannot really be arsed. So instead he stares hard at the road ahead again.

Lighting a cigarette, Conor thinks of her again. Sometimes the need, the hopeless yearning and craving hurt so badly. He knew she would not come back, but still he waited. And now in the darkness, he suddenly thinks back to when he was a little kid and the holiday to Hastings his mum had taken him on. In his mind's eye he could see the guest house on the front they had stayed in. With its capacious front entrance like a snarling mouth, so stark and austere, and its corpulent landlady, who

Conor's mum had said resembled Goering in a dress. Yes, he remembered it all so clearly.

He and his mum had taken a double room on the top floor of the guest house. Spartan, but clean and neat, it was from there that Conor had first spotted the lone herring gull on the roof of the fishermen's huts on the seafront. It had captured his attention as it never seemed to move from the spot. Rain spattered and wind battered, still it maintained its motionless silent vigil.

Whether Conor was on the crazy golf course or seafront trampolines, the bird would be on its spot staring silently out to sea. But unlike the other gulls, it never harassed or dive bombed holiday makers and day trippers for their soggy chips or undercooked hot dogs. No, aloof it stood above the crowd, oblivious to the milling throng around and beneath it. Over breakfast one morning Conor had told his mum about the bird, of how it was seemingly just waiting. She had distractedly replied that it was probably different birds he was seeing. But he knew otherwise.

On the final day of the holiday as Conor was walking along the seafront eating greasy chips as fat as fingers, he saw a group of kids throwing pebbles at the herring gull. But the bird did not flinch, did not move. It was as if he did not even see them. They did not exist. Transfixed, he gazed as ever out to sea, waiting.

The petrol station in many ways somehow seemed to resemble a sickly and vulnerable old man. Remote, desolate, and in the first stages of minor dereliction, it had belonged to the Grangemoor family for as long as anyone could remember. The latest and last scion of the name was Daniel. Joyless, wifeless and increasingly lifeless, this squat and stocky man in his early sixties had had enough; enough of long working hours at the garage for little reward, enough of developers and speculators willing to offer him a pittance for his little piece of ground.

And now sitting in his tiny garage office with its leaking radiator he thought of phoning the kid in London again. Hesitantly he picks up the telephone receiver, and then lets it slowly fall. What was the point of calling, the kid was never in. Daniel ran a hand through curly greying hair and concluded that being a freelance arsonist was obviously a lucrative Profession to be in, unlike working your nuts off in a run down garage for nicht.

Rising slowly from his chair he looks out across the moonlit, floodlit slushscape. Suddenly he turns his gaze to the small station forecourt and idly counts the potholes. He smiles a thin smile of resignation as he recalls how every hole had occurred.

There would have been a time many moons ago when he would have dutifully filled in every hole. But now there seems so little point. Symbolic of this tired antagonism he felt in heart and mind towards the garage, were the three antiquated red petrol pumps, Chelsea pensioners in metal form. And as if aware Daniel was looking at them so disdainfully, the pumps seemed to drop there nozzles a little lower in sad submission and shame.

But things had not always been like this. Many years ago when he was young and possessed of something resembling enthusiasm, the petrol station had seemed kind of exciting, a challenge to Daniel. In moments of reverie he had imagined the garage was one of those gas filling stations seemingly obligatory fixtures in American films of the fifties. Back then in his mind's eye he could imagine Jimmy Dean turning up at his petrol station in his 54 Chewy. Or perhaps a Ford Mustang packed to overspill with sickeningly beautiful and healthy rich college kids, out slumming it for the night.

And as the bell rang out on the forecourt announcing their rowdy arrival, an old 'Gus the gas' type character would emerge from the filling station office wiping oily hands on even oilier overalls. And as he cleans the windscreen of the Mustang and then fills it full of gas he would be cheerily servile, as it did not do to smart mouth the progeny of the local rich and powerful.

And so, the master and slave banter would go back and forth even though by now Gus was dying inside, feeling less than nothing. Finally tiring of the humiliation game the beautiful young things would sling Gus a couple of bucks and then drive off to the roughest bop, hop or bar they could find, leaving Gus with a pained stick on smile on his leathery old face.

Daniel turns away from the window. He had so wanted to be one of those rich college kids, but had turned out to be Gus. Just then his old black and tan cat scratches insistently at the outside door seeking refuge from the cold. Looking at the creature through the door glass, Daniel realises he has clean forgotten its name. He could remember he had owned the cat nine years, could even recall where he had got it from. But its name? Distractedly he lets the cat in and walks slowly back to the tiny office, where once more cold tea and a vague ennui are his.

Sitting down in his chair he decides to do it, to phone the kid again. But once more, as ever, there is no reply. Outside it had started to snow again, wet cloying clumps drifted down. Daniel sips his cold tea and waits. Perhaps the kid was on his way to him?

As much as he tries, Baines cannot get the image of the run down petrol station out of his mind. Although situated on the main London road, it had seemed to him somehow out of place, forgotten, and now in his head a seed was germinating, a dark seed.

He finally pulls the car over into a darkened lay by and switches off the engine. Lighting another cigarette he looks at the snow tumbling from the night sky. Through the white and into the black he sees the red twinkling tail light of an aircraft. He is surprised to see it in such weather, surprised and envious. He watches it until it disappears from view, and thinks to himself that he does not give a shit where the thing was going, he just wished he was on it. Because delude himself as he may, he knew deep down that this was not a life he was living. It wasn't really anything. Draining the bottle dry and smoking his fag to the filter, he muses.

The cold finally won, waking Conor from his brief slumber. Yawning, shivering, he asks sleepily. 'Why have we stopped?' Baines does not reply. He is on a plane. Conor smears a hand across his crippled eyes. They ache constantly in the cold weather; reminding him of their continued unwelcome existence. When he was a child he thought that if he rubbed hard enough at them for long enough they would somehow go away, disappear. Now older, he sometimes when the shudders are really bad, considers taking more drastic action. After all, they cut out cancers and tumours. The darkness in the car makes him feel both calm and uneasy. Instinctively he feels for the knife in his pocket, and then not so instinctively for the crucifix in his other pocket. Which one could save him?

Outside in the black and white everything was so still and

silent. To Conor it truly feels as if he is the last of the last. Flicking his fag butt out of the car window, Baines finally breaks his reverie as he turns to face Conor. 'Do you think a petrol station round here makes much money?' Conor mumbles a reply. 'Why, you thinking of buying one?' Baines sneers at him briefly. 'You're funny. Christ I nearly busted a rib. No, smart bollocks, the thing is while you were in dreamland or devil land or wherever the hell you were at, we passed a petrol station. It looked a really soft touch, you know! An easy job.' A passing cars headlights scythe across Conor's thin face.

'Oh yeah, just like that last really 'easy' job of yours.' Baines sighs heavily, he knows what is coming. 'Yeah, really genius idea of yours to rob Unigate when they had the sodding builders in!' Baines sighs once more. 'How the hell was I supposed to know there was gonna be building work going on there?' This time Conor sighs. 'I dunno, maybe the sight of sodding JCB's all over the dairy yard might have given you a clue!' He rubs aching eyes wearily. A quiet descends, until Baines finally breaks it. 'Alright! I admit it, the Unigate job didn't exactly go to plan, but.' Conor interjects tetchily. 'You mean you actually had a plan?'

Baines ignores the sarcasm. 'Look, I got good vibes about this petrol station, I reckon we can get some real money out of it. This one is different.' Once more Conor replies with a sarcastic weariness. 'Yeah, they are always different.' But his words are only heard by the darkness, because Baines was back on a plane.

The job in the bookshop made Dina happy. The touch, the feel, even the smell of the books pleased her. Of course there were books in the shop that held no appeal for her, but it did not matter, for every tome in the little cavernous shop contained the thoughts, erudition, inspiration and mental perspiration of their disparate authors, and this Dina greatly respected and admired. One day she would be a writer. She knew this, she was not sure how or when, but she knew it would happen.

She had got the job in the bookshop a few months back, just after her seventeenth birthday. That day she had spent a particularly fruitless afternoon in her local job centre and was on her way home via collecting a prescription for her nan from the chemists, when she noticed the job vacancy for 'Sales Assistant' stuck rather hurriedly and obliquely on the book-shop window. With a nothing to lose attitude she had entered the shop.

Needless to say, Mr Breitner the shop owner had been suffi-ciently impressed by her enthusiasm and palpable love of books to offer her the job there and then. To say she was overjoyed would be an understatement. She had simply gripped the job offer by the throat. Truth is that Breitner, an astute, balding foreigner in his mid sixties, had been equally impressed by the fact that Dina was under eighteen, thus meaning he could pay her the bare minimum. But pauper or princess, Dina really did not care, she would be working, touching, seeing, feeling books, reward enough for her.

However, that Breitner was odd somehow Dina discovered in her first few days working in the shop. As she served customers or stocked shelves she would often see him pacing in his small office, apparently in conversation with himself. Sometimes she would try to get close enough to the office to attempt to find out what he was saying, but all she could make out was that he appeared to be speaking German.

Alongside this strange behaviour, she also could not but help notice that he spent an inordinate amount of time just staring out of the shop window, as if waiting for someone or something. And whilst he did this in silence, there was a certain agitation in his features. However, these peculiarities aside, Dina found Breitner to be a polite and considerate employer. Indeed, he seemed keen to foster her love of books and knowledge by encouraging her to take home any tome that was of interest to her. And he seemed genuinely interested in her health and well being also.

So much so that every morning as she arrived for work, he would invariably ask her how her leg was. And this despite the fact that Dina had often told him that although her childhood accident had left her with a pronounced limp, her leg rarely pained her. But she always thanked him for his concern.

In some ways Dina felt sympathy for this strange man there was an indefinable sadness and loneliness about him. Every evening after the final customer had left and they were about to shut up shop, he would courteously thank her for her day's efforts and bid her a good evening, and always there would be a barely concealed sadness in his eyes. However, this snowy New Years Eve early evening, Breitner surprised Dina by asking her politely, but self consciously, if she would care to join him in his flat for a New Years Eve drink. Almost the instant he had made this innocent proposal in his halting ponderous English, he regretted it. Dina's large dark eyes seemed to him Full of unease and discomfort. Breitner suddenly felt very old and very cheap.

Trying to rescue the situation from a drowning silence, he said to her that he had recently purchased a first edition of

Hardy's 'Jude the Obscure' that she may be interested in. The truth was that Dina had not replied to his proposal straight away because she was not sure how to. An element of confusion existed in her mind. To refuse his offer would make her appear cold and ungrateful, and undoubtedly hurt him. Yet she could not help feeling a sense of uneasiness. However, as he was turning away from her, Dina finally found a small voice. 'Yes, thank you, a drink would be nice.'

It was just gone two am, and Lazarus Glick had finally bought sleep, but at such a cost. Outside, the last of the New Year revellers were drunkenly embracing a new shiny decade. Whilst inside, in sleep, Lazarus was reliving an old decade, one which had created what he had become and destroyed what he had once been.

Was it her? Lazarus was trying to see, attempting to make out in the hollow of a wave Esther amongst the heaving throng of frightened humanity being shepherded towards the waiting serpentine freight trains. The wagon doors are being pulled open by Ukrainian auxiliaries. The wagons resemble dark, empty mouths, gaping and insatiable. Was it her? Cajoled and coerced a human tide of despair sates the hungry mouths. Whips and rifle butts at their backs and fear, terror and the unknown to their front, the human cargo with screams and blows are boarding the wagons, young and old, the able bodied and the lame. All are boarding.

'Have you seen her? A small woman, mid-twenties, dark hair, hazel eyes. Her name is Esther Glick, she is my wife. You must have seen her!?'

The old blind Jew walked proudly, his nephew Lazarus on his right arm, Esther on his left. From a distance away across the crowded, chaotic, dusty train station, the stocky SS man sees him, decides he is not walking fast enough. Approaching the dignified old man he orders Lazarus and Esther away. And then a few inches from the old man's unseeing eyes he screams at him 'Schnell! Schneller!' Confused and bewildered the old Jew attempts to obey, but he stumbles and falls. Lazarus tries to lift his uncle up but is beaten away by the butt of a rifle.

Unsteadily the old man rises to his feet. The SS man proudly wearing around his ample girth his 'Gott mit uns' belt, bellows once more 'Schnell!

Schneller!' Heads in the cowed crowd turn and eyes widen, as a crying sun looks on weeping down its rays. From the crowd 'Shema Y Israel' is gasped out. Running as hard as he can, stumbling and exhausted, the man with the dead eyes is watched by a man with a smile and a dead heart. The old man does not know he is running towards the train tracks, cannot see the hurtling train. Lazarus sinks to his knees in the dust; Esther screams an animal scream, and the SS man laughs to see such fun. 'Have you seen her, my wife?'

Deep in the dark heart of the shadow of the crematorium, flames dance and people dance. In a kind of blind frenzy the wedding party sways, shimmers and circles. The Klezmer band strikes up 'Hava Nagila' and they rip it out hard and fast, the circle of joy ripples and bobs like waves. Coming in, going out, and this circle of happiness remains unbroken. In a corner old Lea Rosenthal, defiantly dour, exclaims in a loud voice to no one in particular. 'It was not like this in my day. Back then weddings were respectable, pious affairs.'

Toothless Yankiel Glick, the father of the groom, downs another glass of vodka on the run and cusses back at her. 'A wedding without a band is like a piss without a fart!' She looks at him daggers. But soon they are swept along by the tide, by the manic and mesmerising dance, and still the circle remains unbroken. And in the middle of this clinging, clasping circle of love, bride and groom are raised high on steady shoulders. They had waited so long for now and now had finally come. Now was their time, a fine time, a shining time. And from on high Lazarus looks across at she who is now his life. Esther returns his look. But her large hazel eyes are staring and scared. He does not understand this look it is not one she has worn before. Strong Esther, bold Esther now looks so small and fragile a mouse amongst serpents.

She speaks to him but above the music he cannot hear her words. Her face is now grey and ashen, her lips contorted. He tries to reach her but the circle is moving in, suffocating. Now he is no longer on strong shoulders, he is floating, drifting high above the carnage. He watches as the circle is finally broken, ripped asunder. Tears of blood roll down his cheeks, as the dancing stops and the band are forced to play a stigmata cantata. Bodies have turned to stone, twisted and contorted with limbs entwined, families clutching a final embrace. As in life so shall they be in... Lazarus is blinded by his blood tears. He scrambles over bodies seeking his Esther amongst the chaos. Finally, as a pillar of salt he finds her. And through her death mask face he hears her, hears barely audible gasped out words.

'Lazarus, say Kaddish for me. Say it for our people. I love you Lazarus, never forget that... Stay alive. Survive!'

Deep in the dark heart of the shadow of the crematorium flames dance, but people no longer do.

Sweat-shrouded, Lazarus with his eyes still burning from

looking inward at his own dream rises from his bed of twisted sheets and murdered souls and shivers against the cold. Then suddenly this man with a stone heart, cold heart, no heart sinks to his knees. A huge choking sob roars and racks his body. As shoulders heave and fists clench. From somewhere deep in his soul a keening wail, an animal howl rips out into the silence... She was gone forever.

CHAPTER THREE

Baines drove the car slowly past the petrol station twice. By the third time he was ready. Conor had spent the last twenty minutes trying to talk him out of doing the 'job' without success. Truth was Conor was not averse to robbing the place, but the petrol station looked so on the cusp of dereliction that he just wondered if there was actually anything worth nicking in it. Besides, he was cold, hungry and tired. To him right now even the semi-warmth of the dark and dreary squat seemed preferable to freezing his nuts off in a stolen car in the middle of nowhere.

But Baines was not to be dissuaded or denied. He just kept repeating over and over that he had a good 'vibe' about the job, and that it would be the 'perfect score' Conor just wished he would stop watching second rate American crime films.

They finally parked the car up at the side of the petrol station, around fifty yards from the forecourt and out of sight. The plan was simple. Baines would break into the station and hoist anything worth hoisting, while Conor would stay in the motor with the engine running. And so through a stark, white-dark brightness, he watches as Baines trudges off through the snow towards the front entrance of the station.

Earlier, whilst driving past, he had noticed that there was a small window half open. He made his way towards it. But soon his disappointment was tangible. Although he was skinny, he was not that skinny. There was no way he could squeeze through the small aperture. Peering through its filthy glass, he is not able to see too much, but can just about make out that behind the counter there is a small wall rack with packs of cigs stacked in compartments. Reaching into his trouser pocket he pulls out a Zippo lighter. Then promptly drops it into the snow. 'Bollocks!' Getting down onto his haunches he sinks cold fingers into freezing slush searching for the lighter.

In the car, Conor watches proceedings with a sense of incredulity and mild amusement. 'Now, kids, carefully observe the master criminal at work. Notice his professionalism, and how he always goes properly prepared for every job... What a prick!' for the briefest of moments, Conor just felt like driving off and leaving 'Reggie Kray' to scramble about in the snow with frost-bitten fingers. But the thought passed as quickly as it had come.

Outside, soaking wet and increasingly frustrated, Baines finally locates the errant lighter. It does not work 'Fucking great!' More out of hope than expectation, he walks a few paces in the black to the front entrance door and slowly turns the door handle. To his utter surprise the door is unlocked. Blowing out his cheeks, he smiles nervously and enters the opaque premises.

The smell that hits him reminds him of damp, dried out, then damp again paper, either that or the mustiness of an old church. Cautiously in the gloom he makes his way to the station counter. At its end stands an archaic looking till. Once, twice, three times he tries to open it. But the metal dinosaur is obdurate and feisty and refuses to yield. Cursing, he turns his attention to the wall rack and its cigs. Just then, an explosion of light fractures the darkness. Turning his head sharply, Baines sees the stocky figure of Daniel standing in the doorway, his finger on the light switch. He blinks hard, trying to accustom his eyes to the brightness, and then turns to run, but Daniel's voice with its tone of annoyance Stops him in his tracks.

'What time do you call this? You were supposed to call me first to let me know you were coming.' Daniel eyes the skinny kid ruefully. He did kind of have the look of an arsonist about him. Still squinting eyes against the light, Baines cannot disguise the look of bewilderment on his face. The old man must be mad, or pissed. Never exactly a warrior of the word, the boy merely responds with a muted. 'Do what?' He starts to slowly ease towards the exit. Daniel walks towards him. 'Brian did tell you the deal? A hundred pounds now and another hundred pounds when the insurance company pays out.'

At the mention of money Baines is instantly intrigued. Now he edges away from the exit and back towards Daniel. With a practised slyness he thinks on his feet. 'Yeah, Brian told me a bit of detail but not all, how about you fill me in on the rest.' Daniel eyes him briefly, then motions him to his small office. 'We can talk in there,' Baines follows Daniel inside, slowly closing the door behind himself.

Outside, the temperature was falling, as was Conor's patience levels. Baines had been gone forty minutes now and once more the thought of just driving away briefly revisited his tired mind, but as before he stops thinking of it. Turning the car radio on he plays with the dials and just gets static or foreign stations, and he wonders why at night it was easier to get French stations than English ones? .And on and on the voice on the radio was saying a million things but telling him nothing. Well, nothing he could understand. Indeed, the French geezer's voice was slow torture. It was one of those voices you hear that instantly makes you shudder. Makes you feel a desperate need for a cold shower.

Finally Conor snaps the radio off, killing the killer voice. In the darkness he lights his last fag and idly wonders if all Frenchmen of a certain age had the type of voice that sounds like they are spewing into a bucket. His fatuous reverie was broken by the sight of Baines exiting the front entrance of the petrol station.

As he approaches the car, Conor sees he wears a sly smile on his pale face. Getting into the motor, Baines slaps a handful of cash on the dashboard. Conor looks at the money and then at the boy. 'So, the old place did have some cash then. Christ, you were in there ages!' Baines shakes his head slowly. 'Jesus, you would not believe what happened in there. It was fucking mental!' With a half-smile he faces Conor. 'Y'know, the geezer who owns the petrol station only thought I was a sodding arsonist!' Conor looks at the boy non-plussed. Thinks maybe that the petrol fumes had done for what was left of his brain.

'What you talking about? So, you are saying there was someone in there?' Baines opens a pack of Rothmans he had lifted from the fag machine and slowly lights a cig. 'Christ, Con, try and keep up! Yes Einstein, that's exactly what I'm saying.' He inhales hard on his cig, then continues.

'Look, when I got inside it was pitch black, couldn't see nothing. Anyway, there I'am groping around in the dark trying to open an old till, when, Bang! all of a sudden the lights are on full blast. And there he is, this old geezer standing in the doorway with a face like a slapped arse. I dunno if he is tooled up or something. And I'm not going to hang around to find out. So I start edging towards the door, getting ready to leggit.

But then he starts talking to me. Some old bollocks about how he has been waiting for me to come and do the job.'

Conor interrupts briefly. 'Job, what job?'

Baines sighs impatiently. 'I'm coming to that...Look, bottom line is, it's a case of mistaken identity. He has been waiting for some kid to come down from London to torch the place for the insurance money. So, I became that kid!' Baines smiles and shakes his head ruefully. Conor looks at him and then runs a hand through his lank dark brown hair. 'So, we are going to torch the place. When?' Baines stubs his cig out in the ashtray and faces him. 'He wants the job done now. He has already left by the back door so to speak. But he will be back tomorrow morning, no doubt heartbroken to see his place a pile of ashes.' Baines suddenly looks up to the sky, but the plane is long gone. Conor is quiet briefly.

'But if he has already stumped up the cash and is gone now, why don't we just go? Why bum it?' Baines looks at him as if he has uttered a heresy. 'Are you having a laugh? I want to sodding torch it! And anyway, once the insurance stumps up we get another sixty quid.' He smiles thinly. 'The man is a total mug. I would have done the fucking job for a tenner.' He opens the car door and lets in the night. 'Come on then, let's go... Frying tonight!' He laughs like a drain at his lame joke and gets out of the car. Conor follows him uneasily, sucking in freezing air and crunching coldness underfoot.

Thirty minutes later and flames are licking and lapping at the night. From a safe distance, and obscured by the black, the apprentice arsonists watch the bonfire of Baines vanities with conflicting emotions. Sitting in the car they view their handiwork as it reaches its crescendo. With firelight illuminating his face, Baines is transfixed, mesmerised by the flames. Conor looks across at his face, disturbed and disturbing. The look in Baines eyes is almost one of orgasmic entrancement. Conor on the other hand just feels sick, he has seen enough. Breathless and shaking he drives away rapidly, as behind them petrol pumps play out the finale, exploding orange-red into the black. Conor turns his gaze away from the flames and looks at the trembling sky. And then, for no reason he can think of, he suddenly starts to cry.

Had it actually happened? Dina was silent at the breakfast table. She looks first at the unappetising cold toast on her plate and then across at her grandmother. As ever, the old woman sits with a vacant expression on her face. Only her pale lips move as she utters over and over. 'If thine eyes torment thee, then cast them out.' Dina looks at her grandmother's hand as the fingers twitch and stroke imaginary fur on the kitchen table.

Dina so wanted to reach out to touch that hand, to feel warmth, life. She takes the shaky hand and holds it in her own. It feels limp, cold and lifeless briefly her grandmother looks at her as if seeing her for the first time. And then slowly takes her hand away. 'I'm tired, I want to go to bed.' Her voice is as vague as her dim and rheumy eyes. Dina sighs, but as ever answers patiently. 'Nan, you have only just got up. It's eight in the morning. How about I put the radio on? There might be some music you like. Tell me again about that dancing competition you won when you were a girl.'

The old lady is silent. Dina slowly rises from the table. 'I'll put the kettle on for another cup of tea.' She walks out into the small and spotlessly clean kitchen. That place that always somehow smelt of pine disinfectant and fresh bread, a heady combination. As she fills the kettle at the sink she briefly thinks of Breitner. Thinks of the things he had told her.

From outside in the tiny snow-patterned garden, the morbid song of a crow cuts loose, intruding in upon the quiet. Coming away from the sink, Dina sees that the breakfast table is now empty. In the silence she suddenly feels very alone and very young. Sitting back down at the table, Dina suddenly feels an overwhelming need to cry. But tears to her were a luxury she had not allowed herself for... For such a long time. She bows her head just as a pallid, kindly winter sun briefly smiles yellow across her legs. She looks at her lame left leg. And in this very instant she somehow feels the presence of her mum. Then, for a moment the sweet release of tears are hers.

Somehow, Breitner's flat had not been as Dina had imagined it. In her mind's eye she had expected his home above the book-shop to be cluttered wall to ceiling with all genres of weighty tomes, a veritable suburban oasis of study, erudition and knowl-edge. Instead, the space was dark, sparse and gloomy. Entering the front room, Breitner had smiled nervously as he motioned Dina to sit down on a faded sofa of indeterminate colour or hue. Briefly he hovered around her nervous and clumsy.

It was with a sense of relief that she finally watched him walk away into the small kitchen. In his brief absence, Dina allowed her gaze to pan the room. What she could not help but notice was that the space lacked any sense of homeliness or warmth. It kind of reminded her of what she imagined a room in a hostel might look like, transient and soulless. There were no photos of loved ones in silver frames. No paintings adorning the walls, no ornaments or sentimental keepsakes. There was not even a television.

After a few minutes, Breitner returned from the kitchen. He placed a small tray carrying a bottle of red wine and two glasses onto the aged coffee table, and then poured the drinks. Sitting down in a worn, burgundy leather armchair opposite Dina, he raised his glass and wished her a Happy New Year.

Thereafter, platitudes and trivia were exchanged between them. And after ten minutes or so it was palpable that these two lonely people, more than a generation apart, had little in common save for a profound love of books. In the ensuing silences of which there were many, Breitner drank heavily, nervously. Dina, drinking moderately, watched the metamorphosis gradually take place. With every glass of wine imbibed, this taciturn man became more loquacious as well as more and more agitated. He spoke of his childhood, not in terms of time and place, but in feelings and emotions. He rambled, mumbling and stumbling over his words.

Dina felt that he was no longer even aware of her as a specific person, as an individual with a distinct character and personality. No, she merely felt she had become some sort of receptacle for his melancholic mumblings. And by the time he was half way through the second bottle of red wine, his mumbling words were coming thick and fast. A babble of English and German emanated from his thin mouth. Lucid then incoherent.

'Sobald es anfing, konnte ich den Wahnsinn nicht mehr stoppen.' Dina did not understand his words, did not know how to put back together a falling down man. Instead she sits stunned, somehow paralysed. Who was this man in front of her? A few hours ago he had been her boss, a quiet, polite and reserved person. Now, with the metamorphosis near complete she no longer recognises the sobbing and desperate figure who was seemingly becoming smaller more crumpled and crushed before her eyes.

She felt sick, just wanted to leave, get away. But try as she might she could not move. In her unease, her helplessness, she gazes across once more at Breitner. as if to make sure he was real, that this was real. In the gloom of a dark space, a grey, granite face looked back at her, as he sat rigid in the chair eyes unblinking. And with those eyes of some moribund, beached sea creature, he stared through Dina, as if looking at nothing but seeing everything. Everything as it was all those years ago in those wild east days of mud and blood. And even though the world had moved on from those days because it had to, he had remained the same. Well, almost the same.

Truth was, as each haunting year had passed he had started to feel something akin to contrition. Indeed, there was no doubt that in his heart there was the occasional beat of remorse, and an increasing need to somehow atone. But how does one make reparation to ashes?

Finally, as quickly as the maelstrom had swallowed him up, it released him into drunken sleep. And his stupor also appeared to free Dina from her petrification. Rising slowly, she involuntarily shuddered, the intense feelings of nausea was once more with her. For a few moments she just stood as heavy as stone, staring round a room devoid of soul or warmth. Her gaze finally settled on Breitner. Slumped in his chair he looked very old and very damaged. Cautiously she touched his hand. It was of ice. Feeling strangely vague and disassociated she drifted off into the master bedroom and took a heavy blanket from the bed.

In the front room Breitner muttered in drunken sleep.

'Juden!..In Gottes Namen!' As she covered him with the blanket he groaned and shifted slightly, before falling silent. Dina needed air, needed to breathe again.

Outside in the street, as some party goers waited for now, and as others counted down the seconds as another year died, a small, dark, limping girl sucked and breathed in the night, before sinking to her knees and being violently sick. No one helped her no one came to her aid. As ever, Dina was alone.

The planting of the geraniums was nearing its end. It had been a disaster. Firstly, the weather had been unpredictable. One minute a watery sun and blue skies had been in the ascendency, then, barely an hour later and the heavens would open, releasing rain in biblical proportions. Hassler, from the balcony of his villa, was a sentinel to all that transpired. Lazarus and Yitzhak were never far from his cold, menacing yet silent observation. Rain or shine he was there, watching and waiting. Most worryingly for the pair were the times, generally in the late afternoons, when Hassler would appear on the balcony with a bottle of schnapps in one hand and his rifle in the other.

But despite his close and menacing attention, Lazarus dreaded the moment when the last geranium was planted, for then the back-breaking brutality of the quarry would once more be his. But of more immediate concern to him was that as carefully as he and Yitzhak planted the geraniums, within hours they were dying, if not already dead. And try as they might to revive the moribund plants, it was all to no avail. But despite this, for now the pair were safe, Hassler from his balcony vantage point could not see the full picture, was unable to view the catastrophe up close. However, tomorrow was to be his 'inspection' day. And Lazarus could already feel the noose tightening around his neck.

It was soon common knowledge in the barracks, that the plants, known ironically by the inmates as 'Hassler's Babies' were dead or dying. The religious Jewish inmates attributed their demise as being a divine judgement upon Hassler from God. As the flowers had withered and died then so eventually would he at the end of an executioner's rope. The more secular Jews mocked this view. However, even some of these conceded that the soil of the camp was somehow tainted, evil, thus responsible for the demise of the flowers.

'And it's not just the soil that is poisoned by this hell.' The voice of Manny drifted across the gloom of the barrack. 'It's the skies as well'. He swayed a little as he spoke, the vodka stale on his breath. 'I mean, has anyone in this shit hole ever actually seen a bird here?' He is met with silence. He does not notice. 'It's like even the bloody birds know this place is evil. Even they know the crimes, the horrors being committed here.' And it was true. In Hassler's empire not only was the soil toxic, tainted and barren. So too were the skies.

In the sullen opacity of the barrack, Lazarus and Yitzhak listened to the various viewpoints and gathered no solace or comfort. Indeed, all that the words engendered in their hearts was a fear and trepidation for what Hassler's morning inspection would bring.

So, as it must, night seamlessly moved aside letting in a morning that was chill and stark. Both Lazarus and Yitzhak had spent fitful and sleepless nights. The first part of which had been given over to utter silent despair. But gradually as weariness played tricks on such tired minds, they discovered a spurious optimism, a hope however remote that maybe the geraniums would miraculously revive and resurrect themselves from the blighted and poisonous soil. Or perhaps that during the night Hassler would go fully insane and blow his head off.

But by dawn's first unwelcome light, all straws had been clutched at and proven to be worthless. And at seven am, as was the routine, Overath came to the barracks to take them to the villa garden. However, this morning he had a face like thunder. 'You two bastards are dead, now fucking move!' Chasing Lazarus and Yitzhak out of the barrack, he beat them wildly with his cudgel as they ran. In the hurry scurry chaos, Yitzhak lost a boot in the cloying black mud, but carried on running, too frightened to retrieve it. With his heart beating hard and his mind alternating between numbness and fear, Lazarus knows he is running to his death.

Still a hundred metres from the villa, he could hear the apoplectic, apocalyptic curses of Hassler roaring out. The hour of Lazarus had struck. It was a funeral bell. And now under a flurry of beatings and threats from Overath, Lazarus and Yitzhak, bruised and bloodied are chased towards Hassler, who is waving his Luger around like a lunatic, but whose raging storm has now given way to the first stage of bereavement.

He stands over the rows of his ailing or deceased progeny: a grieving father. He turns slowly and faces the mud spattered, blood splattered murderers of his geranium children. His voice when it comes is flowing, as black and hateful as the mud that was his camp. 'You, you Jews you truly are our misfortune. Everything you bastards touch dies in the dust. God's chosen people? Huh! What God would that be?' He is quiet briefly. Lazarus still breathes hard and heavy from fear and the chase.

He just wishes the mad bastard would get on with it, pull the trigger and put an end to it once and for all.

As an apologetic sun timidly shines through the grey, he feels and hears Yitzhak softly sobbing by his side. Then the strangest thing happens. He feels an overwhelming desire to smile. To laugh at the absurdity of it all, everything was so ludicrous. Here he was about to surrender his life and all because of some dead flowers. He stifled the desire to laugh by looking up at a sky he would never see again. And it was so strange to think that everything would go on without him. The earth, moon, stars, trees, love, hate, all would just carry on.

Hassler's voice, now tearful because of his loss, snapped Lazarus back to his mad reality. 'The Führer is so right! You scum truly are a cancer, a bacilli infecting decent humanity!' Lazarus sighed inwardly and could not help thinking that at least he deserved to be killed by someone who had read more than

'Der Stürmer.' The tears welled heavy in Hassler's eyes now. He gazed down mournfully down at his fallen family. It seemed to him to be a metaphor, to somehow symbolise all that was wrong.

Yitzhak was dead before he hit the ground. His blood and brains splashed warm across the face of Lazarus. Closing his eyes, Lazarus waited, and waited. But it was not a bullet that came, but Hassler's voice, sounding strangely ethereal somehow.

'Open your eyes, Jew! You won't die this day. Every man knows the day of his birth, but none know the day of his death. And so it will be with you also. But hear me, you are marked now. Your days are numbered.' Lazarus blinks hard, blood and sweat has trickled into his eyes. But he can make out the figure of Hassler walking away. His voice sounds distant. 'You know what to do with him?' Overath salutes: 'Jawohl, mein Kommandant!'

Outside the front of Barrack 3, two punishment posts rose from the cloying mud like limbless trees. Needless to say no fruit would ever be borne nor gathered from species such as these. Save for the bitter fruit of human suffering and degradation. But this day God had been doubly merciful to Lazarus Glick. Not only had the supreme deity spared him a bullet in the head, but now he seemingly appeared to perform another small miracle also. It came about like this.

Just as Overath was escorting Lazarus back to the camp, this time more with threat than cudgel, they passed SS Möller by the gates. As ever, the rotund Möller had at his heels his dog Geist, a spectral white beast, a real modern day Cerberus. This hound from hell was trained by Möller to attack prisoner's genitals on command. And these poor, halfstarved wretches had no defence against the huge creature. And the more they screamed the more Möller would roar with laughter. And at the end of the 'game' if he was feeling merciful Möller would put the poor screaming soul out of his misery by strangling him.

That the camp inmates lived in fear of Möller and his dog was an understatement, they positively quaked at his sardonic appearance. So when Möller called out to Overath and then walked over to him, Lazarus feared the worse. Even from five paces away he could smell the booze on Möller's breath. And so could Overath. It was palpable that he had little affection for the man and his crude, boozy, barstool bonhomie. Indeed, Overath preferred to project himself as being a man of taste and culture. So the crassness of Möller was an anathema to him.

Whether or not Overath was successful in this projection of himself was immaterial to Lazarus. To him, Overath was just another brutal sadist in a uniform. That said, amongst the SS in the camp there were varying degrees of sadists. And the vague and aloof Overath was at the lower end. The same could not be said of Hermann Möller, he was top of the sickening pile, Emperor of the mud and blood. For him there was nothing more enjoyable than starting his day with a victim or two. And this particular morning as he swaggered across to Overath, he was eyeing Lazarus as the wolf eyes the lamb.

'So, where are you taking the Yid?' He half spits as he slurs out the words. Overath looks at him with a practised disdain. 'The punishment post, this pile of crap decided to wipe out the chiefs 'babies.' Lazarus stands stock still, alternating furtive, frightened glances between Overath, Möller and Geist. Suddenly from nowhere, Möller swings a punch hard into the guts of Lazarus. He slumps doubled up to the ground. Struggling for breath, disorientated, he gets unsteadily to his feet. Gazing up groggily, he sees the fat laughing face of Möller, the disinterested face of Overath and the snarling bared teeth of Geist. Möller suddenly stops laughing, his voice is mocking.

'Go on Geist, go play with the Jew!' In an instant, the hound was off its lead and pouncing towards Lazarus. Once more he closes his eyes and waits for the impact. But all is silent, save for a small whine and then a whimper. Somehow time seemed suspended, hanging unreal. Suddenly he feels the warm tongue of the dog gently licking the back of his hand. He cautiously opens one eye, then the other. He gazes down at the huge brute of a dog as it almost with tenderness licks his blood and that of Yitzhak from his hands.

Möller watches in total amazement, then mortification, till finally incandescent with rage he explodes with fury. Bellowing and cursing Geist at The top of his voice. Around him this totally unexpected and unusual event is witnessed with secret glances by the wide eyed and open mouthed inmates.

And in hushed, bewildered whispers they are exultant. The beast has been tamed. Yet Geist's 'weakness' is a dagger to Möller's heart. His scream of anger is one borne of feelings of betrayal and comes from somewhere deep down in his soul it reverberates out across the entirety of the desolate camp. And if there had been birds in such a place as this, then surely they would have stopped in flight and crashed to earth such was its depth and ferocity. But after this storm came a calm, as time once more seemed suspended, frozen.

The face of Lazarus is ashen it looks as if all the blood has been instantly drained from his face. Even Overath has for once lost, or temporarily misplaced his vague aloofness. Whilst Geist, ears drawn back hard against his skull and large dark eyes fearful, starts to submissively edge, belly crawl towards his master. Möller, appalled by this weakling he has created, explodes in a flurry of fists and boots. Geist, expecting such an onslaught, skilfully avoids the blows and makes off at full tilt towards the camps perimeter fence.

Shaking with rage, Möller fumbles his pistol from its holster and fires off round after round after the dog, but Geist is long gone, slipping through the wire fence. For a moment Möller's face twitches and his shoulders heave slightly, as if a sob of loss or regret is about to escape. Then, suddenly turning on his heels, he observes across the parade ground a middle-aged Jew who he deems unfit to exist any longer in this world. With a smile that resembles a grimace, he walks over to the man. Looking hard into the man's frightened eyes, Möller simply says, 'Its time.' With that he grips the Jew by the throat and throttles him. It is as emotionless and as casual as that.

Stepping over the fallen corpse, Möller walks away towards the officers mess, where breakfast was still being served. He suddenly had such an appetite. And after he had eaten, perhaps, just maybe, he would go looking for Geist. After all, he was not such a bad dog. And as he walks to the officer's mess he whistles a cheery tune. No, not such a bad dog really.

As if both momentarily in some kind of trance, Lazarus and Overath watch Möller's departure. In his mind Lazarus tries to make sense of what had just happened. Why had not the hound savaged him like he had attacked and maimed so many others? He looks down briefly at his grimy bloodstained hands they still feel warm and wet from the dogs tongue. Had it been a miracle? Do such things exist? His reverie is ended by Overath's curses. 'Move, you Yid bastard!' Harried, hurried to the punishment post, he is pushed, prodded, pinioned to it by an enthusiastic Kapo. This time there is to be no divine intervention, the omnipotent one had helped as much as he could.

Lazarus received twenty five lashes of the heavy whip, and was forced to call out every excruciating stroke. Miss count and the whole procedure starts again. Some way, somehow he does not miss count despite the fact that never in his life has he felt such searing and unbearable pain, but just as the final agonising lash rips into his broken and lacerated flesh, from a cloudless and bright sky a gentle rain soft and soothing starts to fall, a balm for his shattered body.

Now barely conscious and mumbling incoherently, Lazarus

is dragged off to the camp infirmary, where upon reaching its doors a most inexplicable thing occurs. Suddenly in an instant, heavy rolling thunder roars and rumbles across bright and sunny skies.

In utter bewilderment eyes are raised heavenwards as a series of lightening bolts strike silver streaks across the radiantly sunny sky, many of the more mystical and religious Jews feel that this bizarre meteorological happening, along with Lazarus' taming of the hell hound somehow mark him out as special, perhaps even one of the 'just' men of old?

The more pragmatic of their number ridicule such a suggestion. Yet even they are unable to find a plausible explanation for the mornings surreal events. Either way, with his becalming of Geist and the stoicism he displayed on the punishment post, Lazarus had gained both kudos and respect from his fellow inmates. The quiet and reserved young Jew was now a name.

CHAPTER FOUR

The morning coldness in the squat was unforgiving. Swathed in a blanket that has seen better days, Conor sits cross-legged on his mattress. With cursed eyes closed but his mind open, he thinks about God. There had been a time a few years back when he had been in communication with the Almighty, but somewhere along the line they had wearied of each other, reaching the stage where God had stopped taking his calls. Now, to Conor, God just seemed to help those that could, and were able to look after themselves. So, what was the point in praying, imploring and beseeching? You may just as well pray to a house brick or pot plant.

So now the falling down boy had put his faith in having no faith. Instead, he had put hope and belief into somehow transporting himself back to a time, that time before his birth: a place, a space when he never existed or expired, but was suspended in time. Of course he knew nothing of the sciences or theology how could the kid? But he just knew that such a place existed, and he had to find it, for only then would the pain end.

The 'voice' had decreed that the boy was not as others. Had spoken, saying that he would never know the liberation of death. And Conor believed that. And so he must keep searching for that homeland suspended between this life and death, this world and some other.

The gunshot was an explosion that brought down crumbling

ceiling plaster and shattered the now. Stumbling off the mattress, Conor crawls on all fours. Raising his head slowly and warily he sees Baines standing in the doorway with a grin on his face and a pistol in his hand. Conor sneers coldly at him. 'You stupid prick you nearly gave me a heart attack!' getting to his feet, Conor glares at him, 'What the fuck you doing with that? Where the hell did you get it from?' Baines spins the pistol like a gunslinger and crashes down into the solitary armchair.

'When I was a little kid, my old man told me about this geezer who sells cheap shooters in Catford.' With a stupid grin on his face, Baines aims the gun at Conor and then presses it against his own right temple. Shaking his head slowly, Conor merely mutters, 'You are not all there, boy.' Baines smiles. 'That is sodding rich coming from you. You are only slightly less nutty than squirrel shit.' Not losing his smile, he tenderly kisses the barrel of the pistol.

Conor hates that smile, always has done. It winds him up. He hates the gap between Baines front teeth. But Baines says it's cool, makes him look like Ray Davies. But Conor thinks it makes him look more like Jimmy fucking Tarbuck. But today Baines won't be denied his smile, because all is good on Planet Baines. He has a shooter, some cash in his pocket and big plans for getting some more.

Wrapping the blanket around his shoulders, Conor walks across to the feeble fire that is distinctly more smoke than flame. Breaking up an old wooden box he banishes it to the moribund blaze, where with a hiss and a crackle the fire is slowly resurrected. Warming his hands by it, Conor looks over his shoulder at Baines. 'You know, I'm almost afraid to ask, but what the hell do we need a gun for?' Baines rests the gun on the faded arm of the chair. 'You know your trouble, you ain't got no ambition.'

He looks around the bitterly cold and derelict room. 'This ain't a life we're living; it just ain't anything really. A fucking existence that is all it is. I want more Con more than this. You know it would actually be nice just to live somewhere where I didn't freeze my balls off, where I had electricity, running water, enough to eat, enough to smoke, enough to drink. I'm just so sick of this shit hole, sick of living like this!' He gets up quickly from the chair and goes over to the window. Outside in the street below, a geriatric milk float trundles by, passing an old man who appears to be having a spitting contest with himself.

Conor is quiet, just stares into the fire. He is trying to think of something important or profound to say, but nothing is there. Coming away from the window, and with a watery winter sun at his back, Baines somehow looks younger, thinner more fragile than Conor had ever seen him before. He watches as the boy takes from his Parka coat pocket a slab bar of chocolate and twenty cigs. In silence he hands them to Conor with a certain gentleness he does not recognise, that is totally alien to the boy. Turning away, Baines sits back down in the urban skip armchair, and stays wordless. Truth is he suddenly felt very empty. And lost in that emptiness he thought once more of the plane in the night sky, and drifted with it momentarily. Predictably another silence ensued, that neither seemed in a hurry to break.

Outside in a nearby church hall, the strains of an amateur band rehearsing echoes out. With enthusiasm and energy the band rip out 'White Riot' soon to be followed by 'Babylon's Burning' running his hand through his dense brown hair,

Baines rises from the armchair. 'Christ, I can't take much more of this!' Conor looks across him as he paces creaking floorboards. 'I don't think they are that bad, but I guess the bass sounds a bit off.' Baines stops pacing and snaps back at him. 'Not the sodding band! This!' Scowling, he casts eyes around the derelict room. 'We have to get out of here Con, it's eating us alive. What we have here is nothing, actually it's less than nothing!'

Reaching down he picks up the pistol from the filth scaled arm of the armchair. Crouching on his haunches in front of Conor, he looks hard at the damaged boy with the damaged eyes. 'This, what we are doing, what we have got, it ain't enough. Look, I didn't get the gun for a laugh or to feel big or something. I got it so we could stop fucking about and get some real money.' Conor briefly looks at him and then talks to the fire. 'I know that, I'm not stupid. So, what jobs you got lined up? A bank? Building society? You do know that if we get caught we'll be looking at ten years.'

Baines sighs loudly. 'So what, at least we would be sodding warm; have a proper roof over our heads and enough to eat. … Anyway, we ain't gonna get caught. Look, we will just start off with small jobs. You know, low risk; a ton here a couple of hundred there. You see?'

Once more from outside, the raw sounds of the amateur band tear out. Conor finally takes his gaze away from the flames. 'Let me see the gun.' In silence Baines passes him the weapon. Taking it in both hands as if it were a precious artefact or sacrificial offering, Conor points the gun at the flames as if to fire into the fire. He looks across at Baines. 'Y'know, someone is going to have to pay the price. Cos there is always a price to be paid.' Baines eyes him suspiciously. 'What you talking about?' Conor looks back into the fire. 'Nothing, it's just something I read in a book. Perhaps you are right. Maybe it's just how things have to be.' Wordlessly he hands Baines the gun back and comes away from the fire.

The first day back at the bookshop after New Years Eve was difficult and uncomfortable for Dina and Breitner. Both shocked and confused by that evening's events, Dina had seriously considered writing Breitner a letter of resignation and quitting the shop. Indeed she had wrestled with this dilemma the whole of the previous day. However, despite the unnerving and strange behaviour of Breitner on New Years Eve, Dina's love of books and learning had won the day.

She had arrived at work that morning to find Breitner quietly doing paperwork in his office. He had kept his head down as she had entered, barely raising it to say a polite good morning to her. And thereafter he had stayed in his office most of the day. However, now and again as she served customers or stocked shelves, she could feel his gaze upon her, but if she self consciously returned that gaze, he would hurriedly look away.

For his part, Breitner could not for the life of him recall what the hell he had said to Dina that evening. Only that he had this overwhelming belief that he had said too much. Looking through the glass partition of his office out into the shop, he watches the girl as she catalogues books. How much had he told her that evening? How much had she understood? Had he spoken in English or German? Would a girl such as her be able to understand German? Had he told her everything or nothing? His mind was in total turmoil. How could he have been so stupid!

Ever since his youth alcohol had been master to his slave, had loosened his tongue, been a devil pumping through his veins. How could he have been so stupid? He slams his eyes tight shut, as if by doing so he would not be able to see the past, would not be able to hear the cries and screams.

Suddenly, the ringing of the telephone cut across his daymare. Slowly opening his eyes, a solitary tear emanated from his left eye. He felt its tickle as it slowly trailed down his cheek before coming to rest on his dry top lip. Ignoring, indeed oblivious to the ringing phone, he once more looked out the glass at the dark, little lame girl with her books. He suddenly felt an ocean of pity for her. But it was tempered by a cold realism. For a black epiphany had gripped him heart and mind. And he knew now what he had to do. He tries to reconcile things in his mind by shutting out anything resembling weakness or compassion. Over and over he mumbled to himself. 'Who would really miss her anyway? What purpose does she actually serve?'

The constant ringing of the phone was starting to annoy Dina. Why the hell did he not just pick it up? She raises her eyes from a tattered edition of 'Northanger Abbey' and looks across at the office. Breitner sits bolt upright; unmoving, his eyes in his head but a million miles away. Dina recoils the pose reminds her of New Years Evening.

Suddenly, as if breaking the 'trance' he slowly answers the phone. As he talks into the receiver he briefly turns his head towards her and smiles through the Glass. It is not a human smile his face somehow was more of a grimace. All the features that normally compose a face: nose, mouth, eyes and ears were there in their proper shapes and usual places; but somehow in

Breitner's case they no longer constituted a normal human face. Dina restrains a shudder and looks away. Suddenly feeling sick, she drops her books and gasps for air. Slowly she makes her way to the small wash room and splashes her face with cold water.

After a few moments she feels a little better. Opening the small wash room window she breathes in the morning and chides herself for skipping breakfast. From his office, she hears Breitner calling her that a delivery of books had arrived. Looking at her reflection in the mirror she promises it she will eat soon. With that she softly closes the wash room door behind her and goes back to the books.

Old Ishmail the Turk, a block orderly in the filthy and ill-equipped infirmary, tended the wounds of Lazarus. No one knew why he was called Ishmail, it was not his name and he was not a Turk. But this small and wiry Lublin Jew was a good and just man. And somehow from somewhere he begged, borrowed and 'organised' the scarce medicines and extra food Lazarus needed to recover after his beating. Ishmail even had the foresight to hide Lazarus under a pile of blankets when the SS came to clear out the deadwood, or 'help along' those patients who were not dying quickly enough.

And as Lazarus slowly began to regain strength, the obvious question began to trouble him. Why should a man he barely know risk his life and relatively comfortable position as a block orderly, to save him?

Finally, one late afternoon, two days after his admittance to the infirmary, Lazarus hesitantly addressed this question to Ishmail, as the older man cleaned and dressed his deeply lacerated and painful back. In all honesty it was the question

Ishmail had been expecting, and the one he did not have a plausible or logical answer to. Helping Lazarus to sit upright on the primitive plank bed, Ishmail sits down at its foot.

For Ishmail, a paragon of silence, words come hard, he always selects them carefully, as if concerned that by over use he would wear them out. Finally, in a quiet voice he speaks. 'If you are waiting for me to say something heroic or profound, then you will be disappointed. I just did what I did.' Lazarus eyes him closely, this man of indeterminate age. 'And that is it?' Ishmail sighs softly. 'Look, perhaps it's because I see something special in you. You know, some of the old Jews think that maybe you are one of the ′just men`. Imagine that.' He smiles and looks briefly out of the window at the ugly nothingness of the view.

Lazarus shifts slightly and winces at the pain in his back. 'And what do you think?' Ishmail runs a hand across his shaven head. 'I don't know. But I do know that I have seen that vicious bastard of a dog savage men to shreds, yet you? You he licks and whimpers at as gentle as a puppy, if I had not seen it with my own eyes.' Ishmail shakes his head slowly. 'Like they say, perhaps you have something special about you. I know one thing the beating you took would have seen most of the men here off.'

Outside, gunshots and a scream echo out across the emptiness. Such was the prosaic nature of this happening that neither man even looked out of the window.

'How long have you been in this hell, Ishmail?'

The older man smiles wearily. 'Since before the dawn of time, well, that is what it seems. You know, in this place the weak of body, mind and spirit all perish, most within the first few weeks. Are they the lucky or unlucky ones? This hell is truly

Darwinian.' He sighs once more.

'I was here at the birth of this monster. I just pray to God I'm still here at its death.' Up above an insipid and sickly sun streaks a light across his grey skin. Lazarus looks at him as if perhaps really seeing him for the first time. Ishmail continues to talk, his voice muddy and conspiratorial sounding through lack of use. 'What I'm about to tell you I want you to keep to yourself. Thing is, a few days back me and a few friends heard that the camp is to be liquidated, vanished.' Lazarus cuts in. 'What do you mean vanished?'

Ishmail clears his throat with a small cough. 'You know, it is amazing how gold talks, especially when it's speaking Latvian. Take Aras for example. He would sell his soul and that of his mother's just for the ugliest little gold watch.' He slowly rubs his throat, as if all the unaccustomed talking was somehow paining him. He shifts slightly on the plank bed and continues to speak. 'Aras is scared he says all the Latvians are...' Once more Lazarus interjects. 'What the hell have those bastards got to be scared about? It is us who are suffering, dying in this hell on earth, while they live like kings!'

Ishmail replies wearily. 'Maybe for not much longer, for when the camp 'vanishes' so will they. You see, they are witnesses, have seen too much. Anyway, enough about them, the Devil looks after his own.' He is quiet momentarily. 'The point is this, Aras has it on good authority that Hassler has been investigated by the Gestapo, and they are not happy. It seems Hassler has been caught with too many fingers in too many pies. It would appear he is too criminal, even for the criminals!'

He shakes his head ruefully and gazes off into the near distance, as if seeing a past, whilst surviving a present and having no perception of a future. Clutching his stomach, Lazarus suddenly felt an agonising pain in his stomach, another legacy of the beating. It tears a shudder through him, mind and body. As he speaks, his words are a grimace against the pain. 'So, when will this 'vanishing' happen? When will we be their lambs to the slaughter?'

Ishmail replies thoughtfully but with a certain cynicism. 'Yes, it seems as if some Jews are destined to eternally be God's lambs of suffering. But personally I cannot see myself as that Jew who is somehow serene and impassive before death,' he moves closer to Lazarus, then looks around the dark, dirty infirmary with its usual sights and sounds of suffering. 'You know, the bitter irony is that they are not vanishing the camp because of all the brutalities and horrors committed here. No, they are liquidating it because the SS Hierarchy are embarrassed that one of their own most beloved comrades has turned out to be too corrupt even for them.'

He shakes his head slowly. 'So, Hassler will be sent to the Russian front, or else serve a short sentence in a German prison, and his empire and its subjects shall be obliterated. The mud shall reclaim its own. No taint, no remnants to be left.' Again Lazarus shudders against the pain. 'So, when is the slaughter to begin? Are we just to go like animals?' Once more Ishmail is silent momentarily. 'There is no firm date yet when the 'aktion' will be. But Aras has told us that tomorrow at dawn they are to start digging pits in the woods. And he also said that all SS leave has been cancelled. So my friend, we are really only talking about a matter of a few days.' Lazarus once more clutches his aching guts, as Ishmail continues to speak, his voice even lower.

'You have not asked, but I can tell that you are thinking,

why am I telling you all this?' Lazarus smiles thinly. 'Yes, it had crossed my mind.' 'Well, my hell- hound tamer, it's like this... Look around you, look at your fellow inmates. Half are more dead than alive beyond hope, and the other half still cling to the shred of hope that the SS dangle in front of them, that if they work hard and obey orders they will survive. But you know and I know they are just buying an illusion, a German delusion. And they believe this crap right up to the moment they are standing naked in the snow at the edge of a pit.'

Ishmail bows his head then slowly raising it once more he looks hard into the eyes of Lazarus. 'But you, maybe you are different? Maybe nobody else other than you could have turned the savage beast into an affectionate pup. You know, even Overath wore a kind of grudging respect for you on his face.' Lazarus interjects bitterly. 'Well, I wish that respect had manifested itself into the bastard letting me off of a beating!' Ishmail continues. 'Look, the bottom line is my friend that maybe the old boys have got it right, perhaps you are special. Maybe it will be you who are one of the few who gets to survive this nightmare while the rest of us are dust. That is why I want you with us.'

Once more Lazarus interjects. 'Us, who is us? What are you saying?' Ishmail sighs softly. 'You are not exactly quick on the uptake. What I'am saying is that there are some still strong enough here who refuse to die like animals. But who are willing to fight back.' Lazarus runs a hand across his stubbled head. 'How many are there of you? You have weapons, a plan? Tell me?'

From an adjoining section of the infirmary, a piercing scream tears into the quiet. Another animal that used to be a human being was becoming a guinea pig for a pseudo-doctor practising quasi-medicine, neither Ishmail or Lazarus flinched at the horrific screaming. It was as if it did not exist. 'We are ten, with you eleven.' Ishmail gazes sadly around at the infirmary patients in their varying stages of hopelessness and decay. 'These poor bastard's, and most of those in the barracks have no chance. They must just look out for themselves as best as they can. Either that or pray for a miracle of deliverance.'

To Lazarus, Ishmail suddenly looked old, very old. But when he spoke again his voice was somehow youthful, strong and defiant. 'What is the old battle cry? Better to die fighting on your feet than to live forever on your knees. My friend, we have lived on our knees long enough. So, if we are to die it shall be on our feet fighting.' Ishmail is quiet now, as if already fighting this last battle in his mind. Lazarus feels the pain course through him and gasps out, 'The weapons Ishmail, the plan?'

Ishmail breaks from his reverie. 'We have two rifles and eight pistols, purchased at sky high prices from Aras and his Latvians. As for the plan; that is simple. At the first sign of the SS heavily armed and entering the camp, we set fire to the barracks and the admin block... Then as this fucking place burns, and amongst the chaos, we cut through the perimeter wire at the least defended and hidden section. And then my friend, whoever, whichever of us are left will run like hell to the forest. After that, it's every man for himself. God willing one of makes it and survives, one to write and record the torments of this hell.'

The Bookies on Lavender Street was undoubtedly incongruous. Small and squat in appearance, it was nevertheless hewn from an elegant white stone that in its time must have been both desirable and expensive. However, over the long years, that pitchfork bearing devil called time, had dulled such magnificent stone to a street grey, turning pristine to prosaic. Despite this, situated as it was in a select and quiet area of the strange town, the bookies still resembled a moderately successful solicitors practice, or perhaps a small doctor's surgery, then it did an establishment of such a spit and sawdust nature.

For the best part of a week, Baines had taken the morning bus into the strange town and walked to Lavender Street. And there he had assiduously made mental notes of the comings and goings at the bookies. He noted that the tall and lugubrious shop manager would arrive promptly at eight every morning. Fifteen minutes later he was joined in the shop by a plump, blonde middle-aged woman and a rather gormless looking young man in an ill-fitting BHS suit.

Baines noted that there were no other employees. He also noted, and it did not take a genius to suss out, that Saturdays were the bookies busiest day, and thus by definition the most profitable one. And this particular Saturday, Baines stayed late into the afternoon. Seated on a bench in the small park opposite the bookies, he observed with interest that the day's takings were not banked. Instead, at just gone six in the evening, the manager and the two employees had locked the shop up and left empty handed. Under the veil of a steady January drizzle, Baines watches them walk away.

Rising from the bench he stretches stiff legs and turns his face to the sky. He closes his eyes as cold rain slaps and stings his skin. And he smiles an incongruous smile as he thinks to himself how all this planning and preparation is making him feel so fucking real, making him feel like a someone, a 'face'. And as he opens his eyes to the dark, deadpan sky he wonders if his old man is looking down at him? Watching him with pride?

Looking out across the desolate parkscape, he suddenly feels very small and insignificant, a feeling reinforced by the immensity of a sky he once more raises eyes up to. And soon he is lost amongst vast evening scudding clouds. Sinking frozen hands into his coat pockets, he finds reassurance as skin touches cold metal. And now, not lost any more but found, he realises he can do anything. Nothing was impossible: nothing was sacred, everything was profane.

Conor sits cross legged on the mattress. He listens to wind driven rain lashing against rickety windows. He is waiting for Baines but Baines is late; Baines is always late. He idly flicks through a book by stuttering candlelight. It is an aged copy of 'David Copperfield'. He loves Dickens. It always reminds him of his mum and a time when...

He had bought the book earlier that day from a small bookshop in town. He had humoured Baines by telling him early that morning that he was going out to look for a suitable car he could steal for the bookies job. Of course, Conor had no intention of doing anything of the sort, he just needed to get out of the squat for a bit. The gangster talk of Baines, the damp and cloying misery of the place was suffocating him.

It was the first time Conor had visited the bookshop, and now he knew that it would not be his last. The girl haunted him. He heard her soft voice over and over. Saw those tiny hands over and over. In truth he had not noticed at first that she limped heavily until after she had finished serving him and walked away. But he was glad she limped. He rejoiced in her imperfection, it did not matter it made him want her more.

Oh, how he hated perfection, 'normality' but oh, how he wanted it for himself. And there was the paradox. But for now, he put that out of his mind. And that was not so hard, because there was not enough room there for that and for her. For she imperfect she, was now a thing of such beauty to him. Silently he eulogises her at the altar he has created for her in his seventeen year old mind. When she had looked into his face, he had not seen a hint of revulsion in her eyes. Was she just being kind? What did she really think? Did she think anything at all? Or was he just another customer to be politely served?

Looking down at the book, he runs his fingers softly along its well worn cover; then suddenly feeling stupid and weak for wanting to trace the trail of her fingertips that had once touched the book, he stops. Inside, deep within him he can feel the shudder building, growing, as the muddy growl of the voice was awakening from its poisonous slumber. No words, there did not have to be, its mocking hate-filled laughter was enough.

Conor clenches his fists and slams his eyes hard shut, he rocks back and forth on the mattress. On and on went the laughter, first shrill like a drill in his brain, then a deep growling laughter that makes him want to heave. Slowly he gets to his feet and starts to pace that well worn path across dusty floorboards. Pulling the hood of his jacket up, Conor starts to mumbles a desperate mantra. 'Deny reality, this ain't happening Deny reality, this ain't happening... Deny reality, this ain't happening.' Over and over he spills, spews the words out. But it makes no difference.

From somewhere, nowhere, everywhere, the flame voice rips into him; its invective a scorpions sting. 'That girl, the whore in the shop, she hates you! Could you really not tell? Are you that stupid!? You sickened her. Even a cripple is repelled by you!' On and on it rips into him heart and soul, and as the voice intensifies, growing louder, so Conor paces harder and faster, until suddenly he abruptly stops in the middle of the room and clasps hands tightly over his ears, and sinks to his knees in the dust.

'No! You are a lying bastard!' His scream, loud and hollow echoes empty around the room until it finally dies in the dust. All is quiet briefly. Until that which had the first laugh has the last one also... 'Am I?' The flame voice trails off into nothingness.

Breathing hard, gasping and unsteady, Conor gets to his feet. Suddenly devoid of thought or feeling, he walks across to the mattress and picks up the copy of 'David Copperfield'. With a glazed, fixed expression in those eyes, he walks to the hearth and casts the book into the fire. Ephemerally the dying flames find sustenance in the pages, just as once readers found sustenance in the words that now crackled and burned.

Conor stands as if a pillar of salt, watching the consuming flames. Suddenly he feels different. From deep within him a spark of defiance is his. A little voice, calm and reassuring tells him to hold on hope. A small voice that is innate in all human beings, whether or not we want to listen to it... He would see her again.

CHAPTER FIVE

Hassler knew in his heart of hearts that he had been fortunate. But it was cold comfort to a man who was about to lose his empire. Pouring himself another glass of schnapps, he contemplates just why the Gestapo Internal Affairs Office, had not been more thorough in investigating his activities. Whatever the reason, he was just relieved they had left so many of his illegal stones unturned. Because he knew full well that if they had of investigated with more depth he would be facing many years in prison. Instead, in their infinite wisdom, they had decided to 'forget' him by shipping him off to the Russian Front. He smiles ruefully to himself. Perhaps prison was the easier option after all.

In the study of his villa, with its stolen art dripping expensively off every wall, and its precious manuscripts from antiquity stacked as high as an elephants eye, Hassler sits smothered in a shroud of silence. Staring blankly into the nothingness of night, he tries to think of something, anything other than the vast and soulless Russian Steppes which awaited him in a few days' time.

In his mind's eye he could already see the antlike columns of cannon fodder Ivan's: afraid to live and scared to die, because either way Stalin would be with them forever. Hassler drains the schnapps bottle dry, and then thinks of his dead geraniums tears well in empty eyes. 'Fucking murdering Jews.' He launches the empty bottle against the nearest wall; its sad shards glistening in what light there was. The irony, the contradiction of his words were not lost on him, he starts to laugh, rumbling quietly at first, then hysterically. Next come more tears. Then silence. Why did it have to be like this? Why did life have to... disappoint constantly?

He knows his mind is no longer his own, but he is past caring. It does not matter any more, because soon he will give his life for the Fatherland: problem solved. What a joke. In the darkness he scrambles around his desk drawer for a cigarette. Finally finding one, he lights it and sits down at his desk. It was strange, as a child the darkness had terrified him. All manner of night shadows would come to torment him. But now, the velvet texture of night was somehow a protector, a comfort to a troubled mind. Amongst it one could also hide a multitude of sins. Well, at least until morning light.

Hassler stubs out his cigarette in the overflowing ashtray and rises slowly from his chair. Outside, in that hour when night finally succumbs to day, the destroyers of his empire were arriving in covered trucks. Fully armed as if going to war, yet as silent and stealthy as cats, they disembark from their vehicles.

Almost with an air of detachment, Hassler watches them from on high. He knows that firstly they will annihilate his 'subjects'. But the real heartbreak would commence later, when with fire and indifference they would bring his kingdom crashing down around his ears. Suddenly the insistent ringing of the telephone breaks his gloomy reverie. He briefly looks at it but does not pick up the receiver. He already knew who the caller was.

Returning from the infirmary, it had been the first night back in the barracks for Lazarus. But now, as he watches the SS trucks arrive in the camp square, he knows it will be his last. In

Barrack Three, as in the rest of the camp, pandemonium reigns at the first sight of the heavily armed SS troops, immediately heated and desperate discussions break out voices clamouring over voices to be heard. In the morbid, early morning glow, every possible human emotion is played out, because each actor in this drama of impending death still holds in his heart the hope of survival.

And in this sea of voices, this ocean of torment, sweating and fearful bodies seem somehow to dissolve in front of the eyes of Lazarus. He no longer sees the rocking, bowed heads of the religious Jews as they make their last laments. Nor does he see any more the pale, drawn and terrified faces of the young men, whose lives were done now before they had even really begun. Taking a last look at the human carnage, Lazarus, like a ghost escapes the bedlam by slipping unseen through a small window at the back of the barrack. And in this moment he knows he is leaving the dead for the living. Even if only temporarily.

Dropping down silently into cold black mud, Lazarus hears the harsh shouts of the Germans outside the front of the barracks. 'Juden, raus!..Schnell!' The response is silence, save for a low muffled wailing and a few defiant curses. Suddenly, to his right he hears movement. Peering through the gloom, Lazarus sees the figure of Ishmail and ten other Jews moving slowly and cautiously towards him. It was an amazing sight, armed Jews. It was something he thought he would never see. He felt a surge of pride rush through him. Tethered and cowed for so long, the fact that Jews were no longer willing to go passively to their deaths gave him an indefinable sense of hope.

'So, tamer of the beast, you have decided to join us.' Ishmail smiles briefly and thrusts a loaded pistol into the hand of

Lazarus. Gripping the gun tightly was like an electricity bolt of empowerment coursing through his body. He looks hard at Ishmail. 'So, the plan is still the same?' Before Ishmail can reply, a burst of machine gunfire scatters the group to the four winds. Some drop twisting and twitching to be consumed by the ever voracious mud. Lazarus, slipping and sliding sinks onto his belly into the black earth and manages to slowly crawl to the relative safety of the infirmary, as all around him thunderous gunfire provides the imperfect accompaniment to the growing chaos.

Scarcely able to breathe, disorientated and scared to death, Lazarus stands gasping and shaking in the hollow main corridor of the building. Sliding his back down a bullet-ridden wall he sits silently, head in his hands. He tries to think of Esther, his parents, Yitzhak, but ends up thinking only of the murderous madness that threatens to consume him.

Finally gathering his breath, if not his wits, he looks around him. At the far end of the corridor a dead Jew lies on his back, his arm outstretched and slightly raised, he appears to be waving a cheery good morning, or perhaps a desperate goodbye.

Outside, the cauldron sound of shouts, screams and gunfire intensify. And, if he had not realised it already, then Lazarus did now. That the ruse that the SS were preparing pits in the forest was just a subterfuge. They had intended all along to slaughter everyone inside the camp. But, what did it really matter. Either way the Jews were marked for death.

Suddenly, amongst a thunder of boots, Ishmail comes scurrying for his life into the infirmary. Gasping, pale and sweating, he slides down beside Lazarus, who grips his arm. 'Thank God, I'm not the only one left alive!' Resting his rifle at his feet,

Ishmail lifts his eyes as he speaks, perhaps to Lazarus, maybe to God. 'Bastards, they are shooting at anything at moves. You know, some Jews would not come out of Barracks One, so they threw petrol on it and locked the doors, then set fire to it. The screams were unbearable.' His voice trails off to nothing.

Breaking the ensuing quiet, the voice of Lazarus is one of intense agitation. 'What the hell are we going to!? There is no way out of this!' Rising slowly to his feet and picking up his rifle, Ishmail looks hard at him. 'Live! or at least try to, that is what we are going to do... Come on, we gotta get out of here.' Slowly, cautiously they make their way along the debris-strewn corridor. They walk on past open doors whose rooms were now quiet, just ghosts of screams echoing there silently. At the far end of the corridor they pass the dead waving Jew, and then turn left into a smaller corridor.

Instantly they are at the entrance of room twelve. A large white room stands in front of them, a room where various 'experiments' were performed on inmates considered superfluous or merely suitable candidates for death because they had caught the eye of the senior medical officer; for being too short, too tall, wearing glasses, not wearing glasses, for being unshaven, or too well shaved. There never was rhyme nor reason.

As Lazarus stands in the doorway the sight and stench both paralyses and sickens him. Twenty, maybe thirty corpses are piled in stacks top to toe, teeth bared in a grin of death. On them, under them, around them their bodily secretions stain the once white tiled floor. Finally, Lazarus looks away, has to look away. Even though he had seen so many horrors in the past two years, still some sights had the power to shake him to the core; steal, tear away another piece of his soul.

At last walking on, the sound of the hell outside became louder and louder. Just then, as Ishmail turns around to speak to him, an SS man, tall and angular, appears behind them at the end of the corridor. Hurriedly pushing Lazarus aside, Ishmail raises and fires his rifle in one rapid movement. Shocked, surprised, the German crumples almost episodically to the detritus-ridden floor. The last living look, captured forever on his ruddy face is one of utter bewilderment. It could not be possible, a Jew with a gun? Such a beast surely cannot exist. No, unheard of!

Outside in the camp, time had lost all meaning and meaning had lost all control. Everywhere, scenes were being played out that made 'Dante's Inferno' seem a mere comedy. Leaving the rear entrance of the infirmary, and with tunnel vision, Lazarus and Ishmail run out into the mud and blood carnage. They head for the latrines, one of the few buildings not yet burning. It was the one place Ishmail reasoned that the SS with their innate and Germanic fear of filth and disease would not venture into. And in this he was right.

Somehow, some way they stumble and dodge their way unseen to the latrines. Catching his breath, Ishmail speaks quietly, barely audible above the thunder of machine guns and grenade explosions. 'This cannot go on forever. Even those murdering bastards would have had their fill soon.' Breathless, pale and gasping, Lazarus replies wearily. 'You reckon?'

He rests down on his haunches and mumbles as if to himself. 'The Devil and his own do not need rest. They have endless energy for evil.' He looks around himself with a tired desperation. It was strange, he must have been in those latrines a hundred times before, yet he had no idea until now just what they really looked like. Primitive and unhygienic was an under-statement; fetid and foul beyond description. Gazing down at the hard mud floor he realises that all those feet that had trodden it, shaped it, worn it down were no more. The bodies they belonged to did not exist any longer.

As he raises his eyes he does so just as Ishmail leaps back from the small window he had been anxiously peering out of. 'Shit, SS coming this way!' Momentarily he is paralysed, just stares at Lazarus. Finally grasping reality, and then grasping the heavy boarding that covered the deep cesspit, Ishmail hisses desperately at Lazarus. 'Don't just watch me, help!' The reply of Lazarus is one of incredulity and panic. 'What the hell are you doing?' Ishmail snaps back at him impatiently. 'Look, I have lived half my life in the shit, so this means nothing to me. Now in the name of God help me lift this!'

Lazarus hurriedly helps him shift the weighty boarding until there is just enough space for Ishmail to squeeze through. Holding his breath, he quickly lowers himself into the over-flowing cesspit. Looking up at Lazarus he speaks hurriedly.

'Live or die my friend, it is up to you.' Outside the drunken voices of the SS men are getting nearer and nearer. Looking once at Ishmail and twice at the oozing shit, Lazarus chooses life. Rapidly lowering himself alongside Ishmail in the pit the pair just manage to cover the pit with the boarding as the first German, swaying slightly and carrying a bottle of vodka, tentatively enters the latrines. Recoiling, he cannot hide his revulsion. 'In God's name the dirty Yid bastards!'

In total darkness, and with human excrement filling their eyes, ears, nose and mouths, Lazarus and Ishmail are as the dead, not a flicker nor a flutter. Drunkenly, the German kicks the boarding around the latrine. It shudders and reverberates but Ishmail and Lazarus do not move a muscle. Muttering incoherently to himself, the SS man first takes another swig of vodka and then his pistol from its holster. Within seconds he is shooting wildly and shouting loudly 'Fucking Jews! Let's see fucking Moses help you now!'

From outside, his equally drunken comrade calls out to him impatiently. 'Christ, Klaus, give it a rest. There are no Jews in the Shitter!..Now, come on, let's go.' Seemingly, his vodka soaked spleen vented, Klaus ambles off, his continuing coarse invective filling the putrid air.

If Ishmail and Lazarus could have breathed a huge of relief they would have done, but in their present predicament breathing heavily was to be avoided at all costs, especially breathing in. The stench of the pit was truly overwhelming and seemingly getting worse by the minute.

As the voices and mirthless laughter of the SS men trail off into the distance, Lazarus slowly starts to lift the heavy boarding, desperate to escape the sepulchre of shit. Ishmail snaps at him. 'What the hell do you think you are doing?' Lazarus, mind and body drowning in the foul waste of others, peers incredulously through the blackness. 'What does it look like I'm doing? I'm getting out of here.' Ishmail sighs heavily. 'Are you really that much of a schmuck. Look, the place is still probably crawling with SS. We need to sit tight here for another hour or so, just to be certain that.' His words are choked off half uttered.

'Another hour, are you joking?' The stench, the claustrophobia was unbearable to Lazarus, he could barely speak, barely breathe, barely think. In his vexed mind, he tries to make out that the swirling, omnipresent shit is the gently lapping blue beyond blue waters of some distant Tropical ocean. It is not working.

Now even Ishmail that paradigm of calm was losing his cool. 'Am I joking? Do I look like a bloody comedian?' Lazarus looks at him. 'No, lshmail, what you look like is a small man covered head to foot in shit. Now, I don't know about you, but I'm getting the hell out of here.' Frantic and gasping, Lazarus starts to heave the heavy wooden covering, until soon a crescent shaped sickly slither of light creeps into the darkness.

Just then, the silence that had been apparent for a few minutes was shattered by forlorn, lost screams and the violent blast of machine gunfire. Lazarus rapidly lets go of the wooden boarding and sinks back down into the mire... Their disembodied voices fall silent.

In the dour grey cold of an early January morning, Karl-Erich Breitner is sitting at his kitchen table. In between sips of warm tea he speaks a few words to himself, just to check which voice was his today, for in the proceeding days he had noticed, how couldn't he that his own voice would desert him at times to be replaced by the voice of others. One of the voices, the most insistent, had a song-like and lyrical quality to it. And its melodious form with its gentle lilt pleased him. Indeed, he would use the voice that much he feared he would wear it out.

He found that the voice was at its best when he used it to sing. And sing wonderfully the voice most certainly could, it seemed to transcend the normal human vocal range. And so, Breitner would sing Puccini in the bathroom and Bach in the kitchen. He would own the melodic voice and it would own him. And as time passed, he began to wonder if the voice was a benediction from God, perhaps a sign of his forgiveness?

He ponders this daily, hourly, until he reaches the conclusion that this new melodic voice is a reflection of his new soul, purified and free of past sins. And that made him happy. And when he was happy he would use the voice and sing like a bird released from itself. And with this 'release and regeneration' came a mellow Breitner, he had even stopped getting paranoid and sinister thoughts about the limping girl.

Indeed, with a beneficent air he had decreed in his mind that she could remain alive. He realised now that he had been foolish to think she was any kind of threat to him, she was just a silly girl in love with the beating heart of books.

Finally rising from the kitchen table he walks across to the large sash window. Outside in the stark morning light, he sees the blackbird, a shudder rips through him. Perched in its usual place, a low leafless limb of an old Sycamore tree, it looks at him accusingly. Indeed, those gold ringed eyes, such avian haloes, stare hard at him, unblinking and cold. Breitner feels that his legs are going to give way on him; he feels suddenly so dizzy and unsteady. He tries to turn away to avoid those eyes. Breathing heavily, he looks without seeing the tea splashes across the tired brown lino floor, and the grease blackened wall with its out of date calendar hanging crooked and sad.

Slowly, tentatively, and with his stomach churning, he finally gazes back out of the window. But the mute blackbird was gone. Still breathing hard and fitfully, Breitner quickly closes the curtains tight shut. In the resulting darkness he suddenly feels very alone, very vulnerable. For he knew it was only a matter of time before the creature would return. After all it was nothing without its song, its voice. Yes, just a matter of time.

CHAPTER SIX

This day, this January sixth, Dina had decided to wear happiness. But her good mood this sunny Epiphany had nothing to do with wise men from the East. Rather it had everything to do with a certain orange dress that had stolen her heart.

It had all started the previous day when she was casually walking back to the bookshop at the end of her lunch break. As usual, she had eaten lunch at the small cafe by the old river bridge. The elderly Greek couple that ran the place knew Dina as a regular customer, and they liked the polite and diffident limping girl.

At 1:15 every afternoon, she would enter the cafe and order the same lunch; a cheese and tomato sandwich and a cup of tea. She would then take her same seat at the same table and eat in silence, her nose invariably buried in a book. And when she had finally finished both chapter and sandwich, she would dutifully carry her plate and cup and saucer back to the counter, where she would politely smile and thank the old couple. Then leaving, she would slowly walk back towards the bookshop, but not this day. This day, for whatever inexplicable reason, Dina decided to change her route back to the bookshop. And it proved to be a decision of smiling serendipity.

Walking briskly on her unexpected route, she soon found herself at the top of the High Street, right opposite a fashion boutique to be precise. And there through the shiny, superior and smear-free glass of the posh shop front, Dina saw it. There in front of her was some kind of sartorial holy grail. Oblivious to passing shoppers, time, and the cold rain stinging her face, she approaches the pristine glass, her nose practically pressing against its coolness. And there it is. The orange dress was joy, a smile, a slice of suburban sunshine on such a sunless, soulless day. Captivated and enthralled, that is what she was. She wanted, needed that dress. For this serious, shy and bookish girl, such extravagance, such assertion was totally out of character. But she had experienced her first fashion epiphany, and was not about to be denied.

So, with bold Joan of Arc steps, Dina goes into battle, crosses the divide, from the prosaic to the sublime, striding purposefully towards that which is precious beyond compare. And now, at last she stands eyes wide in silent awe, transfixed before the ultra orange garment.

Oblivious to everyone and everything around her, she gazes with awe and wonder upon her perfect fabric aesthetic, and as the gazer gazes, so the gazer is gazed upon her self. From across the store a red slash mouth was sneering into a sardonic smile. And cold grey eyes were narrowed to a point of disdain. The eyes registered a spark of recognition that soon embers into a spark fire of hatred. The hatred, spiteful and malicious, belongs to a tall and slim bottle blonde girl, a shop employee. And while this young woman possesses all the charm and charisma of a privet hedge, she does a well practised line in hating. And her petty cruelty and sadism is that of a budding Lucrezia Borgia. And unbeknown to Dina, this 'Lucrezia', her school yard nemesis and tormentor was once more about to attempt to become her bete noire once more.

'What the hell are you doing here, you weird Spas!?' The voice of the girl has something Reptilian about it. How one might expect an Adder to sound if it could speak. And at the sound of that snake hiss voice, those words, Dina feels her heart being slowly torn out. Turning slowly, she comes face to face with graveyard grey eyes and an even deader sneer. Before Dina could even truly register shock, pain or bewilderment, the hissing voice is at her again, with a burning vitriol.

'You had better go you fucking spas. We don't serve freaks here!' Shamed, powerless, Dina looks across at the store manageress, a smartly dressed woman in her mid forties. The woman smiles pleasantly at Dina and continues to write in a large ledger book. 'Are you hearing me spas?' The blonde girl's eyes narrow to slits as she spits out the words. Dina looks at those graveyard grey eyes and then at the orange dress. No. No, this time she won't give in will not be denied. She suddenly feels strong, a sense of empowerment torrents through her. Her words are faltering at first, then stronger until they are fire and ice, flowing and assertive.

'For two long years you made my life a nightmare. You tormented me, abused me, beat me, humiliated me, but school is over now and so is your hold over me!' The red slash mouth opens in surprise, as do the eyes. She is stunned, silent. It was not supposed to be like this. Dina continues emboldened, 'It's time now. Time for you to make amends for the living hell you put me through.' At last the blonde girl finds a voice, the one she has borrowed from a snake. She cuts hard into the words of Dina.

'You mad bitch! You have not changed at all, still the same nutty, weird cripple.' Dina, with her new found armour, eyes her coldly. 'Oh, I have changed. And you had better believe it. Now, listen, I'm not scared of you any more. So, this is what is going to happen. You are going to get me that orange dress at a fifty per cent discount.' Dina looks first at the dress and then at the sneering face of the girl. Her face contorts into a disdainful glare.

'You're mad! You have lost it big time!' Her voice is even more of a hiss now than usual. But Dina is Boadicea, Joan of Arc now, she will not be denied. 'Okay, let's see what your boss thinks of you threatening and abusing a customer, shall we, cos this 'fucking freak, this spas' is now going to have a chat with your manager.' The girl snarls a hateful grin. 'Go on then, you won't dare.' Dina brushes past her defiantly. 'Just watch me!' With that, she starts to walk a few paces towards the shop manageress at the tills.

The hiss is gone, replaced by a softer, more conciliatory tone. 'Okay, but to get a discount I will have to put a tear in the dress or something.' Dina stops in her tracks, turns and walks over to the dress. She touches it, strokes and caresses it as if it were a living thing. She turns to the girl. 'Okay, but just a small tear I can easily repair.' The girl takes the dress in her hands and takes it into a nearby changing room. She soon reappears. Covertly she shows Dina a small tear she has made in one of the arms. She thrusts the dress into the hands of Dina. 'There, you happy?' She can barely disguise the hatred and contempt in her voice. But Dina does not care, does not mind; she just wants that dress and to get the hell out of the shop.

And now she watches as the sullen faced blonde girl carries the dress over to her boss standing at the tills. Dina looks on as the manageress inspects the garment closely. Finally raising her eyes, she smiles across at Dina and after saying a few words to the blonde girl hands the dress back to her. She then, with a face like thunder, crosses the shop floor back to Dina. Practically throwing the dress at Dina she spits out her bile. 'She has agreed to the fifty per cent off. So, just pay for it and then piss off out of my sight!' Defeated and demoralised, the bully has been bullied. She slinks off to the far end of the shop to continue her solitary vigil of fatuous hating. Dina smiles a small smile of victory and holds the dress close to her chest.

Outside, and with the dress safely tucked inside a posh boutique bag, Dina steps, glides through sunshine rather than around it. Instead of petrol fumes she breathes in huge gulps of happiness. The cold and rain no longer exists, for it was just the figment of another young girl's imagination. Today she would be late back for work. And what is more she did not care, because today was now her double epiphany day. She had fought and finally beaten her nemesis of old, and her reward was a sunburst holy grail. And so now she was wearing the shades and hues of happiness. And it was a style that suited her remarkably well.

In hushed and slightly breathless tones that were totally unnecessary, seeing as they were alone in the gloomy evening squat, Baines informs Conor that he was going to steal a Mini for the bookies job. His reasoning was that it was the ideal motor for a town robbery, 'Cos they are well fucking good, small, nippy and well smart.' Conor is barely listening. He just thinks Baines wants a Mini, because he sees himself on Planet Baines as some kind of Michael Caine in the 'Italian Job'.

Indeed, he spends the rest of the evening whistling 'Self

Preservation Society'. But it is lost on Baines; in his mind he is already spending the proceeds from the Bookies job. Conor left him to his daydreams, as he himself prepared for his usual unwelcome nightly ritual. The mocking voice, the flames, both would soon be his as they were every night.

Why did God not allow him peace, rest? Why could he not just dream of her, the girl in the bookshop? Conor lay on his cold mattress enveloped by threadbare blankets just staring at the wall. He could feel the beat of his heart pulsing in his ears, it annoyed and sickened him. An hour passes, then another. He is tired of wakefulness but fearful of sleep. And this is his tormented nightly limbo.

But finally, without him even being cognizant, he at last succumbs, slips away, unable to fight weariness of mind and body any more. But his last lucid and conscious thought is of her, and he experiences that most painful of human longings. 'If only'.

Rain lashing hard against the window glass brought morning in like a lion. When Conor finally awoke from surreal and twisted dreams, he felt more groggy and disorientated than normal. As ever his sleep had been frightening and fitful, rubbing weary eyes, he shudders hard, both at the continuing existence of his demons and also the prospect of the day ahead.

In the grubby half-light he lights a cigarette and tries to remember. Tries to remember that amongst the voice and the flames and the half forgotten chaos, she had been there, he was sure of it, nebulous and indistinct maybe, but nevertheless there.

The heavy slam of the front door crudely puts paid to his

dream recollections. Baines is back from 'Mini-hunting' and the expedition has not gone well. Rain battered and coughing, he slumps into the dirty armchair with a petulant look on his face. Conor knows that look so well. A tantrum is imminent. And he does not have to wait long.

'You know, I do not believe it! I'm out there for two sodding hours in the pissing down rain, and not one fucking Mini! Unbelievable!' Conor raises his eyes to the ceiling and mumbles sarcastically to himself. 'Yeah, how selfish of the gits round here, not owning Mini's. Especially knowing full well you wanted to nick one. Yep, what a bunch of self-centred bastards.' From the armchair, Baines sighs deeply and takes a packet of cigs from his saturated jeans pocket. The pack oozes like a sponge and cold water trickles down his hand. The sigh becomes a growl.

'That just about sums things up, no fucking motors, and now no fucking fags either!' In a fit of pique and frustration he hurls the soggy pack across the room, where it splatters hard against the paint peeled wall. Perhaps, just maybe, an older and wiser person might have, with a certain cynicism, perceived the soggy mess slip sliding down the broken wall as being somehow a metaphor for his or her life. But Baines was not old and nor would he ever be wise. So, he just saw a wet packet of fags leaving a stain on the wall, in the shape of a poodle, or perhaps Switzerland.

Wordlessly, Conor throws him his pack of cigs. Baines takes one and with wet matches finally manages to light it. With a small nod of his head he tosses the pack back to Conor. And then, as was so often the case, neither exactly being a warrior of the spoken word, a silence ensues; its backbeat being incessant rain-lash smashing against the tired window glass.

Minutes pass, unnoticed and not missed, until Baines breaks the quiet. 'What time is it?' In the dirty morning light, Conor squints at his watch 'Just gone quarter to eight.' Baines rises from the armchair. 'Come on then, time to make a move. We have a bookie's to turn over.' He suddenly seems to possess a fresh enthusiasm, which is more than can be said for Conor. Who, swathed in blankets, sighs heavily. 'You're having a laugh. How we gonna do a job in that, it's pissing down.'

Baines eyes him coldly. 'Don't be such a tart! Christ, it's only a bit of water. Look, we need to get going the bookies will be open in an hour. So, Doris, do me a favour and stop pissing and moaning and get some clothes on!' Baines smiles, Conor does not. 'But you said you couldn't get a motor.' 'No, what I said was I could not get a Mini, so I nicked an Escort instead. Now, c'mon, shake a leg.' He takes Conor's clothes from off the back of the chair and throws them at him.

In twenty minutes they are gone, and madness follows them: For it has nowhere else to go.

CHAPTER SEVEN

At long last the camp was silent. It was pitch black now. A crying sun had disappeared hours ago. Out of pure fatigue and nervous exhaustion, Lazarus had somehow managed to find sleep standing up, his head pressed against the side of the cesspit. Not even the overpowering stench of human waste or the ever present threat of discovery and certain death had been enough to stop weary eyes closing.

Ishmail, on the other hand, had remained vigilant. He estimated that it had been at least a couple of hours since the slaughter had ended. And at least an hour since the SS, their blood lust sated, had driven away in their trucks. So, amongst this, jet black dead night, he takes his chance. Summoning up what strength he could, he slowly heaves the heavy wood covering off of the cesspit. Soon, a different kind of darkness, a different kind of silence greets his eyes and ears. In the gloom he gently nudges Lazarus awake. 'Come on, they are gone.' Bleary-eyed and stiff limbed, he follows Ishmail out of their prison within a prison. Cold, hungry and tired, they wonder what vision of hell awaits them in the camp proper.

Even in this, the darkest of spring nights, the mud of the camp was the camp. And by the light of a pale moon, this black earth gleamed and glistened out its silent menace. And as Ishmail and Lazarus start their slow and cautious descent into its heartland of hate, its grasps and sucks at their every tentative step. Keeping close to the outside wall of the latrine it is not long before they come across the first of the pulses stopped permanently by the SS.

The man is kneeling as if in prayer, his forehead buried, half-consumed by the ravenous black mud. Without a second thought, Lazarus starts to strip the uniform off of the dead man. The voice of Ishmail is a hiss. 'What the hell do you think you are doing?' Lazarus turns to him. 'What does it look like? I'm exchanging shit for blood.' He hurriedly strips off his faecal stained rags and slips into the blood stained uniform of the praying corpse. After his initial hesitancy, Ishmail soon follows suit, swapping his shit smeared rags for those of a corpse.

Moving hurriedly from one charred and ruined building to the next, Ishmail and Lazarus circle the eerily quiet moonlit camp. They look for life, hope. There was none of either. It was just a charnel house, but with flesh still on bone. Indeed, as far as the eye could see or the heart could bleed, corpses were scattered across the jagged, oozing mud. Surveying the scene, Ishmail mutters a prayer for the Jewish dead, and the Jewish living. As his lips move quietly in prayer, he bows his head and thinks of a wife and child buried in the frozen earth of Lublin.

In the past a tear would have come, or a memory or a regret. But now nothing came, nothing at all. Briefly he wondered if he was still alive, was not one of the corpses in the flames and mud. After all, so much of what he had thought, felt and loved had perished. He stopped praying. It all felt so fatuous somehow. For most of the Ishmail he had once been had long since died. What part of him remained alive? It was a shadow, a shell he no longer recognised.

But still there was this inexplicable, intuitive desire to stay alive, to survive. He could not explain it, could not understand it. Perhaps he was not supposed to. Maybe there was nothing to understand. Raising his head he peers through the darkness and sees Lazarus scavenging for food in the burnt out kitchen. He slowly walks over to its still smouldering orange-black shell and joins him. It was palpable that before torching the place, the SS had removed all food and provisions, save for a few charred potatoes. The two men fell upon the scant and rank vegetables, scooping them up from the charcoal floor and eating them ravenously, as if they were the finest au gratin potatoes. However, the feeling of their appetites being sated was ephemeral. Soon the griping, nagging hunger pains were theirs once more.

Sitting on the debris-strewn floor they look at the sky, at the stars, at each other. They look at anything other than the death that surrounds them. Some horrors are simply too much to gaze upon. And so there it is, they suffocate in their silence, just a quiet beyond a normal quiet, an everyday quiet. And it is slowly strangling Lazarus, so he breaks it. 'I found this in the hand of Saul over by Barracks 1.'

He takes from his jacket a blood streaked pistol. 'Bad news is, there is only three rounds in it. Still, that is enough for me, you, and... Well, it's always best to keep one by.' He smiles a small thin smile that is only on his lips not in his eyes. Ishmail looks across at him without speaking. Slowly he reaches into the pocket of his trousers and takes a handful of bullets out. Deliberately he throws one after the other over to Lazarus.

'Pennies from heaven brother, lets just hope they are the right calibre.' Lazarus looks down at his hands and then at Ishmail, his voice is that of a lost child, scared, bereft and alone, a child that can see only uncertainties, craving a reassurance that the older man cannot possibly give him. 'What the hell are we going to do Ishmail?' 'I'm not sure. I'm not sure of anything any more. But I guess I do know one thing. We are on our own. No God is looking out for us.'

The voice of Ishmail sags, as do his shoulders as he gazes out across the muddy sea of carnage, red and brown, brown and red. 'How could he be when he allows this to happen?' Lazarus remained mute, for there was no answer. So, again their silence hung heavy like a veil. An opaque curtain neither could lift, nor see through to the other side.

And as the mourning moon grew brighter despite its pain over what it had seen, so the night grew colder. Yet the two men sit rooted to the spot, framed in its brightness, alone but together. And their souls reflect the mourning moon glistening with despair. This camp of mud was so ingrained in them, such a part of them it would simply not let them go. However, the rumbling of vehicles in the distance decree that this bond of misery must be severed. At the sound of the trucks the pair jump to their feet, Ishmail exclaiming the obvious. 'Shit, they're coming back!' No more words were needed. And so they bolt from this dead camp of dead certainties, to a living forest of living uncertainties.

High up in his crumbling ivory tower, a drunken Hassler views the panicked flight of his last subjects. In an ironic salute he raises his glass of schnapps as Lazarus and Ishmail exit his obliterated, smouldering empire. His rifle by his side, he could have easily shot them as they fled, but the booze had made him feel benevolent, benign, yet ultimately resigned.

Yes, it was over, the emperor was surveying his moribund domain for the last time. The curtain was coming down on this place of mud and blood. In twelve hours it will be as if it and its players had never existed. Well, except for its dethroned ruler and two half-starved scared men running for their lives. Secretly, perversely, Hassler hopes that they survive. For he, right now, with a gut full of schnapps, wanted the whole world to know that his empire had been taken from him, destroyed by the ungrateful, the unimaginative.

Yes, he hoped the two Jew bastards survived. For as long as the camp lived on in the minds of men it would never die. He smiles at such pretentious and grandiose folly. Suddenly the telephone behind him on the desk starts to ring. This time he answers it.

To city men like Lazarus and Ishmail, the forest was something to fear, to be distrustful of, full of satyrs, evil sprites and a thousand other childhood born fears. Yes, the forest was a place to be avoided... Until now.

Entering its crumpled black cloak, not sure if it was to be their safety net or shroud, the pair stumble noisily through the forest undergrowth, falling here slipping there, disobeying the basic rule of forest survival, namely to be as silent and as stealthy as an alley cat. The darkness of the night and the density of the looming glowering pines meant that the circle they were going around in was becoming a spiral.

Tired, frustrated and hungry, not to mention being trapped inside bodies that were increasingly unable to function due to nervous exhaustion, the two men decided to call it a night. Settling down in a nocturnal recess under a particularly large and daunting fir tree, they cover themselves with vegetation from the forest floor and lay down to sleep, but not perchance to dream, but perchance to find a kind of oblivion. But despite feelings of such intense weariness the arms of Morpheus refuses to embrace them.

For every sound, every crack of a twig or shuffling of an unseen forest creature was death awaiting them, whether at the point of an SS gun, or the blade of a Polish Anti-Semite, or the jaws of a wolf. Under these conditions sleep for Lazarus was impossible, even rest was improbable.

Finally he sits up, resting his aching back against the towering tree, in the darkness a thousand thoughts race across his weary mind, as always, thoughts of Esther were predominant and at the forefront of that mind. And yet; and this is what troubled, saddened and scared him. When he tried to see her, visualise her in his mind, to remember her hair, face and body, he could not. And the paradox was that he could see clearly in his mind's eye those that meant nothing to him.

A great aunt he barely knew, a history teacher he had not seen in years. He could see them vividly. So, why could he not see her, she who had been, is everything? Why the hell were they as clear as a bell in his head? Yet Esther was so nebulous and ethereal in his eyes? And he dreaded the day when she would perhaps disappear forever.

Sighing heavily he gazes across at Ishmail, who half buried under forest detritus, has somehow managed to find sleep, albeit of a fitful and feverish nature. In the darkness his legs twitch, hands shake and lips contort into a bare teeth sneer. God only knew what his night terrors were, and the omnipotent one was not about to tell.

Just then to his left, Lazarus hears a soft rustling noise, the sound of feet tentatively walking on twigs and pine needles.

Slowly, he reaches inside his jacket and takes out his pistol. The noise was becoming more distinct the closer the footsteps came. He squints through the darkness but can see nothing. Gently he prods Ishmail awake. The older man yawns, bleary eyed and confused looking. Lazarus presses a finger against his lips and nods his head in the direction from where the noise emanates.

Both men were silent, still, perfectly static as the stealthy footsteps came closer and closer. Lazarus feels his hand tremor and shake as he raises his pistol. Aiming the gun he waits. The soft, padding footsteps, gently crunching pine needles approaches. Finally, out of darkness and cover of the sombre trees comes a dog, a large white dog.

Lazarus is stunned. A few feet away from him stand's Geist. But it is no longer the camp Geist; that canine representative of the Aryan master race. This Geist is thinner, his spectral white coat now matted and filthy dirty, in the eyes of the dog there is a spark of recognition as he looks at Lazarus.

'What the hell are you waiting for? Shoot him, kill the bastard!' The voice of Ishmail was a snarl, vengeful and cold. But Lazarus does not shoot. No avenging angel, he. Instead in a neutral voice he calls over to the animal. 'Come here.' Geist does not move. He merely looks at Lazarus. 'Will you just shoot that fucking dog or do I have to!?' He suddenly makes a move for the pistol. Roughly pushing his hand away, Lazarus calls out to the dog once more. 'Come here boy, now!'

Slowly, half crouching in submission, Geist walks the few paces and lay's at the feet of Lazarus. This brute, this maimer of men now lays cowed and bowed, no longer Cerberus, now a mangy stray, hungry and lost. Looking down at the creature, Lazarus could see dried blood in its dirty coat in two or three places. It was palpable that after his 'exile' from the camp he had had a tough time of things. Tentatively, Lazarus reaches out and gently lays a hand on the back of the dog. It shrinks to the side a little and whimpers softly.

Ishmail looks on with disgust. 'I can not believe I'm seeing this. Do you have any idea the amount of men that vicious bastard savaged?' Ishmail shakes his head ruefully, his voice one of disbelief. 'And you stroke and pet the thing like he is a fucking poodle!' Lazarus is quiet momentarily, looks down at Geist and then at Ishmail. 'He is the monster Möller created. He was and is just a dog.' Ishmail cuts in angrily.

'He is a killer! I tell you one thing, that animal comes anywhere near me and I will cut his throat!' With that, he rolls over on his side and tries once more to find sleep.

All is quiet now, beyond quiet. In the darkness, Lazarus brings out a chunk of dark stale bread from inside his jacket. Pulling it apart he holds out half to Geist. The dog does not need asking twice. He grabs the bread in his huge jowls and wolfs it down in the blink of an eye. Lazarus eats some of his bread and puts a small amount back into his jacket pocket.

Whether out of gratitude or simply for warmth, Geist lay down beside Lazarus. Involuntarily, he reaches across and slowly starts to stroke the animals back, the matted fur coarse against his hand. Geist stiffens at first at his touch, but then relaxes, perhaps knowing that he would not hurt or be hurt any more. And in this still, starless night, if it had been possible or plausible, a white dog scared and scarred would have cried, cried for a forgiveness perhaps gained, and a kind of redemption perhaps attained. But maybe this is just anthropomorphism gone mad. After all, only a mad man could suggest that a mere dog could actually possess such refined emotions and sensibilities. Would it not?

Breitner had not spoken in three days. In that time not so much as a murmur had passed his lips. Puccini was gone from the kitchen and Bach from the bathroom. Now it was silence in the living room staring at four blank walls, more expressive than he. And in his physical and mental paralysis, the shop has more or less been forgotten by him, but not by Dina. Indeed, this child-woman in her orange flame dress had single handedly run shop affairs for the past seventy two hours.

Acquiring a new maturity, strength and self-confidence, Dina was in her element. Whether placing orders for books, talking to suppliers or filling in paperwork, she was professional, accomplished and efficient. However, she knows it is a situation that cannot continue indefinitely. Indeed, when she has time between customers she would go up to the flat and see Breitner. And there he would be as always, sitting on the faded sofa breathless and lifeless, in his own private kingdom of catatonia.

To try and encourage him to communicate, Dina had left a pad and pen on the chipped, teacup-ringed coffee table. But it stood unused and isolated, a white island in a sea of teak, Breitner merely looking at it from time to time, and then looking through Dina. She tried anything, asked everything; but was met with a dead stare. She did not know what else to do, or who to contact. She was pretty sure he had no family. Or if he did he never mentioned them, and so it went on into a fourth day, and then into a week and then into weeks.

And so, as well as running the shop, Dina had more or less become a part-time carer for Breitner. Cooking and cleaning for him during her lunch hour and also after the shop was closed in the early evening. Until finally, after a month had passed since his self imposed verbal exile had commenced, he communicated with her.

After shutting up shop for lunch as usual, Dina had gone up to Breitner in his flat. He was standing staring out of the kitchen window. He does not turn around upon hearing her footsteps approaching. 'It has come back and reclaimed that which is his. I always knew it would, but it would have been so nice if I could have kept the voice a little longer... Just that.'

Turning slowly to face Dina, she notices the merest glint of a tear in his dark blue eyes. As he slowly walks towards her he takes her hand in his. 'I forgive the bird you know. He was only taking back what was rightfully his. Do you see?' There is a flash of intensity in his eyes and voice that the girl cannot comprehend. In the few months she had known and been employed by Breitner, his behaviour had been strange and erratic, but now it was starting to border on the insane.

Indeed, if his manner and behaviour over the New Year had been disconcerting and unnerving, then the past month had shown it to be downright worrying and bizarre. Not for the first time did the thought cross her mind that she really should call a doctor.

The voice of Breitner suddenly breaks into her troubling reverie. It echoes out hollow from the living room. 'Dina, can you come here I need to talk to you.' Walking into the dark and dreary living room which had become even more depressing to her of late, Dina finds Breitner sitting on the sofa, a pair of black framed glasses perched precariously on the end of his long and narrow nose. In front of him on the coffee table sits a beaten-up old grey box file. With a motion of his hand he motions for Dina to sit down opposite him. She looks at him questioningly, wondering what madness will be his this time. She does not have to wait long to find out.

Peering over his glasses, and in a voice borrowed from a cheerful maniac, he declares with a smile. 'Dina, I have decided to give you the shop.' He utters the words so casually that she just presumes it's another form of his growing psychosis or mental illness manifesting itself. So she smiles, a tight nervous smile that soon develops into a tight nervous laugh. Breitner's face straightens.

'This is not a joke. In the morning I will phone my solicitor and get him to draw up the necessary papers.' He looks at Dina expecting a reaction, but is met merely by a bewildered, uncomfortable silence. 'I thought this would please you. I really thought it would be something you wanted.' Sighing, he removes his glasses and rests them on the coffee table.

'I'm sorry, I was obviously mistaken. I was purely thinking that' His words trail weakly away. Finally overcoming her shock and uncomfortable feelings at his words, Dina finds a voice, small and hesitant. 'I don't know what to say. It is. Well, I'm only seventeen. Dunno, it's all just a bit of a shock. I don't know what to say, how to react.'

She looks across at him, this strange foreign man that she cannot comprehend. That he was eccentric she had realised from the start, but now this, this madness. 'Your age is irrelevant, it's merely a number. What is relevant is that you have a genuine love of books, of the written word and knowledge, a rare commodity in these heathen times.'

He sighs gently and somewhat wearily. 'Dina, I'm old and

tired. My mind is.. It does not matter. Look, the thing is, I have no one to leave the shop to: no family I mean. Well, no one above ground that is.' Dina looks at the old man, an expression of confusion on her face. How could he be so seemingly lucid and articulate now, yet for the past few weeks become such an immobile and silent zombie, dead from the neck up?

Breitner sees the look of confusion and bewilderment on her young face, the questioning look in her large eyes. His voice was reticent, strained. How could he admit that while he knew his mind was slipping away, he could do nothing to halt that inevitable slide, 'The thing is... Look, I know that over the months my behaviour has at times been some what. Well, strange. It is just that sometimes I truly cannot explain or understand how things are. It's like.'

Once more his voice trails off into silence and his head slumps slightly. 'Mr Breitner, I dunno, look, this what you are suggesting is such a huge shock for me. It's just so kind and unexpected. I mean, no one has ever really given me anything before. Well, nothing like this anyway. It´s just taking a little time to sink in, I guess.'

Dina suddenly feels very small, very young. She looks down at her orange dress. It was not a suit of armour now. It could not turn her eggshell ego into steel. What was inside her was inside her. She feels an overwhelming need to cry and she has no understanding why.

She bows her head eyes fixed on the stoical carpet, its colour that of gravy. Rising from the sofa, Breitner briefly and self consciously places his hand on her shoulder. Walking to the window he gazes down on sad charcoal roads. Perhaps what he would say to the girl he could not say to her face. He breathes in softly, unable or unwilling to shake off the sudden hopeless conviction that everything was totally fatuous. He could feel a tide of despair slowly start to wash over him, and knows that right here, right now he was not strong enough to hold back the flow any more...Things fall apart.

Closing his eyes, he tries not to look at the parade of shops opposite with there solemn unsmiling and unseeing glass faces. His eyes hurt him now and his left eye twitches. Perhaps he had seen too much, lived too long. Maybe his eyes had reached some kind of saturation point. Maybe they were washed up used up, unable to take any more. He tries to imagine himself blind. It must be like drowning in night.

The voice of Dina breaks into his dark reverie. He had forgotten she was there. 'It is nearly two. I really should be reopening the shop.' She rises from the chair, her small hands meticulously smoothing out the creases in her orange dress. Breitner watches her, his gaze rising then falling, small hands, large eyes, small hands, large eyes. He wonders, if had he been blessed with a child would she have been like this?

'Mr Breitner, I really should be getting back to the shop now.' Dina feels uncomfortable again. Why wasn't the dress a suit of armour any more? Oh, and in her head how she just wants to be Joan of Arc again, strong, confident, empowered, brave.

'Yes, of course you are right, you must go.' His voice is beyond vague, as if an echo from another time, another place. And now, as she walks to the door Dina avoids his gaze. As ever she was glad to be leaving the flat. There was something inherent within its fabric that depressed her. Just what it was about the place that engendered in her such feelings of mental suffocation she was not sure. Perhaps it was just its bleakness and monochrome decor. Or maybe the archaic tired furniture.

Either way, she was more than relieved to leave its dreary confines and head back down to the light and her beloved books. And as she hurriedly descends the stairs back to space and light liberation, she hears Breitner call after her. 'Dina, I will without fail be contacting my solicitor in the morning instructing him to prepare the necessary papers. The future is yours.' His voice traces off, nebulous and hollow. She does not look around, pretends not to hear him. Behind her the flat door softly closes. Positioning himself back on the sofa, Breitner looks briefly at the battered box file on the coffee table.

Outside, on an oblique television aerial a blackbird sings its liquid song. A sickening shudder rips through Breitner. His hands shake and his face blanches. The creature had its song back, why the hell did it not leave him alone now. He sinks down onto the sofa. But from never far away his homeland catatonia offers him refuge once more. He accepts it willingly.

CHAPTER EIGHT

As they drive the nine am same again streets of the grey town, Conor and Baines as was their wont, remain resolutely mute. Indeed, apart from the repetitively hypnotic scrape-squeak of the worn out windscreen wiper blades, the only sound was the frustrated sighing of Conor each time the clutch of the ancient Escort slipped.

That Baines had nicked 'a right pony' was palpable to him as soon he had turned the screwdriver in the ignition, and the tired old git of an engine had coughed and wheezed into something resembling life. Add to this the fact that the car reeked overpoweringly of stale beer and wet Labrador, and one could understand his moody and stubborn silence.

Not that Baines appears to notice any of it. He is elsewhere, somewhere, nowhere. The vodka is not working how it should. It's just making him feel morose and detached. So he gives up reality for distraction, and counts the spots on the fluffy dice that hang forlornly from the rear view mirror. Hearing the rain hitting harder, his attention turns to watching it slitherslide down the window glass, seemingly fascinated by its jagged stop start passage, but locked in an all pervasive sense of distracted detachment, the boy switches gaze from rain to creature.

His hazy eyes settle on a small, black shiny insect crawling along the cracked rubber seal of the car window, each fissure in the rubber a Grand Canyon to the tiny beetle. Its progress across the mighty ravines is further hampered by Baines gently blowing on it. But stoically and with great fortitude against the hurricane, the bug carries on its little life struggle. Unblinkingly Baines watches it, never averting his gaze, his narrow eyes melting into the shiny glistening shell of the insect; as black as Whitby Jet.

Thoughts come and go; mixing the coherent with the absurd. Until all that is left is the absurd. Like why does the bug choose to live in a trash can Escort when it could live in a Bentley, or at least a Capri?

Baines is regressing now, retreating fast. He is six years old and is collecting bugs near his aunt´s house on the marshes. Standing by the waters edge the reeds and sedge tower above him, both protective and threatening, as around him midges swarm as thick as soup, because the beautiful dragonflies there were never to be his, he had to content himself with more prosaic creatures, the names of which he would never know.

But that time and place was just a space to him now, a half-visible fading snapshot. And he wonders why childhood memories are so fragmented and incomplete? For example, why was the only clear recollection he had of his aunt that of her wrinkled, creased face, that stem and unsmiling face with the look and texture of an over-done Yorkshire pudding. Of his uncle he can recall even less. Only that he was a morose and quiet man who always had the faint aroma of piss and peppermints clinging to him, limpet-like.

Both, aunt and uncle were taciturn ghosts silently shuffling around echoing rooms, rarely talking to each other or him. Even to a six year old it appeared to be a house of the dead, a dead house. And as that child he had thought that perhaps that is where one went after death, a silent, red bricked house on the marshes.

The black shiny insect was becoming more adventurous. Climbing its very own Mount Everest, it was now slowly ascending the rugged north face of the car door handle. And if one could have seen its tiny face, undoubtedly grim determination would have been etched upon it. Whereas etched upon the face of Baines, was the look of someone drinking themselves back sober, and now once more gazing at the bug, he ponders the reason for its existence. What purpose did it serve? After another blast or two off of the bottle he is questioning the purpose of his own existence and that of the boy with the weird slanting eyes sitting next him. But it's a question he cannot answer. Maybe they were, would always be just drifting shards. Dust on a grimy mosaic, ready to be blown away at any minute.

Draining the last dregs of the Moscow mineral water, Baines stares out of the rain lashed passenger window. Wiping thin lips with the back of his hand, he wonders if he is going mad or that the vodka is just bad? He ponders this as outside road signs flash by, almost like a countdown. What if madness is somehow catching? What if Conor's lunacy was contagious? Again he looks across at the boy he does not really know, nor want to know, but was all he had in the world.

He tries to figure out what Conor is thinking. What persecuting demons were in his head right now? And what is more, would they become his demons too?

Finally nearing the bookies, the rain at last ceases and a watery sun kisses down pallid rays from a broken sky. As Conor pulls the car up opposite the bookies, Baines notices a pale rainbow arching high above. The 'old' Baines would have probably seen the sudden appearance of the rainbow as a portent, a good luck omen for the forthcoming job on the bookies. But the 'new' Baines, new as of today, merely saw it as a rainbow, and not a particularly impressive one at that.

Conor switches off the engine. The car cannot wait to die. A few yards in front of them a drunken old bag lady argues with herself. She has cardboard hair and nicotine hands. She wobbles, staggers, stumbles, finally taking a header straight into some unsuspecting bushes. The boys watch her descent without comment. To Baines, as he glimpses the ripped PVC coat disappear into the foliage, she is the shiny-shelled car insect in human form. In his somewhat pissed mind the parallels are glaringly obvious. Both, insect and old woman share a struggle for life, for survival, the bug in a clapped out 1971 Ford Escort, and the woman on the streets, in foliage, in squalor.

After a minute or so, the PVC rises swearing from the bushes, her fiery, filthy invective that passionately delivered that it merely serves to unsteady her once more and she plunges back into the defenceless greenery. And there she lays singing for a couple of minutes before she is scraped up, helped up and shoved off by an equally pissed passing pal.

Conor and Baines observe the sad street cabaret in cigarette smoke silence. In all honesty it was a distraction from the job in hand Conor could have done without. Truth was, his head was even more cluttered than normal. As ever, he had bad vibes about a Baines job. But on top of that he had other things on his mind. Namely, that the voice and the flames were intensifying their venomous ferocity, terrorising his every hour whether sleeping or waking.

Then there were thoughts of the girl from the bookshop. And this pained him more, because this seventeen year old pragmatic realist knew that even if he told her how he felt about her she would likely blank him. And as things stood, that was one kick in the balls he could do without right now. But as it was, at this very minute, it was Baines who was at the forefront of his thoughts.

For a while now, indeed, since the garage blaze episode, Conor had had the recurring thought of cutting Baines loose, blowing him out once and for all. He was sick to death of his dumb arse 'jobs', tired of his infantile fantasising and master criminal bullshit plans and schemes. He knew that severing the umbilical cord was going to be tough, but he guessed it was time. However, he had been joined at the hip with Baines for so long he knew no other way, no other life... But... But now with his anticipated share from the bookies job, Conor felt perhaps it was time. His time.

Baines knew it was time. He just hoped it was the right time. As he left the vehicle he did not say a word to Conor, or even look at him. They had spent so much of their union in silence, now more than ever quietitude seemed apt somehow.

As he crosses the street the winter sun sinks soft rays into the gutter puddles he does not even notice. Nearing the bookies he feels the sleeping handgun stir inside his jacket, digging hard into his ribs. This just adds to his amazing and liberating sense of nothingness. Perhaps it was the vodka finally working, wrapping him up into a cocoon of 'fuck it' nothing matters any more. Whatever it was he was past caring, beyond feeling. It was like... Nothing!... All was pointless, prearranged and preordained. What ever.

And if it was to be like a man rushing to the gallows late for his own hanging, so be it. That was cool, too.

But now back in the now, Baines is pulling his Chelsea scarf up tight across his nose and mouth. Lurching, stumbling, he launches himself into betting shop win or lose oblivion. However, unfortunately the 'launch' is more comedic then heroic. Thundering into the bookies, he slips and falls on his arse on the recently washed lino and tiled floor. The ignominy was brief and only witnessed by two. Rising quickly to his feet, Baines holds the gun in white warrior hand and aims it at his audience.

It is often said that when traumatic events occur they appear to somehow unfold in slow motion. Well, not on this day. For the boy with the gun is seriously manic now, a whirlwind with a shooter and a bad haircut, a typhoon in an oversized Harrington jacket. Waving the gun frantically Baines eyes his little audience, to him, they appear nothing more than statues unmoving, forever caught in his time, his moment.

The old statue was small and frail. An early morning punter, he was profligate with his pension yet frugal with his words. But the bookie's was company. A hangout until the boozer opened. Both a sanctuary against the pitchfork bearing devils called loneliness and old age, a reason for not falling down, giving up.

As deaf as a brick he would smile and sagely nod his head when spoken to, even though he could barely hear a word said. His hearing aid then was pretty much superfluous. An aural decoration; beige and archaic, it hummed as serenely as a summer insect. And for this reason it would forever be a June hay meadow in his ear.

Baines looked again at the old man and motioned with the gun for him to move away from the counter. The elderly statue obeys mutely. With granite feet he hesitantly shuffles sidewards, resembling a wrinkled crab that is caught in two minds over whether it should escape back into the sea or stay and guts it out.

Waving his gun in a particularly frenetic and aggressive form of semaphore, Baines turns and faces the cashier. With a jerky movement he forces a canvas bag under the tight, metal mesh grille. The eyes of the female monolith are grey and wide. Heavy with Avon Aqua-Blue eye shadow, she looks nervously at Baines and then at the bag. Then, made mechanical by her fear, this statue, so unsteady on her plinth, starts to fill the battered canvas bag with notes wrenched from the cash drawer.

And all the while he watches her hands, follows the trail of slightly raised veins, meeting up then branching off. Jutting blue branch lines, bodily train tracks... 'For fuck sake, hurry up!' Baines voice roars out raw. The woman statue jolts back and those hands with their slightly chipped cerise painted fingernails speed up, cramming notes into the bag. Baines is still tom between looking at her hands and the clock on the wall, a wall whose colour was open to conjecture, but which once had worn the proud title 'April Forsythias.' Well, that is what it had said on the paint tin.

Tom still torn between looking at the hands on her arms and the hands on the clock. Then he notices it. The second hand on the clock was definitely going backwards Tock-tick, tock-tick, tock-tick. So, even time was turning its face from him, retreating running from him. He suddenly feels a sudden urge to laugh. As irrational and incongruous as it was given his present circumstances, the laugh came. It starts out hesitantly, throaty and soft. Seemingly in competition with the mosquito hum emanating from the old man's hearing aid.

But soon it eclipses the insect in the hay meadow and was roaring forth, maniacal and strange. Its madness must possess an infectious quality because soon the female statue is laughing also. It is a laugh borrowed from a child, one full of hysterical little half-sobs. Baines suddenly looks across at the old man, sees that he is laughing now also, his deafness obviously no obstacle to him participating in the lunacy as well.

In fact, with the humming of his hearing aid and the clacking of his ill-fitting dentures as he grin's his coyote grin, he is adding immeasurably to the music of the madness. Turning back to the woman, Baines sees that her hysterical laughing sob has erupted into a spring flood of uncontrollable tears. The lunacy is complete.

Well, almost. For in the midst of the absurdity she attempts words, words that her contorted mouth cannot pronounce or utter clearly. But to the boy it does not matter anyway, he ain't listening. They are fatuous utterances, expelled on wasted breath. He gazes again at the clock, then again for the last time at the hysterical statue with such grey eyes. Grabbing the battered canvas bag she has placed shakily under the grille, he turns and bolts from the shop. Leaving behind him tears and laughter in equal measure.

By the time he awoke to a dawn heavy with mist, Ishmail had already gone. But Geist remained, snoring dog snores. Lazarus with bleary half-opened eye's, was experiencing that disorientation and temporary confusion one feels on first waking in a strange place. Looking down, he sees the dog tucked hard against his legs for warmth. Truth was he still had ambivalence towards the creature. That white fur now dirt encrusted, had once been matted with blood, the blood of friends, the blood of innocent people. Those marked out for death, picked out by Möller, executed by the hound.

He muses abstractedly about redemption. Man is capable of seeking it and achieving it. Does the same go for animals? He shakes his head at the seeming absurdity of the thought. Turning his head to the left, he sees a scrap of dirty white paper wedged under a stone. He reads the scrawled words slowly.

'All along I said it would be every man for himself. That is how things are and have to be... So, my beast-taming friend, stay lucky. And more importantly stay alive! And if you should, tell the Americans, the British, anyone and everyone who will listen, what you have seen. Stay strong. And if God wills it one day we will meet again when this madness is done.'

Lazarus screws up the paper and throws it to one side. He knows he should not feel a sense of betrayal at Ishmail's departure. After all, the man had more or less saved his life. Yet he could not shift from his mind the thought that the man had just done a runner in the night. Leaving him to? What did it really matter, they would both probably be dead in a week or so anyway.

He leans against the scaly trunk of the tree and raises eyes heavenwards. He thinks of nothing because he feels nothing is nothing. Beside him, the dog is awake now. It stretches out its thin yet still powerful body and yawn's a massive yawn from its mantrap mouth. It turns and looks at Lazarus with its large intelligent eyes protruding from its gargoyle head. A shudder sweeps through Lazarus. It always did whenever the dog looked at him.

Just then, some metres away, Lazarus hears the tell-tale sound of twigs being snagged and snapped underfoot. His first thought is that it is Ishmail, and he has had a change of heart. Rising slowly to his feet he takes cover behind the tree. And soon sees that it is not Ishmail returning.

The German soldier is very young, very drunk and seemingly very lost. Lurching through the trees kicking up pine cones, he mumbles incoherently to himself. Fixed like stone, with Geist at his feet, Lazarus waits.

Just a few metres from him now, the boy soldier stumbles and falls... Again... Lying face down, unmoving in the forest undergrowth, minutes pass. With Geist starting to become restless at his feet, Lazarus slowly takes out the pistol from inside his ragged jacket and softly walks the few paces over to the prone figure. Standing over the soldier he hears him snoring noisily. Swallowing nervously, Lazarus softly kicks the scuffed boots of the boy, there is no response. He kicks harder and aims the gun at head of the boy.

'Get up! Slowly' the soldier groans groggily and turns his head. Looking up, his narrow green eyes widen. 'Who are you? Don't kill me.' His young face is ashen, bloodless; pine needles cling to his left cheek. Lazarus is taken aback at his youth. No more than seventeen or eighteen.

'Stand up! Slowly.' the boy rises unsteadily to his feet. Geist sniffs at his leg and snarls a throaty growl. The kid stares at him and then at the gun. His green cat-like eyes register not only fear and bewilderment, but a knowing look also. He knows the man standing in front of him is an escaped Jew. The rag clothes, the cadaverous gaunt features, the shaven head. No, he could not possibly be anything else.

'Throw your rifle over there.' Lazarus points to some bushes twenty metres away. The boy does not move, remains stock still. 'What are you going to do to me? I never killed any Jew.' He does not finish the sentence. Tears begin to well in his young cat eyes. 'Just do as I say and throw the rifle.' Silently the youth obeys. Seeing the rifle flying through the air Geist thinks it's some bizarre game of fetch. With tail wagging he bolts towards the bushes. Taking his eyes briefly off of the boy, Lazarus bellows after the errant hound.

'Leave it!' Geist stops dead in his tracks. Seizing his opportunity, the boy turns on his heels and starts to run, a blind and desperate zigzag flight, just as he had been taught. Darting in and out of the looming, towering pines he heads towards the dark heart of the forest.

At first, Lazarus does not realise just what is happening, his feet are leaden as is his mind. It is Geist that takes the initiative. Bolting head down, he soon chases down the breathless, terrified boy. Lunging, the dog grips his arm in his powerful jaws and pulls him hard onto the forest floor. Screaming out in shock and pain, the boy tries to get to his feet.

Seemingly able to differentiate between Jewish and Gentile flesh, Geist makes no attempt to savage or maul the kid as he had done so many times in the past to Jewish prisoners. Instead he merely keeps his huge jaw around the boy's lower arm. In a matter of seconds, Lazarus is standing over boy and dog. Glaring at Geist, he bellows out 'Leave!' Slowly the hound releases its grip on the arm of the boy. It flops down limply by his side. He breathes heavily, his creased face tearful. Lazarus looks down at him, a sobbing boy. He looks so forlorn and pathetic this child of the master race.

Ephemerally, Lazarus no longer sees him as German - Germany - Enemy - Progeny of the race that murdered his parents and probably his Esther, too. No, he is broken, a broken child-man, just another victim, but in a different uniform. 'Show me your arm.' The voice of Lazarus is neutral, unemotional. The boy raises his face, the bright cat's eyes now a dull sea green, blank in resignation. Things had come full circle.

Every day in the camp, Lazarus has seen the same look in the eyes of many of his fellow inmates. Many of whom would be dead within a few days. Once more he looks down at the boy soldier. Notices for the first time his filthy neck and ears, and his unkempt dark blonde hair. Without asking again, he reaches down and takes the arm of the boy. The kid winces, half out of pain, half out of fear. Through the coarse and thick material of the military great coat, Lazarus sees and feels sticky oozing blood.

'Take your coat off.' The boy meekly complies. Under the coat he wears just a faded shirt and braces. The gaze of Lazarus is drawn to the left wrist of the boy. It is swathed in a thick, dirty bandage that had once been white. He feels the eyes of Lazarus looking at his wrist, he self consciously hides it behind his back. Lazarus does not pass comment. 'Roll your sleeve up.' Again the boy complies silently.

The puncture marks left by Geist had pierced and bruised his skin but had not reached down to the bone. 'You will need to clean the wound or infection may set in. What were you drinking?' The boy looks at him with a quizzical expression on his dirty face. He answers hesitantly. 'Yes, vodka. Why?' Lazarus runs a hand across his shaven head. 'Have you any left? I can use it to clean the wound.'

The boy slowly takes out a near empty quart bottle from an inside pocket of his coat, and passes it to Lazarus. Who then douses what vodka is left onto a grey looking piece of cloth and starts to clean the wound. This is done in silence, a silence eventually broken by the boy. 'Why are you doing this; if you are just going to kill me?' Lazarus does not reply, just finishes bandaging the wound as best as he can.

Leaving the boy, he goes and sits under a tree. He continues to look at the kid as he slowly puts his coat back on. 'Have you got any food?' Without replying, the boy delves deep into his coat pocket and retrieves some scraps of brown bread and a half-consumed chocolate bar. He passes them to Lazarus. And then watches as the items are ravenously dispatched by man and dog. He cannot but help stare disbelievingly as the human animal and the canine animal devour the meagre offerings in seconds. It had really never occurred to him that any living creature could be so desperately hungry. He looks away, feeling an indefinable shame.

It was strange. A few weeks ago when he had sliced at his veins, he had so wanted an end. And yet when he had thought that the Jew was offering him that end, he had turned and run for his life. A week of psychiatry; decent hospital food and a gut full of stolen vodka had perhaps changed his outlook, but then the white coats had started looking, talking to him differently, had said that soon he would be fit and well enough to return to his unit.

With practised sympathetic faces they asked him how he felt about it. What the hell did they think he thought about it? Had the stupid bastards not been listening? Did they still not get it? It was because of the fucking unit that he had taken the knife to his flesh. But it did not matter now. Nothing mattered. Not any more. Soon he would be shallow or deep in the pine covered earth of this Polish forest...He wondered what its name was?

Not for the first time, Lazarus eyed the boy silently, wondering what the hell he was going to do with him. He knew, just knew he could not kill the kid in cold blood. So, what to do? Tie him to a tree and leave him for the partisans to find? That would be a long and lingering death at their hands. So what, he was of the race that tortured and murdered his people. Perhaps it would be poetic justice, a sacrifice, one of theirs for the thousands of his.

No. Lazarus could already feel his conscience staining a deep dark crimson over that one. It was a dilemma that had no chance of achieving a satisfactory resolution. For, while he knew it was madness to take the boy with him. What else was there? If he was just to let him go, what would then be stopping the kid going to the nearest German patrol. Then he would be dead within the hour. He simply could not take that chance.

From what little there was left of the optimistic side of his mind, Lazarus attempts to salvage a glimmer of hope from a near hopeless situation, it is not easy. In fact, he could not. Indeed, the only two 'positives' he can discern from the slough of uncertainty dominating his thoughts, were firstly, that having the boy close to him would act as an insurance policy. After all, the Germans would not shoot at one of their own. Yes, definitely an insurance policy, perhaps not a top of the range 'Fully Comp' insurance policy. Indeed, it's was more of a 'Third Party Fire and Theft' policy. But nevertheless, it was insurance of a kind.

The only other positive Lazarus can muster is that the boy probably knows the forest and its surrounding farms and villages better than he did. He would know what peasants to go to for food and which ones to avoid, those willing to denounce a Jew to the authorities for a quart of vodka and a few cigarettes.

Once again Lazarus looks across at this child of the master race, this progeny of superior Aryan stock. And how masterful this golden youth appeared in his torn, shit and snot stained oversized greatcoat. How superior this Teuton knight looked with his filthy face, bandaged wrist and dirty unwashed hair. What a fine specimen, exemplar of true Germanic order and efficiency.

Against the backdrop of his guts growling louder than an exploding mortar shell, Lazarus did not know whether to laugh or cry as he gazed upon the silent boy. In all events he does neither. Instead he addresses the kid as he nervously paces the fallen pine cones, feeling as if he is suspended between life and death. 'What is your name?' The boy answers softly 'Walther' his arm hurts like crazy and he feels sick, fit to spew an ocean.

'That is your first name?' He sighs inwardly. Why the hell was this Jew asking him stupid bloody questions? Would it somehow ease his conscience a little for when he put a bullet in his head?

'No, my first name is Karl. Walther is my surname.' As was so often the case, Lazarus suddenly feels a paralysis of the tongue. He looks up at the unprepossessing grey morning sky and then across at Karl. 'I have decided your coming with me.' He rises slowly to his feet, convinced his few words have

128

explained everything. Karl looks at him bemused. 'So, your not going to kill me?' 'If I was going to I would have done it already... No, you will come with me.'

Lazarus brushes pine needles from the backside of his rag trousers and again looks in the direction of Karl. 'Are you stationed around here? I need you to 'navigate' for me. I need you to take me to a peasant who can feed me and give me clothes. And not one who will turn me in for a few coins. You do know this forest, this area?

The boy is silent briefly, looks uneasy, looks as if he has the words but is unwilling or unable to speak them. Finally, he finds a voice. Not big not strong, but nevertheless a voice. 'Look, have you not worked it out yet? I'm a deserter. I have no idea about this area, my unit is stationed kilometers away up north. Lazarus interrupts him. 'So, what the hell are you doing drunk and alone at dawn in the middle of a forest?' Karl gazes up at the slate grey sky, then down at his boots.

'The hospital was going to send me back to my unit. I couldn't handle it. So, I deserted. That was two nights back, been walking ever since. And I have no idea where I am or where I am going. I just know one thing. I'm not going back.' He fall's silent, gazes down self consciously at his bandaged wrist. Lazarus watches him briefly, before slowly starting to walk away. Back towards from whence they had come.

He does not turn around as he speaks. 'None of that changes anything. You are still coming with me. But we need to find that rifle first.' Silently, boy soldier and animal follow Lazarus. And as grey skies give way to sombre amber hues, so their surreal, unreal little trinity is formed.

CHAPTER NINE

Breitner was true to his word. Early one dank, mid-January morning he had his solicitor Mr Phelps; a cheerless, charmless man with the face of a frustrated mole, draw up the necessary legal documents to formally transfer the ownership of the shop to Dina. In essence, the deal was that on her eighteenth birthday the shop and all stock would become hers. The only caveat being that Breitner would remain a tenant in the flat, living there rent free until death finally decided to claim him.

Drifting in a fog of unreality, and with Breitner beside her incongruously dressed in stained blue pyjamas, Dina signs the papers with a shaking hand. Whereupon, Breitner yawns loudly, farts violently, and then mumbles incoherently as he retires back to his bed. It was just gone midday.

Phelps the solicitor looks astonished. But being of the old school, he acts as if nothing out of the ordinary is occurring. As if it were perfectly normal for an elderly foreign man in soiled pyjamas to break wind with the force and ferocity of a minor nuclear explosion, and then shuffle back off to bed when most people are considering what to eat for lunch.

Dina herself is silent, beyond embarrassment. And in this awkward teenage mortification, all she can think of doing is to offer the solicitor a cup of tea and a slice of Jamaican ginger cake, both of which he politely declines. But with a look on his face that appears to suggest he would prefer to poke cocktail sticks into his own eyes than spend any more time than was absolutely necessary in this dank flat, with its bizarre, seemingly unbalanced elderly occupant.

So, in the days that followed, as Breitner remained bed bound in his homeland of Catatonia, barely missing the shop. So, the shop decided that it barely missed him either. Indeed, once more Dina was proving herself more than adept at running shop affairs. It was as if she were made for the place and it for her. But, as ever, come early evening and Dina would feel the black cloak of despondency descending upon her.

And as she locked the shop up for the night, a sinking feeling that did not possess a name gripped her so tight she could barely breathe or move. In short, she knew she was going home to find silence, senility, and suffocating sadness. Her Grandmother's degeneration appeared to be reaching some kind of denouement. And may God forgive her for it, but Dina as she looked at the cadaverous old woman laying in bed, or slumped like a fading sparrow in the armchair, just wished that this person who used to be her grandmother, would, would breathe her last. Because as things were, there were two people slowly dying within the sombre walls she shared with her grandmother.

And again, and again Dina would find herself trying to come up for air. But there was none. More and more the bookshop was her refuge. Even the madness of Breitner seemed modest when juxtaposed against the suffocating, cloying, demanding neediness of her grandmother. In any one hour, Dina would be the old woman's carer, punch bag, sister, mother and nemesis. Love and hate condensed and served out in equal measure.

And the girl just wanted to run away, needed to disappear deep into a world of books. And the only way she could do it was at the shop, her shop. That thought sustained her. But the feelings of guilt never left her, guilt that she could never do enough for her Grandmother. And the darkest guilt was always hers, that one that wished the old woman dead.

'Sweet, so sweet!' Baines quietly mouths the words over and over as he sits cross-legged on his faded mattress. Beside him, the money lay stacked in neat little piles of happiness. He looks down at it thoughtfully, a content expression on his face. Across the room, Conor stands at the window smoking. He is thinking of the bookshop girl. Right now, he has a mind to scoop up his two-fifty and cut the umbilical cord once and for all. Just go to the girl in her shop and blow a ton on sodding books he would never read. But which with there academic and intellectual titles would be bound to impress her.

The thought was beyond beautiful. But the thought was ephemeral. For inside his head the flame voice was screaming at him now, berating him loudly for being such a 'Sad fucking dreamer!' Soon it was joined by other hostile voices, forming a polyphony of hate. Conor closes his eyes tight shut and bites hard on his bottom lip. Soon he can taste the iron blood. A taste he knows so well.

Instinctively he reaches inside his jacket for the blade. Instead, blind snake fingers brush the crucifix, feeling the spiky crown of thorns. The broken body is once again in his hand. He twitches, flinches and lets the Messiah fall. Now his shaking hand digs deeper for the knife. At last its aloof coldness presses his skin. Conor gasps. The blade is reassurance, solace, Excalibur, the only reality that worked.

From across the room, Baines thin voice competes with those

in the head of Conor dragging him back from... 'You know I already have the next job lined up... Well, provisionally.' He says the last word with a heavy emphasis. Baines occasionally liked to use words of more than one or two syllables. He would utter them with a sense of pride, a guileless pretension that invariably made Conor smile ruefully.

But there was no smile today, rueful or otherwise, because the boy suddenly feels so drained and weak. Even the blade in his pocket appears to have temporarily lost its omnipotence. Only the voices in his head remain active, albeit in mocking whispers now. But above them, Baines voice drones on. 'I was speaking to Kenny Brooker the other night, down the dog track. The lucky bastard had just won two hundred quid in two races.'

He pauses briefly expecting a response from Conor. But one is not forthcoming. Instead, the boy just gazes down wearily at the floorboards. One had a chip in it the shape of the Isle of Wight. He follows its dusty grain with his dusty finger, from Cowes to Freshwater Bay and back again. He sighs deeply, as unperturbed Baines continues his banquet of bullshit.

'So, we got talking. As you know Kenny does a bit of plumbing on the side. Well, a week or so back he had a little job across town. This old boy was having trouble with his cistern or something. Anyway, Kenny says the house was well big, but kind of stuck in a time warp or something. And he said that when the job was done and it was time for the old boy to pay, he only went and tried to pay for a ten quid job with a fifty quid note, unbelievable... Kenny reckons he is a Jew.'

With a certain excitement in his eyes and a crooked smile parting thin lips, Baines quits talking. He turns to the boy and waits for a response, waits for something. Finally, disinterestedly, Conor looks up. 'How does Kenny know he is a Jew?'

Tilting his head back on his pencil neck, Baines sighs loudly. 'How the hell should I know perhaps the old boy was dressed as a fucking rabbi. Look, you ain't getting the point. What is the old saying? 'Where there is a Jew there is money.' Trust me, the old Yid is loaded' He lights a Castella Cigar, takes a drag, and then proceeds to cough his nuts up, his face alternately turning crimson then purple. It is palpable that the young Master Criminals lungs had not quite become accustomed to the transition from Players Number Six to a heavier kind of leaf.

Trying valiantly to regain composure, dignity and voice, he splutters out, 'Look Conor, the beauty of it is that he lives on his own, has no security, and is as mad as a fish... No offence meant.' His still crimson face creases into a sarcastic smile, one which is not reciprocated. Instead, Conor remains quiet. The first dustings of dusk darken his long face, reflecting his mood.

The thing is he is not even listening to Baines. Not really. He was root deep in one of his moods, where even his apathy was apathetic. Sometimes when the voices left him he would feel like this. Experience a kind of nothingness that was all consuming. Did not want to see anyone, hear anyone or feel anything. Now such a mood was upon him. And Baines did not exist any more, and as he looked through him to the cash on the mattress, he wonders how much money it would take to make it all end, to make it all just go away.

'Hey, Silly Bollocks. So, come on, what do you think?' Baines voice is like nails down Conor's blackboard. 'I don't think anything about it. Look, ripping a bookie's off is one thing. But turning an old man over... No!' The words of Conor are uttered with a vague assertiveness, calmly. And herein lay the paradox. Inside his mind, as we have so often witnessed, Conor could be suffering maelstroms of misery, cataclysmic tumult and tortures; yet rarely did his voice betray the agonies of within.

Invariably his words would be uttered with a calm serenity and gentleness. Indeed, his voice was the only thing that the boy liked about himself. In fact, he would often find himself modulating his tone; repeating certain words over and over, until he heard back the desired timbre, pitch and texture in his voice. And on these occasions, in his more utopian and childish moments, he would consider a world where the wearing of a mask was mandatory, a legal requirement, thus making faces redundant and obsolete.

He smiled inwardly at this thought, a cool vision indeed. Yeah, bring it on. Bring on a 'Vocal meritocracy' Bring on a world of vocal not visual. Bring on that world where people are judged on their voices not their looks. Then he would be a king. Well, at least a duke or an earl perhaps.

And such were the thoughts, the mental wanderings and musings of this boy. As with crooked eyes and damaged mind he attempts to make sense of seeming nonsense, and comprehend the incomprehensible. Just to understand the hateful world that surrounds him. Just to do that.

'You know, I don't see why I should waste my time on you. You are so wrapped in that fucked up world between your ears, you just don't have a clue what is happening in the real one.' Baines is at him again, his voice tetchy and whining. He looks at Conor briefly, a mix of annoyance and resignation on his face. Then, roughly pulling his coat on he storms out, slamming the door very hard behind him. Whereupon, and in the best tradition of second-rate comedies the world over, a large lump of plaster crashes from the geriatric ceiling.

Its descent is watched by Conor. Its heavy impact on equally geriatric floorboards makes him briefly flinch. And as the dust rises stinging his eyes, it seems to awaken dormant voices, all with something to say, all clamouring to be heard. Slowly, he takes the blade from his jacket and rolls up his sleeve. It was time again, time to cut in and time to cut out. He is glad Baines is gone. Now he could find silence in solitude. No voices. No Baines. No anything.

Lazarus knew he was taking a hell of a risk getting the boy soldier to knock at the door of the peasant's small home. But desperate times call for desperate measures. And things were certainly desperate. The bottom line was he badly needed a change of clothes. He had to somehow shed his ragged concentration camp stripes, and do so rapidly.

As he lay in dense bushes just yards from the front of the hut on the edge of the small village, his mind briefly turned to Ishmail. Once more, his feelings were ambivalent and confused. Why should the man have risked his life and position in the camp for him, only to then abandon him in the forest? Lazarus chided himself for thinking like a child, blaming it on his tortuously empty stomach. Indeed, hunger was gripping him like a vice. It made him dizzy and his guts pained him endlessly. But it was time to stop thinking of Ishmail. What was done was done. No point dwelling or brooding upon it.

Suddenly distracted by a crunching sound, he gazes down

and sees Geist chewing on pine cones. A few weeks ago that would have been the limb or testicles of some Jewish prisoner. Times change, people change. And evidently so do dogs also, even the most recalcitrant.

Just then, the door of the peasants hut starts to slowly open. Instinctively, Lazarus crouches lower in the bushes. Twenty yards away, the boy walks towards him with an expressionless face. Under either arm he carries a bundle. Looking over his shoulder a final time at the peasants hut, he enters the dense bushes. Passing the bundles to Lazarus he crouches down on his haunches.

Hurriedly Lazarus opens both loosely tied packages. In one was the clean, if somewhat worn shirt, jacket and trousers of a peasant. In the other was food, a hunk of bread, cheese and a sausage. All rather aged, but to the starving, pure manna from Heaven.

So, in silence, Lazarus deals out the rations, and they tear into the food as though their lives depend upon it. Crouched, furtive and dirty, it is not hard to picture this trinity as hunter-gatherers five thousand years removed; shrouded by primeval forest. But these particular hunter-gatherers, unlike those that had trod their footsteps five millennia before, were not fearful of malevolent forest spirits or omnipotent, vengeful water deities. No. The spirits that were to be feared for them were those of the uniformed flesh and blood variety, armed with gun and grenade, and with a well practised hate in hearts and minds.

'You know, it's lucky you didn't go to the hut. I reckon the old man would have killed you. Or handed you in.' the boy speaks through his food; his teeth the same creamy white as the bread he chews ravenously upon. Lazarus rests the remaining piece of bread on his knee and looks thoughtfully at the boy. 'What did he say about the Germans and the Partisans?' Karl swallows down the last of his bread and wipes his mouth with the back of his hand.

'Well, the good news is that he says that the Germans rarely come into the forest hunting for Jews. But the bad news is that most days the forest is crawling with partisans and Anti Semites who seem only too happy to do the job for them.' Lazarus is quiet briefly. When he finally speaks it's as if he is thinking aloud. 'It's best to follow the river south. The Slovak border cannot be much more than thirty kilometres away. Of course, we can only travel by night. But even so, we should be able to travel the distance in two or three nights.'

He slowly nods his head as if agreeing with the sagacity of his own words. He rises and looks down at Karl. 'Do you have any money left?' The boy shakes his head. 'No, the last bit of money I had paid for the clothes and food.' 'What about anything worth selling?' Karl slowly slips off the cheap looking wrist watch he is wearing. 'Here, you might as well have this. I'am sick to death of time anyway. Lazarus holds the trash can timepiece in his hand, glances at it and then at Karl.

His tone is both sympathetic and overly optimistic. 'Well, let's see, we could get a fair few Zlotys for it, if need be.' The boy looks at him coolly, his confidence growing enough for him to speak his mind. 'I doubt it the thing is a piece of crap. But you never know, someone might be fool enough to buy it.' His words are lost on a forest breeze, because Lazarus is now silently taking the fetid prisoners rags from his body.

In the dappled light, Karl cannot but help notice the barely healed raised lash marks on the grey-white back of Lazarus. Nor can he help but notice the sunken chest and painfully protruding ribs. Everywhere on his body the scars of anguish and privation are both visible and invisible.

Hurriedly and self-consciously Lazarus covers his nakedness. Against his skin, the peasant's clothes feel soft and cool. At his feet, Geist sniffs at the discarded rags, the dried blood on them rekindle something, a memory, something from another time and place. Finally, he raises a heavy hind leg, and lets out a steaming stream of golden piss all over the soiled rags. Lazarus, snug in his peasant's clothes, looks on. The symbolism is so obvious he can barely be bothered to raise a rueful smile.

By night, the river looks like heavy black tar. In silence the trinity move stealthily along its sad bank. To their right, vast pines loom, touching, shrouding the sky. But not totally. For high above, a spring moon, full and bright lights their way. With the boy's discarded rifle now retrieved and slung over his shoulder, Lazarus lets Karl lead the way.

Earlier in the evening he had given the kid his pistol. And whilst it was a decision he did not exactly regret; equally. It was one he did not entirely feel comfortable with either, hence his decision to make the boy walk along the bank in front of him. That said, he was starting to feel a certain trust in this strange kid who seemed as wearied of the mud and blood as he was. So, while exactly not a kindred spirit, Lazarus nevertheless could not perceive him as an enemy either. Perhaps he just saw the boy as yet another victim of the madness.

So, in the deep opacity of a Polish night, hour fallowed trudging hour. And now as a pre-dawn wind starts to bite root deep, likewise does their ubiquitous pangs of hunger. But this sad, mad trinity marches on. For what else was there? Behind them were only death, time and method uncertain. But a certain demise nevertheless, and in front of them?

Despite the uncertainty, Karl had never felt such a liberating solace and comfort in darkness as he felt right now. There was no fear. Not any more, just an acceptance of the unreality of things. It was like the time after his brother Ralf had drowned in the lake on his Grandfather's farm. For days, weeks after the tragedy, the twelve-year-old Karl had joined the ranks of the living dead, functioning in a daze, breathing in a haze. But no tears, just an overwhelming and crushing unreality had been his.

Fast forward six years, and the unreality is back. But this time it's different. This time if there was to be a death it would be his. And the strange thing was that there was a part of him that did not care to resist it. Yet equally, he knew that he would not be able to acquiesce placidly either. So now he closes his eyes briefly to make darkness darker.

And in shortened steps a fragmented, floating mind, realises that tomorrow is his nineteenth birthday. With a shudder he thinks no more of it. Opening his eyes again he quickens halting steps. Yet his levitating mind refuses to release the unreality. Instead it casts itself back to a time when the black tar river was a clear water stream, and the pearly moon was in its infancy.

He tilts his head to face opaque skies. And his mind tells him that he is older than the black earth under his feet, yet younger than a tomorrow still to be born. Suddenly, from behind he feels a heavy blow that sends him reeling, falling, sprawling down the river bank into the reeds and sedge. He soon feels

Lazarus by his side breathing hard. The coldness of the river casts asunder the feelings of unreality of the boy.

And as the water rises to his waist, the here and now is his again. 'Just shut up and keep quiet,' the voice of Lazarus is a hiss. 'In the trees over there to the left, I saw a couple of flash lights. It's either Partisans or a German patrol.' In the blackness Karl can feel the skeletal limbs of Lazarus pressing into him. He can smell river, dog, fear, night. But can see nothing. And in the darkness he wonders if the cold water will consume him as it had Ralf.

And he thinks of lost thoughts, of lost words spoken. And then clings on hard to the river bank weeds that keep him afloat. Lazarus was slightly above him and to his right. The boy could smell the moth balls on the peasant's clothes he wore; its scent mingling into the algae stench of the river made him want to vomit, made him want to run, to be anywhere other than here. Even into a grave like Ralf's.

In the sickly blackness he tries to free himself, to escape the sapping and cold grip of the river. He had barely made a move before he could feel the bony hand of Lazarus grip his shoulder. 'Get back!' The noise of the splashing water brings muffled shouts from across the river. Yells and curses from obscured Knights of Teuton. Cold voices, bold voices, but not old voices echo out, as their flash lights beam and bounce off the rivers surface like skimming stones.

Seconds later, a volley of rifle shots sting the night air, making it bleed cordite. Lazarus and Karl become river stones, motionless. A few feet away they hear Geist yelp, and then run off into the night. With heads buried into the river bank they are unable to tell if he has been shot. Seconds pass and then minutes. No more gun fire comes. On both sides of the black tar river all is quiet again. And after what seems like an eternity river stones move. But they move differently now. For now a trinity is broken.

One bright, early February morning, Dina's grandmother breathed her last. And the girl felt nothing. And for the ensuing days she continued to feel nothing. But then as the fourth day passed into the fifth, she was hit head on by the truck of guilt. Day and night stinging blows from this unforgiving bastard battered her conscience and lacerated her mind. And now, standing alone in an early morning kitchen, floodgates finally crash open; tears come so hard and fast she thinks, hopes she will choke.

Falling to her knees, she sinks her nails into the cold barren lino, and howls. Howls until finally raising her tear-ravaged face, she screams at the night. 'I am glad she is dead!'

The day of the funeral broke as grey as ash. Since first light a steady drizzle had been falling. As always the weather was sticking strictly to funereal protocol, namely, that all mourners at the graveside should get as wet and cold as possible. Not that there were many mourners attending the laying to rest of the old woman, just Dina and an elderly couple, who appeared to be at the wrong funeral. They shuffled sheepishly, smiled with embarrassment at Dina and the priest and then walked slowly away, gesticulating angrily at each other. The priest carried on with the service, his words neither comforting nor sincere.

He was a kind of ecclesiastical paradigm, as were his words. Dina closed her eyes to the rain and her mind to his words.

He could have been speaking about anyone, her grandmother, the man who owned the greengrocer's on the High Street, Idi Amin, anyone. He was a holy man of more grey than black. And the weather and the churchyard camouflaged him perfectly, so well that Dina could not see him any more. She could not see or hear anything any more. Could only feel February rain on her skin. And now bowing her head, she turns her face against the living and the dead.

As the sad little service finally ends, so does the rain. Sods law. In a voice that is almost her own, Dina thanks the priest. Barely looking at her, his handshake is swift and slimy. She watches him depart across the Ypres mud of the churchyard. Slipsliding every now and then, he grips onto moss encrusted headstones to stop his descent. For once, souls are saving him. Reaching the door of the vestry, he looks back briefly at Dina. She thinks she sees something in his face. A certain look. Had he sussed her? What did it matter? She knew already that she did not wear grief well. Guilt was more her colour.

The wake was a solitary affair. Dina always knew it would be. But still, nothing could have prepared her for the emptiness. She thinks of her grandmother alone in that box, unseeing and unfeeling. Was it just her shell? Had that part of her that had once been well, happy and young escaped? It frustrated the girl that she did not know, could never know.

Rising slowly from the armchair, magnolia walls seem to groan in empty silence. Walking to the kitchen, she takes a cloth and wipes all the surfaces, even though they are not dirty. She catches a glimpse of herself in the chrome of the toaster and quickly looks away. And so, agonising minutes slip away in a haze and bustle of non-thinking and superfluous cleaning, anything to stop her tearing

her soul apart.

After a small eternity she leaves the kitchen and floats unseeing from room to room. Absent-mindedly she trails her small fingers across cold walls, dead furniture and a plethora of other textures that somehow blend into one.

Reaching the front room, she takes a bottle of Cinzano from the wall unit and an Otis Redding LP, and tries so hard to obtain solace, comfort, something, from the remains of the day. But all she finds is the stiff pages of a half-remembered photo album, where long dead and dusty people lived. Forever caught in time. Some smiled, some grinned and some stared unblinking at the camera lens shoved under their nose. But there, always there was her grandmother, young and old and gone.

On holiday at Bognor Regis, or the matriarch with a gin and a glare at family piss-ups, or relaxing in the chair she got with her Green shield stamps. There, always there, young and old and gone, with each turning page. And only the eyes remained free from the ravages of time, dark and aloof, with a gentle cruelty about them.

Dina slams the album shut and gazes vacantly out of the window. Outside, timid shadows were being born under stark amber streetlights. Everywhere was dusk quiet. All that was missing was the tumbleweed. The girl finally comes away from the window and the outside world. Today it troubled her. She felt done with it. Drinking the Cinzano made her warm. But then all too quickly, cold, numb and tearful. And as the evening dripped away in a blearyblur of tears and time unmissed, so a stealthy darkness came, bringing with it oblivion. And thus were buried the final remnants of burial day.

CHAPTER ELEVEN

'If thine eyes torment thee, then cast them out.' All morning the voices in the head of Conor had been in overdrive. And he knew that today, like every day, he would face an unequal struggle against their mocking invective and hatred. And equally he knew that today, like every day, he would use the blade, his only weapon, to fight the futile battle.

And long ago he realised he was slave to the master, captive to the captor. And never for more than a minute was mind or hand far from sharpened steel. Turning his coat collar up against a belligerent east wind, Conor starts to walk the streets he knows so well, knows better than anyone. Pavement gazing was his, was all he knew.

Disembodied shoes and boots ebb and flow before his downcast eyes; human dodgem cars hustling, bustling, hurrying, scurrying. Some weighed down with shopping, all seemingly weighed down with suburban ennui. In his heart, Conor hates himself for hating them. But they were not of his world and he was not of theirs.

At last reaching the bookshop, he raises his head and peers through the shop window. The girl is at the far end of the shop talking to a middle-aged man in a suit. Conor watches her closely, black hair, white skin, black dress, small, so small, a black and white sparrow.

And now his strange amber eyes follow her as she limps to the counter, the customer following closely behind her.

Conor's long face remains impassive as she serves the man, where soon, with a mutual Tuesday kind of smile, the transaction is concluded.

Outside, the boy with his heart of granite and glass hesitates. He watches the man leave. Then look's up and down the street, as if not only expecting to hear the demons that lived in his head; but to see them also. However, as always all those oblique eyes see are shoes and boots, boots and shoes.

Breathing hard and deep he slowly opens the door. A small shop bell announces his arrival. At its tinkling chime he immediately casts his head downwards. But not before Dina sends a shy but friendly smile in his direction. He returns the smile, but his is crippled, pained. And as he pretends he has suddenly gained a massive fascination in the shelves stacked with books on model-making, yoga and Roman mosaics; so Dina pretends to replenish shelves in the adult fiction section.

He so wanted to say something witty and profound; but his brain had turned to slush and his tongue to lead. And now she looks across at the stumbling, mumbling boy with something akin to a sympathetic attraction. And so across the oceanic space of the bookshop she calls across softly to him. 'Books by Dickens are over there, to your left.' Conor is mute, words extinct. But the voice in his head takes silence for a cue. 'Hey creature, the little crippled whore is speaking to you. Ain't you going to answer her?'

The boy is covered in sweat now. With eyes cast to the floor he hides his hands, he does not want her to see how they shake, a pitiful tremble. He wants to reach inside his head and rip the voices out. But from somewhere, somewhere deep inside he finds a calm a composure. Because he knows that this girl, this small dark sparrow, cannot be allowed to know or see what a fucked up little person he is. He must wear the mask don the disguise of a 'normal'. Whatever the hell that is.

Finally raising his head slowly, his voice is soft. 'You remembered about the David Copperfield book?' Dina gazes across at the strange looking boy. She likes the calm gentleness of that voice. 'Yes, I remembered. Actually we have just had an old edition of Bleak House delivered. I thought you might be interested in taking a look at it?'

He tries so hard to maintain eye contact with her. Because that is what normal people do. Yet all the while the voices are whipping up their invective. 'You are fucking deluded! The bitch is disgusted by you. You are less than nothing to her!' Conor feels sick. He swallows hard and tries to smile at those soul-deep brown eyes. But his reply when it comes is awkward and strained.

'Yes, yes I would be interested.' He follows her as she leads him to the back of the shop. Up close she is frail looking then he had first thought; and her limp more pronounced, but right at this moment. Here in the now. He knows he will love her till he dies, simple as that. No ambiguity in a heart and soul such as his.

'Ah, here it is,' Dina takes from the shelf a green fabric-bound book. Although only of a medium size, nevertheless, the tome rests heavy in such tiny hands. With a small smile she hands the book to Conor. In his hands it has become a priceless artefact, such is his touch. Noticing this, she smiles once again. 'It's okay, you don't have to be that precious with it, it's really not that valuable.' He looks embarrassed, blood rising in the cheeks of that long face. She suddenly feels mean for saying it. 'I was just joking. So, have you ever read Bleak House?'

He looks briefly at the book in his hand, and then at her pale face. 'No, never read it. But I have always wanted to. How much is it?' 'Well, cos it's quite an early edition, it's £10. Is that too much? If it is, we do have a cheaper paperback edition.' All this eye contact is agonising for the boy. At last his gaze drops away. He replies through the top of his head. 'No it's fine.'

Christ, how he wants to just grab her by the hand and run from the shop. Because the place, the space, it is all closing in on him. But at least for now the voices were dormant. But still, intuitively, he feels for the blade in his pocket. And she, this girl watches him, wonders who he is, what he is, where he is from.

Whilst thoughts of the funeral had not totally disembarked from her brain, they were nevertheless no longer at the forefront. And so, as she looks at him, so he looks at her. Furtive, nervous side glances. And as she wonders so does he. Doubts crowd his mind. Was she sickened by looking at him? Could she ever be anything other than sickened?

Eyes, his eyes intrigued her, their colour and shape. She did not feel repulsed, did not lean into a cringe. Where others may perceive the reptilian in them, she only saw the eyes of a tortured, tormented boy.

'Do you like any other authors apart from Dickens?' Her voice is light and airy as she smiles at Conor over the top of the cash register. He passes her a nervous smile along with a crumpled ten pound note. And he knows now there is no way out. He was going to have to ask her. 'Er, well, to be honest, I have only read Dickens.' He breathes hard, looks at the floor, ceiling, then back at the floor. Finally he raises his head, and the normally calm gentleness of his voice is replaced by a stuttering hesitancy. 'I, well, was wondering if, if you are not doing anything later, then perhaps. Well, you might wanna come out with me?'

He gasps out the final words staccato fashion, as if firing out wasps from his mouth. There follows a silence he had expected. Finally giving way to an answer he had not. 'Yes, okay, why not. Where shall we go?' The feelings are strange; euphoria, disbelief, confusion and joy, all in equal measure. He somehow manages to hold himself together long enough to reply in a normal tone.

'It's your choice. So, how about we go for a drink? Or maybe the cinema?' She wishes he would let her look longer into those pained eyes. But she cannot help but notice that after practically every word spoken he would look away. 'Look, how about you come back here at six this evening. And we can decide then where to go.' Her final words are accompanied by the ringing of the shop bell; as a rather frosty looking middle-aged woman enters the shop.

'Right, six it is then.' Clumsily, awkwardly, he stumbles out of the shop, in the process, nearly ploughing into the hatchet-faced customer. Dina's amused smile seeing him off on his way.

Outside, long dark curtains of rain hang from the sky, condemned men falling from cloud gallows. It stings and lashes the face of Conor. But what did he care. Forgetting himself, he walks with a head held high. As for once, his voices remain sleeping.

A dozen minutes and a dozen miles away under the same aching, arching, desolate February sky, Baines stares at the house. He is relieved that the rain is at last starting to abate.

His feet loafer shod, Weller-style, are starting to resemble saturated canal barges. And the fifty quid Hillman Imp he had bought that very morning, was springing more leaks than the Titanic; rain seeping through the weary and cracked seals of the windscreen, oozing, forming a confluence with the leaks from holes in the roof of the vehicle, an unholy alliance.

Briefly taking his eyes from both minor flood and the house, Baines switches on the car radio. It fizzes, fuzzes, crackles and dies. It does not work. It could not work. Why the hell should it for fifty quid. He curses under his breath, and then sinks another vodka miniature in one hit. The liquor both soothes and jolts him. Once more he casts eyes towards the house.

It is spacious and detached a paradigm of middle-class suburbia. The street it is located on is eternally quiet and smug. Lime trees form silent sentinels along its full length, bark-clad witnesses, always keeping an eye out in silent observation, but leafless and lifeless now, there spiky fingers groping and grasping imploringly up at the leaden London sky.

Baines looks at them briefly, but his mind has become consumed by the possibility that Kenny Brooker has sold him a pup. After all, for two days the boy had been watching the house, yet there had not been the slightest sign of life from within. He had witnessed a succession of callers knock at the sturdy oak front door. But it had remained resolutely shut. And he was slowly starting to come to the conclusion that either the old Jew was dead. Or he had not existed in the first place. Kenny Brooker could be so full of shit sometimes.

He was just about to call it a day: when it happened. Very slowly the front door started to open. He instinctively slid down in his seat a little. Slipping out furtively from the shadows, old man Lazarus stands pale against the red bricked house. On his face is a blinking look of bewilderment against the light, a sense of surprise that outside a world still exists.

Tall and stooping, he is a personification of grey, as if, without him knowing or caring, cement dust had gently fallen upon him throughout his tormented, wasted years. The grey ingrained in every furrow, crevice and crease of his face. And now, for the merest moment, young and old eyes meet. And the boy tries to read something, anything in those eyes. But he cannot, because they are without life, two lifeless dark lakes... Dead.

A sudden inexplicable shudder rips through him. He fumbles the key into the ignition, revving the tired engine then drives off hurriedly. The silent limes watch him depart a wind swaying there skeletal limbs in a sombre salute. The boy glances nervously in the rear view mirror, but Lazarus is gone. Exhaling hard, he knows he will have to see him again soon. And the shudder sweeps over him again at the thought. But, of course, the young master criminal would swear to God that it was just the cold.

Lazarus declared it a miracle. Karl stayed silent. He just wanted to go home, back to the farm, just wanted the whole damn thing to be over and done with. As if perceiving Karl's silence as a challenge to his declaration of a miracle, Lazarus loftily asserts that they are in the midst of an act of awe and wonder. How else could the dog have found them again? It was 'Nothing short of a.' 'Yeah, a miracle. You have already said so. Four times now.' The voice of Karl is tetchy, muffled by the dense, dark hay.

The haystack they had found refuge in was small, damp and

ragged. Hidden away in the corner of a bleak and desolate field, it offered a temporary sanctuary against their enemy, the sun, which had already risen, giving the dawning day a red disc of trembling warmth, which they would soon endeavour to sleep through. For in their world, days had become nights and nights days. And now, deep down in this tomb of straw; hot, prickly and suffocating, both physically and mentally, tired voices whisper out once more.

'So, you do not think it's a miracle that the dog tracked us for fifteen kilometers in the pitch black of night, and then found us in this very haystack in this very field?' Karl sighs. He could not care less about the dog or non existent miracles. The only thing dominating his thoughts was food, or more specifically, where the hell he was going to get some from.

The pain in his stomach was becoming acute, a dull, constant ache like toothache in the guts. 'If we don't get some food soon, I'm going to eat the dog!' His words are uttered only half-jokingly, for in his eyes the animal is a waste of space, if not a liability exactly, then certainly not a creature that served any purpose. In the stultifying heat of the stack, he feels the heartbeat of Geist against his leg. He nudges the animal hard with his knee, it growls deeply in its sleep, but refuses to budge an inch. Karl sighs, and once more thinks of food, all food any food.

Beside him, Lazarus shifts uneasily in the hay. He thinks of Esther. He has a hole in his chest. The hole is called Esther. And it was too big to fill with words like, 'I miss her so much.' It was a hole that could never be healed, never be filled... Something inside him was broken.

It is the voices of two men that woke Lazarus from his fitful sleep. Groggily, he quickly claps his hand over the muzzle of the stirring Geist. Seemingly aware of the danger, the animal remains silent and stock still. Through the dense straw, tiny slithers of sunlight glints against glass. Glass bottles are being rapidly thrust into the haystack. The coolness of one bottle brushes the face of Lazarus, another grazes his hand. He tries to listen to what the men are saying, but their speech is nervy and hurried and spoken in the local Silesian dialect. Then their voices are gone.

Slowly, tentatively in the darkness, Lazarus takes one of the bottles. Its coolness chill his fingers. Prizing the cork out, he sniffs its transparent contents. The aroma instantly evokes memories, engenders within him a sensation of sliding back in time, time. A time, a decade since, when the peasants from the villages around Krakow, would bring bottles of home made vodka to his father's watchmakers shop on the outskirts of the city, in the hope that they could persuade the old man to trade a few watches for their fire water brew. And on more than one occasion, Yankiel Glick would Succumb to the temptation and swap a few cheap timepieces for a few bottles of the illicit booze.

However, the wistful smile on the lips of Lazarus, soon gives way to a curse, as the left boot of Karl catches him in the solar plexus. Wincing, Lazarus shakes the boy awake. Karl mumbles incoherently and turns onto his side. Lazarus shakes him harder. 'Wake up. I have something to show you.' Karl replies blearily. 'Well, unless it's a huge steak I'm not interested.' 'It's better than steak. It's currency.'

Lazarus strokes one of the bottles and holds it up for Karl

to see. In all there are five bottles of the illicit vodka, liquid bargaining chips. Yawning loudly, Karl opens his eyes to darkness. But here and there tiny filters of sunlight permeate the hay, giving just enough light to see the bottles. 'What the hell are they? Where the hell did you get them from?' Lazarus smiles 'I did not get them from anywhere. They were very kindly donated by some local Poles. I just hope they were Anti-Semites. Now, that would be poetic justice.'

Reaching across, Karl sniffs it tentatively. 'It smells a bit like schnapps.' He passes the bottle back to Lazarus. Who, shaking his head, say's quietly. 'No, what it smells like is bread, cheese and sausage.'

CHAPTER TWELVE

Conor arrives promptly at six. His journey back to the bookshop has been nothing less than tortuous. As ever trying to avoid the busier streets, the boy has assiduously kept his eyes fixed downwards as if afraid his gaze might get snagged on someone if he raises his head. Then, halfway over the old river bridge, it starts. Or more specifically, they start muffled howls of pain and anguish. Then the derisive mocking tones he knew so well, and feared so much. 'No! not here, not now!'

His voice is a hopeless, desperate gasp. He lurches, and then stumbles into the cold granite of the bridge. Passers-by give a wide berth to the strange looking boy who mumbles incoherently. The stone of the bridge feels cold, but he can feel a pulse in its deadness, throbbing and insistent. Suddenly he feels electrical jolts tearing through his head. The pain is excruciating. He slams his eyes shut and waits for the shudder voices. And he does not have long to wait. The flame voice as always is the loudest.

'Repulsive thing from the depths of the pit, you fucking freak, I should cast you back into the fire!' Growls and howls fill the head of Conor. He cannot breathe, cannot think. Staggering along the bridge, he starts to bolt down the footpath that ran alongside the sluggish river. He runs hard, runs fast runs blind. He runs.

Past derelict houses, derelict factories, derelict drunks on derelict benches. But still the voices scream. And the harder he runs the louder the screams. He can no longer make out their words, just feels their venom and vitriol, echoing, echoing, a white noise of hate. Finally, breathless and gasping he collapses onto his knees in the riverbank earth.

Clasping the palms of his hands over his ears, he starts to rock back and forth on his knees back and forth, rocking. Then, like some incongruous white boy Muslim, he presses his forehead against the cool earth, and prays at this riverside mosque. Prays for a crushingly beautiful silence to arise, ascend from the river and flood his mind free, to wash away the voices. Just to do that. In the name of all that is sacred. Just to do that.

By choosing her orange dress, Dina had wanted to wear confidence and happiness. Instead, all she wears is a shade of nervousness and apprehension. For now as she answers his knock at the shop door, she is shocked to see the condition of Conor. He is breathless, has patches of dirt on the knees of his jeans and large flecks of earth on his forehead.

Seeming distant and distracted, he barely speaks as she locks the shop door behind her. It unnerves her. And what also unnerves her is that without even having to gaze up, she knows Breitner will be at his window watching her. These days the only thing that seemed to move on him are those dark blue eyes. His lips seldom did. Catatonia continued to claim him captive. And he appeared to be in no rush for it to relinquish its grasp.

And long since the blackbird had lost all fascination for him. It had stolen back its stolen voice, and he. He was left to his dreams, nightmares that hijacked his sleep. Such images of mud and blood... Such memories.

The Lamb pub was just a stones throw down the street from the bookshop. A slightly squat and self conscious building, it nevertheless wore proudly on its shabby plastered exterior an equally shabby small plaque, which bore the solemn inscription. 'On this site, in the year of our Lord 1554, four religious martyrs; Henry Askwith, James Ball, Andrew Barrington and Stephen Bertola, were burnt at the stake for their religious beliefs.' Directly under the plaque in black marker pen, a heartless wag had added the words, 'Frying tonight!'

Coming in from the cold, Conor and Dina find a snug that is not so snug, and a bitter that is not so bitter. But more importantly they find; bit by bit, scrap by scrap, each other. And with alcohol their liquid matchmaker, layers are gently stripped away. Borderlands are crossed. And barriers, barricades of shyness and self consciousness are systematically dismantled. Lost together now found together. Boy and girl. Beguiled and beguiling. And if such a thing as a soul exists, it's not overly glib to suggest that they found each others.

And now he did it. Somehow, Conor told the girl as much as he could about the chaos that was his life. It was frightening, painful to do. But it was honest. He could not lie to her. It was a river of flowing words from his mouth. And once he had started it was the Nile. Gushing; bursting banks, A flood of his inner most thoughts and feelings. And in his soft voice he told her everything. Well, almost everything.

The voices he could not tell her about. He tried, but could just not find the words, because there are no words capable of describing the indescribable, and as for his belief that he was somehow less than human. He could not tell her about that either. How could he when he did not truly understand those feelings himself. Deep down he knew he was not mad. But equally, he knew he was not sane either.

Under the dimmed lighting of the little snug bar, the girl looked at the boy as the boy tried not to return that look. It was paradoxical. Here he was telling her some of his innermost thoughts and feelings, yet, he still did not feel comfortable or confident enough to look into her face for more than a few seconds at a time.

As for the girl, she liked the boy. He was unlike the few others she had known. She liked his self consciousness, his aching lack of self confidence. In many respects it mirrored her own, and it was such a refreshing change from the arrogance of the crowd. But most of all she liked his voice. That voice. She could not imagine it ever to be angry, harsh or loud, it just flowed, calm, soft and gentle. Not creepy soft, just pleasant soft. And she feels herself comfortable with this boy. She likes this feeling.

When his words stopped and he gently lowered his head, her words began. At first fitful and reticent, but soon with a river flow that matched Conor's. Her quiet voice spoke of her mother, gone for such a long time, and of her grandmother, so recently gone. Then in darker tones she spoke of Breitner, neither living or dead, here or gone. Suddenly perturbed at the dark melancholy of her thoughts, the girl quickly changes the subject, talking instead of life and hope.

With a zest and enthusiasm that was somehow infectious, she speaks about the bookshop and its wonderful and diverse range of books, and how when she is eighteen the shop will become legally hers. She beams a smile that Conor returns. And for the first time he feels truly relaxed and Confident enough to

159

look at her face for more than a few seconds. Really look at her.

And he forgets everything. Who he is, what he is, none of it mattered now. because he knew that he loved her and would always love her with an intensity beyond what anyone would understand. And as she continued to speak, he tentatively, awkwardly held her small hand in his; feeling its strength and fragility in equal measure.

'Hey Kev'.. Look, the freak show has come to town. Fuck me, how could anyone be so ugly with only one head!' The glazed eyes of the drunken young man look across the bar at Conor. His face wears a sardonic sneer.

The man and his friend had arrived in the pub just minutes earlier, staggering, swaying and swearing. The elderly barman had considered not serving them, but had done so out of fear, and in hope that they would have one drink and then piss off, bored by the lifeless, near empty little bar.

But that is not how things were transpiring. Because these two young men, who wisdom had always kept its distance from, were riddled with the same insecurities and prejudices that every drunken Neanderthal the world over suffers from. Namely they despised the 'other,' the 'different'. They especially hated those that they perceived as being weak and vulnerable. Because when they looked at these individuals it was like staring into a cracked mirror.

And with this twisted reasoning and logic, this cruel philosophy, so the two bar stool bully boys picked out their preferred scapegoats for their evenings hatefest, two for the price of one.

Falling descending from Heaven to Hades, so Conor falls into a kind of paralysis, as with each poisonous missile of hateful invective that is fired at him, so he dies a little more inside. 'Christ, you are the best argument for the Abortion Bill I have ever seen. It's fucking unreal man!' In the gleaming gloom, the girl holds his hand tight, tighter, a rage building up inside her small body. Finally releasing his hand, she gets to her feet and walks across the fag burnt brown carpet, to the bar.

'Oi, oi, here come Hopalong Cassidy!' the face of the man smiles, but his eyes do not. His friend, a head shorter, grin's a cretin's grin and reconnects fleshy lips around his pint glass. Now Dina stands in front of the main tormentor, barely reaching his shoulder. Her voice is calm, betraying the anger eating away inside her.

'Why are you doing this? What have we done to you? You do not even know us.' She fixes her large eyes upon his face. It was a narrow, florid face, possessed of too much hatred and too little empathy. Empathy was, and always would be a stranger to him. Lowering his eyes briefly he is unnerved by the intensity of her gaze. And he knows in that moment that he wants her, needed this little crippled girl. Not for keeps. But just for a little while. And the thought both arouses and repels him. The feeling of needing someone so far from perfect makes him recoil.

Finally raising his head he meets her gaze. Now on his lips he wears a distorted smile and in his eyes a tender hatred. Raising his arm with his hand slightly cupped as if to caress her cheek, he instead brings it down hard across her face. The blow sends Dina stumbling to the floor... All is still... Nothing moves... Even the cretin's smile is as if frozen in time.

A tiny rivulet of blood, crimson bright against her white skin, emanates from the mouth of Dina. She lets it form, and as a strange, surreal paralysis claims the bar, so, Conor's breaks.

And a voice he has never heard before rips through his skull. 'You gonna let him get away with that? Do the cunt! Do him!' No longer there but somewhere else, Conor get's to his feet.

'What you waiting for? Cut him!' Whoever he was, whatever he had become, for he would never totally know, the boy now calmly took the blade from his coat pocket. Not ground gazing now, but walking tall and erect, he confronts the man. And although detached, seemingly elsewhere, there was still the memory of a thought in the broken mind of the boy, that this was the moment he had been waiting for, for an eternity.

And now, not hearing anything, but seeing everything, Conor performs his destiny. In a rapid slashing movement he brings the blade down hard across the grinning face of the man. As he does he lets out a yell, animalistic, unnatural. 'Now you are me!' As if in dreamtime, slowtime, the man raises a hand to his ripped face and cries out, to his mother? God? Or to someone beyond listening? And as the blows rain in, so the scapegoat-hunter has become the scapegoat.

And the release the boy feels transcends the orgasmic. Each slash, each frenzied cut of the blade was payback, payback to every sonofabitch who had ever put him down.

Witnessing all, Dina feels a strange sense of euphoric repulsion. At last rising to her feet, she grabs the swinging arm of the boy as he is just about to scythe again at the now prone and motionless figure. Not thinking, barely breathing, she pulls Conor out into the night, leaving behind statues to gaze at the fallen.

Outside, they cross the road away from the pub in a hurried and shocked silence. Finally stopping a few streets away, they turn and face each other, both uncertain of what to say or do.

By the dull light of an Estate Agents window, Dina looks into the soul of her blood-stained avenger.

Suddenly, a smile appears that is pure suburban silver. Followed by a laugh, diamond sharp cutting through the darkness; proving that everything that had happened back in the pub was real, forever unchangeable. Gazing once more into the face of her beautifully ugly boy, she draws closer to him and kisses his lips.

Self-consciously, awkwardly, Conor holds that small body so tightly. And the shaking breath he exhales so sharply is both the death rattle of his old life, but also an expression of the overwhelming need and love he has for the girl, a love that simply defies words. At last slowly pulling away from him Dina looks down at the shining crimson life-stains smeared across her coat.

'Do you think he is dead?' The boy replies softly, but with a cold-faced conviction. 'I hope so. It would make everything right and worthwhile then.' Starting from her eyes and spreading downwards, Dina smiles almost impishly. Then, suddenly and instinctively she grabs Conor by the hand. 'Come on!' Laughing, she starts to run, dragging him along. And as she runs her limp seems somehow less pronounced, barely noticeable 'See, everything is healed now, everything!' And as they run and laugh along a street to somewhere, so seventeen demons fly from the boy, one for every year of his little life.

Imagining himself a different person, Baines looks out vacantly across a watery wasteland of forlorn and abandoned cabbages and beets. But he was no one right now, no one in particular. Just a half-drunk boy in an old allotment shed. Finally coming away from the window, he sits down on the only available seating. An aged deckchair with 'Property of

Margate Borough Council' inscribed into the wood of its frame. Directly in front of the chair standing on an old crate is a stolen road works light constantly amber flashing.

And as Baines stares at it, it somehow makes him feel chilled, funky and psychedelic, like slipping into the skin of a Woodstock hippy. Well, normally it had that effect on him when he dossed down evenings in the old shed. But this evening was different. This evening he feels a growing sense of expectation and excitement.

For the past few hours in fact, for the past few days his thoughts were never far from the old Jew, and his rambling, shambling house. And now as he looks through the flashing amber light, he recalls something Kenny Brooker had said to him about the Jews. According to Kenny, in the war when the Jews were deported huge amounts of gold, cash and valuables were taken by the Germans. But many Jews aware of their impending arrest and deportation had managed to send vast amounts of gold and money to relatives in big cities such as New York and London.

And herein lay the obsession the boy had with the old Jew. What if, maybe, just perhaps the aged Hebrew was one such recipient of the gold and money? After all, everything fitted. His age, location, that big old house, it all fitted. That gaff alone was worth a few bob. Who's to say in every crevice, nook and cranny of the sodding mausoleum, Sterling, Marks, Dollars were not stashed away. Baines smiles to himself. He knew what he had to do now. Yeah, exactly what he has to do.

CHAPTER THIRTEEN

The food Karl had managed to exchange for the illicit booze had all gone by the time they reached the densely wooded Slovakian border. Treading carefully through the darkness, Geist leads the way. Some twenty meters ahead of Lazarus and Karl he adroitly picks a path through the dense trees, his tail a wagging white rudder in the night.

Suddenly, abruptly, Geist stops dead in his tracks. Turning his head sharply to the left he starts to whimper, then to shake. Behind him, Lazarus and Karl instinctively take cover in the trees. Squinting through the black woods, they see a child of twelve or thirteen approaching the animal tentatively from the shroud of some bushes. He cowers slightly as the child reaches out a thin pale arm and strokes his broad head, then without turning her head or taking her eyes off of Geist, the girl child calls out to Lazarus and Karl.

'Come, follow me, I will show you the way.' Stunned, the two men come out from the trees. Karl turns to Lazarus. 'How the hell did she know we were there?' Lazarus shrugs his shoulders and approaches the child. He speaks softly to her in hushed tones. 'What do you mean you will show us the way? Show us where?' Finally turning her attention from Geist, the girl looks at Lazarus.

Her features are commonplace, dark brown hair and eyes, small and thin. Lazarus waits for her reply. But she leaves him hanging, her small face mute. Turning around, she starts to walk along a sloping path through the trees, as above her a patient and kindly moon illuminates her child steps. Her voice is calm in the night as she calls out to the two men. 'Follow me. This is the way, the right path.' Briefly, Karl and Lazarus look at each other quizzically. Either the child is touched in the head, or their unlikely saviour? Whatever their thoughts, they somehow feel compelled to follow the small dark figure. And so, as trusting as weary children, they do just that.

Tracked in an unreal silence, the moonlit path finally leads them to a clearing in the forest. Peering through the darkness, Lazarus and Karl look out across the large man made space. Where, situated in its centre stands four or five sturdily built small wooden houses, all of which bar one were in darkness. Without looking back to see if the men follow her, the child walks across the hard black earth towards the lighted house.

Standing in the shadows, Lazarus gazes down at the ground pensively; whilst a few paces to his left, Karl pulls the collar of his oversized coat up and slowly looks around. It was tangible he could sense it, the strangeness of everything. It was the kind of place where, as his mother would have put it, cats bark and dogs meow.

The child's soft knocking at the door of the house is finally answered by a tall, angular male figure. The pale light that emanates from behind him casts him in silhouette, thus making it impossible to determine his age or features. The conversation between the child and the man is brief, and out of earshot of Lazarus And Karl. But after a few minutes the girl returns to them.

'Father Jan says you can stay. He wants to see you now.'

with that, this ethereal little being just floats off, her child steps silent against the cold earth. Momentarily Karl and Lazarus stand and watch her quiet departure. And then, as if her tiny spell over them was at an end, they walk tentatively towards the house of Father Jan.

Peering inside the half open door, the men stand in the doorway, unsure on whether or not to enter the house. 'Come in and close the door behind you.' The voice of the occupant of the house is calm sounding and pleasant, unlike his appearance. Moving from the shade into the glow of a kerosene lamp, his face is no longer concealed, and it is a face neither Lazarus nor Karl could ever forget.

For, where eyes should have been there were just empty sockets, deep and taut, pinky red with deep blue veins. And his wide face seemed to be an amalgam of ill-fitting features. Karl could not restrain a shudder, as Lazarus recoiled and looked away. Jan senses their horror. 'I think, perhaps I should have stayed in the shade.' His gentle voice has a warmth a humour. Both men felt shamed. This Jan seems able to sense also. He speaks matter of fact.

'I was born without eyes. Rare, but there you are. Better I should have been born this way than someone who would have needed them more than me. What is done is done.' Walking across to the open fire he casts his sightless face towards its flames. As he does, Lazarus takes the opportunity to gaze around the squat little house. It was sparsely furnished, yet warm and clean. He turns his gaze now towards Jan. 'If you don't mind me asking. Where the hell are we? What is this place?'

Coming away from the fire Jan motions with his hand for the

two men to sit down on the only available seating, two rickety looking chairs. 'Please, sit down.' Sitting down on the bed facing them, Jan speaks slowly. 'Well, in answer your question. Where you are is in a place that does not exist. It does not exist to the German's, it does not exist to the Slovak fascists. Neither will venture this far into the forest. There is nothing for them here. And as for the local people we see them only rarely. They call us the forgotten, well, either that or the cursed. Either way, they prefer to stay away, which suits us fine.'

He smiles thinly. Lazarus looks across at him. 'Why do they call you the cursed? So, if you do not have contact with the outside world how do you survive?' Jan rises from the bed. 'My friend, we survive because we 'do not' have contact.' Without waiting for a reply he walks slowly out into the tiny kitchen.

In his absence Lazarus and Karl are silent. But from outside they can hear the constant whimpering of Geist. Karl sighs heavily. 'See, even the dog knows there is something wrong with this place. I reckon we should get out of here. Something is not right. It's fucked up somehow.'

Before Lazarus can reply, Jan returns from the kitchen carrying two bowls of potato soup and a loaf of bread. He places the bowls on the small table that occupies the centre of the room. Then taking two spoons from his jacket pocket he hands them to Lazarus and Karl. 'Go ahead, eat. You must be starving.' The two men fall upon the food ravenously, their first hot meal in days. As they eat, Jan goes to the front door. Opening it fully, he calls out softly into the night. 'Hey friend, come in, there is plenty for you too.'

Geist does not need asking twice. In one bound he bundles through the door into the house, and as Jan feeds him, so Karl and Lazarus lay down spoons in empty bowls. For now their hunger, if not their curiosity sated, they look on as Jan once again sits on the bed and addresses them. 'So, tell me. Not all were murdered at the camp then?' Lazarus and Karl remain silent. Jan continues in the same soft tone. 'You have nothing to fear here, we heard what happened at the camp. News travel fast even to those who have rejected the world.' Lighting an old briar pipe he gently blows the smoke up towards the ceiling.

'You know, when little Hana heard about what happened at the camp, she prayed to her God that someone, at least someone would survive. Because after what happened to her she thinks she is the last Jew on earth.' Karl stifles a cough, as a plume of pipe smoke threatens to engulf him. 'Is Hana the little kid who brought us here?' Jan nods his head. 'Yes, that is our little Hana.' Lazarus can barely hide the incredulity in his voice. 'With respect, what the hell is a little kid doing wandering about a forest in the middle of the night?'

Jan smiles briefly. 'Like I said, waiting for one of her own, waiting for you. And now you have come.' Rising slowly from the bed, he walks to the door. 'Well, for what is left of the night let us find sleep. In the morning you will meet the rest of this 'commune of the cursed' as the locals call us. Goodnight.' With that, he softly closes the door behind him and goes out into the night. For a few minutes or so, Lazarus and Karl remain locked in a quiet neither seemed able or willing to break.

Until finally, shaking his head from side to side, Karl speaks. 'Look, I don't know about you, but come first light and I'm out of here. I just don't trust this place, any of it. And I certainly don't trust this Father Jan, or whatever he calls himself.' He crosses the room and sits down on the edge of the bed.

Rising from the table, Lazarus sits beside him. 'I do not admit to knowing what the hell this place is either. Or whether or not this Father Jan is kosher. All I know is I'm going to take my chances here. I'm so tired, so sick to death of running and hiding. Surely this bloody war cannot last much longer.' He gazes down at the ground briefly and then across at Karl. 'So, you are going to go? Where do you plan on heading?'

'Switzerland. I have an uncle there, he runs a restaurant. I will stay with him till this madness is done, if it ever is.' Karl is quiet momentarily. 'Look, actually, if it's all the same with you, I'm thinking of heading off now. There is still a few hours of darkness left yet. Just wanna get away from this place'

Slowly, almost apologetically he rises from the bed. Self-consciously he stands in front of Lazarus his hand outstretched. Lazarus smiles thinly at the formality, but takes the hand in his, all the time looking at the dirty bandage that swathes the skinny and scarred wrist. He is lost for words, feels awkward. 'I don't know what to say really. Just, well, good luck I guess. I hope that uncle of yours has got plenty of food in.' He smiles once more and then lets his gaze slide to the floor. Sharing his embarrassment, Karl busies himself collecting together his few meagre belongings.

This soon achieved, he walks slowly to the door. Lazarus follows a few paces behind. At the door another uncomfortable little silence ensues. Suddenly the boy feels a strange inexplicable compulsion to hug this Jew that he would never see again. But that would not do. Formalities would not allow. So, instead he merely leaves, with mouth and mind full of words unspoken. And from the window Lazarus watches Karl as the dark, immovable void of night claimed him. Then, looking around this alien room, Lazarus Glick could not shift from his mind the thought that it was always going to be like this, Esther, his parents, Yitzhak, Ishmail the Turk. Everyone he knew would always go away in the end.

At a little after midnight, Conor and Dina leave the world. Entwined and enraptured, they now inhabit a new time and space. And in the wordless dark, imperfections became perfections and insecurities were surrendered to the night. A night whose beauty they knew deep down would never come again. And so as they clasped and grasped at each other, so they did also to every elusive escaping moment. But it was not enough, and soon, too soon, wrapped in each others arms and the arms of Morpheus, sleep took them hostage. But it was a gentle sleep, a sleep without voices, flames, nightmares, and without guilt, inseparably serene.

It was the brute force of a stark easterly wind that eventually roused Baines from his drunken slumber. Since before dawn, belligerent blasts had shaken and shuddered the flimsy yet stoical little shed. Indeed, one particularly violent gust had threatened to cave in the rickety windows, causing the boy to jolt open bleary eyes. And in that startled moment, and in those that followed, he had not the slightest comprehension of where the hell he was.

And it was whilst in this state of post-sleep disorientation, that he first saw it. Curled in a ball at the top of his thigh, obviously failing in a futile attempt to find warmth lay a dead mouse. Baines looks at it once, and then again. His face is blank, registers no surprise. In fact his expression is that of a person who regularly awakes to find a deceased rodent inches from his crotch.

Finally taking the cold little body in his hand he rises from the deckchair. And by what light there is at the window he studies the tiny creature. And wonders how something that was perceived as vermin could be so perfect in body, shape and form. Gently he trails his index finger along the body of the mouse, as if by doing so he could somehow miraculously give back to the rodent that which it had lost.

Suddenly a half-smile patterns his face, as he imagines that soft-boy Conor mumbling a prayer for the departed soul of the mouse. But the smile soon disappears, when once more the bizarre thought crosses his mind, and words come to his lips. 'So, what if this 'thing,' this madness that has fucked up Conor's head, is somehow contagious?' This theory of madness infection by association; insanity by close proximity, was a daymare that rarely left Baines. Day in and day out it obsessed and haunted him, jostling for prominence in his head alongside thoughts, equally obsessive, of the old Jew and his rambling palace of treasures.

Under the calm guidance of Father Jan, Lazarus was soon immersed in the practices and ways of the 'commune.'

Put to work cutting firewood and tending the small herd of livestock, it was not long before he was familiar with all the twenty souls who called the commune home, people such as Jiri the baker, with his port wine birthmark that covers half his face, and silent Samuel, born minus a tongue, but blessed with an ability to 'tell' filthy jokes simply by using his hands and lewd expressive eyes. And Sara, a young epileptic woman, who with skilled and dexterous fingers, creates the most beautiful and ornate embroidery, despite hourly fits that threaten to tear her apart as she lay writhing and convulsing on the ground.

But of all the 'brothers and sisters' of the commune, who had shunned society before society could totally shun them, it was the child Hana who Lazarus felt most drawn to. And as he worked tending the animals or chopping wood, he would watch the silent, nebulous child as she passed by. Often she would look back at him, her restless dark eyes full of words for him, but her lips always resolutely closed. Always.

One stormy late afternoon, just as Lazarus was putting away his tools for the day, he sees the familiar figure of Jan approaching him. With his sturdy staff wedged in his hand he moves with a certain alacrity of purpose seemingly oblivious to the rain lashing his sightless face and tall thin body. Nearing the tool shed, he calls out. 'Are you there Lazarus? I need to talk to you.' And as the clouds emptied down upon the man, and the skies cracked there thunder, so Lazarus could not help but smile. A modern day Moses stood before him, a paragon of unflinching stoicism and fortitude.

Thirty minutes later, warm and dry from the elements, Jan and Lazarus sit in the cosy and welcoming little home of the older man, with its crackling fire and aroma of pumpkin soup simmering on the stove. But once again Lazarus was experiencing the distinct feeling that all of this was somehow too good to be true.

For how the hell was he supposed to reconcile the fact that whilst he sat there safe, warm and comfortable in this 'sanctuary for damaged souls,' just beyond the forest killers killed and mud and blood was doing its best to drown humanity. It did not make sense, none of it. And now, paradoxically, in some respects the safety of the commune was starting to make him feel unsafe. Yet he just could not put his finger on why?

Perhaps Karl had been right after all, to leave, to go away. Just then the quiet voice of Jan breaks in on his ambivalent reverie. 'I want to talk to you about the child, about Hana. Has she spoken to you at all?' Lazarus shakes his head slowly 'No, not a word since that first night when she brought us here. Look, what is it with the kid? What happened to her?' Jan sighs deeply. 'That is what I want to talk to you about, but I'am at a loss at where to begin.'

For the first time since Lazarus had known him, Jan looked troubled and ill at ease. Over and over he turns the small ring that he wears on the little finger of his left hand. 'You know, I have really tried with the girl, but nothing I say or do appears to make any difference. She rarely listens, just spends her days drifting along. Not letting anyone into her silent, broken little world.'

Once more he sighs. 'Do you know what she asked me the other day? She asked me if it were possible for a person to be neither dead nor alive, but somehow suspended between the two.' Jan shakes his head ruefully and turns his face towards the fire.

Lazarus is quiet briefly, uncertain what to say or think. 'Look, Jan, why are you telling me this? What is it you want of me?' Jan does not reply, instead continues talking as if oblivious to Lazarus or his words.

'I will never forget the day she first turned up here. It was early morning and very cold. How in heavens name she got here is beyond me. But arrive she did, and what an arrival, half-starved, half dead. It was dreadful. I still recall asking her name. And do you know what she replied? 'I do not have a name any more. I left it in the grave alongside my people.' Once more Jan falls silent, his chin slumping to his chest.

At first, Lazarus thinks he may have fallen asleep. But soon the voice is back again. 'It was hard. But over those first few days and weeks as we nursed her body, so we tried to nurse her mind as well. But that proved harder. Yet, very little by little she opened up to us, until finally, she took us back with her. Back to a stark March morning when the tenuous thread that joins the living to the dead was severed for the Jews of her village, two thousand innocent souls, murdered in a matter of hours.'

The voice of Lazarus is barely a whisper in response. 'All except one ... How in the name of God did she survive?' Jan slowly turns his face away from the fire. 'You know, I often think the word miracle is over used. But I believe in the case of Hana it's an accurate term.' Yet again, this normally calm and measured man twists the ring on his finger in quiet agitation. His voice when it finally comes is hoarse, emotional.

'She told us that on that morning the Germans came very early, equipped as if they were going off to fight a Russian regiment. With blows and curses they drove all the Jews to the village square. Anyone who showed the slightest resistance was shot on the spot. It was pandemonium. Elderly people and children who could not move fast enough were beaten with rifle butts. Countless children were separated from their parents in the chaos.

Hana said that a little school friend of hers was so terrified that she would not stop screaming. But she finally did when an SS officer shot her in the head with his pistol. The child was standing only a few meters from Hana.' Jan is silent momentarily his sightless face a pale mask.

'Anyway, eventually the killers managed to gather all the frightened and desperate people together at the village square. Then flanked by heavily armed SS and Ukrainian auxiliaries, they marched them off, a ragged, bedraggled mass of moving misery. Hana said that they were forced along a straight white road that led to a small forest. Here two large rectangular pits had been freshly dug. Any hope of deliverance of survival was now gone. They knew what was to be their fate, if they had not known before. The full realisation hits the people hard. All illusions are cast to the cold march wind now.

Hana said that for a few seconds an eerie collective silence swept through the two thousand. Then, as one, a low moan of utter hopeless human despair emanated from their number, finally to be replaced by shattering howls and screams of panic. Mothers clung to their children, some pleaded with the killers others stood paralysed in numb disbelief, and all the while the religious turned faces heavenwards waiting for a deliverance that would never come.' Jan sighs heavily. That it pains this articulate and gentle man is palpable. Lazarus gazes intently across at him and then lowers his head. For no other reason than it seems the proper and respectful thing to do.

'She went on to say that the people were led to the pits naked in groups of a hundred families holding hands. There killing machines awaited them. Some already drunk on vodka others lazing around smoking cigarettes, all devoid of empathy or compassion. And hour after hour the slaughter went on. And whilst those waiting to be killed could not actually see the murders, they were forced to stand a hundred meters from the pits, their view obscured by trees. But they could hear the gunfire and the screaming. One can only imagine the mental torture and agonies they must have felt and experienced.'

'Anyway, the time finally came. Hana and her family were forced to undress, her mother, father, two grandparents and her three brothers. She said that her youngest brother, a child of six, was too frightened to undress. So gently, his mother tried to take his clothes off, but the boy struggled, refusing to allow her just continued to cry loudly. One of the killers, a Ukrainian, more drunk than sober, screamed at the boy, and then at his mother. This just terrified the child further, intensifying his fearful sobs. Finally losing patience, the Ukrainian brought his rifle butt down with tremendous force onto the skull of the child. He fell to the ground, lifeless.

Hana's mother could not even scream. Choking sobs of disbelief dying somewhere between her heart and her throat. Happy and smiling now, the Ukrainian picks up the crushed little body in one hand and thrusts it coldly into the arms of his distraught mother. And with that they are led off to the pit. Her whole family was murdered that day. Three generations wiped out in seconds.'

The voice of Jan trails away to nothing. Once more, Lazarus looks across at him. 'You still have not told me. How did she survive?' Jan breathes deeply.

'You have to understand that Hana and her family were amongst the last to be taken to be shot. So, by the time they reached the pit it was already full of those poor souls who had gone before. She said that many were only wounded and still living, their death throes making the piles of bodies somehow rise and fall like small hideous waves. Finally standing naked at the edge of the grave, Hana said that she felt nothing, because it all seemed so unreal. But she said she did feel the arms of her mother and heard the words of her father mumbling a final prayer.

Gazing across at her grandparents she barely recognised them, their immobile chalk white faces were already more dead than alive... Then came the deafening blast of gunfire. She said she felt a stinging pain in her cheek and shoulder, as half-falling, half-tumbling she plunged into the heaving pit. And there she lost consciousness. For how long, she did not know. But when she came round, night had come and the killers had gone. And the bodies around her were cold and silent now. To her left lay her mother, one arm outstretched towards Hana, protecting her in death as she had in life.

Hana held her tightly and kissed her bitterly cold cheek. She did not want to leave her, just wanted to lie next to her forever. But the freezing March night dictated otherwise. Shivering, naked and totally alone, she extricated her self from the clasping grasps of the loving dead, and rejoins, gives her self over to the brutal mercies of the hating living, for she had no other choice. She knew the killers would be back at first light to cover over their crimes. And so with an aching heart, she left behind all she had known and loved.'

Jan wearily runs a hand through his thinning grey hair. 'She told us that after leaving this place of death, she walked to a small village a kilometer or so away on the edge of the forest. Traumatised, tired and bleeding, she knocked on the door of the first house she came to. After a minute or so a dull light appeared in the window by the door, followed seconds later by an elderly man, the sleepy-eyed suspicion and disdain etched across his lined face were palpable. 'Get back to the grave little Jew there is nothing for you here.'

Shivering, afraid, Hana is just about to leave when the old man's wife appears at the door. Her voice is one of cold compassion. 'Quick, come in, just take what you need and then leave.' In a darkened bedroom the old woman points to a large chest on the floor. Hana slowly approaches it. Opening it cautiously, inside are layers of musty clothes. Quickly going through the garments, she pulls out a small ragged brown dress and rapidly puts it on to cover her nakedness. In silence she walks back into the main room of the small house. Waiting for her, the old woman hands her a bag containing bread and cheese. 'Now, go!' Hana looks at the grim faced old man and then at his wife. She mumbles, stumbles a thank you. And then leaves, as she had arrived. In silence.

'For three days and nights she walked across country, avoiding people, sleeping in barns and ditches, a lost child, totally alone. Until on the fourth day, a cold and sunny morning she found her way to us. God only knows how. But we were happy to give her refuge and sanctuary, but now. Well, it seems that it is not enough any more. She says that now she needs to be with her own people. And that is where you come into the equation.'

Lazarus gazes across at him quizzically. 'Me? I don't understand. I barely know the girl.' Jan smiles briefly. 'Nor she you. But that does not stop her seeing you as the saviour that will lead her to the Promised Land.' Lazarus shifts in his chair impatiently. 'Where are you going with this, Jan? Look, speak to me straight. What is it you want with me?' Jan replies softly, but firmly. 'I want you to take the child to London. She says she has family there, an uncle her mother's brother.'

Lazarus looks at him disbelievingly. 'You are joking!? Look, it may have escaped your attention, but there are crazy bastards out there, killing Jews for a bottle of vodka. Or for what barely passes for an ideology. Either way they are killing Jews in their thousands. In the name of God, London might as well be a million miles away!' He rises from the table and walks slowly to the door.

The voice of Jan follows him. 'You know, if you do not go with her she will go alone. The girl wants to be with her own people. What can I do? I cannot just keep her here against her will.' Lazarus stops at the door. 'This is emotional blackmail. You know that, don't you?' Jan sighs softly. 'It is sad that you see it that way. But I'm just telling you how it is. The child is a headstrong, free spirit, damaged yes, but nevertheless determined and obdurate. With or without you, she will have her way.'

Lazarus bows his head. 'Okay, look, let me think this madness over. I promise to give you my answer in the morning.' Opening the door he leaves. His head full of more doubts than certainties.

CHAPTER FOURTEEN

Lying lost amongst early morning shadows, the gaze of Dina fell from Conor back to the ceiling, before returning once more to the boy. She watches him intently as he tosses and turns in fitful sleep, his lips moving but no words emanating.

She had been oblivious to the recent arrival of dawn. Unnoticed and unheralded, and as stealthy as a thief, it had proceeded to remove from her all thoughts and words. Until all that was left in her mind, yet again, were the recurring images of an eternal shingle beach, and that winters sea without beginning or end, both now so far away in time.

But still she could close her eyes and recall how as a child the sound of the waves rushing, booming and breaking onto the shingle, had reminded her of the noise the weary old train had made as it pulled into the seaside station, a kind of crashing rumbling echo, a roaring herd of buffalo, on and on. And so, like a dream she had dreamt in waking sleep, the sea and the shingle beach were somehow always with her. Root deep. Ocean deep

And now across the breakfast table, Dina wants to say so many things to the sleepy boy. But reticent and self conscious small talk has given way to cold tea and toast silence. And the words were left dying in her throat. But if she could have resurrected them, she would have told him about how for years the sea and shingle had obsessed and possessed her, an ocean of many shades, textures and moods. And now, right now just when this damaged, beautifully strange boy is such a part of her soul, she needs so much to tell him what he is sharing it with.

But no, she cannot. It would all sound too phoney, too pretentious. And he would probably just look away in embarrassment, or worse, think she was just a silly cow. But she did not know him. Not really. For if she did, she would have known that she could have told him anything, absolutely anything. If she had wanted to drone on for hours about Einstein's General Theory of Relativity, he would have sworn to God that it was the most fascinating thing he had ever heard.

Because she was his all, all he wanted, all he needed. But the boy just wished he knew what to say to her and how to say it. Just wished there was some kind of script to follow, because he knew how to hate, but, how to love? That was another thing entirely, an alien conception to him in many ways.

Raising his eyes from the table, Conor watches as Dina quietly clears away the breakfast things. 'So, what do you wanna do with the day?' Placing the plates on the kitchen worktop, Dina turns and faces him. 'I need to go to work. I have to open the shop up. I'm already late as it is.' Conor cannot disguise his disappointment. 'It's just. Well, I thought after last night. I mean. Look, don't go to work, stay with me. Let the old man look after the shop.'

'Are you kidding he can hardly look after himself.' She gazes down at the floor. The eyes of the boy follow hers down to the lino. 'Then just put a note on the door saying the shop is closed. What do you say?'

Staring at a ceiling that was more cracks than plaster, Baines lay on his mattress, seemingly paralysed. Buried under a thin grey blanket he had barely moved in hours. Because. And not for the first time, the dream had been his. Dark and disturbing images; totally unexplainable, of old men in their cradles and babies in their coffins. If there was some profound significance or symbolism in these dreams then they were lost on the boy. To him, they were merely fucked up night terrors. Further confirmation, if he needed it that somehow some way Conor's madness, that insidious insanity, had finally, like a malevolent worm burrowed itself deep inside his head.

And now, with his first movement in an age he attempts to rouse himself from the mattress. But something unseen will not allow it. Breathing hard and fast he tries once more with what little strength he has to lift himself. The sheer exertion makes his pale face redden, and the veins protrude hard from his temples. But it is all to no avail. And he slumps back down amongst the filthy blanket and mattress... He was unravelling. Things fall apart.

It is very unlikely he would have come across the word 'nadir.' But if he had, and was cognizant of its meaning, then he would have undoubtedly realised that his young life had reached that particularly hopeless state. The money from the bookies was long gone, squandered on something and nothing, and now. Now he had this thing in his head, burrowing deeper every day. He swore to God he could feel it squirming, writhing and muttering softly in his ear in some foreign tongue. And so with his eyes closed his distorted thoughts turn to Conor the source, the carrier, the architect of his? He tried to think of an appropriate word that described his private hell adequately. But one did not exist. Words perhaps did not, but feelings certainly did.

And what Baines felt in his mind was an overwhelming

need to destroy in his mind that which was slowly destroying him. Perhaps many things were not functioning as they should between the boy's ears. But his paranoia was in full swing; working overtime. Indeed, the thought was constantly in his mind that maybe Conor and the old Jew were in cahoots, somehow working in tandem an unlikely alliance out to destroy him.

Finally opening his eyes once more, he finds himself desperately fighting for air. So, this was it? How it would end? They had finally come for him. Thrashing and flailing his arms as if waving at someone long gone, Baines tries again to rise from the mattress. But once more a force is pinning him down.

Only this time the force has a face. Indeed it has two faces, for there amongst the soiled watery blankets are Conor and the old Jew, the latter pulling on his ankles and the former with one hand round his throat and the other pushing his head down under the rancid water.

And as he fights and struggles, Baines looks into those strange crippled eyes, expecting to see anger or hate, but he sees nothing, just two empty voids staring back at him. He tries to scream out, but the taker has become the taken. And no voice comes, instead just the increasingly desperate sound of his own breathing, followed by the intense sensation of Conor's hand pressing his head down harder and harder beneath the fetid water.

Now gulping and gasping for life. That life he does not recognise any more, he somehow manages with a huge final effort to break free. Rising then falling, then rising again, he breaks through the watery blankets, casting them aside with a breathless release. And now as he lays floundering, as pale, naked and torn as a fish cast adrift on a riverbank, the worm in his head sings 'Te-ra, te-ra, te-ra' as it burrows deeper, so joyful in its work.

Four hours later, and the boy is still lying spent, washed up on the floorboard riverbank. He has not moved an inch. But his splintered mind has... Tomorrow he will look for Conor.

That Lazarus would agree to accompany the girl on her impossible odyssey was in many senses a 'fait accompli.' Perhaps it was the conclusion of a man who had become careless with his life. Or maybe he felt some kind of unexplainable responsibility for this strange silent child, either way, that same evening they left the safety of the commune.

Amongst solemn and muted goodbyes to the couple from the residents of the commune, Jan handed Lazarus a rucksack packed with provisions. The man himself was unusually emotional. It was palpable he felt helpless in not being able to prevent or dissuade Hana from making such a perilous journey. A journey he knew in his heart neither was likely to survive.

Finally, just as Lazarus and the girl were about to leave, Jan approaches them for the last time. Slowly opening his coat he takes from an inside pocket an envelope, self consciously he hands it to Lazarus. 'It's not much but I hope it helps, even if only a little.' With an equal sense of self consciousness Lazarus takes the envelope and puts it into his jacket pocket. His voice is one of humility.

'Thanks, look I know you have very little, and...' Jan interrupts him gently. 'And what little we have is yours. That is the way we do things.' Lazarus had met people like Jan before. But the difference was that he was genuine. And there was something of the childlike and other worldly in this eyeless man. Who nature, genetics, call it what you will, had cursed. A child like credulity mixed in with a kind of profound wisdom, a strange symbiosis indeed, but an unforgettable one.

And so, as late evening drizzle gives way to midnight rain, palms are pressed, emotions exchanged and final goodbyes said. And without looking back, a tall thin man, a silent waif and a white dog drift away into a coal black forest.

Under arched cathedral skies, two laughing sea children play out the day on a windwhipped shingle beach. And at their happy feet, and on such a winter's day, the icy briny nips at their icy toes. And their memories are now, and their moments are then. But their moments are not forever. For maybe, just perhaps, both know deep down in their hearts that moments were all they really had. But that remain a secret never to be told.

In a late morning haze, they had travelled down to Bexhill on the train. All morning Conor had asked Dina repeatedly what she had wanted to do with the day, until finally she told him. And so now, with her soul immersed in sea dreams she felt like she had come home. But also there present, remaining unsaid and unspoken, was the fact that they both knew they needed to get away from the town, as it was surely only a matter of time before the police paid them a visit.

But now Bexhill was theirs, borrowed for a while. Though some things they did own. Like the winter sun that glared, glistened and gleamed off of the pristine Art Deco whiteness of the Town's De la Warr pavilion, and the young seagulls that shrieked and swooped for the greasy chips thrown them by

Conor and Dina. Each bird was theirs now, part of their story forever.

And on this day partly real, but so overwhelmingly nebulous, the couple drift down empty out of season streets. Hand in hand they peer into fussily decorated genteel tea rooms. And then shoulder to shoulder, pause then pass sad and unsmiling paint-peeled seafront pubs, where inside, hard-faced locals make it known with surly glares that any outsider in the bar is about as welcome as anthrax in the town's beer supply.

And so the afternoon passes, lost in sights and sounds that would never come again. But that would equally never be gone. And as is often the way with memories, it will be the memories of the seemingly unimportant, the trivial that will be the most enduring. Such as the imagery produced by the vision of a frail very old man pushing a wheelchair containing a very fat young woman.

And as the aged man struggles with his heavy burden up a steep hill, his face contorts grotesquely under the strain. Colouring up rapidly it produces a most remarkable and diverse range of shades and hues, from an original ashen grey through to a straining pink. Before finally ending up a deep shade of scarlet that would have been the envy of many an Atlantic lobster.

And now so deeply lost in his Herculean task, he fails to notice that a stray gust of wind has blown the fat woman's hideous straw hat from her head. However, he is soon made cognizant of the fact by her shrill screams and urgent thrusting of a chubby index finger in the direction of the rapidly escaping head wear.

Watching the errant hat being blown further downhill, the

old man is now caught in a dilemma. Should he try and ignore its heroic bid for freedom, and thus avoid the painful effort of going back from whence he came or? He does not get to the second part of his dilemma, because now a chubby finger is pointing accusingly at him, as if suggesting that somehow he and the hat were in cahoots over its perfidious escape bid.

And now, with her blood pressure rising as well as her decibels, the fat young woman demands action. And so, with the last of his meagre strength, the old man heaves and hauls the wheelchair a full one hundred and eighty degrees, but then. Disaster! Clutching and groping for the wheel brake, he discovers it does not exist. Well; needless to say it was soon a case of out of control, hurtling wheelchair- screaming fat woman- and a very tired, red faced old man trying to hold onto both.

Sat a few yards away watching proceedings on a stoical sea wall, Conor and Dina are unsure whether they should help - applaud - or laugh? In the end they do nothing, because soon the rampaging wheelchair, its obese occupant and its ageing captain, no longer at the helm, flashes past them. And the last image Conor and Dina have, is one of a fat arm thrust out defiantly, as the bulky Boudicca in her chariot, negotiates a particularly tricky corner at great speed.

And then, then they were gone, out of sight. But not out of mind. Because they; like the winter sun and the shrieking young seagulls, were memories claimed. And however insignificant they may appear to others, arguably it would be memories such as these that would be the last to flicker, fade and finally die.

CHAPTER FIFTEEN

Finally succumbing to the spat out curses, threats and invective of Baines, the weary and aged car convulsed into life, and now in the sullen darkness, the boy can feel its metallic grating whine. He shudders hard as the jagged and barbed vibration claws at his shot nerves. And in his head the car is a personification of a death warmed up. And now the boy moves slowly his hand on the gear stick. A detachment clings to him. A second skin he is not even aware he is wearing.

An hour later, boy and car are moving at a crawl down streets still and silent. He has long since given up trying to get the car to increase its speed. For like an old beach-ride donkey, tired and forlorn but not cowed, it makes its own pace, or none at all.

Passing under orange glow street lights that splash their illumination and subtle observation out across the red bricked respectability of the sturdy houses, the grey faced boy awaits instructions. Wait's that voice in his head that offers him truth and enlightenment. Days ago, when it had told him that sleep was sapping his strength and sucking all the life out of him, he had stopped sleeping.

And when it had told him that Conor and the old Jew were poisoning his food slowly bit by bit, he had stopped eating. And the voice was more than God. For it told him what he must do. Unlike the divine deity who remained silent. And the voice told him how things must be. And the boy believes, because he is told to believe. And in the darkest corner of his dark mind, the worm sings its little song once more. Sometimes the tune was different. But the words were always the same.

> 'Southern trees bear such a strange fruit,
> with blood on the leaves and blood at the root.'

The body must have been hanging from the tree for days, as decomposition was already quite advanced despite the cooler weather. And the stench of death was everywhere.

Silently stalking through a small clearing at the edge of the forest, it had been Geist that had made the grim discovery. First recoiling, then recalling, the scent of blood and decay of human flesh from its camp days, the dog tentatively approaches the gently swinging corpse. Cautiously it sniffs the leg of the battered and broken body; before letting out a deep and pitiful whine. Then, white against black, it bolts back towards Lazarus and Hana. Who, lit by a silver slither of moonlight, themselves edge towards the grotesque suspended figure.

Gently thrusting a paternalistic arm across the chest of Hana, Lazarus approaches the body alone. Gazing up at the crow-plucked face it is unrecognisable; a grey-black rotting death mask that stares down at its lifeless chest, as if reading the inscription on the placard that is hung with string around the noose-bound neck. Edging ever closer, and with a hand clasped over his mouth and nose to block out the stench, Lazarus squints through the darkness just enough to read the inscription on the crudely made placard. 'This is what happens to Jew-loving traitors and deserters!' A jolt courses through Lazarus, followed by a numb feeling. Trailing his eyes down the tattered greatcoat, he sees what he expected to see: the pathetic remnants of a filthy bandage covering the thin, blackened wrist.

He knew then.

Lazarus buries Karl in a shallow grave, swathed in a silent solemnity. He quietly says kaddish for the boy before placing a stone on the grave. And that is that. All he can do. And now closing his eyes briefly he feels shame, shame that he feels nothing. And he wonders how that can be? Okay, admittedly he had not known the kid that long, but nevertheless, they had spent countless hours together. The boy had lived with him, eaten with him, slept by him, laughed and argued with him. And now? Opening his eyes again, he gazes up at a charcoal sky and wonders when had been the exact moment he had ceased to be a human being?

Breaking in on his bleak reverie, the voice of the girl trails hollow across the night. 'It will be light soon, we should leave here.' Lazarus looks across at the pale little face with those so dark eyes. Suddenly, inexplicably he feels a surge of protectiveness towards this child he did not know. This ethereal little girl nobody really knew, because she would not or could allow it. He replies softly. 'There is the barn of a peasant around a kilometer from here, Jan told me of it. It's safe enough. We will see out the day there, and make a move when it's dark again.'

Instinctively he reaches out to take Hana by the hand. But she recoils as if his hand were fire or ice. She looks away, knowing she cannot bear the touch of another human being. It both frightens and repels her. Simultaneously, both cast eyes downward in a kind of muted embarrassment. Uncertain of what to say or how to act, Lazarus finally turns and slowly walks away. Just as a diaphanous early dawn mist gives way to a fine rain, the pair, cold wet and hungry trudge their way to the ramshackle barn, entrenched in a grey silence. Both wanted to break, but which neither knew how.

And so, as a pallid sun finally rises lazily, sending soft streaks through the spring drizzle, man, child and dog settle down in the hayloft of the old barn. Buried deep amongst damp hay and straw, child and dog soon slip away, finding a sleep that eludes the man. For try as Lazarus might to empty his mind of the night's baggage, still it weighs heavy.

Through a crack in the timber slats of the barn, a slither of daylight flits dirty white across his pale and unshaven face. Gazing out through the crack, Lazarus looks down upon the deserted farmyard. It is eerily quiet save for the song of a gold-finch that proclaims its little kingdom from the top branch of a scrawny apple tree at the far end of the muddy yard.

Easing himself deeper into the straw, it is not long before the omnipresent image of Esther once more invades his mind; so many thoughts of her crowding his brain, bringing with them the old familiar painful and hopeless longing, like a wave of desolation washing over him.

He recalls how, In the first few months after their separation, he would lay on the hard plank bed in the camp at night, and in a childish dialogue with a God that was not listening, he would invent, proclaim and promulgate a covenant with the deaf deity, wherein Lazarus would give up whatever months or years remained of his life just for one hour with Esther.

And somehow, some way this thought, this act had comforted and sustained him, offered him a hope amongst the indescribable hopelessness, that he would never see her again. And now? Now there were no such infantile illusions or delusions. Because wherever and whenever it had happened, Esther was no more. Whether now bone or ash, all he loved was dead and gone. Of that he was sure. So, if his mind had accepted it. Why in the name of God could not his heart?

The bleak and dark guest house at the far end of the seafront looked about as welcoming as the Lubyanka on a wet, cold November night. But the place was cheap and the elderly land-lady, cheerful.

Indeed, she was as warm as her building was cold. And for her part, she liked the young limping girl and the strange looking boy. They were quiet and polite. It did not matter that they had very little luggage. It did not matter to her either that with them being so young it was unlikely they were married. She was not one to pry. In her seventy-two years Lou Elliot had never been given to prying, or to making moral judgements, and she was not about to start now.

Truth was she was lonely. Cancer had claimed her husband five years back. And the voracious, insidious bastard had remained, slowly eating away at her soul, until it had left her with an aching emptiness, a loneliness that manifested itself in many ways, one being that her guest house, unlike so many others in the town, stayed open all year round. For Lou could not abide an empty house. She needed voices, laughter, noise, pulses. She would say that silence is for the dead not the living.

It was strange she had not loved him in ages. Not really. But over the long years, she had gotten use to him and his ways, and in this, had found a kind of comfort and security in the banality of routine. So, when his interminable and intolerable agonies finally reached their inevitable conclusion. And his end come morphine drenched in an airy sea view hospice, Lou fell apart. Fell down. And for a long time after could not get up again.

Without family, and in her hour of need without friends, Lou drifted, drunk and sunk, until a kind of epiphany was hers. No divine lights. No soothing words from the son of the deity. No. Epiphany came in the shape of a dour, dreary and dismal guest house at the arse end of the seafront. One that desperate owners thought they would never be able to shift.

Whether it was just a moment of madness, or maybe an example of the singular sense of humour of Lou, was not quite clear. But, either way, she found a beauty in the ugliness of the guest house, a possibility in its impossibility. But best of all, by buying the property she would be returning to the land of the living. And so, this strange, unlovely and unloved building was to be her unlikely salvation. It gave her a purpose, and paradoxically its darkness and melancholic look lifted her.

To all that knew her, there was no doubt that Lou Elliot was an eccentric and perverse woman. But equally, they knew also that just like the doors of her guest house were always open, so too was her big heart.

Stepping out of the car and then out of himself, Baines walks down the street to the bookshop. On either side people pass by him. But to a disengaged mind, they were no longer real, just images, ghosts of former people. Finally reaching the shop, he glances up at the closed sign on the shop door and mutters a curse. Turning his head slightly he catches a glimpse of himself in the shop glass.

The face that stares back at him looks as if it were falling apart. It was a face he no longer knew. Slowly, he presses his finger tips against the cold glass and traces the outline of his hollow eyes, and then attempts to smooth the reflection of his furrowed brow. He did not recognise any of it, nothing. There was no youthful grace in his face, just the weariness of an old man. At seventeen his youth was gone.

Gripping the door handle firmly he pushes and pulls it frantically. 'Open the fucking door Conor!. I know you are in there.' He bangs his fist on the glass, once, twice. 'Get your arse out here!'

Upstairs in his flat in that faraway land of catatonia, walls are tumbling down and the madness of years old secrecy and subterfuge is starting to unravel. Sitting up in his tomb bed, Breitner resembles a statue, a particularly dilapidated, sweating and cadaverous one. And now, every blow aimed at the shop door, jolts and jars through his body. He had been waiting for this day for over thirty years. And now it had finally arrived he did not know what to do. So, he did nothing, just waited. A statue that closed its eyes, as a distant scent of geraniums filled his imploding sanctuary of catatonia.

Outside, the boy has stopped hammering on the shop door. But he knows that he, who is killing him, lies somewhere deep within those walls. And he knows because the worm in his head insists that that is the truth.

Reaching inside his coat, he takes out a quart bottle of vodka and some purple pills wrapped in cling film, he is not sure what the hell they are. He had got a score of them off of Kenny Brooker a few days back. All he knew was that since taking them he had barely slept, barely eaten and barely thought. And he was okay with that, because everything was for now, everything. For in a disengaged mind, now was all that mattered, and now had become today, yesterday and tomorrow.

The wall was not of the Berlin, Bastille or Warsaw Ghetto

variety. But it was high enough to prove stiff opposition to a boy whacked out of his nut on pills and booze.

However, after numerous fruitless attempts Baines finally manages to scale the obdurate structure. Jumping down into the small back yard of the shop, he looks down at his heavily cut and grazed hands and knees. Rivulets of blood drip onto the grey concrete yard, forming scarlet islands in an ocean of dust and grime. He gazes at it briefly and dispassionately as if it were the blood of another. Then, turns and walks to the back entrance of the shop.

Trying the handle of the rickety back door he finds it locked. Turning his head to the right and then to the left, he takes a few steps back and then shoulder barges the flimsy door open.

Inside the storeroom it is dark, Baines fumbles and stumbles making enough noise to awaken the long dead. Finally, reading the paint-flaked wall like Braille, his bloodied fingers locate the light switch, an aged and dusty strip-light flickers out a weary glow casting what light it can around the gloomy claustrophobic storeroom. The sudden illumination wakens the room's collection of wee beasties. In a corner, the boy watches a large spider. Sees its predatory grace as it skims silently across battered and decaying cardboard boxes, containing half-forgotten books by totally forgotten authors. Baines eyes its stealthy flight from the light, watches it intently, transfixed.

Until, suddenly, from upstairs a thud, dull and heavy reverberates around the small stockroom. Instinctively, Baines feels for the gun in his coat pocket. As ever, the feel of the cold metal reassures and empowers him. Switching off the light, he waits for another thud, his eyes fixed to the ceiling. But with no more sounds forthcoming the boy exits the room, leaving behind a last layer, a final remnant of a kind of sanity.

The thud the boy had heard was Breitner's small bedside cabinet crashing to the floor. After all the days he had spent in his crumbling land of catatonia, the wasted limbs of Breitner no longer seemed able to obey the simplest commands of his half-functioning brain, thus resulting in him knocking over the solid teak cabinet.

And for what seems an age, he merely stares at it, as if half expecting the cabinet to miraculously rise of its own accord. And as his eyes watch his ears listen. The hammering at the shop door had ceased a while back, but still Breitner sits rigid and straight in his bed, his face ashen and his sparse grey hair sweat-matted to his skull. He is not sure why, but the situation makes him think of Eichmann.

He had met him once; back in the summer of 1942. The man had made little impression on Breitner 'A pen-pushing pedantic prick.' had been his conclusion on the top Nazi bureaucrat. 'A nonentity obsessed with Judaism, statistics and trains.' Breitner had read that when the Mossad agents had tracked him down to the Buenos Aires suburbs where he was hiding out, the 'great man' had shit himself, literally. Well; thought Breitner, at least he would not suffer that fate. He had not eaten in days.

Ascending the stairs, Baines thinks of everything and nothing. Calling out, his voice sounds movie-time false, phoney borrowed from someone else. 'Conor, get your ugly arse out here!'

With each step he takes up the echoing stairs, so another layer of reality is a skin best shed. Who the hell needs reality, when you have a gut full of booze and a head full of voices and pills, for this kid, reality was to be avoided at all costs, a dish far too unpalatable to confront or consume.

Swaying and unsteady, he finally reaches the top of the stairs. 'I know you are here. And I know what you are trying to do to my head. But it ain't gonna work Bro!' His movie-time voice has become a defiant snarl. And the gun in his pocket gives him everything. All he needs to become what he has become.

Breitner can hear the voice of the youth outside his door can hear creeping footsteps on the worn-out carpet. Would others come? Would they send only one agent? Once more he tries to swing his thin and wasted legs out of the bed. But it is a Herculean task that is beyond him now. So, this was it? How it would end?

Closing his eyes he sees faces. Faces of those he had known and loved, so few. And faces blurred into a solid mass of those he had killed, so many, and now love, hate, life, death. None of it mattered any more. It was all one and the same.

With an incongruously dramatic flourish, the boy storms into the bedroom of Breitner. Waving the gun frantically, his pill-glazed eyes finally rest upon the bed, and the corpse that lies upon it. Curious, but never compassionate, Baines silently gazes down at the distorted grey face. Watches as cyanide dribbles out of the corners of thin pale lips. He dispassionately pokes the barrel of the handgun into Breitner's hollowed cheek. Finally, a look of disinterest, or perhaps its disgust spreads across the face of the boy. Turning, he walks slowly from the room.

CHAPTER SIXTEEN

Time passed, as is its way. Months went by neither mourned nor missed. And now, as always, Lazarus and Hana were living by their wits, surviving the hostility of local peasants, the frequent German Jew hunts, the ever clawing pain of hunger and the filth and squalor of countless barns and makeshift forest hideouts. But somehow they get by, survive. And now, of a late autumn afternoon they huddle together for warmth in the draughty and tumble down barn in northern Poland. In the distance they can faintly hear the heavy artillery of the Russians as they advance westwards. And now was about somehow holding on, now had no other significance than that.

'It won't be long now. They are getting closer with every day that passes.' The voice of Lazarus is smoky due to lack of use. 'Soon we will be safe.' His words seem as much about reassurance for himself as they do about comfort and assurance for the child. Either way, Hana remains quiet, as was so often the case.

For months Lazarus had attempted to work out this little enigma: this child of one skin but so many seemingly non penetrable layers. And it was not for the want of trying that he had failed to get through to her. But as time went by he had reached the sad conclusion that whoever and whatever the girl had once been, was now lost left behind with her murdered family in that mass grave.

And now he watches her as late afternoon shadows fall, gently consuming the last vestiges of splintered sunlight from her face. And as ever Geist is by her side. It was palpable that the dog had a huge affection for Hana. And it was more than reciprocated. For the child found everything that she needed, that she could not or would not find in humans, in Geist.

Rising slowly to his feet from the damp and foul smelling straw, Lazarus stretches his aching body. Suddenly, a burst of machine gunfire rips into the wooden barn. Instinctively, Lazarus dives back down from whence he had come. Soon another burst of gunfire brings splinters of wood raining down upon him. Lying prone now, he lifts his head slightly and looks across at Hana. She has wrapped a small protective arm around Geist. Both lay on their sides buried deep in the straw. There is no expression of fear on her face, nor surprise. Just a calm look as if she were prepared to meet her second death.

Inching on his belly towards a large bullet hole in the wood, Lazarus peers out. Below, a group of SS men are forcing a huddle of terrified and bewildered Jews into the barn at gunpoint. Most are elderly folk or women with kids. Many are passive, too ground down through hunger and utter despair to resist any more.

At the rear of the group, a tall and elderly man takes from the pocket of his ragged coat, a document. He tries showing it to the nearest SS man. The officer tears the document from his hand and rips it to pieces. He then starts to pistol whip the old man. Blow after blow rains down. Finally, with almost a macabre grace, he falls to the dirt. The officer screams for him to get up. But his threats are met with stillness and silence. For the old man is beyond that. He is dead. Enraged, that whilst he has so much power, the power to raise the dead is beyond him, the officer unloads his pistol into the lifeless figure.

Then, under a barrage of blows, beatings and curses, the remaining Jews are driven into the barn. Behind them the doors are bolted shut and the fires lit. Inside, children scream for mothers and mothers scream for God. While outside, the cruel jeering laughter of the instigators is only eclipsed by the hopeless cries of their victims.

Up in the hayloft, acrid black smoke starts to engulf Lazarus, Hana and the dog. Coughing and half-blinded, Lazarus makes his way over to the girl. 'Come on, we have to try and find a way out of here.' He tries to take her by the arm. But she steps back out of his reach. Lazarus tries once more, but Hana merely steps away further. He looks across at her through the dense smoke; incredulity etched across his face.

'Come on, what are you doing? We have to leave now.' The child stares back at him, a fathomless expression on her small face. 'No. You go I have found the place I need to be.'

He would never be certain whether she jumped or fell. Her descent from the loft was both sudden and silent. Desperately he tries to climb down the loft ladder to reach her, but it is already ablaze. Squinting through the stinging smoke he can just about see the girl lying motionless on the hard earth floor of the barn.

Around her chaos reigns, people engulfed in flames run and fall, as out of their mouths searing screams, unforgettable and beyond animalistic rips through the horror. Those who can attempt to break out through the few windows are met with bursts of machine gunfire, their bodies left dangling half-in and half-out. And all the while all around time hangs motionless. Turning its face against the hell on earth that man creates.

The dense smoke is making breathing increasingly difficult.

Slumped back down in the straw now, Lazarus has left behind the screams and stench of burning flesh. He feels such an inexplicable calmness, such a beautiful acceptance of the inevitable.

His mind flits between images of Esther, his parents and the family home in Krakow. Profound images entwine with the prosaic. He sees the look of a child on the face of Esther when she was pleased or excited, the gentle streams of sunlight that would filter in through always pristine white net curtains of the apartment in Krakow. And closing his smoke filled eyes now, Lazarus hears the voice of Esther. Like an echo across an empty room. It was time to go to her now, wherever she was.

The tugging on his trouser leg was becoming increasingly insistent and forceful. As if someone or something was attempting to drag him back to a world he thought he was done with. Slowly opening his eyes, Lazarus sees the solid white mass of Geist standing in front of him. His huge gargoyle head with its fearsome teeth is attempting to pull him to his feet.

Eventually, not thinking not feeling, Lazarus gets to his feet. The smoke is an opaque blanket now enveloping man and dog. Beneath them, below the hayloft, the fire still rages and the barn is in imminent danger of collapse. Charred corpses lay strewn across the barn floor. Some hold hands, some have hands raised heavenwards for a divine intervention that never came.

Escaping the suffocating smoke, man and dog leap from the hayloft. Out of the frying pan and into the fire. But, unlike Hana's, at least their descent has a soft landing. Indeed, they land fair and square in the middle of a stack of decaying horse shit.

Lazarus and Geist battle flames, billowing smoke and crashing timbers as they make their way towards Hana.

Miraculously, the fire has not touched her. On the contrary, a ring of flames two meters high surround the ethereal child, as she lays motionless on her side, Fiery sentinels guarding her inner final sanctum.

Desperately, man and dog attempt to penetrate the circle. But again and again the heat and ferocity of the flames drive then back. Outside, sporadic machine gunfire still thunders out, cruel and relentless, tearing into what is left of the blazing barn. Lazarus knows time is short. So, with one last surge of energy, and with his face and head covered by his jacket, he runs hard into the fire.

And this time he breaks through. Geist has already managed to find a way through and is by the side of the prone child. And this creature that had once savaged Jews now mourns for one, his low whining whimper beyond piteous. Dumbly, he gently licks her hands and face expecting that to be enough. When he finally realises it is not, he lies hard by the side of the child, pressing tight against her motionless little body.

Stepping towards Hana, Lazarus gets down on his haunches and stretches out his hand to touch her shoulder. In a moment all is forgotten. Well almost. Geist, with teeth bared and a snarling growl from somewhere deep down within suddenly is the camp beast again. He lunges forward at Lazarus, knocking him off his haunches, his jaws grip around his wrist and hand. biting the hand that had fed him.

Lazarus grimaces and lets out a cry of pain. Then as suddenly as his storm of regression to another time and place had come, so it abates, and Geist slowly retreats to the place he has to be now and for always. He lay's back down next to Hana, and tenderly rests his big old head across her dead heart.

The barn is a total inferno now, a shifting orange wailing wall of all consuming heat and death. Whilst all around an acrid swarm of smoke envelopes everything. Lazarus, as if paralysed, stares down blankly at the dead, enigmatic child and the dog lying so close and hard alongside her that he has practically become a part of her.

And the man knows that he must at all costs leave now, or else perish alongside them. Squinting through the opaque and choking smoke, he spies a potential lifeline, a possibility of escape. At the back of the barn, in the very furthest corner he notices a small area not yet enveloped by the flames. Now, gazing down for a final time at child and dog, he does the most inexplicable thing. Slowly and deliberately he crosses himself, just like he had so often seen his Christian neighbours in Krakow do as a kid.

Momentarily, he feels the paralysis again. Breathing hard and heavy, he moves leaden legs and mind slowly. Now, outside all is quiet. The SS have gone. Their task performed. Finally, Lazarus makes his way across to the fire-free corner at the back of the barn. Gasping and weak due to smoke inhalation, he collapses onto the foul smelling floor. Where, with his last vestiges of strength, he stretches his thin legs out and starts to kick away at the barns timber wall. He has no idea if SS will be waiting for him on the other side. And he no longer cares. Just knows that he has to get out. Leave. Escape the smoke that is stealing his breath, taking his life.

But now, with a last desperate lunge of his boot Lazarus finally kicks a hole through the wood. And then, not coming up for air, but going out for it, he pushes his head and shoulders through the gap and breathes life, in huge gasps. Turning his head rapidly from left to right, he sees no SS. Instead, casting eyes skywards he sees a group of crows huddled together way up in a big old oak tree fifty meters away.

Silent and funereal, they watch the blazing barn, dumb witnesses to the senseless slaughter of innocents. Finally, with a weary and desperate effort, Lazarus manages to extricate his tired body through the jagged and splintered gap in the timber frame, and out into a world almost as dangerous as the one he had just left behind.

Heavy-footed, shambling and stumbling he bolts across open scrubby ground at the back of the barn. At any second he expects machine gunfire to cut him down. But nothing comes. And he finally makes his way to the small oak glade where the crows hold court.

In their black majesty they look down from upon high at the broken personage in their midst. In a lugubrious air they begin their discordant chatter, the twenty crows of his conscience. And soon that chatter turns into accusatory squawking roars. 'You left them to die. You left them to die. You left them to die.' over and over. Sinking to his knees, Lazarus clasps his hands over his ears, as the bird's mantra tears through his soul, again and again.

Dina never thought it would be like this. That she would miss the bookshop so little. But days spent with her dark and damaged boy, and the very singular Lou Elliot meant just that. That she rarely thought of the shop or Breitner. But that is not to mean that books were out of her thoughts entirely. No, they were always there in the background. And in her more abstract moods, the books would take on human characteristics, specifically those of Lou and Conor.

Indeed, Lou she would perceive as being an open book, light and airy, a romantic comedy perhaps, definitely all heart and soul, whereas Conor on the other hand was a closed tome, so dark and somehow unreadable. Indeed, she knew deep down that she would never be able to read him, reach him. Not totally, that at best, only half of him would be her's. But it was not enough to deter her love. But was it even really love, Or just some strange fascination, a bizarre compulsion and infatuation that would gradually pass? She did not know.

Conor had once said to her that the only way he could survive, was to not think about thinking. At the time she had not given it much thought. But now she was beginning to see the childish wisdom of his words, the perverse truth of them. Even if at times it appeared an impossible theory to put into practice.

Another theory (If indeed that is what it could be called) that struggled when put into practice, was the 'culinary theory' of Lou. That her cooking was a crime against nature and mankind Dina and Conor were discovering only too quickly. Yet Lou swore by her unconventional cooking practices, whilst Dina and Conor merely silently swore at it.

The theory was basic enough. It simply entailed throwing any ingredients she had at hand into a large pot and then boiling them either, to a slow and agonising death, or a desperate surrender. Whichever come first.

Needless to say, it was not long before Dina tactfully suggested that she take over the cooking duties of the hotel for a while. Not that the duties were that strenuous or time consuming. Indeed, the only other guest in the hotel was an elderly man who appeared to have perfected misanthropy into an art form. He was one of those souls whose hatred had started at self, but had then soon transmitted itself outwards, a wildfire of loathing crossing boundaries of race, religion, gender and class. He merely existed to hate.

Even the warmth and generosity of Lou was met with a sullen hatred by the 'elderly foreign gentleman' as Lou would call him, being unable to pronounce his exotic sounding surname. In the three months he had been resident at the hotel, this irritable and irascible man had barely spoken more than a couple of dozen words to Lou. And they were mostly epithets of complaint and bad humour, invariably accompanied by a glare of disdain. But she tolerated his gruff ways and sardonic sneers because one guest, however unpleasant, was better than no guests and loneliness. For Lou had tasted its bitterness before, and it was not a brew she wished to imbibe again any time soon, too unnatural, too soul destroying for one as gregarious as she.

And so, in these days before the storm, another triumvirate was born, Lou, Dina and the boy, living out little lives as thick as thieves. And in such unreal times they seemed unstoppable.

No slow degeneration, just a rapid descent into the realms of the hopelessly dysfunctional. And now Baines tries to remember just when it was that the worm in his brain had turned. He conjectures hazily that it was probably two days back. But he could not be sure. All he was certain about was that ever since it had turned, the singing had stopped. Only to be replaced by alternately, a gentle whimper and a keening wail.

The voices too had left him. For now, taking with them their

cacophony of chaos and commands, but it was a false liberation, a spurious emancipation, because the damage was already
done, beyond repair.

Welcome to Bexhill. Twinned with... Baines gives the road sign
a cursory glance as it disappears in the rear view mirror. To the
boy with the fresh supply of pills and booze, everything seems
to be hanging by a thread. Minutes, hours, the nine pm sky,
himself. All suspended. There but not there. And now gazing
out at the road in front, his eyes follow the uncoiling tarmac
snake as it stretches out into the distance.

Until now in the shadow light he stares down hard at his
hands gripping the steering wheel. They are the hands of his
grandfather, Strong, iron, skeletal with protuberant sickly blue
veins, robust hands, perfectly suited to smack up the head of
a young boy. To strike and smite for no other reason than that
they could.

He had learnt about Bexhill through Gary Brooker, the
younger brother of Kenny. The two had bumped into each
other outside the Off-licence on Gladstone Street. As ever Gary
was skint and had ponced some fags off of Baines. In fact it was
almost a 'Quid pro quo' thing. Because Gary got some smokes,
and Baines some much needed information.

Ducking into a shop doorway out of the cold evening rain,
Baines cuts to the chase. Manoeuvring the conversation adroitly
away from the piss and wind preoccupation Gary possessed
regarding the theft of motorcycles. 'So, you have seen Conor
recently then?' Gary exhales a fog of Marlboro. 'Yeah, about
a week back. The weird looking bastard was with some little
limping girl. They were getting on a train to Bexhill.'

Baines looks at him questioningly. 'You are sure it was Bexhill?' The boy releases another industrial-strength plume of smoke and slowly nods his head.

'Yeah positive, you do realise you ain't the only one looking for him, don't yer?' Baines feels the worm slowly stirring inside his head once more. 'What you talking about? Who else is looking for him?' The kid looks at him disbelievingly. 'Christ, have you been hiding under a stone? I thought everyone knew, the old Bill of course. They want him on account of his rear-ranging some geezer's facial architecture with a knife, in the Lamb. Apparently the bloke nearly died. He lost a shitload of blood. I heard he needed eighty stitches to his face and neck.'

Baines cannot disguise the surprise on his face. He had always thought that the only person Conor would end up cutting badly would be himself. After all, he was a suicide waiting to happen.

Fag smoked, info revealed, transaction concluded, Gary drifts off into the pissing down rain. Baines watches his departure in silence. Then, like second nature, he pops a pill and chases it down with vodka. Nothing had changed in his mind. He would still find Conor and 'off' him. Because then and only then, would he be truly free... Simple.

Bordered to the east by open farmland and to the west by the dense Katozory forest, the home of Stefan Kasparczak was little more than a timber framed shack. Barely four meters by four his primitive domicile had just one room which served as bedroom, kitchen and bathroom. But it was enough, all he needed, because he was a man of simple tastes. However, 'simple' would not be a word one could use to describe the personality and character of Stefan.

Indeed, it was acknowledged by those that knew him that he was a man of moods and complexities. One minute this stocky middle-aged man would appear to be blessed with a quiet good humour, yet the very next minute light could become shade and his whole demeanour would change, transforming him into a man of dark thoughts. One who it would seem appeared to hold an abstract grudge against something that had not happened yet.

To his neighbours, wary and confused by his sudden mood changes, Stefan was an enigma rolled up in a fifty zloty note. All in all, a man probably best to be avoided. And this suited him down to the ground. The tranquillity of solitude appealed to him far more than the sham niceties and vacuous chatter of his neighbours. And so, Stefan would retreat in upon himself. Self contained in mind and body. Until that is mushrooms, of all things put an end to such serene feelings of solitude.

To the inhabitants of Katozory, October was a highly significant month. For it was at this early stage of autumn that the annual picking and gathering of the fruits of the forest took place, specifically the harvesting of that most versatile fungus with its distinctive cap, the wild mushroom. And not war, weather or worldly woes could or would deter the folk of the surrounding villages from descending upon the forest, armed with buckets and baskets to take from the benevolent forest its bounty, blessed such as it was with countless varieties and species of the revered edible fungi.

From the window of his shack, Stefan can see the hubbub as gaggles of people mainly family groups enter the forest in excited anticipation. And he watches and waits, confident in the knowledge that none will find the choicest and rarest mushrooms, those that live out there days in the densest and darkest heart of the forest.

The reflection that stares back at him from the shallow pool of murky water is gaunt, grey and hollow-cheeked, a skeletal shadow with the face of a muselmann.

Rising unsteadily to his feet, Lazarus feels the familiar sensation of dizziness. Once he feared it, now he falls into it. Lurching to his left, he leans hard against a tree, before slowly sinking back down again to the cold and damp forest floor.

Emaciated by hunger, and exhausted both in body and mind, the man that once was Lazarus Glick lay's down amongst the rotting forest undergrowth and waits to die. His pitiful dance of the muselmann is done now. The aimless wandering and apathetic listlessness all finished with. It would end here, shutdown. But he feels no fear. He is beyond that now. He merely feels a weary resignation, as he prepares to close his eyes upon a world he had no further use for. One he had in truth, left behind an age ago.

And now minutes pass. Or perhaps they are hours. Either way, Lazarus is not aware of there departure. Because in these, what he perceives to be his final moments, he possesses a total insensitivity of the reality around him. And so, through the glazed seeing, but non-seeing eyes of the dying, he views uncomprehendingly the vast October sky above him, watches without feeling the clouds gliding slowly and sadly, there nebulous serenity that of the funeral procession, as these swans of the sky, mourn another soul lost to the madness.

Flickering and fractured images flood his moribund mind once more, indistinct and hazy. Not vivid and razor sharp as in the barn when he thought death would claim him then. No. These images were shards broken and abstract visuals, the out of focus snapshots of a dying mind.

It is nearly dark by the time the last of the mushroom pickers leave the edges of the forest. From his shack, Stefan hears their chatter and laughter fade into the dusk. And now, contrary to the opinion of the many, he feels this to be the perfect hour to go mushroom gathering. And also to attend to other business activities that the imminent darkness will afford him the liberty to perform in total secrecy.

That Stefan dabbled in the black market was not of any great surprise to his neighbours. After all, many of them did also. However, what would have surprised them is the fact that for many years he had been stealing from the wealthier of their number. But that was small beer in comparison to the housebreaking he undertook at the homes of the more affluent citizens of the nearby large towns. Jewellery, cash, paintings, he took anything that had any value. That is if the Germans had not already stripped the place of its finer pickings.

But Stefan was a careful thief and an honest one as well, if that is not an oxymoron, for he would only steal from those who could stand it, could afford to lose a little here and there. In fact, the only thing he required of his criminality was that it gave him food for his belly, booze for his brain and tobacco for his lungs. And to assuage any possible pangs of conscience that might arise. Then a fifty zloty donation to the local church from this former altar boy would sate that insidious creature... Conscience.

Equipped with just a torch, a canvas bag and a small spade, Stefan leaves the brightness of his shack for the darkness of the night. Cautious and methodical, he always used a different route when entering the forest, and then a different track into its lonely and desolate heart. Most times he would go three or four times a week to his stash, either to add to his ill-gotten gains or like this night, to retrieve a few pieces to take to his fence in the city.

Since the advent of the war five long years back, Stefan had deemed it prudent to remove his stash from his shack and relocate it deep in the forest, because the Germans thought nothing of tearing a person's home apart and taking away anything that took their fancy.

As usual everything was as it should be. In the darkness, and on bended knees, Stefan digs down into the sodden black forest earth. At first the sound of a hollow moan does not perturb him at all. As it was quite common for a dying forest creature to come to this dense and inaccessible place to breathe its last, live out its final moments. But again the moan echoes out, this time followed by a gasped word Stefan cannot make out. He springs to his feet, his voice a hiss in the blackness.

'Who is there? Show yourself!' He is met with silence. Raising the spade in his hand as if it were a battle-axe, he moves slowly and tentatively towards where the moans emanate from. Releasing one hand from the spade, he shines the torch in a wide arc, its brightness piercing the night.

About ten metres to his left he sees what he thinks are a pile of dirty and soiled looking rags. Cautiously he walks over to them. Aiming the torchlight upon the rags he soon discovers a human being inside them, a human being more dead than alive. Bending over the prone figure, Stefan speaks softly.

'Who are you? What are you doing here?' He is met with silence. After a few seconds Lazarus half opens one glazed eye then closes it, blinded as he is by the piercing torchlight. Stefan lays down the spade and slowly holds out his hand. 'Here, take it. Go on.' Seconds elapse. Finally, Lazarus musters up enough strength from deep within himself to raise one painfully thin arm. Gently, Stefan takes it and raises Lazarus up onto spindly legs. And then, as the exertion proves too much for him, his matchstick legs buckle and he sinks back down.

In total disbelief at this human wreck in front of him, once more Stefan raises Lazarus to his feet, astonished and sickened by the bag of bones he now holds in his arms. 'In the name of God, what the hell are we doing to each other?' He looks hard into the grey and ashen face as it slips into unconsciousness; and wonders what the hell is he going to do?

Because now, this man that was an enigma to those that know him. This man that was seemingly lightly touched by both God and Devil has a decision to make, a dilemma to overcome. And the irony is that he knows in his heart that whatever decision he makes, he will end up regretting it one way or another.

The voice of the Bringer of Peace had first visited Conor early one morning. Sitting on the shingle beach, the boy had been watching a sea mist consume the horizon, before turning its attention to an ocean that was undecided over whether it wanted to be rough or calm; tea-brown, seaweed-green or an indistinct shade of blue.

Then, then in a tone appropriated from some suburban Maharishi, comes the Bringer of Peace, a voice that rises steadily above the usual clamorous babel of the others in his head. And it's a gentle voice, serene yet insistent, softly chanting a mantra. 'Conor Christie, Corpus Christi, body of Christ, body of Christ. Purge your scourge in the forgiving sea.' The boy has no real comprehension of what the words mean. But the voice is somehow mesmeric, as compelling as the flame voice.

He lies down amongst the rough shingle and lets the voice claim his brain, as the cold sea started to claim his feet and legs. And high above a vast sky of enamel grey starts to close in on him, as if forming a metal band around his head. It's a gentle pressure at first, but soon the steel strip starts to tighten. The pain makes him grit his teeth and screw his eyes shut. The voices in his head are quiet now. Save for one. The Bringer of Peace. But its voice is no longer serene and gentle. It booms out one solitary word which reverberates along the deserted beach.

'Release' Slowly, the pressure of the metal band eases, until bit by bit it finally lifts altogether. Opening his eyes, Conor sees the same enamel grey sky but it's smaller, a shade lighter and a hue softer now. As if the chiding it had received from the bringer of peace had left it suitably chastised and contrite.

Conor slowly tries to raise himself from the lapping waves as if a spell had been broken. But now once more the Bringer of Peace speaks, his tone once more calm and compelling. 'Listen to my words and then do as I say... Walk now. Enter the kingdom of Neptune.' After a brief hesitation, the boy starts to wade out through the bitterly cold waves. His movements are mechanical and his face an expressionless mask.

Deeper and deeper he strides out into the numbingly cold

sea. All is silent now, everything is still. Even the squabbling, shrieking sea birds seem suspended somehow.

Further and further out he goes until sharp shingle underfoot becomes soft sand. And the water is past his waist now, a girdle of cold which numbs him body and mind. 'Stop' Once more the voice of the Bringer of Peace booms out. Conor halts dead in his tracks, his feet sinking deeper into the cloying seabed, and inside his head the changing voice changes again, once more becoming the maharishi of mellow.

'May the sanctifying power of the sea purge you of the scourge, may the power of the kingdom of Neptune embrace, heal and purify you.' Over and over the maharishi voice chants the mantra, an incantation to boy and waves. And as rhythmically those waves ebb and pulse against the shivering body of the boy, the voice continues. 'In one hand take the body of Christ, in the other the blade, because neither can help you now.'

Conor stands stock still, uncomprehending and frozen to the marrow. 'Take out the crucifix and the knife!' The voice now was neither booming nor maharishi, instead merely impatient, tetchy and irritable. But finally Conor gets it, understands. With frozen fingers he delves down into saturated jeans pockets. But the denim has become sodden and heavy; swathing his legs like a second skin making it difficult for him to retrieve the knife. But eventually he finds it, and as ever the cold sharpness reassures him, hardly his weapon of choice, more like his weapon of desperate necessity.

But the search for the body of Christ proved more problematical. Truth was, Conor had forgotten he still had the crucifix in his jeans. But now with rigid blue fingers he delves down deeper and deeper into waterlogged pockets. Until at last, wedged under some loose change and a saturated pack of Players Number Six cigarettes, he locates the body of his saviour and protector, protector? I guess that depends on whether or not we believe in the veracity of the words of the Bringer of Peace.

Either way, Conor now holds in his hands the sacred and the profane, one in either hand. Both architects, players in his mental lock down, shut down, break down melt down. Now, beyond cold and beyond feeling, he awaits further instruction, as around him the grey-brown wall of waves grow higher. And he does not have long to wait, for soon the voice of the sancti-monious Bringer of Peace is somewhere else in his head.

'Cast into the depths all that which proclaims itself truth, but which is in reality falsehood and lies. Cast out into the realm of Neptune every curse, taunt and insult that ever tore at your heart.' The maharishi is in full flow now, spewing out words like bolts of fire, those words a strange symbiosis of the coherent and the incoherent.

'It's time, time to stop gazing upon the mounds of smoul-dering embers of yesterday, time to stop looking into the future and seeing only the past, time to shout down the echoing emptiness, time to plough that lone furrow until you see the light, zinc-bright white at the end of the tunnel. Now wash away the stain the phoney prophets branded upon your soul. Cast out these weavers of dreams and send them back to their webs.'

On and on the maharishi espouses, until finally his voice abruptly terminates. Conor is frozen in time' literally. He no longer moves at all. The sea is he and he is the sea. But soon the voice is back in his head. Only the maharishi is gone, instead the voice is a deep south Negro evangelical, lifted from the summer of 63. 'The time is now. Cast what imprisons you away. Tear it away!' Once more in mechanised movements, Conor raises both arms and hurls the blade and crucifix into the watery depths. Inside his head the evangelical voice explodes. 'Free at last, free at last. Thank God we are free at last!'

Although he had flatly denied it, Dina knew that Conor's voices were becoming more and more varied and voluble. He had done his best to hide things from her. But she could see the subtle changes in him. His silences had become longer, his solitary walks by the sea more frequent. And she could not help but notice that the lacerations on his arm and wrist were now deeper, more frenzied and savage looking. She worried for him. She worried for them. She worried.

Until in the empty hours of another sleepless night, she begged him to get help, to see a doctor. After various evasions he said he would, swore it. But she knew he would not. And so the drift drifted on, unchanging, his private hell remaining private. And seemingly no matter what she did or tried, Dina could not reach that other half of him. For the dwelling space that was his mind; once a building of semi-detachment, had now become fully detached, silent, bleak and unreachable.

But without her knowledge, somewhere deep down inside the boy, call it his soul if you will; a defiance was stirring, embryonic, but nevertheless a will to somehow climb out of the abyss that had been his for as long as he could recall. He wanted a life he wanted to live, for him, for Dina, for them. It was, as the old song goes, 'Time to tear down the walls of heartache.' But it was hard, so very hard.

Baines runs out of pills first. And as it turns out it is not too long before his patience follows suit. He had just spent two days scouring every inch of Bexhill looking for Conor. And it had proved totally fatuous. Now, back in the less than salubrious surroundings of the squat, his vacillating thoughts were: vacillating. Shifting back and forth, to and fro. Paganini's bow has nothing on them, Conor-The old Jew-Conor-The old Jew. Eventually his coin comes down on the side of the old Jew. Like petals pulled from a buttercup. Conor can wait.

CHAPTER SEVENTEEN

For what seems an eternity, Lazarus hovers, flit-floating between the living and the dead. But this time no images no ghosts visit him. Maybe because this time death is claiming him faster than life can hold onto him. And now lying in the sturdy little bed of Stefan's, his breathing is barely audible, and his face a yellow wax mask. Every few hours Stefan would bring him potato soup, water and bread. Apart from this there was little he could do. Either God would take this muselmann off his hands or he would not. And right now, as days dragged into a week, the Almighty did not appear to be in any great hurry.

As with pretty much everything about his character, the relationship Stefan had with God was complex. Many times over the years contact between the two had acrimoniously been put on hold. But their rivers would always merge once more, a bond that could never be truly severed, because at heart, Stefan was still that good ten year old Polish catholic boy, immersed in a child-like awe and wonder of church and religion.

Finally, as the seventh day rises; dreary, drab and unprepossessing, so Lazarus rises also, but not from the grave like his namesake. But from the bed of Stefan Kasparczak; this Jew-saving, Jew-hating thief, and now this sometime Christian, sometime atheist, takes Lazarus Glick gently into his arms and carefully carries him to the chair by the warm stove.

Momentarily both men are silent, as if dumbstruck,

wondering how the hell had they come to where they were at, until finally through dry cracked lips Lazarus speaks. 'What is this place? Who are you?' He takes his eyes from the stove, and looks into the round peasant face of Stefan. 'Me? Who am I? I'm just the stupid fuck who has risked his life saving your, sorry, Jewish arse!' A smile breaks out across his face. Lazarus turns once more towards the stove, his tone vague and distant.

'First Ishmail the Turk and now you, I'm surrounded by saviours.' Stefan looks at him uncomprehendingly. But Lazarus does not elaborate. Instead, just continues to stare vacantly at the stove without speaking. Stefan stokes up the small fire with more kindling. Turning slowly he finally speaks, his quiet voice almost lost amongst the crackling, chattering flames.

'You know, I didn't think you were going to make it. Thought you were a dead man more than once. So, come on, where have you escaped from?' Lazarus runs a hand wearily across his close cropped hair. 'It's a long story... Why did you do it? Why didn't you just leave me out in the forest?'

'You think I haven't asked myself that a hundred times before. I must need my head examining. I mean, not only do I risk my arse saving a Jew. But I go and pick a poor one. One who doesn't even own a pot to piss in.' Once more Stefan smiles a rueful smile.

Just then, a loud knock at the door is followed by a drunken voice. 'I know that you are in there Stefan. Look, I mean you no harm. Just send out the Jew!' Inside the shack, Lazarus stares nervously across at Stefan. Whose voice when it comes is a hiss 'Get under the bed!' Lazarus does not need telling twice. Once more the slurring voice is heard from outside. 'Come on Stefan,

I don't want any trouble. Just send the Yid out.'

Finally replying, Stefan takes a Browning pistol from behind the stove. 'What the hell are you talking about Lesniak? There is no Jew here. There are no Jews anywhere now. You and your friends have seen to that.' Hiding the gun in the waist band of his trousers, Stefan opens the door and stares hard at Lesniak. 'So, come on, you don't believe me, have a look round.'

Lesniak, a tall, thin man in his early forties, cautiously enters. He carries in his left hand a pistol. Stefan eyes him with a certain disdain. 'So, Lesniak how is the Yid-hunting business these days? The thirty pieces of silver must be stacking up nicely by now.' Lesniak remains silent. Obviously used to the barbed comments of Stefan, and for a few moments he stands in the middle of the room, narrow dark eyes shifting from left to right, a predator devoid of conscience and soul.

'Well, I can see there is no Jew here. But I sure as hell can smell one.' Once more Stefan eyes him disdainfully, a sardonic sneer on his lips. 'You sure that ain't your own scent? Cos, I tell you Lesniak, looking at you in this light I swear to God that there is more than a few drops of Hebrew blood in your veins.' The man turns sharply, violently, and thrusts his face a few inches from that of Stefan. 'Fuck you Kasparczak! This ain't over. I will be back.'

With that, he turns hard on his heels and storms out of the shack. Slowly, cautiously, Lazarus slides out from under the bed on his belly. He looks across at Stefan who is at the window, watching alternately the departure of Lesniak and a sky full of thunder. He does not turn around as he speaks. 'He might be a fool, but not that much of one. He knows what is going on here. Judas won't leave it alone. He wants that thirty pieces of silver.

It was like floating, sleepwalking out of a fog. For early one morning it had suddenly struck Dina that; that which had once meant so much now meant so little, her old life, her old ways, the old town. But now Bexhill was done. And it was time to go back to it; home. She had spoken to the boy about her plan to leave at breakfast.

Expecting opposition, she was surprised when Conor agreed immediately with her plan. Truth was he was getting restless. In his mind, just like in Dina's, the time and place of the town had been and gone. Somehow in the last few days it and its sea had lost all meaning. He did not trust it now it had lost its truth and integrity. It had made promises to the boy it could not keep.

Instead, planting in his head clutter and mutter, Neptune and the Bringer of Peace had proved to be false prophets, fucking liars just like the rest. Their sea-soaked promises had turned to rust. And he knew now that he had been a fool to believe them. Perhaps, just maybe, despite all the mocking cruelty that the flame voice espoused from his theatre of bile, he was right after all. The only truth was to be found in the fire.

Lou Elliot did not allow her face to betray her feelings when Dina told her of their decision to leave Bexhill. But inside, inside things are different, for in just the short period of time that she had known the young couple, Lou has become attached, close to them. And now, now the thought of them leaving was...

'When will you go?' As Lou speaks, she does not look up from cutting carrots on the grey kitchen work surface. Standing a few feet away at the Belfast sink, Dina watches but does not see, only hearing the cold water tap with its damaged washer constantly drip onto the stained porcelain. Over and over it echoes tortuously. Suddenly, turning away from its prosaic torment, Dina gazes across at Lou.

'Look, I have been thinking. Why don't you come with us?' The rhythmical sound of knife against chopping board stops dead. Lou is momentarily speechless. She turns slowly to face Dina. 'What? Are you serious? What about this place? It won't look after itself.' The girl walks across to her. 'Lou, the place is empty. The old foreign gentleman left three days ago. There is no one here. Look, just shut the place up and come with us. It will do you the world of good to get away from here for a bit.' Lou is silent briefly, just looks into the dark and gentle eyes of the girl. Finally, she speaks. 'You know, that is the most stupid... And simply wonderful idea you have ever had, when do we go?'

In a dysfunctional mind logic and rationale are invariably nowhere to be found, short on the ground. Not that they had ever been close companions of Baines in any case. But ever since his 'mania' had moved in, whatever he did actually possess in the way of logic and rationality had moved out, leaving him sinking ever deeper into the morass of his own broken thoughts. And now?

Now in a darkened room he stands with a loaded gun pressed against the head of an old man. Always impetuous, constantly a stranger to the concept of taking responsibility for his actions, the booze and pills are dictating play now. 'Where is the fucking money!?... Come on, where is it?' Baines spits out the words in a mix of anger and frustration.

Becoming increasingly hyper, borderline manic, Baines shuttles Lazarus in four-four time from room to room of the rambling house. Gold, sterling or dollars, it's all the same to the bank of Baines, and he wants it, wants it all. Breathless and confused, the old man is dragged through the semi-darkness. Finally reaching the end of yet another soulless corridor, Baines kicks open the door to a large bedroom. Pushing Lazarus roughly onto the double bed, he closes the heavy curtains and switches on the light.

Looking across at the old man he swears to God he has never seen such a grey face. To the boy it resembles an oil filter that should have been changed five thousand miles ago. And now as Baines turns over the bedroom, tipping out wardrobes and drawers, Lazarus sits motionless on the bed, a man out of time; out of place, out of luck. From across the room, Baines suddenly turns on him.

'Look, I have had enough of this shit! Now, where the hell is the money!?' Once more the boy levels the gun at the head of Lazarus. Slowly, somehow beyond slowly, the old man gazes up at the boy. 'Have you seen Esther? You must have seen her?' Agitated, sweating and rapidly losing both plot and grip, Baines swings his arm back as if to strike Lazarus. But then, with a weary yet sardonic expression on his face he lets his arm down by his side.

'Yeah, let's find Esther. Perhaps she knows where the fucking money is.' Looking over at Lazarus with a tired disdain, the boy takes out a half bottle of vodka from inside his jacket and sits down on a chair by the window. Lazarus does not look at him. Lazarus does not look at anything. He just stares straight ahead seeing God knows who or God knows what.

Crippled minutes pass under the stark glare of a naked light bulb. Taking the bottle from his lips, Baines looks at it quizzically, as if hoping that it could maybe give him inspiration or clarification on what the hell, he was supposed to do next. If this was his hope then he is to be disappointed, because all the Moscow mineral water is doing is what it always did: namely, intensifying already strong feelings of vague detachment.

That oh so familiar sense of unreality of the been and gone and here and now. And it was his, always his. Like the worm in his head, the pills in his blood and the gun in his hand.

After what seems like an age, but is in fact just a few minutes, he rises unsteadily from the chair. Turning, he briefly looks out through a crack in the curtains down onto the street below, where a middle-aged woman passes by walking a small dog.

Seeing the slither of electric light piercing the night, she casually looks up at the window. Spying her, Baines gazes for a few seconds before inexplicably waving at her. Momentarily surprised, the woman nevertheless returns the wave. Briefly, unexpectedly, he feels something akin to happiness. He could not adequately describe the feeling. But it was kind of like he felt a backhanded validation, confirmation that what he was doing was right. And it was not just the worm in his head that had sung approval for his actions. No. For now, the woman, representative of all humankind, by acknowledging his 'mission' with that wave of approval, had granted consent to his actions.

Smiling a jagged smile that mirrors his jagged mind, he finally comes away from the window. Just then, the hacking cough of Lazarus breaks in on the delusional reverie of the boy. 'Christ, you should see someone about that cough. It's a real church yarder. Anyway, come on. We ain't finished yet.'

pointing the gun once more at the head of Lazarus, Baines
motions for him to get off the bed.

CHAPTER EIGHTEEN

True to his word, the Jew-hunter Lesniak returns to the home of Stefan. And it is well gone midnight when Stefan and Lazarus are awakened by heavy pounding at the door. Bleary-eyed and half-awake, the two men dress quickly in the darkness

'This is your last chance Kasparczak; send the Jew out!' Shielded by the shadows of night, Stefan slowly reaches for his gun. 'Look, Lesniak, whoever it was that told you I had a Yid here is full of shit. So, just do yourself a favour and piss off home while you still have one. Cos, believe me brother, it wont be long before the Russkies come. And I think they will be very interested in fuckers like you who collaborated with the Germans.'

As Stefan speaks he moves silently towards the window. Outside, the angular figure of Lesniak is illuminated by what pale moonlight there is. In his hand is a pistol. And as ever he is under the influence of alcohol. He seems to sway with his words. 'Don't you know anything you dumb shit. The Russians hate the Jews as much as the Germans do.'

Coming away from the window, Stefan calls out in response. 'Perhaps you are right, but at least they don't murder them. And anyway, it's not going to save your arse. The bottom line is you hunted Jews and then sold them to the Germans. In Russian eyes that makes you a collaborator. Time is running out for you Lesniak,' before the man can reply, Stefan charges the door swinging it open wide. He fires three shots in rapid succession at the head of Lesniak, who stunned and shocked falls silently to the ground. For a few moments in the sullen moonlight, Stefan stands over the body, looking down blankly at a red mass that used to be a face.

Inside, Lazarus stands stock still. The voice of Stefan cuts sharp and tetchy. 'Don't just stand there. Help me bury this piece of crap!'

Under barren skies disseminating intermittent drizzle, Lesniak the hunter of Jews is buried far into the forest in a shallow grave. And now back in the hut, a stark realisation of what has just transpired leaves each man alone with his thoughts.

Presently, Lazarus speaks, his voice calm yet hesitant. 'So, how long do you think it will be till he is missed?' A soft streak of early morning sunlight strikes yellow across the pale unshaven face of Stefan. Rising slowly from his chair by the window, he pulls a small suitcase out from under the bed. 'I have no idea and I'm not hanging around to find out.' Hurriedly he starts to pack a few clothes into the case. Suddenly he turns and faces Lazarus.

'Well, my friend, this is where we go our separate ways. As for me, I will be going to my sister in Katowice; well, at least until this shit blows over. God willing it will only be a week or so till the Russians get here. Then I will come back.' Lazarus is silent, once more his life a succession of partings and goodbyes, and now as he sits on the edge of the bed watching Stefan pack, it's happening again.

Two days later and faintly in the distance, Lazarus can hear the heavy artillery of the Red Army tearing up earth and sky. With every hour that passed the prospect of liberation was inching towards becoming a reality. And he thinks of Esther and all those innocent Jewish souls that would never see it. And he wonders, like he had wondered a thousand times before. What the hell had it all been for? What in the name of God had their deaths achieved? Had it all just been about satisfying the anti-semitic blood lust of the demigods of Hitlerland? Was that it? Was that all it really was about?

Breathing in sadness with every breath and drowning in a blood sea of incomprehension, Lazarus suddenly feels so very tired, body and soul. If he could have slept for a thousand years it would not have been nearly enough. But still the question nags away at him, never leaving him. That question in the head of Lazarus Glick, son of a Krakow watchmaker, that question that haunts him as it has silently haunted many rabbinical scholars and Talmud academics ever since. Namely, if there is a God, where the hell had he been for the past five years?

The existence or non-existence of God was the last thing on the helter-skelter mind of Conor Christie. Indeed, for the past few days since arriving back from Bexhill, the boy had been on the run. Well, perhaps 'run' is the wrong word. It in truth had been more of a desperate and disorganised flee from the police.

It had all started when he, Dina and Lou had left the train station on their return from Bexhill and started the short walk to Dina's place. Stepping out across the sombre housing estate, a steady rain fell from stark and uncaring skies. Carrying the suitcase of Lou, Conor had briefly thought of Baines. The first time he had done so in what seemed like an age. A few paces behind him, Dina and Lou shelter under a red umbrella, chatting about anything and nothing.

Turning his head he looks back at the girl, his girl. He inwardly smiles, because for this boy with his mongrel-Mongol eyes, she is pure perfection. And with her on his mind and clouds on his lids, he does not notice the slow, belly-crawl approach of the police patrol car. And behind its rain-dashed windscreen two faces peer out eyeing the boy closely. Now sure in their minds that they have their man, they bring the car to a gradual halt. Then in a manoeuvre straight out of The Sweeney, the two young officers bolt from the vehicle, doors slamming in perfect unison.

'Conor Christie?' The voice of the older is a shrill shout. From right and left the two men lunge towards Conor. Startled and confused, he instinctively backs hard away. Then, in an act of blind self-preservation, he swings the heavy suitcase at the officer to his right, catching the man squarely in the solar plexus. Then he kicks the other officer hard in the balls. As both men sink to their knees, the boy turns and looks at his Dina. He looks imploringly into her eyes, as if questioning her on what he should do next.

Her response is immediate and stark. 'For God's sake, run! Go, get out of here!' But still he stands looking at her. And as rain patterns across his face he mouths to her. 'I will always love you.' Then, glancing down he sees that the two officers are slowly getting to their feet. Dina sees it as well. She turns once more to the boy, her voice a choke. 'I love you too, you know that. But you gotta go now just for a while.' He looks at her for the last time, and she sees the damaged child in his eyes. She wants to hold him, draw him to her, but times up. Then he is gone.

Awakened, the somnambulist boy runs off, flees from the

police across the heartland, wasteland of the desolate labyrinthine housing estate.

Trawling the back bedrooms of the capacious house, Baines finds not cash, jewellery or gold. No, what he finds is ragged striped pyjamas with a faded yellow star stashed away in a small case at the back of a musty wardrobe. Confined in such dark and dismal quarters, the pyjamas that are not pyjamas reek of piss, sweat, hopelessness and fear. Holding them up the boy instantly recognises it. After all, he is a child of 'The World at War' TV generation. He has grown up with the grainy black and white images of staggering, shaven-headed skeletal ghosts in striped pyjamas that are not pyjamas.

And just as such images of suffering had not moved his callous and unfeeling eleven year old heart back in the day, so now his heart remains unmoved as he holds such a soiled garment of pain in his hands. But he is what he is. Moulded made and manufactured by neglect, non-existent nurturing, and left in a social wilderness by a society that did not, does not, will never give a shit.

Tied to a chair in the darkened front room, Lazarus is a candidate for stone. Unmoving and with a face bloodied and bruised, he watches without seeing the black and white TV in the corner, as it casts out flickering slithers of light and shade. On the screen, a young Ken Barlow argues with an old Albert Tatlock, their fish mouths moving in unison. While down at The Rovers Return, Ena Sharples downs another milk stout as she puts the worlds to rights with an aloof and disinterested Annie Walker.

In the bathroom upstairs, the spaced-out boy is hatching a spaced-out plan. Standing over the basin, Baines, now wearing the pyjamas that are not pyjamas, looks at his reflection in the wall mirror. In his right hand he holds a pair of large open scissors. Wildly, frenetically he starts to hack and cut at his hair, taking it back to his scalp.

Every now and then he stops and takes a swig from the omnipresent vodka bottle, after all, it's thirsty work being mad. Now an oblique smile spreads across his face. The job is finished. Mouse brown hair strews the basin and floor. Once more he looks at his reflection in the mirror and throws another slanting smile, one that could have meant anything, everything or nothing. Then, then he is ready for the performance.

CHAPTER NINETEEN

For Lazarus Glick, liberation finally appeared one sunny morning in the shape of a Russian soldier on a motorcycle.

Around eight am the rider had suddenly appeared on the horizon, a lone figure shrouded in a blanket of dust thrown up from the parched dirt road. On seeing the military figure in the distance, Lazarus had instinctively dived for cover into a roadside ditch and waited. Waited and watched as the motorcyclist came ever closer. Squinting through the hazy sunshine, Lazarus can at last see that the soldier is not wearing the *Feld grau* of the Wehrmacht, but the uniform of the Red Army.

And as Lazarus blinks through old dust made new, he sees out on the horizon more Red Army uniforms, some scattered across the fields and others marching down the dust road. Some ride on trucks, others on the side of tanks. All head towards the village. And above, below and intertwined with the machine roar, Lazarus can hear some of the soldiers sing, their young voices bringing back memories, memories of once being human.

Still laying low he stays in the ditch until the military column has passed. And although these were his liberators, the liberators of his people, what were left of them, to him a uniform was still a uniform, a soldier with a gun still a soldier with a gun. And so this was the liberation of Lazarus Glick. And he tried to feel something, anything. But ultimately all he felt was a huge overwhelming sense of loneliness, a dull and hollow nothingness that went without a name.

And so, sure, the body of Lazarus Glick would soon be liberated, free at last, but his mind? That would never be truly liberated, would always remain captive to it self, held so by all that he had seen and all that he had lost.

'It is widely believed that near this church in the late spring of 1381, the radical priest John Ball preached a fiery sermon to a large crowd. In their number it is alleged was Wat Tyler and his followers. And Ball, it is believed by delivering such a fiery oration did in some respects instigate the chain of events that would ultimately lead to the Peasants Rebellion of that fateful year.'

Huddled in a blanket in a dark corner of the church, Conor Christie reads the faded wall plaque for the fiftieth time and then watches as shadows cast shadows across mouldering medieval masonry. Closing his eyes now to make the darkness complete, the boy contemplates the echoing emptiness of the place and wonders if God had ever actually visited this scene, one of his more obscure, forlorn and desolate outposts.

Swathing himself tighter in the threadbare blanket he lights another cigarette, and then, perhaps if he had known how to properly, he tries to work out yet again the strange dichotomy that was his life, a dichotomy that seemingly produces such an unequal division between an undamaged body and a damaged mind. Yet in the damp, dank darkness of this church God had forgot, the boy cannot afford to think of such dichotomies and divisions of body and mind.

Instead he knows he must get his head together somehow

and find a way of extricating himself from the excrement he was in. And now in the gloom, a match strikes hot gold against cold black as the boy lights yet another cigarette and runs a hand through his lank dark brown hair. He thinks of the girl, a girl in a police cell, a girl in court. His girl banged up. The thought sends a shudder hard through him. And he knows, just knows he has no other option than to man- up, front-up and hand himself in to the police. But, sadly, in the front of his mind where the heavy voices reside, they have other ideas.

Indeed, ever since the boy had entered the church a few hours back, one by one they had awoken from menacing slumber. And high above this vocal carnage, the shrill voice of a child echoes out over and over, a lost child, a never to be born child, its voice a drill inside his head. 'Ashes in the water ashes in the sea, Conor is falling down again one, two, three.'

Throwing the blanket to one side, he tries to stand up, but there is no strength, sensation or feeling in his legs. After a few seconds he slowly sinks back down to the cold stone floor. Then, as quickly as it had come the voice of the child disappears. Only to be replaced by the clamour and babel of countless others. As ever at the head of this vocal vanguard was the flame voice.

'She betrayed you, the cripple girl done you like a kipper. It was her that grassed you up to the police. So, what you going to do about it, freak?' Stunned, drowning in dead air, the boy snarls a reply. 'No, you're a fucking liar she wouldn't do that to me!'

'Am I? Would she not? You just don't get it. All of this, everything is about God and the Devil, good and evil, light and shade, black and white, day and night, life and death, truth and BETRAYAL.'

The last word is spat out venomously. Conor, agitated and desperate, tries once more to get to his feet. However, it is another unsuccessful attempt and he sinks back down onto his knees. And straight away the voice is back at him. 'You are such a mug. She has so stitched you up. Do you not see that? Are you really that stupid?'

Conor thrusts his head in his hands and starts to rock back and forth on his heels. 'It's lies, lies, all lies, she wouldn't do that to me, no way!' His body jerks harder and faster. 'Now get the fuck out of my head. I know what you're trying to do.' Suddenly he lashes out, swings a punch at the church wall. An agonising jagged jolt judders up his arm. He winces and cries out a curse.

The shouts and screams in his head are full on. Hurriedly Conor reaches into his jacket pocket. But the blade is not Excalibur any more. That had been lost to the disingenuous sea. This blade goes by a different name. Breathing hard now, he runs the knife across remembered skin. Raising eyes heavenwards he feels the familiar sensation, that indescribable, indefinable symbiosis of excitement and release. Casting eyes downward he watches as crimson life gently oozes from him. The voices are gone now. His head is empty.

The voices of the two women had become nothing more than an occasional accompaniment to the ticking of the clock on the mantelpiece. And their sparse conversation carries more heavy pauses than Pinter at his best. Sipping cloudy tea and nibbling stale bourbons, Dina and Lou, young and old, each thinking thoughts of a damaged and desperate boy lost somewhere in the night. And try as they might to avoid doing so, the more they thought the more they retreated and withdrew into their solitary chambers of silence.

Of course for Dina, whilst she had huge concerns over the welfare and whereabouts of Conor, it was not her only worry. After enduring seven hours of questioning by the police, to clear her head some she had made her way to the bookshop. Upon opening the shop door a stench like no other hits her full on. Recoiling and clamping a hand over her nose and mouth, the girl walks tentatively, hesitantly through the shop.

Everything was as it should be, as she had left it. Nearing the door that leads to the flight of stairs to the flat of Breitner, the stench becomes discernibly stronger. Opening the door, Dina slowly makes her way up the stairs. With each step she took she knew what she was going to find in the flat. Entering the bedroom of Breitner the stench is unbearable. Drawing back the curtains in the room, the source is found, her worst fears realised.

'Jest to ze, Yitzhak?' The pale teenager in the striped pyjamas that are not pyjamas stands before Lazarus. The words mean nothing to him just a confusing babble. The boy barely understands his mother tongue, let alone Polish. Lazarus looks at the ragged vision in front of him 'Yitzhak?'

For once, the dulled brain of Baines responds with alacrity. For once he is thinking on his feet. 'Speak in English the Germans won't understand what we say then.' Lazarus looks at him quizzically. 'Since when have you been able to speak English Yitzhak?' Baines does not reply. Instead, he moves closer to the old man 'The money, Lazarus. Where is the money? Look, if we are to escape from the Germans we are going to need money' The eyes in the head of Lazarus Glick suddenly ember brightly.

'Yitzhak, tell me. Have you seen her? Have you seen Esther?' The boy is quiet for a moment. 'Yes. Yes, I've seen her. It's another reason why we have to find the money and get to her.' Lazarus leans forward his eyes wide. 'Where is she? She needs money?' Baines sighs inwardly, impatiently. 'We all need money, Lazarus. So, come on, let's get the cash together. You don't wanna keep your Esther waiting, do you?'

With that, the boy starts to untie the old mumbling man from the chair. And in the darkness the voice of Lazarus sound as liberated as his wrists were becoming, more alive than it had done in years.

'I have waited for her for such a long time. You have no idea. I waited and waited. And now, now you say she is finally here?'

As he attempts to untie the final knot that binds Lazarus, the boy answers tetchily. 'Yeah, I said so, didn't I? Look, just sit still will yer?' Finally, the cord snaps, fractionally before the patience of the boy. Lazarus rises quickly from the chair. He is suddenly a man that has shed long years of misery, tom down the walls of heartache. He looks across at Baines, his eyes ablaze with anticipation and excitement. 'Yitzhak, take her to me now.' The flickering TV screen flashes white across the impassive face of the boy. In his head the surreal has become the real.

'Yitzhak, please take me to her. I have missed her so much, and now. Now, I can never thank you enough for finding her. Baines suddenly stifles an overwhelming desire to laugh. And then recoils as the old Jew attempts to embrace him. In his discomfiture he finally finds a voice. 'Come on, let's go. The sooner we get the money the sooner you will see her.'

The attic of the rambling house is cold cavernous and pitch black. Climbing the ladder into the dark space, Baines follows as Lazarus leads the way. With the aid of a torch the pair gingerly step across ancient loft insulation, flat and threadbare now. On either side of them neatly stacked boxes stand, each adorned with flags of diaphanous cobwebs. Aiming the torchlight into a far corner, Lazarus approaches a stack of yellowing dust-covered newspapers. Bending down on his haunches, he moves them to one side. Thereupon he carefully lifts up some boarding.

Watching him in the darkness, the face of the boy is one of impatient anticipation. Finally Lazarus straightens up. In his hands he holds a small case which he slowly opens. Inside sparkling in the torchlight is jewellery, lots of jewellery, rings, broaches, necklaces, earrings, all gold, many with precious stones.

The boy is silent, literally open-mouthed. The voice of Lazarus is soft, wistful. 'There are over seventy pieces here. Each year on Esther's birthday I would buy two items of top quality jewellery. I bought it to one day give to her. And now that day I thought would never come has arrived.' A smile breaks out across his face. Baines looks at that smile and then down at the jewellery. 'So, how much is here? What is it worth?' Lazarus is quiet briefly. 'I have no idea. It was never about the money. You must know that Yitzhak?'

Not even listening any more, the pilled-up boy is trying to do the maths in his head. 'Gotta be twenty or thirty grand's worth here.' Lazarus does not answer. And in the darkness; both, one through love of a woman, the other through the love of money, have suddenly regained a modicum of lucidity of thought and action.

CHAPTER TWENTY

Since leaving the church in the early hours of the morning, Conor has been in a walking coma. Seemingly paralysed of thought and deed, he finds himself on the outskirts of town beside a sullen, swollen river. And now sitting on a damp riverbank, he absent-mindedly searches his pockets for cigarettes. But it proves a fruitless activity. Much like the last thought he had had many hours before, a distorted thought of seeking a future in the past.

Across the river a man and boy, probably father and son are fishing. Conor watches them, seeing normality oozing and secreting from every pore of their bodies. And it's beyond a simple envy he feel's. It's beyond words... He looks away, because to keep looking would tear him apart, again.

Up above a squadron of geese fly overhead. But the boy does not see them. He has already risen from the riverbank and is resuming his coma walk. Head down, his brain is on shut down now because it's easier that way. But somewhere deep down at the back of that brain, so dark and damaged, is a palace, a space of light and beauty, untouched and unsullied by the blackness. And that space is Dina, always Dina. And now opening his eyes and looking both inside and outside of himself in equal measure, the boy realises, if he did not already know it, that she really is everything, total. And neither police, nor no one else will ever keep him from she.

Finally, the coma walk is broken. Quickening his step a

sudden determination grips Conor hard. No longer is he dead pavement gazing, no. Now his head is up as he life-walks, skimming parked cars winging there cold metal, he strides boldly as he stares through passers by, because they all look the same, because they all mean less than nothing, because they are not her. On and on he walks. An old man standing by the bus stop talks to him as he passes. His words are lost on the wind.

A few minutes later the boy enters the estate. Where unsmiling same-again houses on same-again streets act as his guard of some kind of honour. Entering Dina's road now he walks with the same determined step and eyes focused straight ahead. In the distance he sees her house. He is nearly there, nearly safe. Well, for now.

Salt sweat runs down the brow of Hassler streaming into stinging eyes. Wiping his forehead with the back of his hand he then looks at it, calloused and covered in brick dust now. Closing his eyes against the burning sky he tries to recall a time when those hands were manicured and soft and white, those hands of an architect, gentleman gardener, Camp Commandant, killer.

His reverie is crudely shattered by the harsh shout of the British guard ordering him to quit 'pissing about' and get back to work. Muttering and cursing under his breath, Hassler heaves a large lump of rubble onto the wooden cart.

He and a group of other German prisoners of war had been put to work clearing the streets of the fruits of war, clearing the carnage of a thousand Allied bombs in the German town. To his fellow POW's and indeed to his British captors, he is Obergefreiter Breitner. He had stolen the identity, papers and uniform from the corpse of a Wehrmacht corporal he had discovered behind the ruins of a burning church in a nearby village a month previously.

A day later he surrendered himself to the British. And from there after a cursory interrogation he briefly joins the lost flotsam and jetsam of displaced persons, until he is finally interned in a German POW camp, safe as Obergefreiter Breitner. And all is well for a while. Until, until the chance meeting with a ghost.

Lazarus left Poland immediately after liberation. For him, as for so many other Jewish survivors there was nothing left there for them any more. All they had known, all those that they had loved were gone. family, friends, all gone forever.

For him, Poland had long since resembled a broken vessel, a fractured receptacle overflowing with pain, misery, bitterness and suffering. So, now penniless and alone he just upped and left one morning, shedding a skin he no longer recognised or wanted.

Carrying a few belongings in a knapsack, he headed west. In his pocket he still had the address of little Hana's relatives in London. His plan was simple. He would find them and tell them plainly the fate of the child. And if they would listen, could bear to hear it, he would tell them also of the fate of all the hundreds of thousands of other little Hana's, buried now in mass graves or just ashes scattered by a crying east wind across a weeping earth.

Upon reaching the outskirts of the German town, Lazarus also reaches the gates of a Displaced Persons camp. Situated about a mile from the town itself, the camp, a former army barracks, is crowded, cramped and chaotic. Run jointly by the Red Cross and an American Jewish Relief Organisation, the site was a vast landscape of flat grey-brown buildings, of which enclosed within, a myriad of nationalities, languages and people resided. And each one of them had something in common with their neighbour. Namely that, without exception all of them were searching.

Some were seeking relatives lost amongst the carnage of war, whilst others were just living for the day, desperately seeking out enough food to sate emaciated bellies and bodies. But all of them, every man, woman and child was somehow searching for peace of mind, a kind of sanity after the insanity of six years of war. And now Lazarus Glick, tired, broken and alone was one of their number.

On his arrival at the camp, Lazarus had registered in the sprawling administration building and from there been directed to his barrack by a harassed clerk from the Red Cross. Where soon after finding his bed and putting away his few belongings, he wandered out into the maelstrom of bodies and voices. Amongst the milling crowds he looked for familiar faces.

Finally, outside the large dining hall he comes across a couple of Jews, Zionist brothers he had known briefly in Krakow. Hoping against hope he asks them if they had seen Esther or knew of her whereabouts. The two young men just stared silently at him with blank faces. Their heads full of freedom and the Kibbutzim of the Promised Land.

The following morning, Lazarus decided to briefly leave behind the depressing confines of the camp and venture into town. Still being early the roads were relatively quiet, and the few Germans he did pass bowed their heads. Lazarus wondered if it was through a sense of guilt, shame or just disgust. He knew one thing. When he looked into the sullen down turned faces of these citizens of the Thousand Year Reich, he knew he should have felt something; anger, hate an overwhelming desire for revenge. But he felt nothing, not a thing. They were dead to him, walking corpses. Well, almost all of them.

The Lutheran church in the centre of town had suffered badly from heavy Allied artillery shelling. Surrounded by flattened shops and houses, it resembled a large broken tooth as its jagged masonry reached up forlornly into the early morning sky.

Loading its holy rubble unceremoniously onto wooden carts, Hassler now and again comes across mangled and torn prayer books, Once so piously and fervently clasped by hands now probably dead. Straightening his back and wiping his brow, Hassler squints hard against transient dust and stationary sun.

Suddenly in the near distance he sees a tall, very thin young man dressed in ragged clothes. The figure walks slowly along the bomb damaged road, getting ever closer to where Hassler and the other German prisoners of war are working. Raising his eyes from the road, Lazarus gazes idly to his left, sees the dust-covered prisoners in their despised grey-green uniforms. And amongst them he spots a face. He looks again in disbelief. But there can be no doubt. Those eyes so extraordinarily ordinary look back at him, squinting through the hanging brick-dust. And Lazarus knows them, sees the fear in them.

No more arrogance, no more cold detachment, just a kind of primeval fear. And as the dust floats higher it takes time with it. And for a second that could have been a minute and a minute that could have been an hour, the two men stare at each other. Until, until Hassler turns, jerks his head away to look at the ground, the trashed church, the crippled trees, anything just as long as he does not have to look any longer at the past he sees in that face. But it's no good.

And then it comes, the sight, sound and iron stench of blood fills his eyes, ears, nose and mouth, blocking all his senses. Shutting off his brain now he sees fleeting visions of decaying geraniums as warm piss streams down the inside of his leg. 'Arbeit, Arbeit!' The shrill voice of the young British corporal tears out in the direction of Hassler. Drawn back to now, he attempts to obey, starts to load rubble onto the tired cart. Claiming a calmness and sureness that he did not know he possessed,

Lazarus walks over to him and softly speaks one word. 'Hassler!' Hassler does not look up, does not stop working. But inside he is in turmoil. Through gritted teeth, Lazarus spits out. 'Look at me you bastard!' Finally, Hassler slowly raises his head, attempting to regain a little composure. 'You have the wrong person. What is it you want?' Lazarus snarls a reply. 'Time, that is what I want. I want the months and years, bastards, like you stole from me, and when you are finished with that, you can give me back my wife and family.'

He stares at the rivulets of sweat streaming down the face of the now ashen grey Hassler. 'What the hell are you talking about? You are talking like a madman.' Lazarus half-turns to walk away, but then breaks his step and gazes once more at Hassler 'Am I? Let's see if that British soldier thinks so. I am sure him and his superiors would be interested in knowing that they have such an enthusiastic killer of innocent people in their midst.' Once more he turns as if to walk away.

The voice of Hassler is a desperate hissed whisper. 'Wait! Look, what is it that you really want?' Lazarus sneers coldly at him. 'What I want, what I need you cannot give me.' Once more he goes to walk away. The voice of Hassler is now practically a whine. 'There must be something you want, Dollars, Diamonds? Look, it's hard for me to talk right now. Come back here at eleven tonight. I promise it will be worth your while. Are we agreed?'

Barely able to conceal his disdain and contempt, Lazarus slowly nods his head. And with that start's to walk away. The voice of Hassler follows him. 'How can I trust you?' Without turning around, Lazarus replies coldly. 'You can't.'

The girl sitting in the shadows of the ten pm bus station is Tonia today. Tomorrow, as is her wont, she will be somebody else. Huddled up against the world in her fake fur coat she feels safe here at the bus station. It is her second home. Her first is a crumbling bedsit off of the High Street. And there, here, now, when the girl is drunk, she likes to sing. One of her punters told her she sounded like Debbie Harry. But he is a smackhead. Sitting beside her, Baines watches her as she drinks from the bottle, and then wonders to himself why was it that every time he glances at that face it somehow looks different.

'If you ask me, it's a sodding stupid idea.' Tonia wipes red lips with the back of her hand and passes the bottle to Baines. He takes a hefty swig and faces her once more. 'Yeah, well I ain't asking for your opinion. I just wanna know if you are interested?' She looks at him smiling a rare smile. 'You said I could take what I wanted, yeah?' The boy nods his head slowly 'Yeah, of course.' Once more she smiles. 'Okay, but we need to stop off first at my place. I need to check out my wardrobe.'

It was the first time Dina had been back to the bookshop since discovering the body of Breitner in the flat. At his funeral six days later, she had been the sole mourner. Actually, perhaps mourner is the wrong term. Perhaps observer would be more apt. Not that there had been too much to observe. Just an elderly arthritic priest, an absence of flowers and a sky the colour of sheet iron.

A few days after this, Breitner's solicitor had sent her a letter stating that all of the affairs of Breitner were in order, and reaffirming the fact that on her coming of age the bookshop and flat would become hers. Rather than feeling happiness at this further confirmation, Dina merely felt strangely empty. Truth was her head was full of Conor and the precarious situation. It was like she was living two lives now hers and his. As if somehow they had become indistinguishable from each other.

And through the thin grey veil that barely separated one moment to the next, nothing seemed real nothing made sense. And the child in her so craved a positive resolution, a happy ever after conclusion to her and Conor's plight. But the woman in her, older than her years, knows that this is not going to happen. Knows that life just is not like that, and so. as the boy approaches the house this day, she is left in her confusion whether to wave greetings to him from across their abyss, or perhaps goodbye's.

Ushering him quickly into the house, all such feelings of doubt and confusion dissipate. She hugs him, grabs and clutches him holding him fast. Then, pulling slightly away she informs him with a half-smile that if he had been thirty minutes earlier, he would now be sitting in a police cell.

At the kitchen table, that high altar of decision making, the three conspirators conspire. And over the PG Tips and stale macaroons, Lou formulates a plan. As Conor and Dina listen patiently, the old lady takes threadbare brushes from a box and with sweeping strokes paints her blank canvas with colours borrowed from the realms of fantasy.

Barely pausing for breath she paints scanty flesh on the bones of her ideas, ideas which basically amounted to them stealing a high performance high powered sports car and then ripping off a city of London bank of its gold bullion, before hijacking a plane at Heathrow and flying to El Salvador. Her fire-eyed enthusiasm as she articulates her plan is only matched by Conor and Dina's distinct lack of it.

Not sure if Lou is serious or has merely lost the plot Conor gazes down at the floor with a bemused expression on his face, whilst Dina gazes up at the ceiling, sighing inwardly.

An hour later over cold tea and small talk, nothing has been decided. Other than that for now Conor was to hide out at the bookshop. Throughout the many hours of police questioning, Dina had possessed the presence of mind not to mention the flat above the bookshop. It was as if in the back of her mind she had somehow known that it would be needed eventually as a safe haven for the boy. And so it was now proving.

And by eleven pm that evening, Conor was ensconced in the rooms of a dead man. Where armed with a stock of food, a small electric fire and a future seemingly gauged, experienced, and lived on an hour to hour basis, he prepares to sleep. But not before his last waking thought is of Baines, Baines the gobshite, Baines the wastrel, Baines the young master criminal, Baines the...

'What you are now, once were we. What we are now, you too will be.'

Lazarus glances at the inscription carved above the cemetery gates as he slowly passes through them. In the near distance the bomb ravaged church is in total darkness, save for a small slither of moonlight patterning its eastern most extremity. Pulling up the collar of his coat, Lazarus sees a figure move slowly from what once was the central nave of the church. Twenty meters away Hassler calls out through the black. 'Are you alone?' As he poses the question he puffs nervously on a cigarette. Lazarus replies with a sneer. 'No, behind the wall over there I have Zhukov and a platoon from the Red Army.'

Hassler ignores the barbed comment and tentatively starts to walk towards Lazarus. Looking cautiously left and right he holds in his hand a small package. Lazarus looks at the moonlit face of Hassler and then down at the hand that carries the package. And already in his mind he is thinking that if Hassler's other hand goes anywhere near that package, then he will make his move. Standing in front of him now, this Camp Commandant turned Corporal, this exemplar of the 'Herrenvolk' looks suddenly fragile and vulnerable. Lazarus looks at him coldly.

'Give me the package. I have no trust in you.' Hassler does not move. Lazarus repeats the command. 'I want assurances.' Hassler clutches the package hard by his side. Lazarus feels a surge, a wave sweeping through his body and mind, a second liberation, a newly found strength. 'You are in no position to argue. Give me the damn package!'

A weird stunted laugh emanates from Hassler. But his eyes do not laugh. Instead they remain fixed on Lazarus, a strange look behind their banality, a look of a once possessed arrogance, superiority and hatred for the Jew in front of him. But in that look is also a new found look of fear, knowing the damage this Jew could do him, but albeit predictably it is his old time arrogance that wins out. 'You know, I have been going through all the long forgotten faces in my mind, and I came across yours. I can place you now. You are one of those bastards that murdered my geraniums.'

Hassler cannot see, is not able to comprehend the absurdity of his use of the word 'murdered' in such a context. But Lazarus can and he can barely contain his anger. 'You talk about the destruction of a few fucking flowers! How many human lives did you destroy? How many poor innocent bastards did you murder?'

Hassler does not feel the first blow, does not even see it coming. Neither does he feel the frenetic flurry of kicks and punches that follow. Every blow is a reflection of a pent up pain, misery, suffering, heartache. On the ground, Hassler is in a foetal position, motionless, silent as the blows with boot and fist continue to rain down. Until finally, still weak after years of brutal treatment and starvation, Lazarus slumps to his knees; spent. And there he stays for a minute or two sucking in the night in massive gulps. Side by side lay victim and perpetrator. For now, their roles reversed.

Wiping blood from his eyes, Hassler gets unsteadily to his feet. Whereupon, and inexplicably he reaches down and gently lifts Lazarus to his feet. And as he bends, heavy rivulets of blood drip from his gashed face and head onto the younger man. Now, and once more equally inexplicably a rueful smile animates the battered and swollen face of Hassler.

'I knew I should have bloody shot you over those geraniums.' Lazarus does not reply. Instead, walking away a few paces he drops once more to his knees and is violently sick. Finally straightening himself once more he faces Hassler. 'No more words. We have nothing left to say to each other.' Breathing hard he wipes his spew-stained mouth with the back of his hand. 'You probably have a hundred different excuses, thought-out justifications, and maybe even apologies for all you did. But I do not want to hear any of them. Now, just slowly pass me the package and we will go our separate ways.'

Hassler does not move. Instead, he gazes down at the package in his hand and then into the face of Lazarus. 'It's strange, not once have you asked me what is actually in the package. Not once.' Lazarus sighs deeply. 'It's not strange at all. You need my silence. So, in the package is either a gun or money. And seeing as you have not shot me yet, it must be money.' Again the German smiles a thin smile 'Smart Jew. But how can I trust you?' Lazarus once more sneers a reply.

'Look Hassler, not all men are created in your image. Some, most in fact, are decent people with compassion, mercy and integrity. Qualities that are a foreign country to a piece of shit like you, God why the hell am I wasting my breath on you, it's..!' Impatiently Hassler interjects 'Spare me the moral indignation. Look, as you said earlier, we do not have any more words for each other, so let's just conclude this business. If I give you the package you forget you ever saw me. Agreed?'

Lazarus looks into the swollen and blood stained face. And then nods his head, words no longer his allies. Slowly and silently Hassler hands over the package. In the hands of Lazarus the banknotes fold and bend lightly through the thick paper.

He speaks softly as if to himself. 'In one hand I take the blood money and out of the other fly's away my soul.'

Hassler sighs. 'Don't be so melodramatic. This whole war has been one big robbery; blackmail, theft, corruption, embezzlement. It's had it all.' His voice is rueful, or maybe sardonic. 'Anyway, how you reconcile your conscience is down to you. We are done now.' With that he slowly turns and goes to walk away. Lazarus follows him with his eyes. 'What I do not get is, why you didn't just buy my silence with a bullet? It would have been just one less Jew.' This time Hassler remains silent. Until at last turning round he faces Lazarus.

'Why kill a hypocrite? I mean chances are he will do it himself sooner rather than later. It's a guilt thing you see. There will come a day when he just cannot stand it any more. You see he will always wonder why he survived while so many better than him perished. No, I truly believe such a person will remain silent. Also, if he chooses to be foolish enough and open his mouth, many people will ask the obvious question. Just why did he take a good sum of money off, of a suspected Nazi war criminal?'

As the footsteps of Hassler fade into the darkness, Lazarus closes his eyes and listens until they are no more.

The girl with the Debbie Harry voice, smoothes down the front of her dress and turns to Baines, 'How do I look? 1940's enough, Jewish enough?' The boy shrugs his shoulders and ushers her into the house. Inside, from one of the reception rooms they hear the mellow sound of jazz. The girl smiles warmly. 'Look's like the old boy is having a party!' Turning to face him in the near darkness she can smell the stale booze on the breath of Baines. 'Look, just let me do the talking, yeah?' He snaps, slurs at her.

Entering the room, they find it in darkness. Lazarus sits in an armchair, his eyes closed but not sleeping, his hands gripping the arms of the chair, like the condemned man in an electric chair.

'Well, I said I would bring her and here she is.' Baines fumbles with a small side light until finally conquering it. At the burst of light Lazarus jerks forward out of his Miles Davis reverie. He sighs laden with age as he rises from the chair, his eyes as wide as one without age. 'Esther! Musisz sie w koricu, czekalem tak dlugo.' He falls heavy like a stone into the girl's arms. Awkwardly, self-consciously she holds him in those thin arms. Sobbing, grasping, clutching he sinks to his knees, his arms wrapped around her slender legs.

And as he mumbles tearfully words, she does not understand, she looks across at the boy questioningly, but he is wearing a look taken from one of the young dudes, as he again listens to instructions from the worm in his head. While in the background Miles Davis is wallpaper music now, playing to an audience past caring, no longer listening.

She does not know why, but the girl starts to tenderly stroke the head of Lazarus. The sparse, silver hair is soft to the touch. It reminds her of the hair of a baby, her baby, the one she… 'It's dance time, time to dance.' Baines wrecking-ball voice booms out across the memories and tears. Going over to the stereo he flips idly through the record collection of Lazarus. 'Shit, crap, never heard of it, old bollocks.' Finally, he chooses an LP that looks slow-danceable.

Clumsily he puts the disc on the turntable and drops the stylus, crashing it onto the vinyl with a squeal. Soon the sound of jazz-smooch fills the room. 'Come on then, I've brought your woman to you, just like I promised. Ain't you going to dance with her?' Slowly Lazarus disentangles his limbs from those of the girl. No longer sobbing, no longer broken but complete, he looks at his 'Esther' and speaks softly as he gently strokes her cheek.

'Kochanie, ja jestem tak szczesliwy, ze nie wroci bedzlenny razem ma zawsze.' Taking the girl in his arms they slowly start to dance. Both trapped in a world not of their making, a make believe world neither will ever be privy to. And as the music ends so to does their lives. They slump to the floor still holding still entwined. Above them, Baines looks down as viewing them from another room, from another time and place. Finally, he looks down at the gun in his hand and mutters softly, 'I kept my promise old man. Just like I said I would.'

CHAPTER TWENTY-ONE

In the room of the dead man, Conor can hear the sound of customers in the shop below. He hears their footsteps and the sound of soft chatter.

Dina had had to reopen the shop a few days back. Money was tight and becoming tighter. And as Conor listens to the everyday voices of the mainly middle-aged, middle-class customers, a stark realisation suddenly hits him, that he will never be like them, will never have the comfortable stability and security they take for granted. He will never be that bright son studying medicine at uni, will never be will never have, and this realisation is not a first time caller to him, no, of course not. But its previous visitations had only been to remind him of the bleak hopelessness of his present.

Now this realisation was showing him a future without a future. And it was incredibly strong, clear and utterly ruthless in its stone cold certainty. And he shudders as this cold blade of nihilism sears into his guts.

Lost amongst the ashes of his thoughts, he fails to hear Dina enter the room. She sighs softly to herself as she notices he is sitting in exactly the same position, on the edge of the bed staring out at rooftops, as she had left him three hours ago. Slowly she sits down next to him, placing a cup of tea on the stained bedside cabinet. 'Here, drink this. And don't let it get cold this time.'

He turns his head mechanically to face her, as if it's operated by an automatic swivel. And with a thin distracted smile he acknowledges her existence. And then with a dry mouth he goes to speak, but no words are his. Slowly he turns his gaze back to the window. Once more she sighs inwardly. She knows all the signs. Soon she won't be able to reach him at all. The voices would have won again.

And not for the first time and nor will it be the last, the girl feels totally lost and helpless. Another victim of a madness he could not seem able to conquer, quell or control. But the fragile looking childwoman is a fighter. No quitter, she. And now gently she wraps a thin arm around the shoulder of Conor. And once more in her head she is lover, mother, friend and protector, yeah, an Amazonian in the guise of a sparrow. Whatever it takes, whatever it costs she knows she will never leave him... Ever.

Lazarus never saw Hassler again. And on a bitterly cold day in 1947 he finally crossed the Channel to Dover.

Travelling light in possessions yet heavy in memories, he makes his way by train to London and there to the address of the relatives of little Hana. But all he finds on arriving there is a bombed out shell of what once must have been a very fine house. In his broken English, Lazarus asks a group of kids playing on a nearby bomb site if they knew where the inhabitants of the house were now?

He is met with blank stares and shoulder shrugs. Picking up his small case, Lazarus looks up at a tom winter sky that reflects his mood. Then he walks, walks stark grey London streets. Until tired feet and numbed brain tell him he cannot walk any more.

In a nearby pub called The Red Hart; George Albert Baines

holds court. He is the unofficial bar stool sage in residence. Fount of all knowledge, keeper of all wisdom, this is his domain his beer-soaked kingdom of pissed punch-ups, bullshit bonhomie and petty criminals. A land where the immortal words 'You're my best mate, you are,' are slurred and delivered seconds before drunken fist connects with drunken chin.

And it is into this underclass underworld, as day gives way to south London night that Lazarus Glick, with his tired still emaciated body that holds the pain of a thousand years, stumbles into.

With all eyes upon him, he enters the gloom of fag smoke and loud voices now hushed. Face forward, head slightly bowed he reaches the bar. Behind which stands the middle-aged landlord, who is doing his very best not to resemble one of his beer barrels. Short and rotund, he looks at Lazarus, unsmiling.

'So, what can I get yer?' Self-consciously and in his fractured English, Lazarus orders a beer and takes it to an empty corner table. Eyes that were once curious and suspicious now look away. Save for one pair. The bar stool sage does not like strangers in 'his' pub. It puts bubbles in his blood, especially strangers with foreign accents.

'Ain't seen you around here before.' His opening line is about as original as his fashion sense. He smooths down the heavy creases in his de-mob suit and looks hard at the painfully thin young stranger. Resting his beer glass on the small table the sage sits opposite Lazarus. Leaning back in his chair he somehow manages to crease his face into an expression that is hostile yet welcoming, aggressive yet friendly.

Lazarus replies nervously. 'No, I do not come from here. I'm from Poland.' 'Thank Christ for that, I thought you was a sodding Kraut.'

And so, the two men; oil and water, chalk and cheese, talk. Talk small, talk big. They talk. And by evenings end a strange bond has been formed, perhaps not an affinity, but a bond between the two, nevertheless.

The home of George Albert Baines is a small Victorian terrace a stones throw from the docks. And here he lives with his wife Annie and young son Michael. And in his castle by the river the sage is lord and master. And seemingly, well at least at first glance his appears to be a benevolent reign. So when he mentioned over a couple of bottles of brown ale that Lazarus come stay with him and his family, it seemed more of a benign order than a suggestion, an order that Annie, used to the domineering ways of the sage, instantly agreed to. And so, it was a done deal, Lazarus moved in that very evening.

Contrary to the opinion of many who knew him, George Baines did possess a heart. Not that he was ever one of those that ever wore it on his sleeve. No, in his case it was invariably to be found buried deep under a heavy coat, cardigan, flannel shirt and string vest. But it was there. And every now and again he would allow a glimpse of it to be seen. And ever since meeting the thin and broken young Jew, that heart, for whatever reason had been making more of an appearance than was the norm.

Of course, upon approaching Lazarus in the pub, the primary intention of the sage had been to fleece the young foreigner. But the strangest thing had happened. As words were spoken and Lazarus told his story in hesitant and halting English, the hidden heart of the sage slowly started to break cover. And his monochrome life, and world of ration card hardships shifted, drifted into a paler than pale insignificance, as Lazarus bared his crushed Jewish soul in the stale and smoky saloon of the Red Hart.

Sharing a room with young Michael Baines, Lazarus and the boy soon become close. And when the nightmares of mud and blood and the wild wild east visit the man, it is the small hand of the boy gently resting across heaving shoulders that soothe, if only for a while. And to the boy, the man gave hours, time that the sage due to his residency at the Red Hart could not give. And these hours were spent walking and talking in the park or by the canal, where the boy would ask the man about Poland and the war. And Lazarus would briefly and painfully reflect then gently deflect the questions of the boy away. He was nowhere near ready yet to confront that abyss.

And so, talk would be of the future not the past. An abstract future hazily planned against a backdrop of apocalyptic bomb site vistas. And as they gaze this starkness in Pinteresque pauses each paints a future that will never be, can never be. But it does not matter. Not here, not now, because the joy is in the dreaming, the planning, the imagining. And as the boy imagines so Lazarus would gaze at his eyes, as iridescent and shiny as a starling's wing, but in those eyes is also coldness an inscrutable aloofness he has seen before in the eyes of another child. Images of Hana flash across his mind briefly.

And it is true both children possessed such a cold and indecipherable look. And in the case of the boy it is often accompanied by a darkness that is both disturbing and unsettling. And this is nowhere more evident than when young Michael shows Lazarus some of his drawings. Crayon pictures depicting a child like vision of Armageddon. Where buildings burned, war planes plummeted and broken bodies lay everywhere.

And as carnage reigned, so a malevolent blood red sun beams down. Glancing down at the drawings Lazarus recoils; and wonders what the hell would make the boy draw such horrific scenes... The answer would not be too long in coming.

As every story has more than one side. So, as briefly mentioned before, there were two distinctive sides to George Albert Baines also. Firstly, there is his public facade; that of erudite barstool sage, always ready to offer informed advice and acquired wisdom. And then there was his private persona, that side of him only his family had the misfortune to see, a side driven by bitterness and frustration, a frustration that bled into his soul just a little more with each passing day.

You see, in his mind he was wasted, because he was more than just a back street pub sage, more than just a docker working his balls off for peanuts. And in his many moments of despair he would say to himself over and over that he was born into the wrong class, wrong country and wrong time. Indeed, to the sage his life just seemed to be a succession of wrongs with too few rights. And it was not as if he had not tried changing things. He had; time and time again. But the circle had become increasingly vicious.

They said he spoke the wrong way, had gone to the wrong school, came from the wrong side of the borough, once more too many wrongs.

At work at the docks, behind his back, his workmates called

him 'the doorman' on account of the countless doors of opportunity that had been shut in his face over the years. And that was it. How things were, are. And this horseshit of inequality stacked up built up, and the constant rejections and frustrations made him. Made him what he was, bitter, cynical, angry and unpredictable. And it was this anger and unpredictably that invariably manifested itself in the form of domestic violence he inflicted upon Annie and young Michael. Those who least deserved that blind, hopeless wrath.

And the scenario was always the same. After an evening at the Red Hart where as ever the sage had ruled the roost from his bar stool throne, he would leave at closing time and out in the sobering night air, reality would hit him like a truck, a searing and stark realisation that it was all artifice, a charade, a farce. His life was a sick pathetic joke. And his Red Hart kingdom was just an empire built on sand.

Catching his reflection as he passes shop windows on his way home from the pub, he would stop and stare even if he had told himself countless times not to. For staring back at him was the truth. He was nothing, a nonentity, a lost and insignificant bitter little man. And the surge of hopeless anger would sweep through him. And so to the sage came rage. A blind rage without direction barely controlled.

Reaching home, he is a powder keg of frustration and Annie and Michael are the inadvertent sparks. Come morning after a hell night, the sage is contrite and shamed for all he said and did. And for the rest of the day he wears the subdued coat of remorse, just as Annie and Michael wear their cuts and bruises, and the occasional broken bone.

Of this side of his character Lazarus had seen nothing. For since his arrival, the sage had managed somehow to keep the various demons that possessed him in check, this coming as a blessed relief to Annie and Michael. So, it came as an unexpected blow to them both when late one Sunday afternoon as they sat down to eat dinner, Lazarus informed the family that this would be the last meal he would share with them. After allowing the family time to overcome their initial shock and disappointment, he informed them that while he would be eternally grateful for their kindness and Generosity in taking him in and giving him a home, he nevertheless felt it was time for him to move on.

In response to their questions of 'What will you do?' 'Where will you go?' He was suitably vague. After all, he could hardly tell them that he had bought a house twice the size of theirs north of the river, with the blood money of a minor Nazi war criminal. So instead he merely told them that through the local Jewish community, he had made contact with a distant cousin who lived in Bethnal Green and whose existence he had known nothing of, and this make believe cousin had a spare room he said Lazarus could have for as long as he needed.

Throughout all of this the sage had remained silent; wearing an enigmatic look on his ruddy face, a look that Lazarus cannot read. As for Annie and Michael, they are shocked and disappointed he is leaving. Indeed, Michael, so often cold and detached, appeared inconsolable; tears welled in his eyes and his body shook. And before Annie could console the boy, he dashed from the dining table and bolted into the bedroom.

At six the following morning before the family were up, Lazarus left the house. But not before leaving five £50 notes on the kitchen table. Enough for the sage to buy his little terraced house. Or perhaps start his own small business. Maybe he could even pay for that good education his class and status had deprived him of. Either way, Lazarus just prayed to God that the money would not end up in the coffers of the Red Hart.

Finally closing the front door softly behind him, Lazarus cannot help but see the irony. Here he was leaving behind people he cared about, after he himself had been left so many times in the past by those who had cared about him.

Later that day with his meagre possessions, Lazarus moved into the rambling shambling house that would be his prison of memories for the next thirty-odd years. Yet paradoxically within its dust-heaped walls of painful memories, he would somehow find a kind of calm sanity as he would become more and more lost inside his very own private hell. Until, until he would meet the latest of the Baines line, the late seventies model. And, well, you know the rest.

The voice was soulful, doleful, bleak but clear. It had told Conor that the walls of the bedroom of the dead man were moving inwards, and so consequently, it had instructed the boy that at ten minutes past the hour every hour, he was to pace across the room from left to right counting and measuring the distance. And this he duly did. And it was so. The walls were closing in on him, in all senses.

Down below in the shop, Dina could hear his walking, his metronomic march a pedantic pace never missing a step. Back and forth and back and forth in a four-four time only he could hear.

Time and again she had spoken to him until she was blue in the face, telling him that the walls were not closing in. And now in her desperation to convince the boy, she asked a local builder to check the walls for movement. The man, with a look of incredulity on his face, gazed at Conor and Dina as if they were from another planet. 'Trust me, the walls are fine. They ain't going any place they will see us out that's for sure.' And then he had left. Left Conor and Dina to another day of silence, pacing, silence, pacing.

CHAPTER TWENTY-TWO,

'And amongst the mocking shadows of sadness I'am the slaughter man, the murderer of your hopes and dreams. And before me came another slaughter man, who murdered all of mine.'

Baines watches the flames flicker as time flits and drifts by in a Valium and vodka haze. He has no idea why he has torched the home of Lazarus Glick. Perhaps the worm in his head had ordered it? Or perhaps the booze in his blood had deemed it appropriate to consume the house in flames? What can be discounted is that the boy saw any symbolism in his action. For as he stares transfixed at the devouring orange blaze, his booze-addled thoughts are of self-preservation.

The flames are merely a burning blanket that would cover and then obliterate the scene of his crime. In no way were his actions of a compassionate nature. In no way, despite his perverse satisfaction in feeling he had performed a merciful act by reuniting Lazarus with Esther, could he nor would he ever have the foresight or perception to realise that by casting Lazarus to the flames to be reunited with his Esther, he was also reuniting him with the six million of his people who in one way or another had been turned into ashes; each one a name, a person, a soul, a loss.

Starting up the tired old engine of the Hillman, Baines takes one last look at the blazing house. In the late evening black, the bronze of the fire reflects flickering across his pale deadpan face. Suddenly in the near distance he hears sirens wailing as flashing blue lights appear. Turning his head slowly to the left, the architect of the chaos glances at the two fire engines through glazed eyes.

And the sense of unreality of it all It is. It is... Unreal. And he wonders that if he were to close his eyes and count to a hundred, whether on reopening them he could be someone else, someone good. Even if for only one day. Weller. Yeah, Paul Weller, that is who he would be. Just for one day, twentyfour hours of doing the right thing, saying the right thing, wearing the right clothes. Yeah, up on the Marquee stage spreading the groove around some.

Suddenly, his pissed-up reverie is interrupted by a sharp and heavy tapping at the car window. Startled, the boy opens his eyes and jerks his head to his right, and sees the police uniform, the grim face, the end, and for the umpteenth time its time, time to step outside of himself again. Raising the gun slowly and deliberately, Baines watches himself fire through the glass at the uniform and continues watching as the face of the uniform explodes into a hundred red pieces. Then it falls backwards in a slow, silent stagger before crumpling to the tarmac.

The boy watches the blue descent as it seems to take forever. Then the sound of hoarse, coarse shouting kicks in a different kind of reality. Slamming the car into gear, he revs the engine and pulls away.

Lou was gone. As unexpectedly as she had come into the lives of Dina and Conor, so now, as equally unexpectedly she had departed. She had not said goodbye, had not left a note.

'Like the perfect stranger you came into my life, and then like the perfect Lone Ranger you rode away, rode away.' No. No perhaps not. The thought of old Lou with a mask and on a horse was too bizarre to contemplate. Yet the lyrics stuck in the mind of Dina. And she missed the old woman. Hated the uncertainty, despised the fact that she had no idea why Lou had upped and left without a word, nothing.

She did not tell Conor about Lou leaving. There seemed little point, because in the room of the dead man the walls were still closing in. And the boy was closing off little by little. And tears came fast and furious to the strong girl, but the boy never saw them. She would battle and bottle the bastards up to make sure he never did, because someone had to be strong. But it was so hard to be strong.

And although she missed the old woman, she missed Conor more. But both were gone one way or another. And the loneliness the girl felt was tangible, all-consuming. During the days it was not bad as she was preoccupied with the shop, but the evenings. They were a living death, partly spent with Conor in a ticking bomb silence, partly spent at her home, such a morgue of memories.

And, so now, under lengthening spring evening shadows, Dina finds herself, as so often these days, at the cemetery, Home of both her mother and grandmother. Kneeling by the headstone of her mother on the damp, soft lush grass, a hundred thoughts crowd her mind. But her jaw stays slack, unable to articulate any of them. All she does know is that if wishes were fishes, she would wish her mum back to hold her tight and to tell her what the hell to do. But now all that, was left her to was to cry. Because in her head it was like she was listening to some never ending song with an achingly sad melody that would choke her; getting her every time.

And not one hundred vivid and bright orange dresses or a thousand books would be able to lift her veil of tears. And now in these desperate moments she wonders if somehow some way she is joining Conor in his madness. Was it a price she must pay for loving him? And she thinks this over and over, until all cried out this tired old woman of seventeen years lay's down once more upon the grave of the mother she had barely known. And as light gives way to dark, Dina sleeps amongst the silent.

As is often the case with those who have loved and lost, when after the loss weeks give way to months, so in the grieving minds of those who have lost and been left behind, a saintly haze descends upon the image of the one who is gone. And when the one who has been left behind thinks of that saintly image, he or she cannot see the flawed and tarnished brass of reality. No. All they can see is a glittering and golden image perfect in every respect. And when on occasion they speak of that golden image, it is invariably in almost reverential tones, an illogical, irrational eulogy to the ghost of a memory.

And each had loved and lost in their different ways, Dina, Conor, Baines and Lazarus, all of them. And memories of the loved ones who had left them were such heavy millstones around such frail necks. But life goes on, as the empty platitude tells us. The days are there to be got through as we bear the unbearable. For it's not the condition of being strong. It's the condition of being human. Sink or swim. And the bottom line is that we will always try to swim, because the fear of death is always greater than the fear of life, whatever the situation, whatever the circumstances we hold on grimly. Because ultimately the alternative is... There is no alternative.

Baines sold the jewellery of Lazarus to a Camden Town fence called Terry. A man of around forty who possessed more than a passing resemblance to a disgruntled amphibian. And as he slowly counted out and handed over the tenners, the boy fully expected to see and feel traces of pond slime on them.

Terry had paid two grand for the jewellery. Baines knew he was being stiffed, the gear was worth at least double that, but Terry was the only fence he knew. And anyway, beggars can't be choosers. Truth was the boy was past caring. Everything was beyond fucked up, everything.

And now in a damp flat that smelt of cat piss and creosote, taking crumpled tenners from an amphibian, the boy closes weary eyes and with a final thread of something akin to decency, coherency and lucidity, he thinks to himself that he should feel something, anything for the three lives he has taken. But his brain refuses to cooperate. Instead, he floats out of himself up to the ceiling.

Where opening burning eyes he looks down on himself, searing through muscle, flesh, sinew and bone. He sees nothing there. He is empty. Only his head is full, crammed tight with manic voices, a shrill singing worm, and Conor, always Conor.

Something was calling Conor home, because this was not his home. This was just the room of a dead man. Four walls closing in ready to bury him. And with Jesus in the red corner and the Devil in the blue corner, the boy is just about ready to cut loose, to try and run once more from the carnage between his ears.

Nervous and pacing faster than normal, he has been waiting for Dina to come up to him all morning. It was not like her not to come up to him. Throughout the morning he had heard customers tapping lightly on the door of the shop. But he had not heard the familiar sound of the shop bell. And now as the hours pass so his anxiety grows. As inside his head voices awaken, haranguing him and mocking him in equal measure.

'Well, she has finally done it. She has blown you out, mush. What a waste of fucking space! I told you not to trust the bitch. They are all the same. You never listen, that is your problem... The slut is probably with another geezer already.'

On and on the toxic voices rumble and mumble their poison. Chaotic runaway trains on the fractured tracks of his mind. Now, ultra conscious of every sound and movement, the boy paces once more. Suddenly a sound enters the room, a sound like waves crashing onto shingle. And as he stops pacing a coldness brushes past him, he hears a voice; soft, wistful, faint and brief. Just a few words in a language the boy does not understand.

And as the words trail off so the coldness dissipates. Finally leaves, if it were ever really there. Conor stands rigid as the voices temporarily depart. Finally, he slowly starts to move again. His crippled eyes stare wildly in confusion and fear as he walks towards the window counting his paces, his voice rising steadily. 'Eins, zwei, drei, vier, fünf, sechs, sieben.'

As he calls out ever louder the scent of geraniums fills the room, faint at first then stronger and stronger. Then, despite the coolness of the room flies suddenly appear, their repetitive buzzing the celebratory song of an unseen decay. As the flies swarm his head, Conor continues his pacing. 'Eins, zwei, drei,' thoughts explode in his mind shrapnel jagged, so fragmented and disconnected. Sweat streams into his eyes as he suddenly stops pacing.

Above him the flies buzz louder still. Interrupting pointless jerky flight, they close in on him just like the walls. Crumbling to his knees, the boy howls a helpless, hapless, hopeless wail.

It would be the final act. Time was up. Even Baines in his permanently pilled and pissed-up state knew it. It would only be a matter of time till the police caught up with him. After all, they were funny like that, they seemed to take particular exception to one of their unarmed officers being shot in the head by an out of control seventeen year old.

Truth was, in many respects it was a surprise to him that they had not tracked him down already, because beyond dysfunctional now, Baines even if he had been able to, did nothing to avoid capture. Indeed, he could barely remember shooting the officer. The incident was now only a hazy cloud of a spent memory to him. Taking its place alongside the other nebulous memories that flitted through his addled mind.

Back in the squat now, he is practising death. For hours on end he has remained still and silent on his soiled mattress. Beside him lay the detritus of his life; empty booze and pill bottles, and a few crumpled tenners. Most of the money he had got for the jewellery was gone now. Blown on horses that could not comprehend the concept 'to run.' And on a Brighton whore with cold hands and a name he could not recall. But with nimble fingers he would not forget, for as he had lain sleeping in the squalid flop house, so she with her agile fingers had adroitly had it away with a big chunk of his cash. No tart with a heart, she.

And so, as a worm starts to sing once more in his fevered mind, so the boy with automaton movements finally arises from his filth, and once again surrenders to the rhythm of its song... An accompaniment to a denouement.

CHAPTER TWENTY-THREE

Three days and three nights the girl lay at the grave side of her mother. Cemetery gates are opened cemetery gates are closed. People came and people went. But she remains an object of curiosity and sideways stares. Finally, on the morning of the fourth day she rises from the grave. No epiphany, no other-worldly visions or manifestations precipitated her rising. Perhaps they are just reserved for believers.

No, something as earthly as rain hastened her back onto unsteady feet, and now soaked to the bone, a bone child. She shelters from the downpour under a wilting tree, and shivers as her mind attempts to engage once more with a world that was becoming a stranger to her.

Thirsty, hungry and cold, the blue child rises from green grass and squint's brown eyes upwards to grey skies. Beyond cemetery walls cars roar and stray dogs howl, but she feels no affinity with such events. And she knows she is losing her grip letting it slip, but she cannot stop it.

As the rain abates as quickly as it had arrived, Dina bends down and scoops up a handful of saturated and cold earth, she has an overwhelming need to feel the cold earth against her skin, to feel what her mother and grandmother feel. In that way, in her mind she would be one with them again.

Slowly, with eyes still raised heavenwards she starts to smear the cloying damp earth onto her face and body, its coldness making her start. Behind her, fifty yards away she does not see the battered old car pulling up in the cemetery car park, its squealing brakes torturing the silence. Inside the vehicle, the pale and sickly looking boy stares out across at Dina through dead-rimmed red-rimmed eyes. A faint smile briefly etches itself across his dry cracked lips. It is more then he could have hoped for, its solid gold serendipity.

The womb is dark and warm. But it's not one of life and blood: but one of dead metal. It is not a space for nurturing life. No, little by little the metal womb is destroying it, stealing it away. And now, scared, desperate and forcibly foetal, Dina has no idea how long she has been in the boot of the car of Baines. Has no idea of where it's heading, nor what his intentions are, but as the minutes pass so the air in the womb becomes more and more scarce. And what air is left is pervaded with the stench of old rubber and motor oil.

So, in the darkness the girl tries to limit her breathing to small shallow breaths. As in her mind she goes over and over recent events, of how the boy had grabbed her in the deserted car park, of how he had screamed at her demanding to know where the fuck Conor was, of how she had remained silent and defiant, of how she had tried desperately to break free from his pincer grasp. But despite her frantic attempts at escape he had roughly bundled her into the boot of the car... That was?

She tried to think how long ago that had been. But in the metal womb tomb time had lost all meaning. At the beginning she had tried banging her fists against the metal in the hope of someone hearing. But no one does for no one can. But frantically in her blind panic, Dina continues slamming and punching the obdurate metal with her increasingly bloodied hands... Nothing... No knight in shining armour.

So now alone in the utter darkness she lies curled in a ball, resigned to her fate. And it's kind of okay. It's cool, because she feels so very tired now. And a warm fleecy blanket of calm envelopes her, and it's like she is floating, weightless. Until suddenly, with a squeal of brakes the car comes to a shuddering halt bringing the girl back to a here and now she thought she was done with. But now in the quiet, she hears the footsteps of Baines crunching gravel as he walks towards the boot of the car.

Conor finally leaves the flat of the dead man at around midnight. Empty and spent, the voices have departed now leaving just his echoing footsteps desolate amongst the silence.

And now, after walking empty streets for an hour or so, the boy makes his way to the park. Sitting on a moss-covered bench, he peers through the darkness watching the midnight foxes scavenging trash bins; living out ephemeral little lives as best they can. Before either mange, starvation, or some apathetic prick in a speeding tin box on wheels terminates their existence.

Just then from somewhere in the night words come to the boy from he knows not where. 'Nothing I ever do or feel ever feels like I felt it with you.' Over and over he softly spews the words, a mantra that precipitates the tears forming in his eyes. He has no idea where the hell the words come from, but he knows just what they mean. They mean Dina. Everything always comes back to her. Sinking his chin down onto his chest he silently mouths her name, bittersweet on his tongue.

By first light the foxes had gone and so had the boy. Tracking a familiar path he had walked the short distance to the home of Dina. Where upon arrival, he is met by shut windows and curtains drawn like closed eyelids. She is gone. Conor slumps down on the front doorstep. And all he can think about is that the voices are right. How could they be wrong. He is less than nothing. At that, and right on cue, they commence their berating of him.

'You have fucked it up again. So, what is new, he fucks everything up. Yeah, a real King Midas in reverse, everything he touches turns to shit.' Haunt, taunt and rage. They do not let up, do not quit it for a minute. And as ever there is only one way to silence them.

And so, the tired old ritual starts again, a cold blade against warm skin, and as the last screaming and mocking banshee voice departs, so the boy slumps forward, a small death his.

Drunken, Baines roughly pulls the blue child bone child from the metal womb tomb. Desperately like a fish out of water, Dina gulps in the cool air. Drunken, the boy starts to push her deeper into the dense woodland a gun at her back. Confused and disorientated she stumbles and falls. Drunken, cursing, he drags her to her feet and presses the barrel of the gun against her head. But oblivion does not come. Just a voice like a deep, dark, distant growl.

'I ain't playing any more games, now where the fuck is Conor?' Before Dina can reply, if indeed she had intended to, Baines has rammed her hard against a tree. In the gathering darkness old bark presses deep into young skin. Breathing hard, his vodka mouth slams against her flesh. She tries so hard to break away, but he is frenzied, kissing lips, neck, hair, breasts.

And all the while the gun barrel presses harder, deeper against her left temple. Drunken, with his left hand he paws her body tearing at her clothes. But she no longer resists, for she cannot, because she is no longer there.

Finally sated, but not content, Baines pulls away, turns away, unable to look any more at that which he has defiled brutalised. But it's impossible. Time and again his eyes are drawn back to her as she sits at the base of the tree unmoving. And she seems smaller and more fragile than before. And at this moment he does not know whether to love her or despise her, destroy or save her. Whether to possess or dispossess, own or disown this crippled child-woman. Finally, his confused and distorted reverie is ended by the worm, no longer singing its song. Its lyrical voice replaced by a harsh and rasping tone.

'What the hell are you doing? I don't believe you are mooning over some bitch that is not real, that does not exist. Are you really that stupid that you would be sidetracked by a no one, a nothing, a nobody, now just walk away, but every now and again glance back over your shoulder and survey the carnage you have left behind. And smile. Wear it as a badge of honour... Now, find that fucking boy!'

If the plan of Conor was to walk himself into a state of near physical and mental collapse, then it was working. Hour after hour he had trekked nowhere streets searching for her, nothing, not a sign. But now he finally rests. Feeling the loneliness of ten lost souls he slowly lights a cigarette and watches the trains noisily thunder across the viaduct.

Now standing alone in the derelict and vandalised children's playground, he closes his eyes and tries to locate an original thought in is mind. Just any thought he had not thought a thousand times before. But it is futile, hopeless, groundhog, just recycled images over and over. Dina, Baines, Dina, Baines. Saint and sinner, the sacred and the profane of his little world, If only he could, no, no more maybes, what was the point? He...

Suddenly, just then in the swirling darkness he is no longer alone. For there, as if appearing from nowhere stood a tall man with a brown dog. His looks are those of everyman, a composite of the average. And in a soft, hollow voice he says his name is Cody. Conor, taken aback at his sudden appearance, does not reply, instead just looks at this man of indeterminate age. Well, perhaps his age is not so indeterminate, for soon he is exclaiming in a matter of fact tone that he is a thousand years old. And his dog barks as if to validate and verify the statement of his master.

Inwardly Conor sighs, but something compels him to listen. Listen, as licking the air like a lizard, Cody starts to speak once more. He tells the boy that he is here to bear testimony. To pass onto Conor the wisdom he has acquired in his millennia of life. And so, with pale grey eyes that had professed to have seen so much life but were somehow lifeless, Cody turns to Conor once more. 'You know, over the decades and centuries I have seen all that there is to see. Nothing new under the sun you may say.

In my thirteen lives I have witnessed all, both the good and the evil in mankind, the beauty and the ugliness of humanity. I have read assiduously the works of the greatest philosophers and theologians. And I have listened to the words of the wisest men and women through the centuries.' The voice of Cody suddenly trails away. Gazing out across the prosaic urban vista that surrounds them, he finally fixes his gaze on a spot far off on the horizon. Slumping slightly forward, as if the weight of each one of his thousand years were pressing down on him, he finally resumes speaking, his voice alternating between sandpaper and silk.

'Facts truths, believe me, they are rarer than an honest politician. People throughout the ages are always seeking the truth, demanding it. Perhaps there is no such thing as truths, just interpretations. Anyway, what truths there are, are all around us if only people would open their eyes to them. But most people do not want to really know the truth if it does not suit them... Truly, as things stand, as they have always stood, the only conclusion that can be reached is that there is no point, no logical reason for the existence of mankind, this creator of wars, pestilence, misery, no, there can be no cogent argument for, nor justification for his continued existence... Unless.'

All the while Cody has been speaking, Conor has been silent, silent and confused, he has watched and listened to this strange apparition of a man. And he has no idea what the hell to think. Is he for real? His internal questioning is rapidly brought to a halt by Cody. 'It's a well known fact throughout the ages there have been countless false messiahs, supposed saviours of humanity who have proved to be no more than charlatans, purveyors of false hopes, deliverers of nothing.'

Once more Conor is silent, his eyes fixed on Cody. 'The Jews, perhaps the Jews have got it right. They say that in every generation thirty-six just men, the Lamed Waf are born to take the world's suffering upon themselves.' finally, impatient and tetchy, Conor breaks his quiet.

'Look, just who the hell are you? What are you? And why you telling me all this weird stuff?' Cody replies calmly and slowly. 'All those dark times, you remember? Black places where you tried to escape from, when you cried to die. You screamed out silently from the darkness, calling out for someone to take away the pain. Anyone, God, anyone, just to make it all go away. Well, all the time I was there with you.'

Tears well in Conor's eyes, tears of rage and frustration, he blurts out his pain. 'How the hell could you have been there? And if you were there, why in the name of fuck didn't you help me!?' Cody replies softly. 'Help you? How could I? Don't you get it, don't you understand that I'm just an observer. All that happens, all that occurs is preordained, the blessed and the cursed. Things are what they are... But.' He suddenly falls quiet. 'what?' Once more the boy stares hard into those lifeless grey eyes.

A faint smile creases Cody's lips. 'Like I said, perhaps the Jews really have got it right. Maybe in every generation there are a select few who take upon their shoulders the suffering of the world. And if this is the case, why should these individuals just be claimed by the Jewish faith? I mean, wouldn't it be logical if all faiths are represented?'

Conor sighs somewhat wearily. 'Look, where are you going with this? This means less than nothing to me.' Cody is quiet again briefly. 'You still don't see where I'm going with this? Okay, so you remember all those times when you called into the darkness, 'Why me?' what if the answer to that question is that you are the one, one of the Lamed Waf of your generation your faith, always to carry the suffering of the world within his soul.'

Confused, weary and annoyed Conor responds angrily.

'What the hell you saying, I'm not Jewish!' Cody sighs loudly. 'Have you actually been listening to a word I have said, look that is the whole point of my argument, why should it only be the Jews that have their Lamed Waf? Why can't other faiths have their sacrificial lambs of suffering, I mean, maybe, just perhaps you are the just man of your faith, your God.'

Holding back his angst and frustration, the boy finally explodes. 'There is no faith, there is no God, there are no just men, no, it's just every bastard for himself. You are so full of shit. Now just get the hell out of my head!' A sudden rush of tears roll down his face, and when they clear, he is alone... Cody and the dog are gone.

'Men and women ponder thy mortality, for thou art but tiny blades of grass in a vast and infinite field.'

The weather that early autumn day was perfect. A gentle zephyr breeze stirred lightly, warmed by a serene October sun that beamed down with an avuncular-like benevolence. It was the kind of weather that makes one wish to bottle it and carry it around forever, not that such meteorological concerns were on the mind of Dina. But if they were, she would have prayed that a huge deluge of rain would fall from the heavens and wash her shivering body clean.

Because for the past two hours she had lain self-blaming, shamed and naked on the floor, for unclean she felt and could not shake off that feeling. And three showers and near flaying of her skin with a hard brush could not remove the stain, the taint of him. And now closing her eyes and she is back there again, making her way out of the sun-dappled woodland, her body aching and hurting but her soul aching and hurting more.

Finally, she had limped past a cluster of old oaks that had seen it all before, and then she had reached the clearing at the edge of the wood where Baines had parked the car. But it and he had been long gone. Looking down at the tyre tracks in the mud, Dina had felt a sudden rage, an anger surging through her like a jolt of electricity. And then without even realising it she had howled, screamed, started scratching and scraping at her skin, attempting to eradicate every last memory and touch of the drunken boy.

But already in her mind a dark realisation is forming, a swirling maelstrom of thoughts and emotions. Guilt, anger, hurt, humiliation. And finally, revenge. Scowling, sneering, jaw clenched tight shut, she sees the face of Baines in every tree trunk, branch and leaf. Until from somewhere deep down inside herself the hurt and hatred gives her a kind of strength.

At last she rises slowly from the bathroom floor. It is dark now and in that silent darkness Dina dresses. Yeah, the hatred is so strong she can feel it, taste it. No longer is she that fragile bone child hoping that her mother's grave will open up and swallow her alive. And no longer does she need an orange dress as a suit of armour. Because now, she who had lost all hope, sense, direction and meaning in her young life, felt a galvanisation, a sense of purpose she had rediscovered through pain.

A rediscovery attained alongside a renewed and more defined sense of love and hate. So, while it is the desire for vengeance that is giving her strength, she barely knew she possessed, what about the love part? That is easy, simple. She so totally missed her beautifully ugly boy, and now it's time to get back to him. To stop the graveside odyssey, to shake the cobwebs of madness

and doubt from her mind... As if that were truly possible...
Anyway, just the need to find him, before...

By now, and it will come as no great surprise to learn, that deep
in the heart and soul of Baines lies a half-open wound. The
consequence of which being that the more booze he shifted
down the back of his throat, the more the wound gaped open,
oozing out its poisonous pus of malice, bitterness and frustration. And now apart from a few brief moments of lucidity
and sobriety, the half-open wound, poked and prodded by
the worm in his head, ceases to be able to close at all. Instead
staying perpetually open, it's a weeping chasm seeping out
paranoia and hatred for a world, a time, a place he no longer
understood, if he ever had.

'And all that really matters is...'

Looking at his reflection in the car's rear view mirror, Baines
touches his thin face with the tips of his fingers. And there is
no getting away from it, his skin is turning yellow. Even the
whites of his eyes are white no longer. In passing he informs
the worm about his yellowing skin. But it had merely replied
that he should not worry as a future of economic prosperity
and a cure for the world's ills lay in the far east, and were the
Chinese and Japanese not yellow?

It then went back to its white noise singing, leaving the boy
to reconnect lips around the neck of a bottle, a bottle that
stops his shakes and numbs the pain in his bloated, moribund
liver. And now sitting slumped in the front seat of his old car,
the mind of the boy vacillates between thoughts of Conor and

Dina. And as he does so his cancerous paranoia intensifies and grows, like a toxic weed whose tendrils bind throttle and suffocate the life out of the last tenuous and threadlike grip he holds on reality.

Finally draining the bottle dry, he starts up the irritable old engine of the car and after getting fresh instructions from the worm, he heads east towards the town, his yellow waxy skin seemingly indistinguishable from the yellow glare of the street lights that illuminate his crooked path.

CHAPTER TWENTY-FOUR

'Folie à Trois.'

The lake on the edge of the town is chemical blue. No fish can live in its vast shimmering cobalt expanse. Not one creature could exist in its man made unnatural waters.

Situated in a disused quarry whose topography resembled a dark-sand moonscape; well it did through the eyes of a child, the lake had once been everything to the drunken boy. Playground, meeting ground, battleground, it speaks, reeks of his childhood, reeks of long ago puerile pacts and broken boyhood allegiances. 'Thick as thieves us we'll stick together for all time. And we meant it, but it turns out just for a while.' The words of the song echo through his mind, jostling alongside faces of long forgotten friends and foes, actors in a memory.

And now shrouded in an early morning mist, Baines, gin bottle in one hand, gun in the other, sits on the sloping sandy bank of the lake and remembers, remembers a time that may or may not have happened. Remembers that hot summer's day when he had pulled the drowning boy from the lake. Remembers those crippled eyes and long pale face. Remembers the boy dripping wet, gasping, spewing out chemical blue... That was... He tries to recall how many years had passed since that first encounter with Conor? He closes his eyes as if this would somehow aid memory in his addled mind. It did not, instead a voice not that of the worm reverberates harsh and grating between his ears.

'Greetings from the abyss, London calling, London calling to the faraway boy... You know, you are to blame for all of it. You should never have pulled him from the fucking lake!' The voice seems to choke, gag on its own vitriolic bile and then dissipates.

Opening his eyes again, Baines feels he has somehow lost minutes, hours, days, but knows he is too lazy to try and retrieve them. Instead, he gazes up at the sky where a sun momentarily blinds him, its rays bouncing, shimmering and shining off of the surface of the chemical lake. It briefly affords the lake the incongruous appearance of some tropical lagoon.

Suddenly feeling an inexplicable weariness, the boy lays back on the sandy bank of the lake. He has decided. Well, more accurately the worm has decided for him that he will wait at this place, this place where it had all started. Because the boy would come eventually; he had to. It would always be somehow calling him back.

For days after, Conor had looked out for Cody and his dog, but without success. He was just left with the man's words. Words that intrigued, fascinated, but ultimately confused and bewildered him. Certain words such as, 'messiah' 'just man' 'sacrificial lamb of suffering' resonate again and again. Unsurprisingly, the voices mock him for even contemplating that the words of Cody held any validity or truth. And equally unsurprisingly, it is the rasping and belligerent tones of the flame voice that leads the chorus. Pacing faster now, Conor attempts to block them out. Soon his walk becomes a run and days, months, years fall from him like scales from a fish. And he wants to stop running but he cannot.

Past the chippy, along the canal, feet become yards become miles. His running is 'Gump-esque' pumping legs, fast arms slow brain. And as like so many times before the girl is everywhere and nowhere. She is in parked cars she is by the canal she is in the shadows, near but too far away. And still he keeps running.

Until lungs bursting, heart pounding and with eyes wide open shut, he at last stops running. And before him in the near distance stands the old quarry. Looking around himself he is not sure how he got there. But it does not matter, because at last he is finally...

Tired of walking, Dina had hailed the taxi outside of the train station. She soon regretted it. To say the taxi driver had body odour issues was an understatement. He stank to high heaven. Not only this, but soon in broken English he was regaling Dina with full and graphic details of his recent hernia operation. Sighing, the girl winds down the window. Not only to release the stench of the man's body but also his words.

At last reaching the road that leads to the quarry, Dina can take no more. Hurriedly paying the man the fare, she bolts from the taxi. In front of her a white road winds serpentine before her. At the end of it lies the quarry, its dark-sand vista cold, eerie and uninviting. Slowly, and with a certain amount of foreboding, the girl starts to walk along the white road.

To her left in a sparse field, gulls and crows, black and white, squabble over such slim pickings. As she walks a fine rain patterns her face, but she notices it not. Nor does she notice the cold easterly wind that has seemingly sprung from nowhere. And as she walks ever nearer. she is not sure why she is heading to the quarry and its chemical lake.

Only that, only that a few months back, Conor had told her of its existence. Had informed her of the enormous importance the quarry had played in his childhood. And for one of the very few times since she had known him, as the boy told her of the place his voice lost its gentleness and calmness, to take on a whole new expressive and animated tone. He had briefly spoken of happy and sad times at the quarry, of spending moments there in light and shade.

She had asked him to elaborate, but Conor had clammed up dropping his eyes from her gaze. And that was that he had never spoken of it again. But now, here on the road, the girl feels, knows she will find him at the quarry. It had to be, she had searched everywhere else. And so, on she walks, the fine rain becoming heavier turning the white chalk road to slush.

At last Dina reaches the perimeter of the quarry. Ignoring the rusting and defaced KEEP OUT sign, she wriggles through the antiquated barbed wire fence. Scrambling through the dense ravine gorse, she gazes down at this English Babi Yar, her eyes fixed on the shimmering chemical blue lake.

And as she stares down at it, through it, the rain ceases giving way to a sun, a strange sun that alternates from a pallid yellow to a pure blood red, and the silence. That is all consuming. Not a bird, not a movement, not a sound, not a breath. And now lost in that silence, the girl closes her eyes, momentarily forgets where she is. But soon she is forced to remember. Hearing the snapping and crunch of trodden undergrowth she suddenly opens her eyes.

There standing in front of her, so close that she can smell

the booze on his breath, is Baines. He eyes her with a mix of confusion and disdain on his face. 'What in the name of fuck are you doing here!?' Dina looks at his face that face and feels a tremendous surge of hate and anger shudder through her. The boy feels it, sees it.

Then without his eyes leaving hers he slowly takes the handgun out from inside his Harrington jacket. Calmly he presses the barrel against Dina's temple. The girl has been here before, but this time she does not close her eyes, instead she stares hard into his face, to see what she can see. To try and see something, anything in his eyes, a spark of. But his eyes are faraway somewhere else, at a distant place only he knows.

Then it happens suddenly; in one rapid movement, Baines has taken the gun from her head and thrust it into her hand. Slowly he raises her gun carrying hand to his head. And pressing the gun barrel hard into his left temple he speaks, his voice a slurred and weary growl. 'Go on, do it, pull the trigger! What you waiting for?' Once more Dina looks into his eyes. But if she hopes to see some kind of contrition or remorse in them then she is to be disappointed. For none is present there. How could there be when the boy is incapable of feeling or displaying such emotions. They were a totally foreign country to him, a no man's land.

But now, when his voice comes again it's no longer a growl but more of a whimper, a mumble whose echoes are consumed by the breeze. 'You shoulda done it. You shoulda pulled the trigger.' Oh, and she wants to, wants so much to pull that trigger. But she does not. Instead she gazes down at the handgun nestling in the undergrowth where she had cast it. Then she looks up at the grey-blue aching sky.

'Why did you do it, why?' Her tone is imploring, desperate. Baines is silent; just stares down into the quarry ravine as if the chemical blue lake had stolen his eyes and voice. She wants to hurt him, do him real harm. Her fists clench her throat burns. She wants to relive again all those thoughts and feelings of hate and revenge she had felt after he had raped her. But, but somehow. she cannot... It's all a tragedy, their tragedy.

And as she tries to reconcile this, make sense of it in her mind, so the boy invades her reverie just as he had once invaded her body. 'You don't get it, do you? All this, everything, it's all down to Conor. It's his fucking madness. He's toxic, a cancer that has infected me and you. Don't you see? This worm in my head, you lying on your mum's grave like a lunatic. Him! He caused all of it.'

Dina looks at him coldly. 'And what you did to me, that was Conor's fault too!?' Baines does not reply. Instead, bending down he retrieves the handgun from the undergrowth and puts it inside his jacket, the metal clanging against his ubiquitous vodka bottle. Dina watches him. 'That's shit.' He turns and looks at her. "What is?' 'That somehow Conor has mysteriously infected me and you with madness. That is total crap.'

Looking out across the chemical blue lake once more, Baines speaks quietly, as if to himself. 'And as it was in the beginning so shall it be in the end... He was drowning. Christ knows what the silly little prick was doing in the lake in the first place? Anyway, there I was just sitting on the bank on my own, when I see him thrashing about in the water, his head keeping disappearing under the blue. Dunno, something came over me; I wanted to see him drown, wanted to see someone at the exact moment of death.' Dina cuts in softly, 'But you didn't let him die. You must have felt something other than wanting to see him die?'

Baines looks at her briefly. 'I dunno, what the hell I felt. It's just that. Anyway, after about thirty seconds or so, I swam out to him and pulled him to the bank.' He is quiet momentarily. Dina looks once more at the pale boy with the deadpan face. 'Did he tell you what he was doing in the water?' Baines shakes his head. 'No, like I said he didn't say a word about it. But I reckon he was gonna top himself, but bottled it at the last minute.'

As they talk, haemorrhaging from a mottled grey sky, the rains return. Self-consciously Baines takes Dina by the arm and leads her to a nearby workman's hut to escape the deluge.

At the far end of the quarry by the moon sand of the lake, Conor Christie gazes into a past he sees as clearly as the present, a present where as time passes he wonders if he will ever see Dina again. And from a dark corner of his mind a small voice echoes out. 'You once cast a loving and bright sunlight across her hours. Now you just cast a dark shadow across her days.'

If the voice was supposed to provoke a reaction then it failed. Instead, Conor continues to gaze into the blue. Every ripple on its unnatural surface seems to be a memory, a face, a time lost. And now, just like then, he feels something unseen compelling him to enter the chemical lake. But this time unlike the time before, he resists and moves slowly away from the bank.

Mumbling, stumbling he thinks of Dina, thinks of Baines, thinks of Cody's words. He thinks. And not for the first time his mind is a spiraling helter-skelter of thoughts of today's and yesterdays, of things past and things yet to come. Once more his eyes are drawn back to the blue, as if he is looking, searching for answers or perhaps solace. It offers none.

But it had once or at least pretended to. For then back in the day, it had spoken to the boy. Told him in a beguiling tone emanating from deep down in its glistening blue, that if he would succumb, surrender to it, give himself over to it totally, then the lake would be sure to grant him another life; a better life, a new life where Conor can be that boy he could have been, should have been. And oh, how the boy wanted to, needed to believe it.

And so, when the day came, when the time was right, he took his leap of faith. Entering the cool waters on that warm June morning he had strode out into the deep, into the unknown. Beneath him sand succumbs to his every step. Above him a turquoise sky starts to acquiesce to a bank of gathering grey clouds, shifting fast as if pushed by some huge unseen hand.

On and on he walked the chemical blue a snake bite on his skin. Looking around he fails to see the boy at the far bank of the lake. But the boy sees him, a sardonic sneer on his face. Continuing to walk Conor finds his steps slowing as the lake threatens to consume him. Finally, he stops as the chemical bum started to scorch his chest and neck. Standing stock still he is waiting, anticipating the voice of the lake to beckon him, welcome him, save him.

Instead, all he is met with is a low rumbling growl of mocking laughter rising from the lake. He waits and listens. But the earlier beguiling and seductive tones of the lake are gone, replaced by cruel laughter. Salvation is not to be found here, it never was, just like the sea at Bexhill had years later. And now, with the boy lost in the agony of betrayal, the chemical blue continued to claim him. Involuntarily, he starts to splash and thrash against the tainted water as it threatens to swallow him alive.

It drags and grasps at him, its poison stinging, eyes, ears, nose and throat. Gripping Conor hard it pulls him under. Behind closed eyes brightness comes, a thousand pinpricks of light. Then, suddenly out of nowhere, arms, hands, a body starts to pull him up through the blue. An eternity of lost minutes later and the two boys are safe on the sandy bank. On all fours, Conor heaves, retches, spews out that which had reneged on its promise to him. Gasping, he collapses onto his back.

Beside him Baines lies breathless staring up at the grey-turquoise sky. 'What the fuck were you doing trying to swim in that shit?' Conor turns his head away slowly. 'I wasn't swimming. I was. It doesn't matter.' The boy falls silent, as the grey finally conquers the turquoise, far above the blue.

As the rain stops, so tentative conversation starts. Leaving the workman's hut, Baines and Dina walk through the damp, sparse vegetation of the quarry. They walk single file along a narrow path that leads down to the lake either side of which dense and belligerent gorse bushes scratch and pull at them. The tentative conversation that had sprung up between them had obviously been some form of verbal mirage, for soon they fall silent again. Slowly, cautiously Dina leads the way, even though she does not know the way or where it will lead. A few paces behind her Baines follows, his eyes never leaving the small, slight, limping figure in front of him.

As much as he tries to resist the confused thoughts as they again start to crowd his mind, they are irresistible; pushing, shoving and jostling like passengers on a train bound for nowhere just going round and round. And once more as he watches Dina, he feels the overwhelming need to possess her, a malignant tumour of unnatural desire. 'Find what you love and kill it. Or let it kill you.' He had read that somewhere and had liked it. Of course, it was horseshit, but to the boy it had a certain nihilistic rhythm that appealed to him.

And he thinks to himself again that she should have pulled the trigger when she had the chance.

Reaching the end of the winding narrow track, the girl looks over her shoulder at Baines and then out across the lake. Through her eyes it suddenly starts to rise, bubbling and hissing like some venomous liquid in a warlock's cauldron. And Indistinct amongst the miasma she thinks she sees shapes, bodies, faces, hazy and nebulous. Suddenly above her the sudden scream of a seagull breaks the spell. She looks across at Baines, and knows by the expression on his face that he has seen what she alone thought she had seen. Flashing with confusion and disbelief their eyes meet briefly now. And then as if in unison those eyes switch back to the lake. They watch like statues in a dream as waters rise and the miasma threatens to engulf all.

'It's like the end of everything. Or just the start' Dina's voice slowly trails off.

Baines, rigid, wide eyes staring, takes a step back as if to survey the unreal scene better, as if observing a funeral pyre from the past. For now, rising slowly from the chemical blue are the faces of those who have gone before, those that were loved and hated in equal measure. Lost souls found again.

And at their head the boy thinks he sees the figure of the old

Jew, his grey face angst-ridden, his dark eyes somehow both accusing and forgiving, still searching, still looking for she that he had loved and lost. And behind the old Jew, Baines sees the outline of his father, as in life so in death, lurching drunkenly. The boy goes to call out to him. But no sound emanates from his mouth, save for the silent scream of slaughterhouse sheep.

Alongside Baines, Dina peers through the miasma, sees her mother and grandmother clutching hands, wringing hands, gripping hands as if their souls depended on it. Like the boy, she too tries to call out to them. And also, just like the boy, her voice is nothing but a scream of silence. And still the faces of the loved and the unloved hover in the miasma, forming a phalanx of phantoms.

Suddenly, there rises from the lake a collective moan of half-crazed voices, somewhere between a sob of utter human despair and the howl of an animal. 'Is it far?' And everything is driven by oppressive and crushing soul sadness, no, actually beyond that, more a desolate devastation of the soul, as the old saying goes. 'Any crime or damage against the soul is irreparable.' Maybe that is true, or perhaps it's not.

Either way, it's not something weighing too heavily on the mind of the boy and girl. For children once more they are. Scared, frightened. And they hope that merely by closing their eyes and clasping each others hands tightly the daymare in front of them will desist, depart, because this surely cannot really be happening. This there very own personal little apocalypse.

But hand-holding, eye-closing don't cut it, nowhere near enough to abate the tempest, and as toxic waters keep rising, so from the east comes a wind that is the Devil's own and older than time, Its icy blast slash-crashes to the bone. But somehow the children stand firm against its malice and spite. It whips wails as it slashes young skin, but strong, stoical they take it. Two little lost souls alone on the watchtower.

Huddling closer and closer together against the force, they seem to melt, merge into one. And as they do, so the haunting moans from the toxic blue waters seem to become less and less audible, until with a final desperate gasp they are gone lost on the east wind.

On the other side of the quarry, Conor sees all, hears all feels all. Beside him is Cody. When the tempest was at its height he had suddenly appeared, literally from nowhere and now they gaze out across the lake as the east wind howls out its final pain and the last of the souls disappear under the disturbed and bubbling surface of the blue.

Slowly Cody's eyes follow the desperate descent of the souls then equally slowly he turns away. 'Perhaps that torment awaits us all. Maybe that is all there is?' Conor eyes him coolly. 'I thought you knew. I thought you knew everything? I mean, you said you'd seen everything, lived for centuries?' Cody smiles faintly. 'And so I have. But I'm yet to die. That particular pleasure or pain awaits me.'

Once more his eyes scan the now becalmed lake, as if it were now content, sated by its returning souls. The east wind too is now easing, its pain and anger spent, for now. Briefly a curtain of silence falls between the two, as each ponders a next word a next movement. 'You know, I have waited such a long time for this, almost as long as I have waited for you.' Cody's soft tone is torn apart by the harshness of Conor's.

'Waited for what? What the hell are you talking about?' Undeterred, Cody continues. 'Have you already forgotten all I

298

have told you? Specifically about the Jews and their belief that.' Sighing hard, Conor cuts him dead. 'Jesus, not that again, look, how the hell can I be some sort of fucking saviour when I can't even save myself?' Cody replies softly and patiently. 'I'm not saying that you should be the saviour of all mankind. No, what I'm saying is that you should save those that you can.' Conor sighs inwardly. 'Save who?'

Before the words have left the boy's mouth, then Cody is gone. All that remains is his faint disembodied voice. 'You don't need me to tell you that.' The boy calls after him switching his head rapidly from left to right. But there is nothing.

CHAPTER TWENTY-FIVE.

After the tempest, Baines and Dina stay clasping each other tightly, as if pulling away would somehow mean a kind of capitulation to something unseen. But when the time is finally right they slowly ease apart from each other. And the look left behind and its residue that remains means that things between them would not could not ever be the same again.

And for the girl, her young heart is now shards, fragments that belonged to too many people. And a girl's heart cannot be expected to accommodate such numbers, because it hurts too much, and as for the boy. Well, Baines is Baines. Most things for him remain on the surface, but not all things. He feels different now; feels like he has never felt before. And it's a feeling he cannot explain, a feeling without a name.

Alternately he wants to think of a future and not a past. But it's all too much. And so, he reverts to type and reconnects lips around the neck of a bottle. And as he gazes from girl to lake and back again, he wonders if either is truly real.

And later as shadows slowly start to lengthen across the quarry moonscape, so Dina realises, just feels that these will be her last days on earth. One way or another it's all going to end. And so as she thinks of times past and time present, so time stands perfectly still, unflinching and suspended.

Peering skywards she is back in the metal womb tomb, she thought the end would come then, but realises now that it was only a kind of dress rehearsal for today 'As I walk through the

300

valley of the shadow of death' Dina's voice trails off. She can't remember any more of the psalm. But it doesn't matter. And now she gently takes the bottle of booze from the boy's hand, and as she does, she mouths 'Life doesn't matter at all' smiling, she cups his cheek with the palm of her hand and then takes from the bottle and drinks of its bitter juice. Then like silent quarry ghosts, they walk away, baby steps theirs.

And on they walk, the young suddenly becoming old. And they know not where they walk, entombed in an end of life haze. And heads that were once so full of noise are quiet now. Not serene, just silent. And the worm has long since vacated the boy's head. His life's work achieved. He had led Baines but had now left him to walk over his own grave. Yes, his work was complete. And... And, oh fuck, how the hell could it have come to this?

Below the boy and girl the lake is perfectly still now, as inoffensive as Anthrax. And beneath its surface memories of souls twist in torment. There but not there. And on and on the boy and girl walk; walking right out of this life. High above seagulls circle; sad, sombre suburban vultures, staring down upon the stupidity of humans who have forgotten how to live, laugh and love.

Suddenly, Dina feels the hand of Baines squeeze hers harder. Following his gaze, she watches his pale face blanch even whiter, then tracing that stare, her heart speeds as she sees the figure of Conor fifty yards away slowly ascending to the top of the ravine. And oh how she sees a difference in him. No longer is he the pavement-gazer, eyes cast downwards looking but not seeing the fag butts, dog shit and yesterdays papers.

No, now he wears his head high, for he held lofty ambitions

to be the saviour of dead and living souls, even if most had pawned those souls long ago and now had nothing to redeem them with. But Cody's words which at last he understood resonated and reverberated and he couldn't let them go. They had even finally silenced his clamorous voices.

And now he stands stock still, staring alternately over his shoulder, and in front of him at Dina and Baines. And. And. they both somehow look so old and frail, wasted.

Slowly, as if walking on shards, Conor approaches them. Wondering all the while why Dina is with the boy, as stings of jealousy pulse jagged through him. Silently from behind red-rimmed eyes, Baines gazes at Conor and then through him. And when his voice finally came it's not much more than a gasp. 'It's been a long time. But now you're here, a someone from nowhere, a no one from somewhere.' He smiles a drunken smile at his words; then rasps a laugh before coughing hard and spitting out blood, ' redness searing bright against his thin pale lips.

'You know, I had so many plans and schemes in my head for this moment when I would finally be face to face with you again. And now, now I realise just what a waste of time it all was. Cos none of it any of it is your fault. You just are and always will be that fucked up kid whose sorry arse I dragged out of the lake. And trust me, for everyone's sake I just wish I'd let you drown.'

Conor stares at him coldly. 'Then why the hell didn't you!?' Before Baines can reply, Dina steps forward and takes Conor's hand in hers. Its warmth burns and chills him equally. 'I have missed you so much.' Her words brush his face and he can't suss out if they are a caress or. 'Missing me? Is that the same

302

as loving me?' The girl bows her head, as if an invisible weight were bearing down on head and heart. 'I will always love you Conor, you know that. .It's just...' Her voice flakes fades away towards the lake, drifting, her gaze following.

Conor doesn't chase after her words; too fearful of what he might find. Instead, he turns and looks once more at Baines. He tries to read his face, but it's just a ghost mask looking back at him. Gone was the face he had known forever but never really known, just to be replaced by a spectre. And as the drunken boy raises the bottle to crooked lips, so Conor sees Cody's dog standing a few yards behind him rising on its hind legs. And as the animal starts to speak its voice belongs to neither man nor beast.

'You have heard the words of my master. And now the time has come to act upon them. Be of strong heart and put right all that is wrong. Remember, you have been chosen.' With that, the creature dissipates, disseminating into a thousand windblown fragments. Blinking hard against this bizarre vision, Conor looks around himself, to his left to his right, his expression one of dazed confusion. Any moment he expects hopes to see the figure of Cody. But there is nothing

Instead, his eyes rest upon Dina at the edge of the ravine. Slowly, self-consciously, he walks over to her as she gazes out across the toxic blue. His voice is soft, questioning. 'I waited and waited for you. Why did you leave me?' Dina looks briefly at the boy and then over her shoulder at Baines who sits lounging on a large stone.

'Things were... I dunno... Kind of chaotic. Stuff was building up, stacking up in my head. It's hard to explain, but every morning I would wake up to the same grey and empty picture, and everything I thought or touched left me feeling kind of dirty. And I felt so alone.'

She looks at Conor and then at the ground. 'I just wanted what I was feeling to go away. And in my chaos, in the madness I felt, I thought the only way I could be free of it was to go to my mum, just to' she chokes back a sob, and tears of a remembered hopelessness well in her dark eyes, as her voice cracks. 'I miss something, someone I never even really knew.' The boy watches, sees her visibly crumple. Instinctively, he wraps an arm across her shoulder and pulls her to him.

Behind them, Baines looks on at the pair a glazed view through the bottom of a near empty bottle. And far behind nebulous eyes and fractured perception, the scenario acting out in front of him is one he is having big problems handling right now. And so, under big hungry skies, he feels, falls, feels out of touch, out of time, and out of booze. But he stays. Stone-rooted, and waits, waits for the end of this time, his time, their time. And as he waits, from above a sun screams down its stinging rays, streaming, searing onto him into him, this boy of glass.

Later on the cusp of dusk, unspoken words still linger in the air. For the three are quiet, funereal, as if mourning the dimming of the light. But sitting alone at the lake's edge, Conor Christie reclaims a lost thought. A child's thought that had comforted him so many times so long ago. The thought being that if you really think hard enough, stare long enough at something it will eventually shift shape; change into something that you want it to be.

And so. the boy starts staring into the small fire that crackles and spits close by him. He stares at the past, thinks he sees faces in the flames, and like some apprentice shaman he gazes harder into its shifting brightness and tries to invoke memories amongst the flashing, flitting embers.

Lost in this reverie, Conor fails to notice Baines approaching him from behind. Without saying a word he drops the handgun into Conor's lap. Surprised, he cautiously eyes the gun and then Baines.

'I've told you before I don't do shooter's' He hands the gun back to the boy. Baines takes it, a strange sardonic sneer on his face, and sits down next to Conor. 'Yeah, but like I've told you before, you don't mind using knives, do yer?' He slowly puts the gun back in the pocket of his Harrington jacket, and then absent-mindedly picks dried mud spatters off of jeans that are beyond salvation.

That done he turns once more to Conor. 'Not that a knife is going to be much use to you this time not when the old Bill tum up' Conor's eyes shift rapidly from the fire to those of Baines. 'What the hell are you talking about!?' Baines looks out across the now darkening lake. 'This is where it all started, and this is where it's gotta end.' He falls silent. Conor's voice is insistent. 'Look, what's all this crap about the police showing up?' Once more a sardonic darkness patterns the face of Baines. 'It ain't crap mate. They're on their way. I called them from the phone box down the lane ten minutes ago.'

The look on Conor's face is a mix of horror and incredulity. 'You fucking idiot, what the hell do you think your playing at!?' Getting to his feet, Baines starts to pace, his agitation growing. 'You just don't get it, do yer!? This is where it all started. Where white became black and black became white, where your madness became mine. You know, when I pulled you from that fucking lake, I unleashed something, something dark and sick. By saving you I was infecting me.'

Becoming increasingly annoyed and animated, Conor strides purposely across to Baines. But before he can speak or act a wailing wall of sirens can be heard crying there scream in the near distance. Fleetingly, the boys look at each other and then in the direction of the sirens. Without a word, they bolt to the workman's hut. Inside, Dina sleeps, in repose her small frame stretched out along the wooden wall bench. Jolted roughly awake by their noise, she looks sleepily from one face to the other.

'What is it? What's happened?' Avoiding her eyes, Conor glances coldly across at Baines. 'Ask him. He's got it all planned, he's got it all sussed out to be a re-run of Custer's last fucking stand!' The girl looks at Conor uncomprehendingly. 'What do you mean?' Sighing, Conor turns to her. 'What I mean is that this prick has only gone and called the police.'

Dina shifts her gaze from Conor to Baines, a look of incredulity etched across her face. 'Is this true? Are you mad! What were you thinking of?' Suddenly, Baines laughs out loud, an incongruous and strange laugh which soon dies in his throat. He glares at Conor and then at Dina. 'You're just like him. You just don't get it, do yer? Don't you see we're all fucking mad: and he is the infection the cancer' He glares once more disdainfully at Conor.

Rising from the bench, Dina snaps angrily at him. 'You're talking such bollocks. Look, enough of this crap we need to get out of here.' Pushing her back down on the bench, Baines takes out the handgun and points it at her, and then at Conor. 'No

one's going anywhere. This is where it finishes. It ends today.'
From outside they hear the sound of noisy car brakes squealing
in protest, and sirens screaming a final wail.

Out of the surreal, unreal ether a voice comes, metallic
sounding. 'Okay, we know you're in there. Just come out
now and this can end peacefully.' Baines sneers coldly. 'Yeah
right, no fucking chance of that.' With that, and using the
butt of the gun, he smashes the glass of one of the hut's small
windows and starts to fire wildly in the direction of the metal
voice. Surprised, stunned, Conor and Dina shift to the back
of the hut.

From outside, the brief unreal still is broken by the voice of
metal, its tone appeasing but firm. 'Come on, don't be stupid,
things haven't got to be like this.' Inside the hut Baines paces,
mumbling to himself. 'Yes, they have you prick they can't be
any other way.' Beside him in the cramped space, Dina and
Conor have become shadows, silent and unmoving, temporarily frozen.

Suddenly, out the corner of his eye, Baines sees the figure of
a tall, thin young man standing by the door, grey, everything
about him grey. Turning his body, the boy looks at him square
on. 'Who the hell are you?' The young man replies softly, his
Slavic accent unmistakeable. 'You don't recognise or remember me?' The boy eyes him suspiciously. 'If I did, I wouldn't
be asking, would I?' As the words are exchanged, Conor and
Dina look on, seeing but not seeing, understanding but not
comprehending.

The tall, young man suddenly steps forward as if to approach
Baines. Raising the gun, the boy levels it at him. 'Just stay where
you are!' A mirthless smile creases the face of the young man.

'Go on, pull the trigger. Kill me twice.' Narrowing his eyes Baines looks more closely at the man. 'Just what are you talking about?' Again, the young man smiles without a hint of joy. 'Of course, you don't recognise me, what was I thinking of. You just know me as old, dead of heart and of mind. A stupid old Jew you could trick and steal from. Not to mention murder.'

The blare of the metallic voice jolts into the boy's brain. 'This isn't a game. You are surrounded by armed police; now do the sensible thing and throw out your weapons, and then with raised hands slowly leave the hut one at a time.' Looking towards the door again, Baines sees nothing. Lazarus is gone. He also doesn't see the blow to the side of his head, but he certainly feels it.

Falling back onto the wall bench, Conor stands over him 'Give me the gun! You might wanna turn this into the fucking Alamo, but we don't!' He lunges hard at him, grabbing at the hand of the dazed boy, as he spits out the words. Sprung from his daze Baines fights back, wildly swinging punches at Conor as the two struggle over possession of the gun, looking on Dina is unsure what to do, as from outside the metal voice drones into a verbal blur. Unintelligible; it reminds her of Charlie Brown's teacher in the Peanuts cartoon she watched as a kid.

And nothing is real to her any more. This shit must be happening to someone else, not her. And looking down at the two boys struggling over the gun on the hut floor she suddenly feels an overwhelming desire to laugh. Or perhaps cry. Or even just sink to her knees and pray to a God she doesn't believe in any more.

But she doesn't do anything, instead she walks calmly over to the prone and fighting boys, and as if opening a pair of obdurate curtains she pulls the pair apart. 'Give me the gun!' Her voice is calm, quiet, her gaze steady. Baines his face bleeding, looks down at the gun and then at the big dark eyes in the small pale face. He hesitates briefly before handing the gun to the girl. She turns to Conor.

His words are those of a weary child. 'So, what now, what will we do?' She cups his face in her hand and then looks down at Baines, who breathless and bruised sits slumped on the wall bench. She speaks softly. 'Perhaps he is right. It is all over... Everything left lying and dying tattered and torn. All we have left are the last beats of our pulse.' She smiles ruefully at her own impromptu eloquence, the words given to her by another.

Outside the metallic voice starts up its blah again but no one is listening any more. Once more Dina speaks softly as she takes a coin from the pocket of her jacket. 'It's time. Heads we live, tails we don't. Take the coin and hold it to show that we all agree.' The boys hesitate to take it until Conor finally does. Holding it briefly he holds it out to Baines. 'Come on then, take it. You're the one that dug this fucking hole.' Tentatively, Baines at last takes the coin. First looking at it as he turns it over in his palm, he then hands it to Dina. 'You do it. You toss it.'

She looks at them both. 'And so, we're all agreed on this?' Baines sneers as both boys nod their heads. 'Yeah, let's end this bollocks.' Taking the coin between thumb and forefinger Dina tosses it high. And as it ascends, a sky outside that had briefly forgotten them patterns a sun slither from which a single ray traces the upward flight of the coin through the window of the hut, glints it, catches it as it reaches its zenith and again as it starts its fast descent. Six eyes watch it. Watch it as it lands perfectly upright, vertical on the wooden plank floor.

They look at each other bemused and mystified. Baines breaks the stunned silence. 'What the fuck?' Cautiously he stretches down to collect the coin. Grasping it between thumb and forefinger he attempts to pick it up. It doesn't budge. He tries again, pulling harder. Still it won't move. He looks across at Dina and Conor, and then takes a penknife from his jeans pocket he tries to slide the blade under the coin but is unable to. Shaking his head in exasperation and disbelief he straightens up and once more turns to Conor and Dina. 'This ain't true, it can't be happening.. Dunno, perhaps it's a sign from God or something.'

Conor cuts him dead. 'Don't talk bollocks.' Baines sneers at him. 'Well, if it's bollocks, you try picking the sodding thing up.' Sighing, the girl tries to lift up the coin, but like Baines she too is unable to. 'This is too weird. Perhaps he's right, may be it is a sign or something. I mean how else can it be explained?' This time Conor sighs. 'Look, whether it's a sign, or some kind of sodding miracle, what the hell does it matter, the thing is we've gotta do something. Either surrender to the bloody cavalry out there, or...'

His words trail off into emptiness. But soon Baines finishes the unspoken sentence. 'Or we top ourselves?' There is silence briefly. Even outside all is quiet now, another respite from the metallic blah. Looking away from the boys, Dina goes over to the broken window and gazes out at the dark blue wall of bodies; some in patrol cars others positioned in strategic places eighty or so yards from the hut. Again, the girl feels an over-whelming desire to laugh at the absurdity of it all. How had it come to this? As she ponders the unanswerable, sitting on the wall bench Conor mutters over and over. 'Right now, there is nothing so there's nothing to lose.'

As for Baines, he is silent still staring down at the coin. Not so much an Excalibur stuck fast in a stone, but a small tarnished disc stuck fast to rotting floorboards. Finally taking his gaze from the coin he starts to pace the hut his hands trembling, shaking; his mind needing peace his body needing booze; and he has neither. Suddenly he stops pacing and turns to the other two. 'I've had a thought.' Conor sneers at him. 'Christ, I bet it's lonely.'

Baines ignores the remark. 'Hey, fuck it, let's tell 'em we have a hostage, and unless one of the plod's goes down to the off licence and gets us sixty Rothman's and two bottles of vodka, we'll off the hostage.' Rising from the bench, Conor shakes his head disdainfully in the direction of Baines. 'Christ, you do come out with some old shit sometimes.'

Coming away from the window, Dina gazes over to Baines and then to Conor. She wears on her face a half-smile a last chance epiphany illuminates her eyes. 'No, I know it's mad, but it might just work.' Conor interrupts flippantly. 'What, getting pissed on vodka and smoking ourselves to death.' Dina approaches him he sees the brightness in her eyes. 'No, smartarse, look, it's worth a try, this hostage idea of his.'

She takes Conor by the hand and they sit on the wooden bench. 'Look, it's simple, you just tell the police that you two have taken me hostage. Slowly walk out the door with the gun pointed at my head, then give them a list of our demands' stopping his pacing, Baines cuts in. 'Demands? Hang on, it was a joke; I was just kidding. We came here to die not to find a way out, a way to live.' Conor eyes him coldly. 'No; in your fucked-up head you came here to die, cos you couldn't leave the past alone, couldn't just leave it where it belonged.' Baines responds angrily. 'Fucked-up head? That's rich coming from you. And who was it that fucked with my head?' Voice raised, Dina once again steps in between the pair. 'For christ sake, will you two just stop it, this isn't helping!'

Outside, there is a reinforcement of riot shields as the metallic drone picks up the rhythm once more. And this time the drone is more insistent with a sharper edge. Closing her eyes, Dina tries to hear in the voice that rhythm that beat, a tempo, a hope. But she hears nothing, a babble of threats and false promises. Moving away from the window she approaches Conor. 'So, you have the gun. Let's do it.'

CHAPTER TWENTY-SIX

At around seven in the evening, the sky began to burn hard in the west. Its violent colours enhanced as dark shadows of dusk crept across the old quarry. Outside the workman's hut, Conor stands slightly behind Dina, the handgun pointed at her head. In front, around a hundred yards away, riot shields twitch and a metallic voice lays silent. A few paces behind Conor and Dina through the slightly open door of the hut, the boy can hear the noise of Baines,

'Tell 'em I want three bottles of vodka. And I only want Smirnoff, I don't want any of that other cheap shit, and I want a hundred Dunhill King size, and if they ain't..' half turning his head, Conor hisses through clenched teeth. 'For fuck's sake, shut up!' In a whispered voice, Dina speaks to him. 'Go on, do it, tell them what we want.' Self-consciously, Conor looks down at the dirt at his feet and then up at a burning sky, anywhere rather than the blue wall in front of him. However, after a few moments, the boy finds a voice, albeit tentative and hesitant.

'Okay... Well, it's like this. I want a car, I don't care what type just so long as it's got a tank full of petrol...' Once more Baines calls out from inside the hut. 'Tell em to get us a Mini Cooper.' Conor ignores the comment. His confidence growing, he continues. 'On the back seat, in a holdall, I want ten grand, and I want it in well used twenty quid notes. You get us that without any tricks or bullshit and she lives. If you don't, she don't. You have two hours to arrange it.'

With that he slowly starts to walk backwards with Dina, the gun still aimed at her head. She half turns to him. 'Do you think that they believe it? You know, that I'm your hostage?' Conor shrugs his shoulders. 'We'll soon find out.'

Back inside the hut, they hear the echoes of the metallic voice reverberating. 'Just don't harm the girl in anyway and I will do my best to meet your demands.' From the bench Baines coughs, spitting out more of his life, and sneers. 'Yeah, course you will you bullshitting bastard.' Conor eyes him coldly. 'What's your problem? This hostage gig is your idea.' Baines sighs loudly. 'What part of, I was only joking don't you understand?'

Dina walks once more over to the window. 'Well, either way it is what it is now.' She feels the chill of approaching night on her face through the broken glass. She no longer feels the desire to laugh or cry now. Instead she just feels that familiar feeling of nothingness clouding her mind. Skimming her gaze over the top of the police cars she lets it sink into the kingfisher colours, the burning orange sky, the chemical blue lake. And she knows now she cannot capitulate to the feeling again. Not here, not now.

Conor's voice suddenly breaks into her reverie. 'Are you okay? You look so pale.' She smiles weakly at him. 'I'm okay, I guess. Just want all this crap to end.' He gently rests his open hand on her shoulder. 'Yeah, you're not the only one. If it wasn't for that prick none of this would've happened.' He glares across at the now sleeping Baines his head slumped on his chest.

'Folie à Quatre'

In the darkest corner of the hut, Lazarus manifests himself

314

once more. And in death he had never felt more alive. Well, not since he and Esther. He gazes unseen at the three children in front of him, and briefly a surge of something akin to pity flows through him. For him, them, were they not the same? Broken, lost, irredeemable?

Briefly his hollow ghost eyes scan back and forth over those painful and wasted earthly years, until dark decades merge into one black mass of despair, one which he mentally casts upon his own funeral pyre, and watches bum. And as the last dark remnant is consumed by the flames, so he knows now what he must do, what his final act must be. Only then in his mind could he hope to find true peace. And perhaps also find she, her, the one the murdering bastards had stolen from her on the whim of a deranged mind. But perhaps this was it. By performing this last act, it would somehow earn him a kind of redemption, redemption for? Redemption for some crime he wasn't even cognizant of committing?

And so, so in that dark corner he silently watches the three children, the three players who would be part, would be integral to his earning redemption. And perhaps, most importantly by saving that child who had ended his earthly existence he would be performing the ultimate act of forgiveness. Surely that would be enough in the eyes of God to allow him to be freed from the torment of his own private shadowlands... And... And to finally find his woman, his Esther.

And this thought lifts, sustains him as he finally steps out of the darkness of the corner. And as a cold draught against their pale young skin, so his presence is felt by the three children. And as the hut feels appreciably colder; so the girl swears she can smell the scent of lilies. The sudden chill has awoken Baines

315

from incongruous sleep. Opening his bleary eyes he sees the figure of Lazarus standing over him again.

Instinctively the boy recoils, pressing his back hard into the timber wall of the hut. 'Just leave me the hell alone.' His voice agitated and fearful draws the attention of Conor and Dina away from the window. This time the spell is broken and they too see the figure of Lazarus. Wide-eyed, disbelieving, they gaze upon him, two worlds meeting in silence, a silence tentatively broken by the staring girl.

'Who are you? What are you?' Lazarus replies softly. 'It's not important for you to know my name, nor I to know yours. It's enough for you to know I'm one of the passed and I'm here to help you.' He turns his gaze from the girl and looks briefly at Baines. 'That even includes you.' The boy returns the look with narrowed eyes. 'Don't believe him, it's all part of the madness. It's head games, just bullshit, don't you see that? I mean, how can a fucking ghost help us!?'

His words hang heavy in the air ignored by all. Conor, suffocating in the unreality of it, stays lock-jawed merely staring at that which he cannot understand and thought never existed. It is left up to Dina to speak once more. 'Look, sorry, but this is just all too weird. I just don't get any of it. I mean, how can you help us? What can you do?' Without replying, Lazarus goes over to the hitherto immovable coin and easily lifts it from the floor. Casually he hands it to Dina.

'You see, whatever is seemingly impossible in your world is possible in mine.' The girl eyes him briefly and then turns to the two boys, before facing Lazarus once more, her expression a mix of bewilderment and wariness. 'Tell me... Who are you?' Lazarus nods his head in the direction of Baines. 'One day perhaps he will tell you. But for now, it doesn't matter. The only thing that does is getting you out of here and away from them.' He casts a glance in the direction of the police.

Shaking her head slightly, Dina asks softly. 'But I still don't know why you're doing this, why you want to help us?' For a moment Lazarus is silent as he looks into her face. And as he looks, so she sees for the first time his eyes, sees the lifetime of hurt that still haunts them. And she suddenly feels a need a compulsion to weep, as involuntary tears well in her eyes. But with a strangled cough she chokes back a sob and bows her head. And for the most ephemeral of moments she reminds Lazarus of...

He looks away. 'It's enough for you to know I have my reasons. Now, enough questions.' He moves away from the girl and goes to the window. 'It's time to get you away from here.'

As night starts to unravel its dark cloak, so the police flood the quarry with lights, under whose glare the old hut stands illuminated and isolated, resembling some decrepit, ancient actor on a spot-lit stage playing out his final scene. And behind that scene on this derelict stage, he who in life had held so little control over events, circumstances and the actions of other's, was now in death in control of everything. Well, almost everything. The puppet had become the puppeteer, a controller of destinies.

And now Lazarus suddenly felt so strong, stronger than he had ever felt before. But with this strength, this power came a feeling of repulsion. Repulsion because now he had a tiny inkling, a sense, a small scale realisation of the power the murderers, those lords over life and death had felt, had held as they decided who would continue to breathe and who would perish.

A shudder of revulsion courses through him, reopening decades old scars that couldn't, wouldn't heal even in death. Rescuing him from himself, from such ugly musings, Dina's voice, nebulous, both near and far away echoes out. 'And as we hesitated time rushed onwards without us.' Baines eyes the girl silently, and then with mouth gobbing and hands still shaking, he rises from the bench and fronts Lazarus.

'She's right, times running away running out. So, come on ghostman, you promised to save our arses. We're still waiting for the miracle.' Conor sighs, sneering across at Baines. 'Just give it a sodding rest, will yer?' Lazarus smiles thinly at Conor. 'No, he is right, I promised to get you safely away from here.' Baines cuts in sarcastically. 'Yeah, well, while we're still young would be nice.' Lazarus ignores him and stands silently by the window. He is soon joined by Dina. As she begins to speak a spotlight streak of dirty yellow patterns across her face through the broken window.

'You know, I still don't know if you're real or you're just a figment, a fragment, or just a vision from the madness?' He turns and smiles softly at her. 'I'm as real as you are.' She returns his smile. 'What's it like? I mean to be, to have passed over? There are a thousand things I wanna know, wanna ask you.' Lazarus briefly looks out of the window, as the boys listen in. Finally he faces Dina. 'You ask me what it's like to pass over? Well, forget walking towards a white light. Forget your earthly concept of time and space. And forget.'

He is suddenly interrupted by the drone voice and the sound of a car being driven up to the hut. Wordlessly Conor and Dina watch from the window as the Cortina is driven to a halt about twenty yards from the hut.

'As you can see, I have kept my side of the bargain. The car has a full tank of petrol and the money is on the back seat. Now it's down to you to keep your side of things.' Before any response from inside the hut is possible, from summer night skies snow begins to fall. In amazement, Dina turns to Lazarus 'summer snow? Is this somehow your doing?' Lazarus doesn't reply, but a faint smile curls his lips. Shuffling in the darkness, Baines joins them at the window, watches as the snow intensifies. He shakes his head slowly 'Christ, just when I thought things couldn't get any more weird and fucked up.'

Outside it's ten below now, and the snow no longer falls as flakes but as big and hard as bullets. Hurrying and scurrying, the summer-clad blue wall run for cover as moonscape becomes snowscape and summer becomes Siberian winter. Now muffled and entombed in the back of a police car, the metallic voice drones incredulously,

'What the fucking hell?' And as his words die, so from skies now the colour of forgotten blood, the blizzard is born. And in the light white swirling darkness, a hundred uncomprehending eyes flit and flicker, fearful and amazed. In the hut silence is far from golden. In fact, just the voice of Baines rings out, sings out 'Where the skies are bathed in blood, there's cataclysmic overtones A-P-O-C-A-L-Y-P-S-E The apocalypse!'

Twisting words stolen from a half-remembered song, the boy laughs, expecting to hear his laughter echoed by the worm in his head. But he hears nothing. For the creature had long since packed up, shipped out and moved on. So, the laughter of Baines hangs alone; sad and mirthless.

Outside, unfettered, unleashed, the blizzard reigns supreme

319

its belligerence and hostility threatening to blow away the world, their little world.

Yet detached somehow from this theatre of the bizarre, Conor Christie gazes with a thousand yard stare, dispassionately watching the players playing the parts handed out to them by a nameless host, some closet ghost both seen and unseen. And he wants to feel something, anything, but his head is not in the clouds; it is a cloud, nebulous and floating, unable to make rhyme or reason, sometimes his head is here sometimes not. And amongst this semi-paralysis, this mental torpor, the boy feels that it is all second-hand; somehow it has all been lived before, if not by him then by someone else.

And he thinks briefly of Cody and his words again, tries once more to find meaning, sense and solace in them, but finds none, finds only more questions than answers. Until finally the sound of the intensifying blizzard crashing against the walls and roof of the hut jolts Conor back to something resembling reality. Turning his head sharply from Dina and Lazarus, he fixes his gaze on Baines.

Broken Baines, stumbling shambling Baines a spitting shadow boy now, mumbling incoherently about guilt and blame life and fate. And about a boy who infected him with his madness as surely as if he had infected him with a dose of the clap. Coughing violently, Baines shivers against the bitter summer snowbound evening. Then turning his back on Conor, he sobs into the wall, fractured, broken.

Deep in the guts of the blizzards blast, and in minutes resembling centuries to confused and bewildered minds, the decision is finally taken by the metallic voice, in his capacity as chief brick in the rapidly fracturing blue wall, that it's time to retreat, tactically and temporarily of course.

And so, as they depart, so the malevolent snowflakes as big as a man's hand, continue to fall hard and fast, whipped and whirled on the gale force wind, until earth and sky somehow seem one, a seamless imperfect blanket shrouding and enveloping this insane little world. As all the while inside the dark hut, curious and disbelieving eyes witness the departure of the police in stunned silence, a silence finally broken by Dina.

'I can't believe that they've gone, just like that.' Tears well in her eyes and she starts to sob. Not with joy or with sadness, but involuntarily uncontrollably as though someone something has taken her over, a soul spasm. It's a feeling she has felt before, but never with this intensity. And in the darkness Conor takes her hand in his, squeezing it softly.

Beside them, Lazarus closes his eyes, a soft smile on his lips, as if conjuring a memory. 'I feel her, she's coming. I know it. She's finally coming!' Dina and Conor look at each other quizzically, and then at Lazarus. He glow's, there is no other word to describe it. And now through disbelieving eyes, spirit form becomes mass. And once where there was translucence, now muscle, flesh bone and sinew forms. Eyes wide, the girl tentatively reaches out to touch Lazarus. She feels the solidity, the warmth, the life.

Suddenly confused and fearful, she backs away. Lazarus doesn't notice his face is an animated sequence of movements. Calm, agitated, excited, until finally his features express a kind of rapture. The look one sees on the face of one who is gripped in the intensity of a profound religious experience. And here in the gloom his bodily movements become expectant, nervous and jerky. He cannot settle, he won't settle. And in a voice cracking with emotion, he cries out into the darkness. 'I never gave up hope, Esther. Not once. All through those endless days that no human being should have to endure, I never doubted that this time would come.'

A silence as heavy as sheet iron briefly descends. Lazarus looks with urgency to his left and right as if sensing a presence. 'Esther, I know your there. Come to me darling. It's our time now.' From the shadows a faint ethereal purple mist slowly moves to the centre of the hut. Conor and Dina look on in awe, a silent astonishment neither can understand but both will remember always. For as some unseen force gives mass, form and life to the burgeoning mist, so that same force takes it from the ashen and motionless figure of Baines.

And as he weakens, flickers and fades, so the mist saps and sucks his energy, his life force. Crudely tom from his rapture, Lazarus looks at the mist he believes to be his wife and then across at the rapidly expiring boy, a look of absolute horror spreads across his face 'No, in the name of God, Esther, not like this!' Frantically, his gaze shifts once more from Baines to the mist that is second by second, little by little taking on human form. 'Esther, no, please, we can't, this isn't right!' Salt tears fill his eyes, blinding him, tearing a wounded soul asunder.

But he makes the decision, puts in place the resolution that tears his heart out, but which he knows is right. Kneeling by the side of the prone boy, he takes in his hand that hand that had terminated his earthly existence. He expects to feel repulsion, recoil at such a touch. But he doesn't. Instead, he feels something strange something he can only assume is some kind of paternalism. A feeling he hasn't felt since the child Hana.

And now looking into the pale blueish face of Baines,

Lazarus speaks softly, as if revealing a secret. 'Look boy, it's not your time. You may think you're done with this world, but this world isn't done with you yet. The thing is none of this matter's. All that really counts is that somehow some way you eradicate from your mind the past. Learn from me, I never could, was never able to.'

Slowly the boy's eyes flicker open and a brief spark of recognition brightens their dullness momentarily. When he speaks his voice is a gasp of weary bravado, a tired final defiance. 'I ain't scared, so don't think I am. Don't you see, there's nothing of this fucking world I'm going to miss, nothing.' Before Lazarus can reply, a muted shriek of anguish and shock rips through the opacity of the hut.

Turning his head, he sees the look of horror on the face of Dina. Following her gaze what he sees tears his guts from him. For the mist is no longer, its translucence is mass now, human form. But it is not the form of a woman, his Esther. No, the form is male. The form is Hassler/Breitner. He is dressed in civilian clothes, a garb unfamiliar to Lazarus, yet totally familiar to Dina. Looking around he briefly surveys his surroundings. Finally, his eyes rest upon Dina and then on Lazarus.

'And so, in life now in death also,' Lazarus eyes him coldly. 'What are you doing here, Hassler? Our business was concluded a long time ago.' Dina turns to him. 'Hassler? His name is Breitner.' Lazarus looks at her quizzically. 'You know him?' Before she can respond, Hassler/Breitner interjects. 'What does it matter? What's in a name anyway?' He looks hard at Lazarus again. 'Me, you, the Aryan and the Jew; we're so similar, both looking for the same thing, redemption, salvation, and an end.'

Lazarus sighs deeply 'Still singing the same old songs, I see.'

By his side, Dina cannot contain her surprise and curiosity any longer. She looks hard into the face of the German.

'Hassler, Breitner? Just who are you?' Lazarus cuts in coldly. 'I'll tell you who he is, was. He was the camp commandant of a concentration camp in southern Poland, a bastard who cried over dying bloody flowers, but who thought nothing of murdering innocent and defenceless men.'

The girl looks stunned. 'Is that true what he's saying?' Hassler avoids the question and the intensity of her stare. Lazarus answers for him. 'Yes, it's true. He is a murderer many times over.' Dina squeezes the hand of Conor tighter as a shiver passes through her. The brief ensuing silence is cracked by the weak and wheezing cough of Baines. Hassler briefly looks down at the boy and then turns his gaze upon the other three. 'Enough words. Enough talk about things passed, things that cannot be changed.' Lazarus eyes him with disdain. 'How convenient, just airbrush past crimes from memory.' Hassler ignores the comment, merely mumbles to himself. 'It's the memories that shout me on.'

The cryptic comment is lost on Conor. Instead, he stands at the broken window looking vacantly out across this incongruous suburban summer tundra, as the vicious unforgiving wind whips and wails. And once more it's his. That oh so familiar feeling of detachment, self-imposed marginalisation.

And so, he looks and waits gazing out across the blizzard blitzed old quarry, he waits for Cody, looks out for him. He needs his wisdom, words, presence. But once more he receives none of these things. Instead just hears the faint remnants of unwelcome voices echoing in his head. And now as he at last comes away from the window, he walks across to Baines and looks down upon the face he knows so well, has known forever, a face old and young, alive and dead. He goes to open his mouth to speak but realises there is nothing left to be said.

It was not only words that were becoming scarce. For now also the actor's movements have slowed, becoming infrequent and lethargic. An indefinable apathy is worn heavy in the darkened air, as if some unseen force is sapping and sucking the life energy out of the actors in their denouement. Only Lazarus appears to retain a sense of energy and purpose. Once again he turns and faces the increasingly fading figure of Hassler. Lazarus looks at him intently.

'My wife, you know where she is, don't you?' Hassler doesn't appear to hear him, instead his face momentarily relaxes. Ravines of flesh becoming smooth clear. His voice sounds almost evangelical. 'It's my time I have waited an eternity for this moment. My final chance for a kind of redemption' Impatiently Lazarus interrupts him. 'You speak so much of redemption Hassler. And, you know, it's the only thing we have in common. We are forever seeking it. So, now it's your chance to get a slice of it. Where is she?' Hassler smiles thinly.

'Can't you feel her, sense her presence?' Lazarus snarls back at him. 'Enough games Hassler. If you know something, tell me!' Just then, the soft voice of a young woman enters the madness. Conor and Dina look at each other once more in bemusement. Looking round, Lazarus immediately recognises the slim and slight figure drifting out from the distant dark corner. And as she approaches him, this woman who would remain always young, smiles that smile he had waited all those long years to see again.

Overcome, emotional, Lazarus trembles, shakes, then drops

to his knees sobbing like a child. He tries to talk in between the sobs, but the words are trapped somewhere down deep in the memories he had stored up in his crippled soul. Kneeling also now, Esther embraces him like a mother reclaiming a lost child. Both strangled now by a paroxysm of pent-up emotion at last released, they once more attempt speech. But realising words are fatuous, they just clasp each other ever closer ever tighter: until they merge into one, consumed in love.

And as they do, flesh, bone and sinew reverts once again to an ethereal mist, a pure pristine mist as white as the roaring snow blizzard outside. Conor, Dina and Hassler look on as the mist slowly, gently dissipates, until, until it is no more.

Just then, the dim and fading voice of Lazarus is heard for the final time. 'Rise up boy. I've told you already that it's not your time. Now, you three go. Go live!' As his words trail away into nothing; outside the blizzards fury is suddenly becalmed. And just as it is, at the far end of the hut, Baines slowly and groggily emerges from the clutches of that which had held him down. Still pale and weak, but alive, he gently sits up straight on the wooden bench. Gazing across at him, Dina smiles a smile of non-comprehending relief. She wants to hug him and tell him. She isn't sure what... It's an abstract feeling, not words.

Then, turning slowly to face Hassler, she asks with a total look of incredulity on her face. 'What is all this? What the hell has happened here?' Even as she asks the question, so Hassler is disappearing in front of her disbelieving eyes. Nebulous and fading away his voice is an echo. 'You still don't understand? Can't you see that all of this, everything is about reparation, redemption. And I'm still not sure I have done enough... Either way, it's over now. It's done.' With that, he fades, disappears into the ether.

'Lost, caught up in the hurry of time.'

Standing unsure and silent, uncertain of what to do next now that the spell has been broken, Conor, Dina and Baines look at each other questioningly. Pale, stunned looking, Conor runs a hand through his lank hair. 'Did any of that really happen? I mean, what the fuck was that all about?' No one answers because they have no answers. Instead Dina turns away and gazes outside at snow that has turned to hope and night that has turned to day. All she knows deep down, very deep down is that they were not telling the story any more, the story was telling them.

CHAPTER TWENTY-SEVEN

Walking across the now sun-streaked floor, Conor slowly opens the door of the hut. Outside, everything that had once been is now no more. The huge snow banks and drifts that had threatened to bury and consume them were now gone, replaced by a glistening, gleaming new sun. Walking out into that sun, the boy approaches the car the police had left as part of the 'hostage' deal. Peering through the window of the Cortina, he sees on the passenger seat a small brown holdall.

Taking the bag from the car he rests it on the bonnet and unzips it. Reaching inside it he pulls out handfuls of cash. 'Jesus Christ. They really did believe that hostage bullshit!' Carrying the holdall he walks back into the hut. Smiling, he shows Dina the money. 'Can you believe it, they actually fell for it.' Dina returns his smile. 'Have you counted it? How much is there?' He places the holdall on the bench. 'About five grand I reckon.' Her smile gradually fades and is replaced by a look of seriousness.

'What in the name of God are we gonna do, Conor?' She sighs, shaking her head wearily. 'I just don't know what to do any more. This... Everything is out of control, beyond mad. It's like we are two little hopeless, helpless leaves drifting endlessly on some crazy fucked-up stream.' Awkwardly, but with a tenderness he would, could only ever feel for her, Conor gently cups her cheek in his hand. 'Look, whatever we do, one thing is for certain we can't stop here. It's just a matter of time before the police come back.'

Just then, Baines' hacking cough intrudes upon their hushed tones. In unison Dina and Conor look across at him. This pale shadow, this ancient seventeen year old returns their look. 'The Jew was right. You gotta leave this place.' Dina sits down next to him: watches as a filter of sunlight catches his blood-less face 'What about you? He meant for you to leave here as well.' Baines wearily shakes his head. 'No... Nothing's changed nothing at all, it's like I said this is where it ends.' The girl sighs audibly. 'So, that's it? You're just going to give it away, give it up. It doesn't have to be like this.' This time it's his turn to sigh. 'You ain't listening. I'm just done with it, done with it all.'

Dina turns to Conor, prompting him with her eyes. Responding, he approaches Baines. 'So, where are all those big dreams you once had, of being someone, something? Are they 'done' too?' Baines merely shakes his head wearily. 'Dreams are just dreams bruv. That's all they are.' He shrugs his shoulders. Defeat in his eyes, in his voice. 'Look, enough talk, it don't change shit, I've made my mind up, I'm staying, now just you two do yourself a favour and get the fuck out of here before the old Bill come back.'

Awkwardly, Dina and Conor just stare at each other, unsure of what to do next. Baines looks over at them. 'Well, don't just stand there like a couple of spare pricks. Get out of here. Go.' Finally, Conor gently pulls Dina towards the door. 'He's right. It's time for us to go.' Stopping at the exit, she faces him. 'Go where?' Before Conor can reply, Baines cuts in. 'As far away as possible from this fucking place. Look, when they come back and ask where you are, I'll tell em you have family in Scotland and that's where you're headed.' A small smile creases his lips.

'So, for Christ sake don't head north' Dina smiles also. 'Wales. Ever since I was a little kid I wanted to go there, but we could never afford it.' Conor holds up the holdall. 'Well, we can now.'

Slowly opening the door of the hut, he looks back over his shoulder and sees Dina self-consciously hugging Baines goodbye, and hears her halting words. 'It's not too late. Come with us. What's stopping you?' Baines doesn't reply. He has no more words. Merely looks at the ground. Watching on, Conor feels something, something without a name. And in his soul, he knows he will never again see this broken-down boy he had unwittingly helped break, this kid with who he had shared life, fate, hate, sadness and finally madness.

But now as he looks across at Baines for the last time, he realises they were never really friends. No, they were more than that, but less also. And so now, as he slowly walks over to Baines, Conor feels a profound sense of unreality in heart and mind. He knows that whether for good or ill it's the end of something that will never come again.

So, there they stand, face to face, toe to toe a silence of strangers, their hallmark, trademark, bond, but bonds are there to be broken. The voice of Baines is self-conscious, awkward. 'Dunno what to say to you, what is there to say other than the usual bullshit when people part, you know, good luck, be lucky, take care. All that crap.' He falls silent. Conor coughs nervously, hesitates.

'Look, what Dina said is right, it ain't gotta be like this, you can come with us.' Casting eyes downwards, Baines shakes his head slowly. 'No, like I said, I'm done. I will take my chances here.' As Conor slowly goes to walk away, Baines tentatively holds out his hand. Conor looks into the face of the boy and then down at his hand. He sees how it shakes. Finally he shakes that shaking hand. 'Look no blame, no regrets, no nothing. Now get the fuck out of here and live. Be lucky, be whatever you wanna be.'

Baines' words are accompanied by a tired, faded smile. Conor wants needs to find words, the right ones. But just now when he needs them most, none are forthcoming. And so, so, there is nothing left to do but slowly turn and walk away. But something in his head won't allow it, won't let him leave it this way. And again the words of Cody visit him. Those he had purloined from the Jews. And they were words he had ruminated over ever since they had been uttered.

'He, who saves one life, it is as if he had saved the world entire.' As if seeking guidance, in the words, he looks out at Dina who stands by the car now. Approaching her, he speaks in hushed conspiratorial tones. 'You're gonna have to help me.' Dina looks at him quizzically. 'Help you in what?' Conor briefly glances over his shoulder back towards the hut, then turns his gaze back on Dina. 'I can't do it. I can't just leave him here to die or get nicked by the police. Look, I know he is a prick, but he's a killer, he's facing a life sentence banged up.'

She looks at him somewhat wearily. 'Well, what do you suggest? I mean, we have practically begged him to come with us, but all he wants to do is stay here. And the thing is we're just running out of time. It's only a matter of time till the police come back.' Conor nods his head slowly. 'Yeah I know.' Moving closer to him, Dina speaks softly. 'Look, this is gonna sound mental, but there is one thing that might just work. A while back when he was pissed, he spoke this weird shit about a worm in his head. He said that this worm controlled everything.

Anyway, the thing is he said that this thing had left him, just disappeared one day; and ever since things had been even worse for him. He said he felt alone, abandoned, betrayed.'

Somewhat impatiently Conor interjects. 'Dina, where are you going with this?' the girl sighs. 'Look, What I'm trying to say is that perhaps if we try and convince him that somehow this worm has said that he must leave this place, has ordered it that he comes with us. Look; I know it's bloody mad but what isn't mad with us?' Once more she sighs and looks down at the ground. 'Look, I dunno; maybe what I suggested is worth trying or maybe it's not. All I do know is that you're not coming up with an alternative and time is nearly up. To be honest, after all the craziness we have seen and been through what I suggested doesn't seem so out of the ordinary to me.' She smiles weakly.

The boy looks at her intently; his crippled eyes narrowing further. 'Yeah, okay; I guess right now there's nothing; so, there's nothing to lose.' Dina nods her head briefly. 'But just leave the talking to me. Okay.'

Seventeen, seventeen paces separate. Separate life becoming death and the dead becoming memories.

The sound of the single gunshot rips out exploding into the near suburban silence. And seventeen paces are covered in a blind panic as Dina and Conor run back to the hut. Slumped on his side along the bench; Baines oozes life from a gaping head wound. Stunned into statues, Conor and Dina just stare down at him momentarily unable to process in their minds what has happened.

Finally; as if in slow motion Dina slumps down beside

Baines. Sobbing and grey-faced she takes his hand in hers. 'Oh, God, no.' instinctively she holds his bloodied head against her chest. Powerless, Conor looks on, dazed and bemused a part of it, and not a part of it. And all he can think about is how much blood there is, and how thick, cloying and reeking of iron it is. And now his mind goes back to the pub. That night when he.

No. He cannot look at it any more. So, he shuts off, shuts down, closes in upon himself. But it's okay because he has been here a thousand times before. Dina, her dark eyes huge in her small ashen face turns and talks to him. But her words are fractured and mangled somehow, just like the head of Baines. And inside his head now Conor screams at Cody. 'You said I would be some sort of saviour, and he would be the one I save! But you're full of shit. You lied!'

And now in this place time has lost its hurry, it merely hangs leaden and unmoving dressed in dark colours. Finally rising from the body of Baines, Dina walks as if in a trance from the hut. Outside she bends and gathers whatever battered and benighted wild flowers have survived the blast of the blizzard. Walking back into the hut she gently places them on the chest of Baines. Bending down she kisses his cold cheek.

Wordlessly, Conor watches, watches as she, as if somehow floating goes outside to the boot of the car. And gripped in a stranglehold of numbed dumb inertia; the boy watches as she lifts the boot and takes from it a can of petrol. Solemnly and silently she douses the body of Baines with the contents of the can, all the while her lips moving as they mumble a Christian kaddish. Finally taking a box of matches from her jeans pocket, the girl sets the fire. Then as the flames begin to spit and rise, Dina her fire task complete turns to Conor and says softly.

'Come on, it's time to go.' But they don't go, can't go, not yet. Instead they watch silent and sombre this sacred conflagration; this funeral pyre. And so, transfixed for the longest time they look on under crucible skies as orange becomes black and back again. Until finally with shared thoughts of a lost boy Dina takes Conor's hand in hers and all is quiet. Words have merely become unnecessary baggage.

As fire becomes embers becomes ash; it finally is time. Time for these reclaimed children of the maelstrom to leave this place, this story. They need a fresh start in a shiny new world they can play in: far removed from this place and all that's gone before. And oh , how they need a world that is an 'oyster and not a clam.' to paraphrase the words of a wise young Weller.

And so, after one last look back at the smouldering of a life that they must leave behind now, boy and girl slowly get into the Cortina and drive away.

An hour later hitting the motorway westward, Conor snaps on the car radio and soon the strains of 'I fought the law.' by The Clash thunders out, fracturing the quiet and filling the void, and as if in unison their thoughts are the same but unspoken, thoughts of a young master criminal who never could and now never would think enough of himself to make something of himself. And as both motorway and their lives stretch out before them, Dina and Conor think the thought no more. For they both know that their only hope of finding a kind of peace and redemption lay in letting go of what had been and gone and grasping hold tightly on what was to come. Because ultimately all that they would need could be found in each other. You see, by loving each other and losing themselves in each other, it was the only hope they had to truly break the madness, and so in these daydreams of children, in such innocent and unworldly minds, they believed... And it was enough... Because it had to be.

THE END

THE END